OFF PLAN

WHISPERING KEY
BOOK 1

MAY ARCHER

Cover Art: Cate Ashwood
Cover Photo: Wander Aguiar
Editing: One Love Editing
Professional Beta Reading: Leslie Copeland
Proofreading: Lori Parks

1

FENN

"'*Come to paradise*,' they said," I muttered as a drop of sweat ran down my leg beneath my baggy shorts, all the way from my balls to my flip-flop. "'*Sunshine year-round*,' they said."

Nobody ever told you Florida was the gateway to hell until it was too late.

"Morning, Fenn!"

I poked my head out from under the hood of the blue Jeep I was trying to pull back from the brink of death, just as the screen door slammed against the house behind me. I watched an enormous pair of black shitkickers *thump-thump-tha-thump* down the stairs and hit the cracked concrete driveway.

"Heya, Beale." My eyes narrowed as I took in the bearded giant approaching me. At six six, my cousin was a solid four and a half inches taller than me. His neck was as thick as many people's thighs, and this morning he sported a dopey, angelic smile, despite the humidity clogging the air. I was immediately suspicious. "You seem remarkably cheerful. What's up?"

"Up? With *me*? Nah. No. Nothing. *Not. A. Thing.*" Beale cleared his throat and took up a position with his ass against the front corner of the Jeep, massive biceps folded over his tree-trunk chest. He cleared his throat again. "Not a thing that's, uh… up. How about you?"

I pursed my lips. Important fact about Beale: the man couldn't keep a secret to save his soul. Knowing this, I didn't press for details. I just made a noncommittal noise and turned back to the engine.

"Me? Oh, I'm just *super*. Nothing I love more than a predawn summons from Rafe to come work on his car." I wiped my damp arm across my even-damper forehead and lowered my voice to approximate my oldest cousin's pissed-off growl. "*'Kick out whichever sorry asshole's warming your bed, Reardon, and come over! My engine won't turn, and I've got stuff to do.'* He's a charmer, your big brother."

"That's funny," Beale chuckled. "'Specially since you haven't had anyone in your bed since you and Gerry, back on New Year's—"

"Hey! That was *one time*, and it wasn't *my* bed, and I thought you and I agreed it would never be discussed." I shot him an accusing look. "Beers were had, Beale, and he's practically the only gay man on the whole island I'm not related to."

Pickings were *slim* on Whispering Key, and that was the damn truth. Pickings were even slimmer since the only kind of loving, long-term relationship I was interested in was with the perfectly restored classic Dodge I'd parked next door. The car, at least, came with a repair manual, and I could trust her to get me from point A to point B, whereas humans were nearly impossible to *ever* fucking understand and totally impossible to trust.

"Right, right. And your moment of weakness didn't have anything to do with you being a sucker for that 'Auld Lang Syne' song—"

"*No.*" I folded my arms over my chest. "It did *not.*" Jeez. A man got drunk and babbled about old acquaintances not being forgot just *one time*, and suddenly it haunted him for his whole life. "And that's *another* fact you swore you'd never mention." I shook my head sadly. "I thought family was meant to stick together."

Beale chuckled, then cleared his throat and looked guiltily back at the house. "Yeah, well, speaking of that... maybe give Rafe a break, you know? He's been having a hard time with Dad, and you know he hasn't been the same since Aimee left—"

"Nope." I pointed a wrench at him. "Not buying it. Aimee's been gone a *year* and Rafe's still in the mopey asshole stage. When a man is dumb enough to fall in love, he shouldn't be allowed to mope for more than a couple hours *maximum* when it inevitably ends. Then he's gotta learn his lesson and move on."

"*Awww.* Have I mentioned recently how glad I am you came and found us all those years ago? You're like a life coach, Fenn Reardon! A terrible, *terrible* life coach."

I rolled my eyes.

I was sorry for Rafe. I *was.* It probably sucked being the oldest brother, especially in a family like the Goodmans. Probably sucked having to share your name with your dad, so even at thirty, you were still called Young Rafe whenever there was a chance someone could confuse you with Big Rafe. *Truly* sucked that Aimee had left without ever really *talking* to him. But we'd all had our hearts broken, right? Some of us were just wise enough to get over it and stay over it.

"And no matter how much you bitch and moan, I know deep down you *like* working on engines, and you *like* being helpful." Beale smiled that sickly sweet smile again and looked at me fondly.

I wiped my greasy hands on a rag and peered at Beale's face. "Okay, seriously, man, what's *wrong* with you? Are you constipated or having a stroke? Am *I* having a stroke and I haven't heard? If you've found another stray cat that needs a home, you can fuck right off. You know I have no room for an animal." Besides which, Beale's cat Marjorie was an absolute *terror*—a pit bull with ginger fur—and nobody had time for that.

"No, it's not that." Beale shot another look back at the house, then licked his lips, and his smile fell away entirely. "The thing is, I've got this *feeling*, Fenn—"

"Ohhhh. Come on, Beale, no." I made a vicious swipe through the air. "We're not doing this now." Or ever.

"No, but *for serious*, though." Beale's blue eyes were as solemn as if he were standing in a fucking church instead of baking in the sun on his dad's driveway, kicking at the scrub grass growing up through the pavement. "I've got that heavy feeling in my chest and that tightening in my gut I get when a storm's coming. Like a portent from the Universe. And I don't know yet if it's good or bad, but change is coming, and—"

I shook my head, torn as ever between laughing and smacking him. "I'm not dropping down this rabbit hole with you again. I refuse."

I loved Beale Goodman like a brother. Loved him unreservedly, the way some people love dogs and cats and screaming infants. He was the giant, hairy love child of Rambo, Ned Flanders, and a sideshow fortune teller—big-ass boots and straining muscles; wide, earnest, blue puppy-dog eyes; a totally bizarre faith in ghosts and woo-woo fairy magic. The man commanded a phalanx of stray animals and woodland creatures Snow White would have envied, for God's sake. I'd defy anyone *not* to feel protective of him. I'd kill anyone who *breathed* on him wrong.

But when the man talked about *feelings* and *spirits* and *portents*, I wanted to kick his ass my own damn self.

For the record, Beale was *not* psychic. Not even a little. He wasn't even like that guy on TV who pretended to be psychic but was really just hyper-observant. There was zero talent involved in Beale's premonitions, and no pretense either, just a heaping helping of anxiety wrapped up in hoodoo he'd learned in the cradle.

His mother—my dad's sister, Mary, may she rest in peace—might've *claimed* she had "the sight," but she *didn't*, as I'd tried and failed to explain to Beale a hundred times.

In fact, she *couldn't*.

Because it wasn't *real*.

Therefore, the only thing she'd passed down to her middle son was an overreliance on all things mystical: auras and crystals, horoscopes and motherfucking *portents*.

And, real talk? I loved Aunt Mary like my own mother—hell, more than my own mother, who only remembered my name when she prayed for me on Sundays—but if Mary had any kind of psychic ability, it would've been hella handy if she'd used her special powers to find us a treasure, or predict the cancer that took her, or give her sons and me a heads-up that her husband was gonna get even batshit-crazier in grief after losing her than he'd been when she was alive.

And if the Universe was sentient enough to be sending out *warnings* to certain people, I could only conclude it hated *me*, because it hadn't sent me a warning for any damn thing, ever, as evidenced by the fact that I lived on a forgotten island with my hick cousins and my wacky uncle, and hadn't had sex since January.

Just sayin'.

"But, Fenn—"

"But, Beale," I interrupted in a pleading voice. "We have had this conversation approximately seventy thousand times over the past five years, man. You know I prefer to get my storm warnings from the news."

Beale's forehead creased, and he darted a glance back at the house. "But—"

I clapped him on the shoulder as I made my way to the driver's side of the car. "Look, if you're talking about real storms, your gut's a liar. Nothing but radioactive sunshine in the forecast today, which is why *some of us* are smart enough to get our shit done early, so we can spend the sunset hanging at the only chilly spot on this entire godforsaken island."

Beale's puppy-dog frown lightened somewhat. "By the rocks?"

"Naturally. I've got two dozen bottles of my favorite craft-brewed stout sitting in my fridge, and you're welcome to join me! As long as we talk about reality and not your..." I made a circle in the air with my wrench. "Whatever this is."

"But my mom always said ignoring a portent's as stupid as—"

"Ignoring a hurricane warning. I know. I know she did. But look around you, buddy. It's only April. Not a hurricane in sight." My gaze trailed over Beale's head, to the little house with its dilapidated white siding and the rusting, blue-and-white awning hanging over the living room window. "And if you're talking about metaphorical storms, that's already come and gone, too. Your dad got the money to keep us and Goodmen Outfitters and the entire town afloat. Somehow."

Personally, I was still having trouble believing anyone had entrusted Rafe Goodman, Senior, with large quantities of money. I wouldn't trust my uncle to bring me change from a vending machine without finding some insane way to "invest" it on the way back. I just *knew* he had to have sold, bartered, or mortgaged something to get the money, and given how few things he had left to mortgage or sell... it was kinda suspicious.

But whatever, right? As I'd been told every time I'd asked, it was none of my business.

I turned the key and the Jeep's engine whined louder than a dog at dinnertime. *Fuck.*

I hung my chin to my chest. "Think Big Rafe's got any money left to spare for his son's car? Pretty sure she needs a new ignition coil."

Beale ducked his head around the side of the hood and rolled his eyes. "You kidding? Rafe wouldn't take money, even if Dad offered."

I grunted in agreement. "Your brother's smart. Anything Big Rafe offers comes with more strings than a piano and more questions than answers."

"Hey!" Beale glanced at the house and lowered his voice. "Keep it down, would ya? Dad's sitting right in the kitchen, drinking his coffee."

"And?" I shot back, moving around to tinker with the engine again. "Not saying anything I haven't said to his face, as you know. Fact: we still don't know how your dad came into money all of a sudden, and he won't tell anyone. I heard through the grapevine that he tried *three* banks and none of them would loan him five bucks. Next day, Big Rafe's talking about getting up some kind of *extravaganza* over at the pavilion for Labor Day with a concert—a *concert!* Like anyone besides Lenny Wilkins and his *kazoo* would agree to play a concert in *Whispering Key!*—and he's making it rain dollar bills over the motel."

I waved a hand toward the two-story yellow cinder block monstrosity I called home, just visible from the Goodmans' house through a tree break between the lots.

"In the past three months, he's hired people to come over and redo the roof, start fixing the pool, and repair the walkway to the beach. And what the hell *for*, Beale, when we haven't had a tourist stay on Whispering Key in decades? Why isn't he using his super-secret stash of money to do something *useful*, like buy another boat so we can offer more tours, since that's the only money we have coming in? Or to fix the bridge to the mainland? Or—"

"More boats would mean us leading more tours, and you barely tolerate the tourists."

"I like the tourists just fine! It's the *charming* them I don't like. The pretense. The tall tales and the fake smiles."

"Maybe Dad gets that! And maybe he wants you to be happier living over there," Beale suggested, nodding at the motel.

"Oh, God!" The laugh I gave in response started way down in my stomach and probably sounded a little deranged. "Shit, Beale. That'll be the day, when Big Rafe worries about my comfort. He still refers to me as 'Mary's nephew,' you know." Or worse, *Mary's brother's boy*, even though my dad had been gone longer than Aunt Mary.

"Because you *are*!"

"Sure, Beale. Sure." There was no arguing with his relentless need to see the good in things. Put Beale Goodman in the fucking jungle with nothing but a pocketknife and some chewing gum and he'd MacGyver you a tent, a cooking fire, and a satellite radio made out of coconuts or some shit. Put him on a boat stranded in the ocean and he'd make you a sail out of seaweed and steer you home with a compass made out of fishing line and pocket change. But if you put him in a room full of people, he floundered like a fish on a line, because poor Beale actually *believed* the things people said and took them at their face value.

It was adorable and horrifying at the same time.

I, myself, had zero delusions about where I fit in the Goodman hierarchy. I was an employee, for sure, since I helped run Goodmen Outfitters' one and only tour boat, running tours from the mainland. And I was family when I needed to get roped into shit, like impromptu Jeep repair. But beyond that?

"What in the name of Jacob Godfrey's ghost do I care if the pool's fixed?" I demanded, pulling my sweat-soaked T-shirt away from my chest. "I'd much rather have Rafe fix the plumbing." *In fact, I'd much rather see him tear the place down and start over.*

Beale shrugged. "The motel was nice once. I've seen pictures. Mid-century architecture and all that."

"Yeah?" I peered through the trees again, trying to see what he saw, but I couldn't get there. Like many of the buildings on the key, the motel had been built in 1940-something, around the time the Berlin Wall was being constructed, and had approximately the same level of charm. Faded blue and yellow letters on a white sign spelled out "The Five Star Resort" atop a rusting steel pole in the front parking lot. Eight of the thirty-two rooms had a view of the Gulf of Mexico, and those rooms were the first to flood every time there was a bad storm, since the door locks caved at the first sign of a breeze. Every mattress in the place was older than I was, and the decor was pictured in the dictionary next to the word *dingy*.

Beale rubbed at the back of his neck. "He tries, you know? My dad."

Typical Beale.

I considered an appropriate response to this.

I wanted to say, "*Tries to do* what, *Beale?*" because if it didn't involve pouring endless hours into researching shipwrecks and lost treasures, or pouring endless *dollars*—dollars he didn't have—into funding every treasure hunter with a decoder ring and the map off a cereal box, or deluding tourists with talk of all the Whispering Key ghosts, or trolling the internet for the next big get-rich-quick scheme, I didn't believe Big Rafe tried very hard at much.

But then again, who the hell knew what Big Rafe was trying to do? He was *never* forthcoming about his plans, not to his sons and sure as heck not to *me*. Everything was shrouded in secrecy. When he'd announced that Goodmen Outfitters was facing bankruptcy last Christmas due to his own financial mismanagement, all of us had been shocked, and my youngest cousin, Gage, had been so pissed, he'd gone back to Southwestern Florida Tech three weeks early. When Big Rafe had decided to run for mayor the month after that, he'd informed the family by standing up at the council meeting and declaring his candidacy. Young Rafe had been so upset, he'd walked out.

But I didn't say those things to Beale. Instead, I said, "*Maybe* he tries, but your dad is three sandwiches shy of a picnic. He's been muttering and smiling to himself for weeks, and whenever anyone asks, he says it's 'secret mayor business.'" I rolled my eyes. "Whatever the fuck *that* means, right?"

"Wow." Beale coughed. "Yeah, that's... *yeah*. Who's to say, really?"

I narrowed my eyes and silently watched Beale focus his attention first on the tree overhanging the driveway, and then on the toes of his boots. He darted a glance up at me, and his whole face flushed when he saw that I was looking at him.

Aha. Now we were getting somewhere.

"What?" he demanded.

"You tell me."

"Nothing to tell! I know nothing," he insisted. "Why would anyone tell me anything? Young Rafe's the oldest and most responsible. Gage is the... the smartest. You're the best at fixing things. I'm just... me."

I made a noncommittal noise. Beale was brilliant at a lot of things, whether he saw it or not. Plus, he was the *nicest* Goodman. Rafe and Gage were so pissed off, they likely weren't talking to their dad, and every evil mastermind needed a sidekick, right?

I tilted my head and said nothing.

Beale shot a glance in my direction and kept running his mouth to fill the silence. "I mean, I definitely *would* keep a secret. I'm capable of keeping secrets. I don't blab."

I frowned and tilted my head in the other direction.

Beale swallowed convulsively. "I don't, Fenn! Especially when it's important! Especially when lives are at stake."

I blinked. *Lives were at stake?*

"Especially when the whole fate of the island rests in the hands of the Goodman family," Beale whispered. He pressed his lips together in a bid to stop the flow of information.

I nodded slowly. "Of course. You'd be a silent *fortress*, wouldn't you? Especially if your dad had found a totally legal means of obtaining money...?"

"Yes!" Beale agreed, relieved. "Yes! Like a grant! Or an investor! Or both!" His face crumpled. "*Shit.*" He glanced guiltily at the house.

But I didn't care about Big Rafe's possible reaction to Beale spilling the beans. I was too stunned by Beale's words. "A grant? A grant for *what*, Beale? And an *investor*? For the motel? Who invests in rubble?"

Beale's eyes widened and mine narrowed further.

"Wait, not an investor for the motel? What, then? The business? The *island*?"

Beale shrugged helplessly.

"*Christ on a cracker*, how do you invest in an island?" I ran a hand through my damp hair, not caring about the engine grease. "What are the terms of the investment? What happens when Big Rafe defaults, or whatever the fuck you call it? Do they take our homes? Do they take over *the island*? Can Rafe even legally take investments like that on behalf of the town without—"

"Can and have!" a voice from behind me boomed. Then in a wryer tone, added, "I can see we've reached the expiration date on your secret keeping, Beale. It was a fun ten minutes while it lasted."

Beale ran a hand over his face and muttered, "Damn."

I closed my eyes and forced myself to turn around to meet my uncle's gaze. He was a big guy despite his age—six feet tall and as barrel-chested as Beale, with his bulk all stuffed into a navy blue T-shirt emblazoned with the word *MAYOR* across the front in white letters. But where Beale and Rafe Junior were all muscle, Big Rafe had run to fat long before I'd met him. Unlike Beale, Big Rafe had black hair almost untouched by gray and dark eyes that hinted at the Cuban part of his heritage. Also unlike Beale, Rafe's eyes glowed with acquisitive passion. There was always *more* out there, *better* out there, and Rafe Goodman, Senior, was gonna fucking find it.

I heaved a heavy sigh. "What are you doing this time, Rafe? And more to the point, what's gonna happen to the rest of us when it backfires? Nice T-shirt, by the way."

He ran a fond, protective hand over his shirt. "Disrespectful as ever, Fenn Reardon. And it's none of your concern. It's *my* job to take care of my family. Young Rafe's car fixed yet? He had to take my truck to do errands."

I shook my head and told myself I wasn't upset by his dismissal. It really *wasn't* my business. I didn't *want* it to be my business.

"Afraid not. She's gonna need a new ignition coil as far as I can tell. Best confirm that with a real mechanic."

Rafe's jaw tightened. "You *are* a real mechanic. Didn't you just yesterday change the oil in Ms. Beecham's Datsun? And figure out why Orry's car was making that chirpy noise?"

Yeah, and it had taken me a week, working on it every evening and a whole Saturday, when it would have taken a real mechanic a fraction of that time.

"Please." I snorted. "I'm an unemployed geologist playing at being a tour boat captain. I enjoy working on my own car, but a wrench and my dad's old car repair manuals do not a mechanic make."

"Sure they do" was Big Rafe's compelling comeback. "Anyway, you're the closest thing we've got."

I snorted. Just like the Concha was the closest Whispering Key had to fine dining, and this three-ring circus was the closest thing I had to family.

I tossed my rag down onto the engine, wiped the side of my face against my shoulder, and swiped my greasy wrench on the side of my shirt.

"Anyway. Always enlightening talking to you, Uncle Rafe, but I've got a party going out on the boat later this afternoon, and I promised Jim I'd take him to get some paint before I left. I'm gonna go and get cleaned up." I hooked a thumb toward the motel. "Bachelorette party coming up from Coral Gables, so the tips should be great." Even though I'd have to throw a whole bunch of phone numbers away afterward.

"The tips are gonna be Beale's today," Rafe said, folding his arms. "Need you to do a favor for me this morning."

Beale and I exchanged a look. Beale looked a little sick and a little guilty.

So he hadn't spilled *all* his secrets yet.

Damn it.

"What favor?" I demanded.

"Need you to get changed and drive to Sarasota. Immediately."

"Sarasota? This morning? No can do. I just told you, I'm *already* doing a favor. I promised Jim Pickles I'd bring him to the hardware store, and it's over an hour each way in traffic, even assuming the bridges are all down. Besides, what the hell's so important in Sarasota?"

Once upon a time, eight or ten hurricane seasons ago, Whispering Key had been connected via a bridge directly to the mainland. That bridge had sustained damage that made it structurally unsound, and all these years later, the funding to repair it kept getting delayed due to environmental studies and labor disputes. Nowadays, the only land route from Whispering Key to the mainland involved driving over a drawbridge to the slightly larger island north of us, and then heading east over one of its two bridges. In early summer, with so many pleasure craft out on the water, it sometimes felt like the drawbridge was up as much as it was down, and Whispering Key was cut off from the rest of the world unless you had a boat. Or gills.

Rafe rocked on his heels, way too fucking delighted with himself. "New guest arriving this morning. You need to pick him up from the airport, since Young Rafe's already gone to help Jim pick out his paint colors, and you're the only one with a functioning car until you can get the parts you need for this piece of shit." He kicked the Jeep's front tire fondly.

"Wait. New *guest*?" I glanced over at the motel like it had somehow become habitable since I walked over here an hour ago. "What kind of idiot is coming here voluntarily?"

Rafe pretended not to hear me. "Gonna put him in the west wing, second floor I think," he mused. "Sunset view over the water."

"The... the *west* wing?" I sounded bewildered because I was. "Rafe, there's only *one* wing, and it's all shitty. Remember? We talked about how the plumbing is—"

Rafe waved a hand. "Mason knows he's going to be staying in the employee quarters. It'll be fine."

"There *are* no employee quarters!"

"You're an employee," he returned mildly. "You're quartered there—"

"Because my alternative was sleeping in Beale's bunk bed listening to him *snore*!"

"Hey!" Beale said, wounded.

"—ergo it's the employee quarters." Rafe nodded, like this settled things.

"Just because you say *ergo* doesn't mean you're right, FYI." I seriously hated when people thought using Latin words made their arguments stronger. "It's a dilapidated old motel. Did someone book it by accident? Beale, come on. You can't go along with this. We could be sued, or—"

Beale shrugged nervously and didn't meet my gaze. "If the guest's okay with it, Fenn..."

But another thought had occurred to me, and my eyes widened with dawning horror. "If he's a guest, why're you putting him in our nonexistent employee quarters? Please tell me you didn't hire someone to work for Goodmen Outfitters when we can barely afford—"

"Fenn, *Fenn*. Jesus. You need to stop doubting so much. I think you must get this from your mother, since Lord knows your father never worried about a thing besides his car and his whiskey in all the years I knew him." He rolled his eyes, and I gritted my teeth. "No, Goodmen Outfitters doesn't need another employee. We need *guests*, though. Tourists. Families. Day visitors. We need to get this island back to where it was in its glory days."

"Which days were those?" I folded my arms over my chest. "Was Kennedy president? Or are we talking pre-Spanish colonial period?"

"For your information, there was a time *in my memory* when Whispering Key was *the* vacation destination. Families came and stayed for *weeks*." He stared at something above the tree line, some *time* that existed only in his memory. "They had bonfires on the beach. Folks got together every night— tourists and locals alike!—to watch the sunset down at Powder Point. They'd stroll down Godfrey Pass eating ice cream from Luisa Oliveira's shop and ride the carousel, or watch movies at Godfrey Park. There was music and laughter nearly every damn day."

I looked at Beale. He looked at me. We both shrugged.

Whispering Key had been a forgotten island for the five years I'd lived here—and *way* longer, based on the look of the place. Godfrey Pass was seven miles of road that ran the length of the island and through a town center comprised mostly of empty storefronts and a boarded-up, graffiti-covered carousel. I'd never heard of Luisa Oliveira, and the only places to get ice cream without heading to Publix off island were Omar's Sundries, and Pickles', the world's tiniest grocery store.

I opened my mouth to say something—something cutting about how a lot of things had changed since those good old days, and the past was the past—but I wasn't a *total* heartless bastard. The happy, dreamy look in Big Rafe's eyes wasn't one I was used to seeing unless he was talking about some treasure his ancestors had dropped off the coast a couple hundred years before, or how he was gonna buy a stake in some almost-guaranteed mind-blowing get-rich-quick scheme for a low, low price.

So instead of arguing, I nodded once. "All right. So what's your plan here? You're trying to get folks to visit the motel? Do some advertising?" I tried not to sound as deeply skeptical as I felt. "Gonna be hard. The beaches are gorgeous, but you know that's not enough. Tourists need more." Like running water and furniture that wouldn't disintegrate under their hands, for a start.

"I'm *aware*, Fenn," he sighed. "Leave it all to me."

Words to strike fear in a man's heart, right there.

"They're gonna want those shops you talked about, and entertainment, and restaurants, and cafes," I persisted. "The Concha isn't gonna cut it no matter how good Lety's cooking is, you realize. Tourists don't love to buy their lunch at the same place they buy live bait, as a general rule."

"Precisely." Rafe nodded approvingly, like I'd displayed more intelligence than he'd thought me capable of. "We need small businesses to relocate to Whispering Key. Chefs and bakers, bartenders, artisans. All the kinds of folks who were here before."

I frowned. I was possibly mildly impressed by his foresight. Against my will, you understand. "So..."

"So, in order to get those people to move here, we have to have *services* for them. Like schools—"

"And decent housing. And medical care," I interjected. "Yeah, okay. I follow you. That's a fuck of an undertaking, though. Shit, Rafe. And you can't possibly have people start coming here before—"

"Sure I can. One bite at a time." He headed back up the steps to the house. "Name's Mason Bloom. JetSet flight 1443. Arrives at 11:29," he called over his shoulder. "Don't be late. Be *nice*. And for God's sake, change that shirt. You look like a criminal."

"Rafe? Get back here. Rafe, what have you done?" I demanded. I started for the stairs to follow him, but tripped on a crack in the concrete and landed flat on my back. My wrench went flying, too... and came to land directly on my face.

"*Jesus Christ*! My eye!" I yelled, pressing my hands to my face.

The only response was the completely unconcerned slamming of the screen door as Rafe went inside.

"Portents in the air," Beale whispered, wide-eyed. "I'm tellin' ya."

And this time, I couldn't even tell the idiot to shut up, because I felt them, too.

2

MASON

"What you need to do is get off your couch and stop overthinking," my brother said in my ear.

"Micah." I pulled my third hard-sided black suitcase off the luggage carousel at Sarasota Bradenton International Airport with a little grunt and set it down beside two smaller pieces of the swanky, designer four-piece set I'd spent an arm and two legs on just the week before. "I didn't call for a big-brother intervention, okay? Safe to say that's *never* why I call you."

"No one *thinks* they need an intervention, Mason. That's the first law of interventions! But we miss you, and it's been four months since Victoria... you know." He cleared his throat. "Did what she did. So—"

"Anyone ever tell you you've got a gift for euphemisms?" I glanced around to make sure no one was close enough to overhear, then said quietly, "I think you mean four months since my fiancée left my ass for another guy?" And not just any guy but *Gunner*, our engagement photographer—honestly, with a name like *Gunner*, the writing had been on the wall there—who'd stolen Victoria off to cavort with him in the jungles of Central America. "Might as well call it what it is. First step to treating a disease is knowing what you've got."

Micah huffed out a breath. "It doesn't need to be *treated*, Mason. This was never about *you*; it was about Victoria."

"Meh. It was kind of about both of us. Vic said she hadn't been really happy in a while, and I guess I was sleepwalking through it, so that's on me." I still felt a dull, guilty sort of ache about not seeing the signs. I felt even guiltier about the fact that, while I missed having someone around, and I missed the future we'd planned... I hadn't really missed Victoria as a *person* very much at all. In fact, I'd started thinking some of the accusations Vic had leveled at me before she left were kinda true.

I *didn't* really feel deep passions, and that probably *was* why she'd never felt deeply passionate about me.

There might actually *be* something broken in me from growing up the way I had, that meant I could never love someone fully or be loved in return.

She might even have been right about me being too obsessed with status... although that one I was pretty sure she'd enabled a whole lot. *She* was the one who'd taught me about wearing tasteful but expensive clothes, after all, and taking exotic-but-not-flamboyant vacations, and driving luxurious-but-not-ostentatious cars—all the stuff that got her likes on Instagram. *She* was the one who'd introduced me to her parents' friends at their Water Mill garden parties, and encouraged me to think big about my career and the future.

Don't get me wrong, I'd gotten on board with that shit *real* fast, because to people who were important and wealthy, those fancy things were like a shorthand for "I'm important also. Take me seriously," and for a guy who hadn't known cashmere *existed* until he was past his second decade of life, that feeling had quickly become addictive. But you couldn't teach a man a better way of living and then blame him because he'd listened.

Not that blame really mattered now, anyway.

"That's not why I called either, though! I have some exciting news."

"Uh-oh." Micah's worry turned to suspicion. "You saying *exciting* when you're in this mood is a little terrifying. Am I talking to the Mason who thinks reorganizing his polo collection is exciting? Or the old Mason, whose brand of excitement involved construction chutes and lube?"

I sighed. The trouble with having a family who loved you was that they never forgot the shit you pulled, even half a lifetime and several big-deal degrees and certifications later... and they never let *you* forget it either.

"First off, it was coconut oil, not *lube*. If you're gonna tell the story, get it right. Second, this is not a *mood*. I'm starting a new chapter of my life." A chapter I liked to call *Dr. Mason Bloom Takes Charge of His One Goddamn Life and Lives Fearlessly.*

Catchy, right?

Ironically enough, living fearlessly was scary as hell. My stomach had been flopping around like a fish on a line for the last two weeks. This either meant I was on the right track or coming down with some form of gastrointestinal illness. It was so often hard to tell.

Right or wrong, though, making a change was *necessary*, because as much as I'd learned to love the lifestyle Victoria and I shared—the fun Instagram poses, the little luxuries and privileges, the *shoes*—when Vic left I'd realized just how much of that life hadn't really been *mine*—not the Water Mill friends, not the exposed brick loft Vic had *adored*, not the ho-hum position at the well-established suburban family practice that paid for it all.

Four months post-breakup, I realized life without Vic felt empty because I hadn't *chosen* any of it. I'd slotted myself into a life *she* wanted, and I'd been *perfectly okay* with it at the time. But there was no structural integrity in a life that could come crashing down when a single pillar was knocked out from under it. There was no structural integrity in "perfectly okay."

Perfectly okay was the kind of life you slid into. Perfectly okay was when you didn't have a plan for the future, or when you settled for living someone else's dream because it was safer that way. Perfectly okay was a trap, and I'd escaped it.

Not everyone was so lucky.

I scanned the crowded area for my remaining suitcase, and my gaze snagged on a man leaning against a pillar across the room.

Whoa.

I blinked double time, because it was like some higher being had been listening to my thoughts and conjured up a real-life cautionary example, just to tell me I was on the right track. *There*, in the flesh, was the kind of bitter-looking human who'd probably just let life happen to him. He reminded me of my idiot teenaged self. The ghost of the Mason Bloom who might have been.

My eyes traveled up and down the guy's form from his over-long, sun-streaked hair, to his thin, stained T-shirt, to his plastic flip-flops, and I felt my lip curl just a little in distaste. He had handsome features from what part of him I could see—the dude was wearing sunglasses indoors, which wasn't weird *at all*. The cut of his jaw was sharp, the line of his nose was straight, his muscles that popped beneath his sleeves when he folded his arms over his chest were thick and well-defined. But the man scowled at the floor with malevolent intensity, like the linoleum had personally offended him and he was ready to make it pay. He sneered at anyone who walked too close. He held himself rigidly distant from every other person in the baggage claim like a feral animal who'd bite with the slightest provocation. All in all, I felt like I was watching an episode of *Criminal Minds*, because *this* was the kind of guy whose mug shot would flash on the screen while the actors said, *"Our unsub is a drifter with anger issues. He's killed before and will kill again."*

And okay, yeah, that wasn't the kindest thought I'd ever had, but whatever. I disliked him because I'd almost been him. And because I never wanted to be like him again.

Serial Killer Guy's gaze drifted in my direction and he caught me staring. He thrust his chin in my direction like he was two seconds away from throwing down with me, right here in front of carousel six.

Charming.

I ran a hand over the front of the button-down shirt I'd ironed that morning, and straightened to my full five feet ten inches. There was zero chance I'd actually get involved in fisticuffs—for one thing, I hadn't thrown a punch since high school, and for another I'd rather let him kill me than show up to my new job all mussed and wrinkled—but I wouldn't show weakness to Serial Killer Guy either. I made sure he looked away first.

"I'm excited that you're excited. Really." Micah injected his doubt into my moment of badassery. "Just maybe don't do anything too rash. No drunken revelry, okay? No weird tattoos? No swan dives?"

Micah's words coming on the heels of seeing this alterna-Mason-Serial-Killer-Guy made me clench my teeth in annoyance... which probably made me a shit person. I mean, if there were anyone on the planet who'd earned the right to give me shit, it was the brother who'd spent most of his adult life living like a monk so he could take care of our sisters and me, right? The guy who'd bailed me out of trouble so many times as a teenager, I couldn't count them? The man who'd give me a *kidney* if I needed it, without a second of hesitation?

Thing was, I had no use for a kidney. I just really wanted to be treated like a competent adult.

"Micah, I haven't been drunk in half a lifetime, okay?"

"Half of *your* lifetime, maybe."

I blew out a breath. "Are you doing that thing where you wind me up on purpose?"

"Not my fault you're stubborn as a mule and easy to rile. It'll be worth it if I get you out of the house and, more importantly, out of your own *head*."

I sighed but found myself smiling ruefully, too, because Micah's shit-talk was laced with so much love and humor and comforting familiarity that I wondered for a second if I'd made the wrong choice, moving thirteen hundred miles from it.

But then the automatic doors to the parking lot *whooshed* open as someone left with their bag, and a wave of tropical air flooded in, so sticky-wet I could *smell* the humidity and feel my hair start to curl despite the Kevlar-esque pomade I'd put in it this morning. And then I remembered why this was exactly the right choice.

Florida was *paradise*. Coconut-scented, beach-in-my-backyard, fruity-drinks-with-umbrellas, *should-we-take-your-yacht-or-mine?* paradise.

And I might not be a passionate man, but I knew how to work hard. I knew how to make a plan, and how to bring it to fruition.

When my old friends and colleagues checked my Instagram stories or caught up with me on Facebook, they would *not* remember the scrawny little kid in hand-me-downs who'd done anything for a dare, or *tsk* in pity at the poor fool who'd had the beautiful fiancée and lost her—they'd see a man living the dream on an island with an exclusive, five-star resort.

And in three short years, I'd leave this place for whatever bigger and better opportunity presented itself, and not tied down by what anyone else wanted for me.

"Mason?" Micah prompted. "Are you even listening?"

"Yes, of course," I lied. "You confessed that you're a shit-stirrer who annoys people for fun. I don't know how Constantine tolerates you."

Micah snorted. "I got him young and trained him up!" he said, in a loud voice that meant he wanted his boyfriend to overhear. "Now he hardly notices that I'm old and annoying. Right, Connie?"

Predictably, I heard a muffled scuffle that I knew from months in their company was Constantine jokingly knocking his arm or shoulder or hip into some part of Micah, setting them both off-balance so they fell into a wall or piece of furniture, followed by laughter, and, sure as day follows night, the sound of kissing. And more laughing. And moaning. And more kissing.

Adorable, right?

Wrong.

"Jesus Christ, can you two control yourselves until we hang up, *please*?"

I wasn't jealous of Micah and Con, I'd just never really understood public displays of affection. They were so very... public. And also... affectionate. They made me uncomfortable. If you wanted to be intimate, how hard was it to wait until you were alone?

There was a staticky noise, and then Micah was back.

"Sorry, sorry! Con just got home. You're on speaker now."

"Hey, Mase!" Constantine said cheerfully.

"*Peachy*," I muttered. "The speaker will make it better. Gay porn *in stereo.*"

"No, no! No porn. This is an affection-free zone, starting now," Constantine said solemnly. "I swear, I don't even like this guy."

"Same," Micah agreed.

Constantine was sitting on his lap, I just knew it.

"Look, Con and I were talking, and we want you to come over and hang out with us tomorrow," Micah began. "You can tell us your exciting news."

"I can't."

"Aw, come on, Mase!" Constantine wheedled. "Don't be like that. You don't even know what we were planning!"

"No? On a springtime Saturday? Might there be a farmer's market?"

They said nothing, but their silence was *guilty.*

"One where we'll stroll around, like I've never seen your little town before, and talk to your crackpot neighbors, like we can't already predict every damn thing they're going to say, and you two will ply me with baked goods like I'm a hog heading to slaughter, hoping I'm too high on carbohydrates to object when you sit me down for a Come to Jesus?"

"That's not..." Micah began.

"Yeah, fine, that was the plan," Constantine admitted. "But that doesn't mean it won't be *fun*! Besides, your whole family's coming. You've always enjoyed it in the past, right? Didn't you always wanna live in a small town? Maybe now that Victoria's no longer in your picture, you could move here full-time."

"Con," I said gently, "People change. Dreams change. Some folks are perfectly happy in a small town, but some of us want more."

Con sniffed. "In my opinion, the only people who don't want to live in O'Leary are people who haven't been here yet. It's a great place. Plenty of hot guys..." Con seemed to remember he was talking to a straight man and added, "And plenty of nice women, too. I even dated a couple, once upon a time. O'Leary's basically a bisexual paradise!"

"Someone needs to lock you down to write the tourism slogans, Connie. Massive oversight there." I rolled my eyes. "Seriously, guys, I appreciate what you're trying to do, but..."

I looked around the area again and frowned. Still no sign of my bag, though the crowd was beginning to thin out, and I swore I'd seen the same two bags going around the belt twice now, neither of which was mine.

Shit.

"But, what?" Micah prompted.

"Huh? Oh. But I can't come." I ran a hand through my hair without thinking, disturbing the pomade, and felt my wavy hair spring free like a convict presented with an open cell door.

Double shit.

Now I'd need to fix myself up before I got to the resort.

"If you can't even concentrate on a simple conversation, Mase, you're worse off than I thought. I'm coming to your apartment—"

"No, Micah!" I said, more forcefully than necessary. "You can't. That's, um... my exciting news. You remember the job opportunity I mentioned a few weeks back? The one I found on MedLister?"

"No."

"Sure you do. On an island—"

Micah made a rude noise. "You mean that scam you mentioned at the party after Olivia's recital?"

"It's *not* a scam."

"Well, it's not a real job opportunity." The amusement in Micah's voice was thick. "*Come work on an island no one's ever heard of, where international law probably doesn't apply! We'll pay you a billion dollars once you sign your life away!* It's like 'Come to my van by the river and I'll give you some candy,' but for grown-ups."

I set my jaw. "*No.* It's *not*. It's a position as a doctor on an island in Florida, where regular old domestic and state laws apply."

I was pretty sure.

"But—"

"A job where I'd be running a practice *on my own*, with almost total autonomy, which is a huge step up from being the newest, youngest doctor in a suburban practice in case you didn't know."

"Sure, but—"

"And, though the initial base salary is… not exactly impressive, you can't put a price tag on the networking I could do while living and working on an island with an *exclusive resort*. Who knows what sorts of people I might meet and treat? The potential for the future is *unlimited*."

"Yeah, but—"

"And, *yes*, there's a three-year contract, but that's only if the chosen applicant wants to take advantage of the private grant that will pay off their med school loans, because this island is just far enough from the mainland to qualify as a rural, underserved community. And it comes with a three-month probationary period, anyway, just to make sure it's a good fit for both parties, so it's hardly *signing my life away*." I paused in my tirade. "So… yeah. Not a scam. A great opportunity. The opportunity of a lifetime, really."

In the silence that followed, I could practically feel the twin rivers of shock flowing through the phone line.

Con spoke first. "I mean. That all sounds great for *someone*, Mase, but you live here. Near your family." He forced out a chuckle. "You have a whole wardrobe of cashmere sweaters, and you'd never use them in Florida. You can't fuck with the sweaters, Mason. I wouldn't recognize you anymore."

I swallowed. Every one of those sweaters had been chosen by Victoria. I'd donated all but one before I left.

"Well, *I* still think it sounds like bullshit," Micah insisted. "If it really worked like that, everyone would apply for it and it would be incredibly competitive. There's gotta be a catch."

I squeezed my eyes shut against a flare of hurt. "Does there *have* to be? Really? Once again, your expert knowledge of *everything in the universe* astounds me, Micah. Maybe it *is* incredibly competitive. Maybe I'm qualified anyway! I'm not *just* Micah Bloom's kid brother, you know. I'm an autonomous human being with actual skills. How do you know I wasn't put on the short list because I'm not only a good doctor with great references, I also aced my phone interview with the resort manager?"

"On the short list," Con repeated softly. "You applied for the job?"

"I..." I took a deep breath and let it out. "Yeah. And I got it."

"But you never said—" Con sounded upset.

"Mason, for fuck's sake, you can't seriously be thinking of *taking* it!" Micah exploded. "That's... that's just... it's not *reasonable*! You, a man who has literally stood in the toothpaste aisle for fifteen minutes debating the relative merits of *Minty Fresh* versus *Fresh Mint*, cannot tell me that this is in any way a logical choice! Victoria moved off to Belize, so now you've decided you need adventure, too?"

"No." I ground my molars together. It stung more than it should have to hear him reduce my motive to something that childish, when it was actually the exact opposite. "I want something that's *mine*, Micah. A life I choose for myself. Success I earn for myself."

Micah was silent for a minute. "Fine, then. Fly down there. Take a vacation. Clear the cobwebs. Bring Toby along. Make sure the place isn't, you know…"

"A front for the mob," Constantine said in a hushed voice. "Or some kind of sex-trafficking operation like on *Dateline*. Or run by serial killers who like to hunt humans for sport."

"Jesus," I groaned.

"Not quite where I was going, Con, but… yeah," Micah said. "Let's go with that."

"Let's not." I pushed down the niggle of anxiety his words conjured. "Let's assume that your very competent younger brother has taken care of everything and the serial killer population on Whispering Key is a nonissue."

I mean… it was slightly possible that I'd been too excited by my new plan—and too busy closing out my life in New York—to research things as diligently as I might have, but I was trying to look at that as part of the adventure. The resort's website had shown fruity drinks, miles of white-sand beaches, and a list of amenities that would make anyone's head spin, so how bad could it really be?

Besides, I had three months to back out if it didn't work for me.

No. Fear.

I took a deep breath and forced myself to calm down.

"Whispering Key," Micah grumbled. "Sounds fake."

"Sounds like an episode of *Scooby Doo*." Constantine still sounded unhappy. "You're basically asking for mysteries and hijinks."

"Or crashing waves and fruity drinks in coconuts," I countered. "I've thought hard about this. I need a fresh start."

"But *why*? Mase, our family's gotten through tough times by sticking together. By supporting each other."

I dragged my loafer against the linoleum floor. "I know it, Micah. But you have Con now. Lauren and Leandra have their families. I love you, you know I do, but I want something I pick, not something I fall into. Something I can point to and say, 'See that thing? I did that. *Myself*.' So if you want to support me, support me now. In this."

Micah made a noise that managed to express surprise and hurt and capitulation all at once. "I... I always support you, Mase."

"We both do." Con sighed. "And we're going to throw you the going-away party of the century. No carbohydrates spared."

"About that." I sucked my top lip between my teeth and hesitated. "I, ah, actually already... *left*. I gave notice a couple weeks ago and flew out this morning. I called to tell you that, before you went all *Dr. Phil* on me."

Silence reigned, and I winced.

"I know, I know!" I rushed on. "It's a little bit crazy. But my choices were acting immediately or overthinking myself into a coma. I wanted to do this my own way. Low-key, with zero goodbyes. I'll be back so often, you'll hardly even miss me. Okay?"

"I guess it has to be," Micah said slowly. "But you'll call if you need help, right?"

"I won't need help! Everything's going to be *great*," I assured him... seconds before the conveyor belt stopped with a muffled *thunk*, and I realized I was the only passenger still waiting for luggage.

Fuck. Not off to a good start.

"But if you do—"

"*But I won't*," I insisted, turning in place and looking around for someone to ask luggage questions. "Hey, I've gotta go. The resort is sending a car to pick me up, and I don't want to keep the driver waiting."

Not that I was expecting a limo or anything, but I imagined one of those suited livery drivers was waiting outside, standing by his town car in the heat, holding a little sign with my name. It was so much more than anything little Mason Bloom, sleeping on the pull-out in his grandmother's living room, would ever have thought to expect for himself, and I was gonna enjoy every minute.

"But if you *do*—"

"Yeah, Micah. Fine," I agreed impatiently. "If I join the mafia or end up on the news, I'll definitely call you."

But as we hung up, I vowed to myself I wasn't going to request his help for anything short of that.

There was a little desk set off to one side of the baggage area with a JetSet airline logo hanging in front of it, so I headed in that direction, doing a push-pull routine with my luggage that occupied way too much of my brain for me to have situational awareness about anything else, which was why I didn't notice the other guy standing in front of the counter until it was too late.

"I'm just asking you to do one simple little thing," Serial Killer Guy was telling the pretty blonde behind the desk. His voice was gravel-rough, and it made a shiver dance up my spine. I could feel frustration pouring off him in dangerous waves, so I was pretty sure the woman could, too.

"So you've said, sir. Three times." She tucked a strand of hair behind her ear and pursed her lips. "And I've told *you* that it's against our policy to use the PA system for people who aren't customers of our airline. I don't have the authority to make an exception."

The other person behind the counter, a man with ruthlessly styled hair and a perfectly knotted tie, nodded emphatically in support, which seemed to help the blonde stand a little taller.

Serial Killer Guy all but growled as he loomed over the desk. "But I'm looking for someone who *is* a customer of your airline. Get it?"

The blonde's voice quavered. "We can neither confirm nor deny whether any person has been a passenger of our airline. *Sir*. So I don't have the authority to—"

"Make an exception," he bit out. "Yeah. Got that. Loud and clear. So who *can* make an exception..." He looked pointedly down at her name tag. "Rachel?"

The woman looked down at her name tag like it had betrayed her somehow, then shot a glance at her coworker.

"I suppose I could call Shirleen," she said dubiously. "What do you think, Bertram?"

Her coworker shrugged agreement.

"Super! We're making all kinds of progress now. Call Shirleen," Serial Killer Guy instructed, nodding toward the phone on the desk. Then he added the world's least polite "Please."

While Rachel got on the phone, Bertram noticed me hovering in the background and gave me a wide smile. "Can I help *you*, sir?"

I pasted on an air of unconcern as I walked up to the counter, even as Serial Killer Guy's attention swung in my direction.

"Good morning! I'm afraid there's been a mix-up with my luggage. Here's my claim tag." I pulled a sheaf of tidily clipped receipts from my pants pocket, then dug out my wallet. "And here's my ID. The bag looks exactly like these." I nodded at my suitcases. "I'm afraid I'm in a bit of a hurry. Traveling for work, you know?"

"Yes, sir." The man's smile grew warmer. "Thank you, sir. I'll look into this right away." He scurried off through a swinging door behind the desk.

I could feel Serial Killer Guy watching me through those stupid sunglasses again, and it made the back of my neck prickle with awareness. I tried ignoring him, drumming my fingers on the countertop and pretending I couldn't hear the blonde arguing with Shirleen about corporate policy, but it felt wrong and dangerous. When you had a hungry hyena within biting distance, it wasn't prudent to simply pretend he wasn't there.

"Can I help you?" I asked, whipping my head around to catch him staring.

The guy didn't so much as flinch. His head moved up and down like he was checking me out, and when he got to my face, his lips twitched like something about me amused him. "Nope."

I set my jaw. I had never met someone so immediately and thoroughly *infuriating* in my entire life. I got along with a wide variety of people—doctors generally *had* to. But everything about *this* man—his appearance, his attitude, even the way he popped the *p* in *nope*—was precisely calibrated to drive me crazy.

And that was probably why, with no trace of reason or caution, I found myself shooting back, "Have you considered trying to be polite? I find a friendly smile and not *looming* over people goes a long way toward getting them to help you."

"Yeah? Have you considered minding your own business?" Serial Killer Guy shot back in his rough voice. "I find that when prissy little fuckers don't judge people they've never met, that goes a long way toward me not wanting to kick their asses."

He tilted his sunglasses down to give me a severe look, revealing a spectacular black eye that was painful to look at. Judging by the way purple-blue striations were leeching into the red, this guy had been in a fight mere hours ago.

Right, then.

I pushed my lips together and turned my attention toward the swinging door, praying Bertram would come back soon. As in, immediately. Picking fights with serial killers was nowhere on my plan for the day.

"But, Shirleen, you don't understand," the blonde was arguing into the phone, darting suspicious little glances at Serial Killer Guy, and I felt rather than saw the man deflate a little, like the air had been let out of him.

"People should do things because they're the right things to do," he muttered, "not because someone gives them a fake smile and dresses nicely. Not because they think they might get something out of the deal."

I swallowed. "Are you talking to me?"

"The fuck else would I be talking to? *Duh.*"

Do not engage, Mason. Ignore him, Mason. Remember why you're here, Mason.

My head snapped back toward him of its own volition. "I don't know. To God? To Rachel? *To the voices in your head*? Just trying to *mind my own business* over here." I noticed he'd pushed his glasses back into place, but I could feel his gaze anyway, cutting through me like a laser. "That's not how the world works, FYI. People are nice to you when you're nice to them. *Quid pro quo*. That's *Latin*," I added smugly. "It means—"

"I know what it means, Loafers." He darted a glance down at my caramel-colored, Italian leather shoes, and somehow I had the ridiculous urge to cover my feet so he couldn't see them. "News flash: the *real* world does *not* work like that. Outside of *Loafer Land*, people don't care about pretense and pretty words, they care about who you are and how you treat them when you have nothing to gain from the interaction."

I gaped. How... incredibly...

"It's *not* pretense!" I hissed. "My default isn't *rudeness*, so I'm not covering anything up! I'm a decent person, so I act like one. Simple as that."

"A decent person," he scoffed. "I saw you watching me back there." He nodded toward carousel six. "All judgy-judgy, looking at me like I'm spoiled milk. Was that you being a decent person?"

"What? I..." I felt my face go hot. "I wasn't judging you." My voice lacked conviction. How to explain that I'd been judging the alternate-universe version of *myself*?

"Thought so." He sounded so self-satisfied that I felt my blood boil with the need to commit violence for the first time since I was seventeen. "For all you know, these are the nicest clothes I have because I give all my money to starving children!" He sighed wistfully. "Pretty sure that makes *you* an *asshole*, Loafers."

I frowned. "Wait. *Do* you give all your money to starving children?"

"Fuck no. Just don't give a shit about what I'm wearing." He grinned broadly. "But you didn't *know that*, so you're still an asshole."

My brain buzzed, and I had the distant thought that Victoria had been wrong about my ability to feel passion, because I was feeling pretty fucking passionate now.

Though I'd guess this hadn't been exactly what she was talking about.

"FYI, there's nothing inherently noble about poverty. And I've learned to take pride in my appearance precisely because it shows other people I value them and myself," I sniffed, giving his flip-flops a scathing look. "It's a pity others are not so enlightened."

Serial Killer Guy gave a disturbingly deep chuckle that sounded like it had been startled out of him. "Someone, alert the media! *Man in Florida Airport Claims One True Path to Enlightenment Is…*" He leaned closer, until I could feel his breath against my face and the only thing keeping me in place was sheer force of will. "Loafers."

It was not funny. It *wasn't*.

It was also not funny that his breath against my skin sent another very annoying chill down my spine. Stimulus was stimulus, regardless of the source, and I knew that, but I still jerked away like I'd been sprayed with acid. I wasn't used to reacting that way to *anyone*, let alone someone as horrible and… *male*… as Serial Killer Guy.

"How about if you stay on your half of the desk, and I'll stay on mine?" With the side of my hand, I demonstrated cutting the desk in two and drew an imaginary line across the shiny floor between us. "Let me introduce you to the concept of personal boundaries. This is a wall. You stay over there. Got it?"

The guy's smirk said he'd achieved exactly the result he'd hoped for: making me react.

Grrr.

But before I could make up my mind to retort, let alone think of something to say, Rachel hung up the phone with a *bang*.

"So, *apparently* my supervisor says we can make an exception for you or whatever. Because JetSet is committed to serving." She barely repressed a sigh. "Just write down who you need me to page and where you want to meet them."

"Thank you. *Finally*," Serial Killer Guy said, taking the pen and paper Rachel offered, not noticing or caring the way her nostrils flared.

"Sucks," I said, giving her a small, commiserating smile. "When you don't have the authority to change things, and then your supervisor *does*. Makes you look like you don't know what you're doing, when you're really just upholding the policies *they* created."

She gave me a grateful smile. "Yes! Thank you. That's exactly it."

Serial Killer Guy finished writing and slid his paper toward Rachel before turning toward me. "Look at you! Loafers McGee, Man of the People. Are you running for office?"

"The wall is soundproof. I hear *nothing*," I remarked in a low voice to no one in particular.

Serial Killer Guy snorted.

The swinging door behind the desk opened and a frowning Bertram appeared.

"I'm so sorry for the delay, sir! It seems your bag ended up on a flight to Ohio instead of Sarasota." He grimaced. "I've put in a request for it to be transferred here, and we'll deliver it to you *momentarily!*"

"Momentarily," Serial Killer Guy repeated dryly. "Lotta moments between here and Ohio."

For once, he wasn't wrong.

"When you say momentarily, you mean..." I prompted.

"Three to five business days." Bertram was a picture of disappointment.

"And since today is Friday..." I let the words hang there, and Bertram didn't rush to fill them. I sighed. "Right, then."

"I can't read your writing," Rachel complained. She thrust the paper toward Serial Killer Guy with a grimace. "Does this say *Boom*? Is this a practical joke, sir? *Is this a bomb threat, sir?*"

I snorted and Serial Killer Guy shot me a glare.

"I'll have your bag forwarded to you as soon as possible at your Florida address," Bertram said, passing me back my claim stubs. "Thank you so much for flying with JetSet, Doctor..."

"Are you kidding?" Serial Killer Guy handed the note back to Rachel. "It's clear as day. It says..."

"Bloom," Bertram and Serial Killer Guy concluded together.

Serial Killer Guy turned toward me, and for the briefest second, his jaw went slack with the same kind of dismayed shock I knew had to be written all over my face.

"Bloom. *Mason* Bloom." He said this in an angry-but-resigned sort of way, like I was no worse than he'd expected, but significantly worse than he deserved. A statement, not a question.

I nodded slowly anyway. "And you... You can't be my..." I swallowed. "Ride?"

"Welcome to Florida, Loafers," Serial Killer Guy said, his lips parting on a very false, very *feral* smile.

Well, fuck.

3

———

FENN

Of all the shit ideas Rafe Goodman, Senior, had ever shat, the one right now trailing me to the parking lot was the shittiest.

"I was expecting a sign," Loafers mumbled, like the world had conspired against him somehow. "You were supposed to be holding a sign."

All I could think of was Beale and his signs, his stupid *portents*. But there was no way the Universe could have engineered this level of tomfuckery. This was all decidedly man-made. And I knew exactly which man had done it.

"Yeah? Well, you were supposed to be..." I stopped and turned to look at Loafers when we reached the back of my Charger. He was red-faced and sweaty already, his brown hair stuck to his temples as he attempted to haul three rolling suitcases across the uneven asphalt. I'd debated helping him for a hot second, then remembered that adversity built character... and this guy *sorely* needed some.

"Actually, I have no idea what you were supposed to be. I didn't know you existed until a couple hours ago." I heaved a dramatic sigh. "Looking back, it was such a peaceful time in my life."

I still wasn't sure exactly what Rafe's plan for his newest "employee" was, but I was pretty sure the guy at the baggage desk had called Loafers "*doctor*," and given the shit Rafe had said that morning, a picture was starting to come together in my mind—a picture I did not like or approve of at all, *thankyouverymuch*, especially when it involved this pasty snob with a silver spoon up his ass.

Loafers glanced up at me, his green eyes all cranky like he was trying to be intimidating and didn't know he was failing miserably. "Uhhhh… why are you stopping?"

I leaned against the side of the Charger. "*Uhhhh…* because this is my car?"

"You… Your…" He blinked at my baby—a vintage 1968 beauty in racing green, which happened to be the only useful thing my dad had left me—and blinked again. "Did you not bring the town car?"

"The town car!" I hooted, truly amused for the first time that day. "No, Loafers. My town car's in the shop. Along with my limo, my flying unicorn, my horse-drawn carriage, and my magic fucking carpet." I popped the trunk, leaned a hip against the quarter panel, and nodded toward his bags. "Get crackin'."

"But I…" He looked from his three suitcases—two large, one gigantic enough to hold a child comfortably—to my trunk, which already contained a spare tire and a bunch of my tools, and then to me. "I have concerns."

"Understatement," I agreed mildly. "Hope you have some rope in one of those bags so we can tie something to the roof."

"Who in the world travels with *rope*?" he demanded.

"Let's see. Mountain climbers? Magicians? People with healthy sex lives?" I ticked off on my fingers.

He scowled and wiped his forehead with the arm of his shirt. "Well, I certainly do *not*."

"Have a healthy sex life?"

"No. I mean, *yes*! I mean..." His face flushed deeper, and he kept his eyes trained just above my left ear. "I do not travel with *rope*."

"Color me disappointed."

He ignored me and pointed to the child-sized suitcase. "This bag is clothes. This one is toiletries and shoes, and the other is basic medical supplies. And my last bag is missing."

"Yeah. Caught that." But despite my better judgment, I found myself repeating, "Basic medical supplies? For what?"

He straightened, not unlike a porcupine with its quills standing on end. "Mr. Goodman suggested I bring supplies I like and am familiar with until I got to the clinic and could order more."

Oh, yeah. The picture was coming in clear now.

"He wanted you to buy your own medical supplies," I repeated. "For the *clinic*."

"That's what I said." Loafers frowned. "He told me I'd be reimbursed."

I grinned with no humor whatsoever. "Well, if Big Rafe—sorry, *Mr. Goodman*—said it, it's gotta be true, right? Just out of curiosity, did he say *how* he'd repay you? Monopoly money, maybe?"

"What?" His eyes were bewildered, and his voice went up at the end, like the shiny Loafers-veneer was about to crack. I was kinda curious what would happen when it did.

"Never mind." I waved a hand negligently. "Chop-chop. This shit isn't gonna load itself, and I'd like to get back to the island before the bridge goes up." I shot him a look over the top of my glasses before shoving them back into place over my eye, which was throbbing in time to my pulse.

One more thing to blame Rafe for.

Loafers frowned even harder, then blew out a breath and assessed the trunk like he was trying to solve a math problem. "Right. Yes. Okay."

He grabbed the handle of the largest suitcase and pulled, but nothing happened—the bag was clearly heavy as fuck and came almost to his waist, so he had no leverage.

"You know it might work better if you—" I began, but he cut me off.

"Don't bother. I'll do it myself."

"Awesome." I folded my arms over my chest and settled in for what promised to be a long show.

I tried not to notice the way his eyes raked over my arms disapprovingly, or the way his lips pursed when he stared at the grease-stained shirt I hadn't bothered to change before running Rafe's stupid errand.

Why should I care? If I had a nickel for every asshole who disapproved of me, I'd own Whispering Key and then some.

Loafers tilted the bag on its side, grabbed a different handle, bent his knees like a sumo wrestler, and heaved one corner of the bag onto the bumper. Face straining, he tried to lift the back end of the suitcase, and the front end slid onto the ground.

His face was so comically disappointed, I couldn't help laughing. And when he glowered at me, I only laughed harder.

"How much does it weigh, for God's sake? How'd you manage to get it on the plane in the first place?"

Loafers set his hands on his hips. "It weighs a hundred pounds, and I paid two hundred and fifty dollars extra, that's how."

"Damn." I whistled long and loud. "Here in the real world, that's a lot of money. You must really love your clothes— Wait, what am I saying?" I asked the cars around us. "Of *course* you do. Loafers without his loafers is like Superman without his—"

"Remember that wall from earlier?" Loafers made a slicing motion in the air between us. "I can no longer hear or see you."

He bent over, ass out, lifting with his knees, and managed to wrestle the suitcase—and I mean full-contact, bonzo-gonzo, *garbage* wrestling, that had the car bouncing like *much* more interesting shit was happening inside it—into the trunk. The whole time, he was so careful to ignore me, it was clear he was aware of every breath I took.

Which was, well… fucking hot, if I was being honest. And I couldn't help but notice that Loafers, while still being a prissy little fucker, was nevertheless passably cute, with all that hair wanting to curl and those greener-than-green eyes.

An ember of lust flared in my gut.

I didn't have to like the guy in order to fuck him, after all. And I just might be willing to risk my dick getting frostbite for the chance to see the cold-as-ice man on his knees with his mouth around me.

I'd definitely be fantasizing about it.

"There." Loafers looked at his handiwork with a satisfied expression. "Told you I could do it."

"Gold star for you." I yawned and looked at the other two bags, then checked my nonexistent watch. "Tick tock. Time's a'wastin', Loafers."

He made a disgruntled noise but got to work loading in the other two cases—one more in the trunk and one jammed in the back, behind the passenger's seat—while I got in the car, set the ancient radio to the classic-rock station, and rolled down the windows so it was slightly less sauna-like.

Loafers got in beside me, slammed the door closed, and glared in my direction.

"All settled?" I asked mildly. "*At last*?"

"No thanks to you." He rubbed his hands against the legs of his pants, leaving damp, dirty trails on the beige material. His shirt was wrinkled, dusty, and almost completely untucked from his pants. "I certainly hope you're more helpful than this with the guests at the resort. What exactly do you *do*, anyway? You certainly don't behave like a livery driver."

"A livery driver?" I grinned. "Fuck, no. I'm a tour boat captain, Loafers. I occasionally fix cars when people need me to. We don't get much call for livery drivers on Whispering Key."

Mason scowled. "*Really.* Do you expect me to believe *all* the guests rent cars to get to the resort?"

He managed to make it sound like *I* was lying, when in fact *he* had no grip on reality.

"The *guests.* At the *resort.* What, exactly, did Mr. Goodman tell you was happening here?"

I could feel the man's eyes boring into me from the other side of the low console like he wondered if I was being deliberately obtuse.

I flicked him a glance. "Being serious here. You'll find that Big—uh. *Mr. Goodman*—tends to play his cards close to the vest. I was told to come and get you. I know jack shit beyond your name."

Loafers sank down in his seat, and his chin went up mulishly. "Well, I'd think it was all fairly self-explanatory. I'm the new doctor for Whispering Key."

"You." I glanced over at him, at the khaki pants that still had a crease down the center front of each leg, and those shoes that were probably worth more than the car we were riding in. "Are Whispering Key's new doctor?"

He sniffed. "Is that so shocking?"

"Fuck, yes. Are you out of your mind? What would possess a person like *you* to take a job in a place like *Whispering Key*?"

He folded his arms over his chest. "I assure you, I'm perfectly qualified for the position. I graduated top of my class in medical school, I have excellent references, and I have years of experience dealing with a wide variety of emergent situations. Broken bones. Infections. Lacerations. Bruising." He made a motion toward my eye and frowned. "Speaking of which, you should really put ice on that, you know."

"Yeah." I eased the car into traffic. "I know."

Loafers sighed and unbent one tiny fraction of a millimeter. "Look, I realize there'll be limitations to what I can do, but I think that would be true for any medical professional, especially since Mr. Goodman implied the facility would be relatively small."

"Small," I repeated in dawning horror. *Try nonexistent.*

"Yes. Small for an island with a five-star resort, I assume he meant."

Oh, sweet baby Jesus and all the fucking angels. "A five-star resort?"

"Pardon?"

"Think, Loafers. Did he say *a* five-star resort? Or *The* Five-Star Resort?"

"I..." Loafers flushed. "*Whichever.* I was possibly a little overly enthusiastic and I didn't do as much research as I normally might have before accepting the position. I honestly have no idea how many five-star resorts there are on the island."

None. The answer was *none*. At least not the way he was thinking about them.

Oh, God. Was this funny or tragic? I honestly couldn't say.

I made a strangled noise, and Loafers hesitated, like he wondered if I was about to pass out. "Keep talking," I instructed.

"But there's nothing else to say!" Loafers lifted his hands and let them flop uselessly back to his lap. "Clearly you have an issue with me, but if my credentials were good enough for Mr. Goodman, they should be good enough for you and for the guests at the resort. I'm a hard worker. I'm an achiever. I'm up to the job." He gave a firm nod, and I wondered if he was trying to convince himself or me.

Thing was, I had no need or desire to be convinced.

My hands tightened around the steering wheel, and I imagined it was Big Rafe's neck.

"Look, if you need an apology for earlier, I... I apologize, alright?" Loafers spat the words all fast and wheezy, like he didn't want them in his mouth any longer than necessary, and I turned to look at him in surprise. "I wasn't as kind as I could have been back at the airport. I was possibly a bit judgmental."

"Possibly?"

His eyes narrowed. "But *you* weren't kind *at all*."

"As apologies go, I've heard better."

"So we got off on the wrong foot," he persisted. "It happens. And I acknowledge that it's partly my fault. I'd really like it if we could rewind this morning and start over. I'm not at my best, you're *clearly* not at your best." He made a vague motion toward my eye and my shirt. "But just because a person *looks* like a serial killer doesn't mean they *are*, and I know that. And if we're going to be stuck together for the next three years of my contract, I'd rather not make an enemy on day one. So…" He thrust his hand toward me and pasted on a fat smile. "Nice to meet you. I'm Mason Bloom."

I knocked his hand away and pulled the car to the curb in front of a strip mall with only the tiniest screech of tires. "Are you kidding me?"

He blinked. "About…? Oh! Sort of? I mean, in my defense, you've got that black eye, and your shirt is *filthy*, and you looked like you wanted to murder someone. Possibly several someones. Possibly *me*. So, you know—"

"Not *that*." If I'd looked like a serial killer, it was probably because I *had* been plotting murder, and that was even before I'd heard *this* bullshit. "We're gonna be working together for *years*? You and me? Under contract?"

Loafers' green eyes went wide. "Uh. Well. Yes? I mean, *I'll* be under contract, anyway. Mr. Goodman applied for a private grant on behalf of Whispering Key that will pay off my medical school debts once I've completed three years of satisfactory employment. I know we won't be working *together*-together, since I imagine doctors and tour boat captains don't often mingle, but we'll likely see each other from time to time, so we could be—"

I shook my head emphatically.

"—friends? Friendly acquaintances? No?" His voice got softer until it trailed off altogether, and his face shuttered. "Fine. Forget I offered."

I pinched the top of my nose so hard, a jolt of pain lanced through my bruised eye and I hissed. I smacked the steering wheel with the heel of my hand. "*Fuck!*"

This was Rafe's secret mayor business. He hadn't done anything that would make the lives of the people on the island better, oh no. Instead, he'd lured this prissy asshole down to the key under false pretenses so he could check a box on a form, and now we'd be stuck paying him for *three goddamn years*.

I knew fuck-all about doctors' salaries, but I knew those shoes weren't cheap.

So, yeah, my serial-killing career was gonna start with Big Rafe. That is, if Loafers didn't kill him *for* me, once he learned the score.

Loafers opened the car door and got out on the sidewalk.

"Oh, for fuck's sake!" I scrubbed a frustrated hand through my hair. "Get back here, Loafers. I'm not actually going to hurt you, dumbass—"

He ignored me. He tilted the seat forward so he could reach his suitcase and started rummaging around in it.

"Seriously? If you wanna change your clothes, you do it on your own time. I have plans." Plans involving the cold, shaded sand at the rocks near the motel and possibly an entire six-pack of beer so I could attempt to forget this shit-show. "Get your ass back—"

He clicked the seat into place, plopped down beside me, and slammed the door. Before I could react, he reached over and deftly removed my sunglasses, tossing them onto the center console.

"Hey!"

He crushed a white plastic bag in his hand, twisted himself to get a knee on the seat, and leaned over to place the bag gently but firmly against my eye. I gasped at the cold, but my eye stopped throbbing in seconds.

"An ice pack," he said unnecessarily, dropping back into his seat. "You're welcome. If you'd like me to drive so you can see better—"

"You? Drive my car?" I snorted. "That'll be the day. Nobody drives her but me."

"Ah. You're one of *those* guys." He put his seat belt back on and stared out the windshield. "Figures."

I ran my tongue over my teeth. His hair was getting curlier every minute he spent in the humidity, and he looked rumpled and sweaty and *human*. Not a *total* asshole. Plus, my eye really did feel better.

"Thanks," I said. "For this."

"You're welcome." Loafers turned in his seat and gave me a critical once-over. "Just to say, if you're going to go around getting beaten up, I might be a handy person to have around."

"I didn't get beaten up," I grumbled. "I... dropped a wrench on my eye."

"You—" His forehead wrinkled in disbelief.

"I'm not repeating it."

"But how does one—"

I glared at him over the console.

"Right. Anyway. Is there any way I can convince you to give us a fresh start? Since we'll be colleagues?"

He looked so damn *hopeful*, the poor bastard, all dressed up in his stupid, stupid shoes, wanting to be *friendly*.

How the hell was I supposed to tell him he'd made a monumental mistake in trusting my uncle? Where did I even begin?

Then again, this wasn't my responsibility, was it? It was Rafe's and it was Mason's. Time for Big Rafe to deal with his own shit.

I shook my head slowly. "Why don't you hold off on making any firm plans about that, okay? I have a feeling you might change your mind in time." As in, exactly as much time as it took to drive to Whispering Key and find out what he'd tied himself to for the next thousand-odd days.

"If you mean that I might leave during the three-month probationary period..." Loafers sat back in his seat and shrugged. "You should know that once I'm committed, I'm *committed*. Unless Mr. Goodman has *invented* the resort—" He snorted at the very idea.

"There's a three-month probationary period," I repeated slowly around the ice pack. "So, as long as you leave in the first three months, there's no harm, no foul."

"But I won't, is my point. Not unless there's some kind of emergency. Or I suddenly win the lottery and can pay off my loans." He rolled his eyes. "And I don't plan to give Mr. Goodman any reason to terminate my contract in that time either, so I'm afraid you're stuck with me."

We'd see how long that lasted.

We drove down the road in silence for long minutes while Loafers stared out the window eagerly, like he'd never seen a palm tree before. It was kinda weird and also weirdly hot.

"What in the world...?" Loafers pointed at the road sign in front of us. "Cooter Key Bridge? Is that a tasteless joke?"

I snorted. "Nope. Real sign, real place."

"No," he breathed.

"Yep."

"But... *cooter*. Like, as in a..." He made a rolling motion with his wrist, like he wanted me to finish his sentence. "You know?"

I fought the urge to smile. "As in a cooter," I said blandly.

"Yes! Exactly! Who names an island after a..." Loafers snort-giggled, like a thirteen-year-old boy discussing porn, not a cold-fish doctor with more luggage than common sense. *"You know."*

His green eyes lifted to mine and... oh, damn. They were dancing.

Dear Universe, if you're even remotely as real as Beale says you are, do not make me *like* the cute, soulless doctor.

But because I'd started developing masochistic tendencies the minute Loafers wandered into my life, I couldn't help teasing him. "It's named that because of its shape. *Duh.*"

His jaw dropped and he stared at me. "You're telling me the island is shaped like a... And they named it after..."

"Aren't you supposed to be a doctor?" I demanded, tossing the now-melted ice pack to the floor at his feet and enjoying myself immensely for the first time all day. Possibly all week. "You can say the word, Loafers."

"Of course I can!"

"Go on, then."

Loafers cleared his throat. "They named the island after a *vagina*?"

"Wait, what?" I clasped a hand to my chest as we cruised to a stop at the light just before the bridge. "A vagina? Dear God! This is the *South*, Loafers. We'd never be so crass!"

"But you said..."

"A cooter is a turtle, obviously. A freshwater *turtle*."

His eyes narrowed. "Is not."

"Is, too. Surely you've heard of the coastal plain cooter? The river cooter?" I leaned toward him and lowered my voice. "The red-bellied cooter?"

"You're making that up."

"I would never lie about cooters," I told him solemnly. "Google it if you don't believe me."

"Maybe I will!" He pulled his phone from his pocket.

"Do it before we go over the bridge, though, 'cause that's where the signal starts to get spotty."

"Does it?" He frowned, but his expression cleared quickly. "Well, I guess that's more of an amenity than a detraction for people vacationing on the islands, right? Forced to be offline? Not chained to social media?" He pushed a hand through his hair, and a few dark waves fell on his forehead.

"Mmm. I definitely don't know anyone chained to social media," I agreed.

"Right. No." Loafers slid his phone away. "Me neither. So, ah... what were we talking about?"

"Cooters?"

"Yeah." His face went even pinker. "You were educating me. Because you have experience with a wide variety of... them."

I laughed. This whole conversation was incredibly immature. And *fuck me*, I liked it.

"Actually." I gave him a sideways look just to check his reaction. "I have no experience at all. In fact, you might say my knowledge of cooters is purely theoretical. In all senses of the word."

"Oh. Right." His brow furrowed. "Meaning..."

"Meaning I know jack shit about turtles, and also I'm gay."

"You're... *Ohhhh*." His expression cleared. "That's cool! Same as my brother." He paused. "I mean, not about the turtle thing, just the gay thing? Though probably the turtle thing also."

"You're babbling, Loafers."

"Sorry, right." Another pause. "I'm, ah... I'm straight."

He said it gently, almost apologetically, and I wondered if he thought me outing myself was the world's lamest pickup line.

Which it absolutely had not been. Especially since it hadn't worked.

"My heart's breaking, Loafers." I rolled my eyes. "But don't cry for me. Somehow I'll survive."

"Oh, no! I mean... I didn't... It wasn't because..." His face flushed a deep red, and he took a deep, calming breath. "You shared with me, so I shared with you. As a friend."

"Thanks for explaining how friendship works," I said dryly, and I promptly packed all my thoughts about Loafers on his knees into a tiny little box in my mind and locked it firmly.

It was a damn shame. I had no illusions that Loafers would last more than an hour on Whispering Key, but I could've made that hour really, really *memorable*. I had exactly one life rule, though. One and *only*. I didn't do straight guys.

Ever.

And I don't just mean I didn't fuck around with them, because *duh*. I mean, I didn't pine for them. I didn't fantasize about them. I didn't even let myself *look at them* too closely, since the looking always led to the fantasizing and then to the pining.

I'd learned that lesson the hard way in Texas some five years back, with broken ribs that had landed me in the hospital and a broken career that had landed me in Whispering Key. It was maybe the one mistake in my life I hadn't been doomed to repeat, and I wasn't gonna start now.

But when Loafers started tapping his finger against the doorframe, passionately mouthing along to the *it ain't me*'s in "Fortunate Son" like he actually hadn't been born with a silver spoon in his mouth, I felt a tiny bit of sweat break out on the back of my neck.

Thank God for probationary periods, huh?

"So, why are we going to, ah, Cooter Key—" Loafers choked.

"You're gonna wanna learn to say that without laughing." I sounded uptight, even to my own ears.

"I wasn't laughing!"

He so was.

"So why are we going to *this place* instead of Whispering Key, where the resort is? Is this a hidden entrance only locals know, or...?"

"Real hidden," I agreed. "You have no idea."

Loafers shut up again once we were over the bridge and heading south. Cooter Key, despite its weird name, was actually pretty, with lots of cute houses and water views. A tourist-trap shop displayed "I Heart Cooter" T-shirts, and Loafers tried to maintain his dignity by clapping a hand over his mouth to hold back his snicker, but I totally heard him anyway.

There was a happy, tropical vibe to the place that I guess I'd sorta stopped noticing, given that most of my time on Cooter Key was spent cursing the fact that I needed to drive through the island at all. Seeing Loafers getting all hyped over it made me look with fresh eyes. I wondered for a second if Whispering Key might have looked like this, too, if not for all the misfortune and mismanagement that had befallen it. In an alternate reality, it might actually be the place Loafers was expecting to find.

Which might have been the stupidest thought to ever cross my mind.

It was like thinking SpongeBob SquarePants might've been a male-model-turned-billionaire-philanthropist, if not for the way he'd been born and the shit he'd had done to him. We were shaped by those things the same way landmasses were shaped by volcanoes and erosion and idiot humans tromping all over them. You couldn't undo it, and it was stupid to try.

I cleared my throat. "We're in luck. Bridge is down." I nodded at the dull green drawbridge in front of us spanning the thousand-foot inlet between Cooter and Whispering Keys, the one thread that kept us tethered to the rest of the world.

Loafers dragged his eyes from the sparkling water. "Is it not always?"

"Nope." I pointed out his window. "See, that right there is the Gulf of Mexico. And this"—I hooked a thumb out my window—"is an intracoastal waterway. If you're a richy-rich yacht owner living over *here*, and you want to take your sixty-footer out *there*, this bridge is in the way, so you call and have them lift it temporarily."

"Ah." He gave me those big, green eyes and nodded seriously. "I'll keep that in mind for when I buy my yacht."

I couldn't tell if he was kidding. Probably not.

"So," I said, as soon as the Charger's tires touched the pavement on the other side of the bridge. "Here we are. Welcome to Whispering Key, land of dreams."

We drove slowly down the winding street, past a collection of single-story homes. Most had yards that desperately needed mowing. One or two had boarded-up windows.

He frowned. "Hurricane damage?"

"Nope. Some of those have been empty for a long while. Big Rafe tries to get out and mow the yards once or twice a year." Or have one of us mow them for him.

I watched the sunlight spilling through the open window play over his stubbled jaw and rumpled shirt, and waited for him to ask follow-up questions, to realize Rafe had played him so I didn't have to spell it out. For him to resume being an asshole, since that would be really convenient for me.

He didn't, though.

Because Beale's Universe hated me.

So instead, I kept running my mouth.

"The road we're on is Godfrey Pass. Spans all seven miles of the key from north to south. That, ah... street on the left there is Margot Lane, which curves up to the highest spot on the island, Godfrey Promontory. Views for days, which is why a few millionaires built mansions up there, once upon a time."

"Yeah? Like, Bill Gates, or—"

I snickered. "Think last millennium, Loafers. You ever hear of Lovey Bricknell? She owned one. Or maybe she still owns it? Not sure if she's still alive or whatever."

Loafers' jaw dropped.

"*The* Lovey Bricknell? The movie star from the fifties? The one who starred in *Rose Colored Dreams* and *My Baby's Coming Home*? She's definitely alive!" He leaned over the console and stared out the driver's window like he thought he might catch a glimpse of her.

"Hey! Easy, tiger. I'm not crashing my car while you fanboy over an eighty-year-old who hasn't set foot on the island in decades." I set a hand on his chest and pushed him back to his side of the console, wishing I couldn't feel the heat of his body through his shirt and that his expensive cologne didn't make my stomach clench.

Attraction was a bitch.

"Oh, *wow*. My best friend Toby's a huge fan, and he forced me to watch them all back in coll—" Loafers' gaze swung out the passenger's side, and he grabbed at my arm. "Holy shit, stop the car!"

"What? No. Why?" There wasn't another soul nearby and nothing out of place.

"The water!" Loafers looked up at me, all pleading and wide-eyed. "It's so *blue* over there!"

"Uh, yeah." I glanced out the window and tried to pretend I couldn't feel all five points where his skin hit mine. "That's 'cause it's deeper over there. It's water, Loafers. That's what it does."

"*Please*," he begged. "Stop so I can take a picture?" And Jesus Christ, I was the weakest person on the fucking planet, but I rationalized that the guy had a nice ass and he'd given me an ice pack, and I'd done a lot more for a lot less reason, so I stopped.

Loafers opened the door but only took one giant step toward the beach before he looked down at his shoes and frowned, like he'd only then realized the utter incompatibility of loafers and Whispering Key Beach.

There was a metaphor there, if the poor sap could only see it.

But Loafers just stood there, sucking in salt air like it was fine wine and enjoying the view like it had been made just for him while the wind caressed his hair.

I shifted in my seat uncomfortably. "I'm *aging* here, Lo—"

"Oh my God! Look! A dolphin! A fucking *dolphin*!" He pointed at the water and crowed like he'd summoned the creature himself. He fumbled his cell phone from his pocket. "They don't have *those* back in New York."

He gave the camera a big cheesy grin that sparkled brighter than the water, and my unwelcome attraction turned to lust that sizzled up my spine.

And that, ladies and gentlemen, was my cue to get this show on the road. Playing tourist had been cute and all, but the sooner Loafers got a reality check and got *gone*, the better for my peace of mind.

"Get back in the car."

"Yeah, hang on. I'm just posting this."

"*Now*, Loafers."

"Coming. Is marine life one word or two?"

"What?"

"Like, wildlife is one word, so I'm... never mind. Found it."

"Loafers. *Now*."

"I hear you. I'm coming." He didn't move a muscle except for his thumbs, and he mumbled something that sounded like, "Hashtag-adventure, hashtag-new-home, hashtag-Whispering-Key..." He frowned at me through the open window. "Hey, did you know Whispering Key doesn't have a hashtag? Like..." He shook his head. "How's that even possible?"

Of all the things Whispering Key didn't have, a hashtag was the thing I cared about least.

"I told you I've got shit to do, so get your ass in the car in the next three seconds, or you're walking the next six miles to the Five Star. And I will throw your suitcases full of fancy shoes into the Gulf."

"Chill out." Loafers got back in the car and slammed the door. "I don't know how you became so jaded to that view. And the way the breeze glides over you? It's *magic*. Wanna see?"

He held his phone over the console, showing me his selfie.

The water was frothy white and turquoise, and Loafers looked windblown and carefree.

"That thing in the water is a clump of seaweed, not a hashtag-*dolphin*." I pushed his hand away. "There's your magic."

Loafers blinked down at his phone dejectedly while I shifted back into drive and pulled back into the middle of the road. "Are you sure?"

"Friends don't let *friends* miscaption their photos."

And friends also didn't let friends go on thinking Whispering Key would be their hashtag-new-home when it was actually a hashtag-nightmare.

"Okay, Loafers. Real talk. Big Rafe…" Is a liar, a swindler, a crook. "He exaggerates."

"Yeah? Like, how?"

"Like, about Whispering Key. The thing is—"

"Um, I believe that man is waving at you," Loafers interrupted. He nodded toward a small, white clapboard building off to our left that bore the sign Omar's Sundries, and a middle-aged man sunning his substantial beer belly in a folding chair in front of a gas pump, who waved enthusiastically in our direction. "Is that Omar?"

"No, that's Dale Jennings," I said, annoyed at the interruption. I held up a hand to return Dale's wave. "His family owned the station before Omar bought it. As I was saying—"

"Does Dale work for Omar now?"

"What? Ah, no. When his mom sold the place, Dale took his share and bought a motor home. Parked it out back. Now he pumps gas and socializes. Omar doesn't mind. Look, the thing is—"

"He really seems quite eager to talk to you," Loafers said. He pointed at Dale, who was still waving wildly.

Fuck.

I sighed and pulled the car to a stop on the far side of the road. "Look, Dale's a talker," I warned Loafers as I rolled down the window. "I am *not*. Do not engage, okay? You and I have a discussion to finish."

Loafers nodded.

I turned to Dale with a smile. "Afternoon, Dale."

"Heya, Fenn! Scorcher out here." Dale took off his cap, which read *Wish You Were Beer*, pushed back his thinning hair, and put the hat back on.

"Sure is. You staying cool?"

Dale grinned broadly. "Body like this can't be anything but hot, Fenn." He put his hands behind his head and rotated his ample hips in an exaggerated bump and grind. "Specially since I started takin' my supplements." He looked over my shoulder at Loafers. "Heya. I'm Dale Jennings."

"Mason Bloom," Loafers said brightly. "I'm the new doctor for Whispering Key."

Dale's eyes widened. "Ya don't say!"

"Yup. Just arrived today, as a matter of fact."

"Well, alright!" Dale exclaimed. "Doc, how much d'you know about *ferrymones*?"

I covered my face with one hand and groaned so only Loafers could hear me. "Why, Loafers, why?"

"I'm being *friendly*," he hissed. "Try it sometime." To Dale he said, "Uh. Pheromones?"

I could sense Loafers looking at me, expecting me to explain this, but I shook my head. Dale and his *ferrymones* weren't the sort of thing you could explain in a two-second whisper. Besides which, if Loafers had kept his mouth shut, we would have been halfway down the street by now.

"I mean, I know what pheromones *are*—"

"B'cause I been taking a hundred percent pure mating hormones, what've increased my virility 'n' sexual potency by seventy-one times the national average according to clinical studies? And I asked my doc over on the mainland if he could get me a prescription for 'em, but he said they're not an actual medication, which can't be the truth. I figure it's because they're too strong for the government to let us have 'em. In fact..." Dale pulled his T-shirt away from his body and took a cautious sniff. "They ain't too much for ya, are they?"

Loafers tilted his head to one side, considering. "Um, no. Did you say you're *taking* pheromones? As in, you're ingesting them?"

"Ingesting!" Dale looked affronted. "I'd never! I just swallow 'em right down with orange juice."

"That's... never mind." Loafers twisted to put a knee on his seat and leaned earnestly toward Dale, bracing a hand on my door and getting all up in my space in the process, smelling like the beach and expensive cologne. "Look, I know we've just met, Mr. Jennings, but I promise you, that's not how pheromones work."

At that moment, I couldn't give two shits how pheromones worked, or whether Dale was spewing sex hormones over the whole island. I cared *very* deeply, however, about the sex hormones that were gonna be unleashed *right in my damn car* if Loafers didn't move. I wasn't sure which of us would be more horrified if that happened.

I leaned as far back as I could and elbowed him lightly in the gut. "Hey. What were you saying earlier about personal boundaries?"

Loafers ignored me. "Those supplements could even be dangerous."

"Dangerous?" Dale bristled. "I'll have you know, I'm a picture a'health. Just look at me! Your friend needs to mind his own, Fenny."

"Right? Dr. Bloom—" I punctuated his name with a shove to his shoulder "—is gonna sit back down now."

Loafers elbowed me back, exponentially harder than I'd nudged him. "Do you *mind*?" he hissed, like *I* was the one crawling in *his* lap.

"Yes, I really fucking do." I pushed Loafers again, and he smacked my hand away.

"Mr. Jennings—" Loafers stuck his face out the window and leaned his elbow against my shoulder in the process.

"*Ouch!* Quit it," I muttered, twisting away. "Get back in your damn seat!"

"I'm doing my job." He turned back toward Dale with a broad smile. "What exactly did your doctor say?"

Dale frowned. "Well, he said they were sugar pills. But he wasn't here when Barbara Patenaude nearly ran herself into the pump one time, 'cause my ferrymones overpowered her. So what does he know?"

"Dale. Was this before or after Ms. Patenaude's daughter took her for cataract surgery?" I asked, cursing myself for getting involved at all.

"Cataracts got nothin' to do with it," Dale said stoutly. "Anyway, I wanted my doctor to test my blood, but since the bridge went out—"

"The bridge?" Loafers asked in confusion.

"Bridge to the mainland. Been gone... what, Fenn? Few years now?"

I nodded. Before my time.

"So we mostly do for ourselves," Dale continued. "Oh! 'Cept that time when Gage Goodman cut his hand real bad and they sent a chopper. Remember that, Fenny? Took an hour. Thought Big Rafe was gonna have a conniption fit."

"I remember."

"Yep. So alls I can tell you's what I know: I started taking the ferrymones, I felt better and stronger than ever, and Barbara was *overcome*." He smirked and adjusted his hat. "Pret-tee clear what happened."

Loafers peered at Dale out the window, and his tongue danced at the corner of his mouth like he was deep in thought.

I sighed and closed my eyes. If I didn't see it, it couldn't tempt me, right?

That lasted two seconds.

"The thing is, Mr. Jennings, what if those pills *are* sugar? No, no, hear me out!" he urged. "What if they're not doing anything but boosting your own *confidence*, which in turn is, um... changing your biochemical—" Loafers waved a hand. "—signature patterns?" He cleared his throat. "And that, um, is causing you to become so—" He coughed lightly. "—irresistible?"

Dale lifted a skeptical eyebrow.

So did I.

"You mean I'm making the extra ferrymones *myself*?" Dale whispered, clearly intrigued by the idea.

"Not to put too fine... or accurate... a point on it..." Loafers coughed. "Yeah."

I blinked, just a little bit impressed. Everyone on Whispering Key had heard Dale preach the good news about his *ferrymones*. Most of us ignored him, some folks called him a fool—because he was—but not a soul had thought to suggest that he was sexy enough without them.

"I see what you're saying, Doc." Dale tapped a finger to the side of his nose, and his little eyes focused on Loafers intently. "Alright, then. I could stop takin' 'em on a trial basis, just to prove they work."

"Good thinking." Loafers nodded sagely. "I think you'll find nothing changes!"

"Can you get back in your goddamn seat now?" I demanded in a low voice.

"Could you stop being a child?" Loafers sat back in his seat, scowling. "I'm *helping* someone."

"You're harming *me*." I made a show of rolling my shoulder at the same time I casually adjusted my shorts, which had gotten way too cramped suddenly. "I'm probably all bruised now. And you could have dinged my bad eye."

"Did I?"

"Not the point."

Dale's gaze ping-ponged back and forth between us. "So, how long you two been friends?"

"Ten minutes," Loafers said sweetly, at the same time I said, "Too long."

Dale shrugged. "Where you gonna be hangin' your shingle, Doc? 'Cause I've had this mole on my right foot for ages, and I'd sure love for you to take a peek at it. Looks kinda like a jellyfish with tentacles, but it *swells* when the tide comes in. Is that normal?"

"When the tide... *no*! Definitely not." Loafers looked a little bit horrified.

"Great!" Dale slapped the edge of the window frame twice. "I'll come find you first thing Monday, then!"

"See you then!"

"Loafers..." I put the car back in Drive. "Don't make any promises, okay?"

"What do you mean?" He blinked at me warily. "About seeing patients?"

"Remember what I was saying? About Rafe exaggerating things? Look around you. What do you see?"

The road ahead curved left, taking us away from the beach and closer to the bay, and suddenly the street widened and the town center appeared in all its faded glory. Two-story dingy white Victorian buildings with peeling gingerbread-covered railings running the entire length of the second floor stood beside smaller, brightly colored single-story storefronts with wide awnings over dirty, empty window fronts. The signs on the fronts of the stores were either faded or missing entirely.

I pulled into a spot next to Mickell's Arcade and stopped to let Loafers get an eyeful.

"Is it... not tourist season?" he asked hesitantly. "Everything looks closed down."

I sighed. "Loafers, it's *never* tourist season on Whispering Key. Not anymore."

"I don't understand."

"I know. Look, that there is the Godfrey Inn." I pointed to a three-story building near the docks with a wide front porch and plantation shutters that were missing a few slats. "Miss Thelma hasn't had a guest in this millennium. And the building next to it?"

"The Tate Gallery?" Loafers peered at the sign through the window.

"Yeah. No relation to the one in England, in case you were confused. It's been closed for maybe seven years, since Shannon moved up to St. Pete Beach. Mickell's here hung on until Jeremy shut it down two years ago, but he still opens it up sometimes, like on New Year's Eve, for us to play pool. Wynott's secondhand bookstore is in that Gothic building across the square, but trust me when I tell you, do *not* go in there asking for anything that made a bestseller list in this millennium. Pickles' grocery store down the road is open whenever Jimmy feels like working. We've got a coffee place down the way called Bean Me Up, but Scotty only opens it on weekends. The Concha's open every day." I pointed to the narrow orange building across the street. "Food's amazing, but there's a *very* limited menu—basically whatever Lety feels like making that day—but it's a good option if you don't feel like hauling your ass an hour over Cooter Key to the Red Lobster." I turned my head to look at him. "Are you getting the picture?"

"That this part of the island is a ghost town?" Loafers nodded, concerned. "Why, though?"

"No, not this *part* of the key. This *is* the key. Everything from those houses we passed when we came over the bridge all the way up to the other end of the island where the *Five Star Resort* is." I made air quotes with my fingers. "And as for *why*... A whole bunch of things, I guess. Short version is there was an accident a few decades back, and a tourist died. Tourism slowed a bit, nobody knew how to pivot, and businesses shut down or didn't keep up. The place started feeling stale, so tourism slowed more. And then more.

Throw in a malevolent spirit and a couple big storms, including the one that knocked out the bridge from Whispering Key to the mainland, like Dale mentioned, and here we are."

Loafers ran a hand over his face. "A malevolent spirit?"

I sighed. "A stupid legend that's the least of your concerns. See that red shack, over there by the docks? That's the home of Goodmen Outfitters Adventure Tours, the company my uncle—*your* new boss—and his brother started an age ago. Goodmen Outfitters used to really be something back in the day. Kinda like Whispering Key itself, I guess. They sold everything from diving equipment to mountain climbing gear—supplies for whatever kind of adventure you could dream up. These days, that shack and the crew boat next to it—the *Mary Anna*—are all that's left. Big Rafe and my cousins and I use the boat to run charter tours off the mainland. We take frat bros out to drink Four Lokos in the sun over spring break, or take bachelorettes out to drink champagne and listen to stories about ghosts and buried treasure. Before he got himself elected mayor of this island, that was *all* Rafe Goodman was in charge of."

"But... what about the resort? Don't *those* guests want to take tours?" Loafers sounded a little desperate, and I almost felt sorry for him. Denial was a powerful drug.

"There *are* no guests. That's what I'm trying to tell you," I said gently. "You were played, Loafers." I patted his shoulder.

Loafers pulled away. "What you're saying is impossible." He crossed his arms over his chest.

Ah. So it was gonna be like *that*, was it? Served me right for being nice.

"Impossible but true. We have no schools, no restaurants, no easy transportation. The businesses failed because the tourists went away, and the residents left because the businesses failed, and now here we are. If you came to Whispering Key thinking you'd be making easy money at some cushy resort..." I broke off, shaking my head. "Look, you have every right to be angry. And I'll take you back to the airport whenever you want, okay?"

Loafers scowled. "I can't just *leave*. I wouldn't do that. I told you, once I'm committed, I'm committed." Still, his gaze tracked over the worn buildings in disbelief. "What you're telling me is *crazy*. Gulf-front property like this has got to be worth a bajillion dollars for the beaches alone. Any land developer would jump at the chance to buy all that abandoned property from the owners and make the island into McMansion-ville, complete with waterfront condos! There's no such thing as a *bankrupt* tropical island."

The anger that had been simmering in my gut since this morning—anger at Rafe, anger at myself for doing his bidding, anger at seeing this island through new eyes and being forced to acknowledge just how pitiful it was—rose to the surface. "And yet, the proof is all around us! Are you one of those flat-earther people, too, Loafers?"

"My name is *Mason*." He put his chin in the air. "And I'd like to speak to Mr. Goodman now. Please take me to the resort." He waved a hand imperiously.

"You're joking! Big Rafe lied. You don't owe him anything."

"I didn't ask your opinion. Does this look like the face of someone who's joking?" he demanded, pointing a finger at his chin, and I couldn't help but take a long, long look, as instructed.

His cheeks were flushed and damp, his hair was disheveled, and his lips were bright red, probably from pushing them together so hard. I could see, in that second, exactly what he'd look like, crawling out of my bed after a long, thorough fuck, and my cock twitched in my shorts at the very idea.

Which pissed me off even further.

Why wouldn't this man accept the fucking *inevitable* and leave without prolonging this mutual torture?

"Fine," I said, shifting the car into gear. "You wanna continue this charade, it's your funeral."

But I had the sinking feeling that if I didn't get Loafers to leave Whispering Key immediately, the joke might just be on me.

4

———

MASON

You were played, Loafers.

I sucked in a deep breath, letting the tangy salt air soothe me slightly, and hoped the rushing air would block out the sound of Fenn saying those words in that deep, rough voice and pitying tone.

Really, what kind of a name was *Fenn*, anyway? At least as stupid as Gunner. Maybe stupider.

I glanced over and saw his knuckles were going white on the steering wheel, the tendons in his forearms popping beneath his skin like *he* was somehow mad at *me*, which was logically inconceivable. It was none of his damn business whether I stayed or left.

I swallowed and stared out the car window at the beauty of the scenery and the weather-battered buildings hung with No Trespassing signs.

Mason Bloom Takes Charge of His One Goddamn Life and Lives

Fearlessly. What a joke. What a clusterfuck of enormous, never-before-seen proportions of clusterfuckery.

Didn't it figure that the *one time* I did something without thinking and *overthinking*, it ended up with me on a third-world island with a tour guide who provoked the crap out of me? I was an easygoing person. Ask *anyone*. Laid-back with patients, laid-back with my family, laid-back with my ex. But I couldn't remember the last time I'd been so fucking *angry*.

"How much further?" I demanded.

"Two minutes. Still enough time to turn back."

I set my jaw. "I'm *not* turning back."

It was tempting. Like, *very* tempting. But I'd signed a contract, and I took that shit seriously. I wasn't going to walk away from this job until I'd talked to Mr. Goodman and given him a chance to find someone to take my place.

And honestly, even if I hadn't felt honor-bound to stay temporarily... where the fuck was I going to go from here? I had less than nothing in New York to go back to: No apartment. No job. No girlfriend. Hell, even my *car* was with Toby. And when I thought about what my brother would say when he found out, how *sympathetic* he'd be and how I'd never live it down?

Yeah, there was *no way* I was leaving Whispering Key without another job lined up. If the idiot next to me could handle life on this island, I sure as fuck could, at least for a few weeks. Wouldn't be the worst experience of my life by a long shot.

"I'm going to take control of this," I said under my breath. "*Fearlessly.*"

Fenn turned his head and gave me a look that might have been amusement or maybe concern over my mental state. "Stubborn, noble, or dumb as fuck? Hmmm. Smart money says a little of each."

I ignored him and turned my head so I could rub at the spot between my eyebrows. I could feel a headache brewing like an impending storm.

"It's only gonna get worse," Fenn warned. "You have no idea what you're in for."

I dropped my hand. "Your concern is touching. Truly. Could we drive in silence for a minute, please?"

"More walls, Loafers?" He shot me a wink out of his good eye—a flash of blue-green like Gulf water in his tan face—and dropped an arm between us like a curtain. "Have it your way. I'd rather listen to this anyhow."

He cranked up the radio and started singing the world's most deliberately off-key version of "Hey, Jude."

I scrubbed two hands through my hair. "Silence means different things to different people, apparently," I said mournfully.

Fenn was too busy singing the *Nah nah nahs* to hear.

And, okay, maybe I *was* dumb, because I found myself wanting to laugh. Possibly hysterically.

"Turn it *down*," I insisted, reaching for the dial.

Fenn wrapped his hand around mine in a firm grip. "Don't touch another man's knob, Loafers."

"I didn't... I wasn't..." I felt my face go hot, and I couldn't say why, exactly. "You're disgusting. As if I'd touch your... *knob*."

"*I'm* disgusting? Loafers, you're the one who's getting double entendres from innocent conversation! First the cooters, now this?"

I pulled my shoulder away, furious. "My name is Mason. Ma-son. Two syllables. It shouldn't be hard to remember, even for you."

"*Even for me.*" Fenn whistled through his teeth. "Call me crazy, but I feel our friendship withering before it ever got a chance to truly blossom. Ah, well. Easy come, easy go." He paused. "So, Mason, huh? An appropriate name for a guy with a fondness for walls. Your mom must've been predicting the future when she named you."

I rolled my eyes. "Meanwhile, your name is, what? *Fenn*? Like a marshy swampland? Perfectly appropriate for a guy who's—" I floundered for a second, trying to think up a word insulting enough "—*you*. Were you always going to be dense and foul, I wonder? Is it nature or nurture?"

Fenn laughed a rumbly laugh, and for a second his blue-green eyes crinkled at the corners in a way that was... objectively not unattractive. Like, for a guy.

And... wow. When had I started noticing shit like that about people?

Fenn hissed in pain and cupped a protective hand over his bruise.

"*Fuck.* It's Fenn with two *n*'s, not one, Loafers. Though, honestly, the guy I'm named for was a treasure hunter my dad idolized, so I'll take the swampland."

Interest caught despite myself, I frowned. "Why? What's wrong with treasure hunt—?"

The car gave a loud *bump* as the tires left the paved road and hit a patch of concrete liberally covered with pebbles and scrub grass. We were in a barren parking lot in front of a two-story yellow stucco structure that reminded me a lot of the building where my dentist's office was located back home, right down to the dark-tinted windows and the long outdoor corridor running along the front and sides.

"What are we doing?" I demanded, leaning over the dashboard to peer up at the building through the windshield. "Is this Mr. Goodman's office?"

Fenn snorted. "This, Loafers, is my home. And *yours*, I guess. For as long as you stick around."

"My—" I looked at the building again. Despite all I'd seen of Whispering Key already, I hadn't expected... *this*. Even the Bates Motel had looked decent enough from the *outside*. "There's been a mistake."

Fenn hooted. "There have been several. Most recently, the one where you decided you weren't leaving." He shut off the engine and popped open his door, standing and stretching in a way that made his thin T-shirt ride up over a set of abdominal muscles that would have made a useful teaching tool for medical students. Then he bent down and looked into the car, where I was still buckled firmly into my seat. "Ya comin'?"

His tone was exactly halfway between laughter and commiseration, and it was enough to have me reaching for my own belt and getting out of the car. I'd be damned if I was the source of his humor *or* the object of his pity.

Of course, I found as soon as I stood that my pants were stuck to my legs like cling film. I stuffed the sweat-damp tails of my shirt back into my waistband and glared at Fenn over the top of the car. "You live here, too?"

"Yep. We're neighbors! Isn't that great? I'd organize the others to bring you some casseroles, except I hate casseroles... and there *are* no others."

"No others." I pushed a hand through my hair. "Meaning..."

"Did you go to *remedial* medical school, Loafers? No tourists means no one is using the motel," he said impatiently. "We have the place to ourselves, such as it is."

He nodded behind me, to a sign atop a peeling white pole that cast an enormous shadow on the ground like a harbinger of doom.

The Five Star Resort.

Fuck. My. Life.

"I need to speak to Mr. Goodman," I said tightly.

Fenn leaned his forearms on the roof of the car, watching whatever expressions were flickering over my face. A little smile danced around his mouth. "You sure do. But first, let me give you the tour! Bet you'd like to know what the Wi-Fi passcode is, right?"

I nodded, wiping the sweat off my forehead. "What is it?"

"N-O-N-E. As in, there's no password, because there's no Wi-Fi." He tapped out a rim shot on the top of the car, pointed finger guns at me, and *fired.*

"Hilarious. *Where* is Mr. Goodman's office?"

"The tour's barely begun! You look hot, Loafers. Let's check out the ice machine over in the breezeway."

He pointed to a large archway in the center of the ground floor of the motel that was completely pitch-black, like that one spot had absorbed all the light around it.

I suppressed a shudder.

"Let's not. Mr. Goodman?"

"I'll have you know, that ice machine was here before men landed on the moon, and it still works. Same with the washing machine. And at only five cents a load, it's a total bargain."

"Great." I folded my arms over my chest. "I'm sold. Is the tour done now?"

"Might wanna watch out for the dryer, though," Fenn continued, proving he was much better at ignoring me than I was at ignoring him. "Last time I opened it, there was a giant snake in there. Roberta and I decided it'd be better if I hung my clothes to dry."

"Roberta?"

"The snake."

"Of course." I shuddered again, for real this time.

"Feel free to renegotiate," the asshole said cheerfully. "You might have more leverage, given that you're wearing the skin of her brethren on your feet."

"Her brethren? My shoes are *not* snakeskin! They're Italian —" I looked down at my shoe, and a tiny pair of reptilian *eyes* looked back. "*Gaaaah!*" I did a little jig in place, kicking my foot like a cancan dancer to get the little *whatever it was* off me.

Fenn burst into laughter so loud it rang around the deserted parking lot.

"Shut up! Did you see that? Holy shit, was that a... a snake? Was it a spider? Is it *poison*?" I demanded.

"That was a *gecko*," Fenn wheezed. "A tiny, *harmless* little hashtag-gecko. Like on the insurance commercial, but without the British accent? The poor baby just wanted a selfie with you and you terrorized him, Loafers! Where's your love of hashtag-wildlife gone?"

I ground my teeth together. "You're enjoying this *way* too much."

"Well, I'm not *not* enjoying it, Loafers," he said, wiping his eyes. "And that's the damned unfortunate truth."

"What the fuck does that mean?"

Fenn sniffed and sobered. "It means I'm ready to go back to the airport when you are."

My molars creaked. Fenn Reardon *was* a serial killer. The kind who *annoyed* his victims to death.

"I'll go find Mr. Goodman myself." I set off across the cracked concrete toward the motel. There had to be some kind of office attached, right? Probably right next to the nonexistent cabana beside the nonexistent hot tub I'd been promised?

"The Goodmans' house is the next lot over," Fenn called from behind me. "Rafe does all his *mayor business* from his home office. Through the trees to your right. Can't miss it."

"Fine."

I stalked off in that direction, and I heard Fenn's flip-flops smack the ground as he followed me.

"I thought you said I couldn't miss it," I said without turning around. "I don't require an escort. You should go take care of your important plans."

"And miss this show? Not a snowball's chance, Loafers."

Right. Fuck my life. Again.

I stepped through the little stand of trees bordering the right edge of the lot and spotted a little white house on the other side. The front yard was mostly driveway, paved in the same cracked, dingy color as the parking lot next door, and the building itself looked like a child's drawing of a house—two big awning-topped windows flanking the front door, and a steeply peaked roof with a single window above. It looked remarkably like the house where I'd grown up, though with a lot less grass and a lot more palm trees.

A beefy giant of a human sitting on the stoop with his boots propped on the railing jumped to his feet when he saw us coming and extended a hand. "Hey. You must be Mason! I'm Beale. Ah... Beale Goodman. Big Rafe's my dad. Nice to meet you."

I found myself smiling just a little, because it was impossible not to when the guy was flashing me a bright grin and a pair of big, innocent blue eyes. "Same to you. I need—"

"We're not here for chitchat, Beale. Loafers isn't staying." Fenn stepped around me, grabbing my wrist before I could shake Beale's hand and towing me up the stairs behind him. "Rafe out back?"

"We?" I snorted, grabbing my arm away. "There's no *we* here."

"No, wait! You can't go in, Fenn!" Beale moved to block the door. "Dad's talking secret mayor business in the living room! He and Gloria kicked me out."

"Yeah? Well, his other *secret mayor business* has finally come home to roost—" He pointed at me. "—so I don't give a shit if Rafe's on the phone with the queen of England or God Almighty, he can damn well deal with his mess."

"Excuse me." I folded my arms over my chest. "First off, who are you calling a mess? *I'm* not the one who looks like a freakin' serial killer. Second, my conversation with Mr. Goodman is none of your damn business."

"A serial killer," Beale repeated, looking back and forth between us. "What?"

"Fenn gives off a vibe," I explained, somewhat defensive.

"Ohhh." Beale nodded. "Fenn's intense. But his aura is really white, you know? Pure but protective. Kind of like Marjorie, this mama cat I rescued, who growls anytime you come near her kits, even though they're over a year old and plenty capable of taking care of themselves. Fenn's more afraid of you than you are of him."

Fenn narrowed his eyes and jabbed his cousin in the chest. "You. Shut. Your. Fool. Mouth."

"See?" Beale smiled beatifically. "He *sounds* all '*Grrrr.*' But he wouldn't hurt a fly, would you, Fenn?"

"Oh, I'll hurt *you*," Fenn assured him. "I'll hurt you bad. When you least—"

"You know, you might be right," I interrupted. "Fenn really *is* like a cat. Misanthropic. Nonspecifically bitchy. Peeing on everything… metaphorically speaking, I'm fairly sure."

Fenn folded his arms over his chest, mirroring my pose, and stared me down with eyes a hundred times bluer and more intense than his cousin's. "What color is Loafers' aura?"

"*Loafers?*" Beale lifted one eyebrow. "You mean Mason?"

Fenn ignored him. "Bet it's brown, 'cause he's full of sh… oes." He snickered to himself, like toilet humor was the height of comedy.

"You," I bit out. "Are a *child*. A very annoying child." To Beale I said, "Is there any way I can see Mr. Goodman, please? It's extremely important."

Beale hesitated, and Fenn grabbed my wrist again, before I could evade him. "Come on while Beale's busy *thinking*."

He towed me into the house—a typical layout, with two rooms in the front, two in the back, and a staircase in the middle—and directed me into the boxy yellow living room off to the left, where a broad-shouldered man with a shock of dark hair and a voice that managed to be cajoling and demanding at the same time stood by a bookcase with a phone to his ear.

"Marvin! Marvin, you need to stand *firm*. Remember what we discussed? It's the Whispering Key Labor Day *Extravaganza*! We spare *no expense*, understand? I don't care what the nodcocks at the bank say."

A redhead in a blue, floral dress with a wide lace collar and bows at the neck and waist jumped up from the sofa as soon as she spotted us.

"Fenn!" she scolded. She braced her hands on her bony hips, which set her reading glasses swinging from the chain around her neck. "You can't just walk in here! You know your uncle uses this room to make phone calls since he doesn't get any reception in the office."

"I know, but I—" He paused and gave a little gasp, clutching his hand to his chest. "Gloria, have you done something different to your hair? It's *majestic*."

She patted her unnaturally tight curls, which were topped by yet another bow, and frowned. "Why, not a thing. I've been having Joanne do it this way since I saw Reba McEntire wearing it back in 1987."

"Reba never wore it as well as you're wearing it today," Fenn said in a tone of hushed awe that made me laugh… and then cover it with a cough. Fenn shot me a look that was part amusement, part warning.

"Really?" Gloria turned to look in the mirror hanging by the door, and her pale cheeks blushed. "Why, Fenn Reardon, aren't you just the sweetest?"

"No, ma'am. You are." There was an unmistakable ring of truth in his voice. "Let me be the first to introduce you to Big Rafe's newest employee! Gloria Frye, this is Dr. Mason Bloom. Loafers, this is Gloria, the woman who *really* runs this island."

"Oh, you!" Gloria turned an even deeper red and held out a hand for me to shake. Her palm was damp, which was no surprise given the heat of the day. "Nice to meet you, Dr. Bloom." She hesitated. "Will you start taking patients soon? I have a few questions of a personal nature…" She licked her lips and leaned closer to me. "…about a problem with my foot? And I hate to trouble my doctor over in Sarasota. She's always so busy."

"See, Ms. Frye, the thing is—"

"Oh, no! You call me Gloria! People on Whispering Key don't get real formal, do we, Fenn? You'll get accustomed to it soon enough, Doc." She blinked guileless blue eyes up at me, and I hesitated.

I forced a smile. "I mean, I guess I—"

"Rafe!" Fenn yelled, saving me from answering. "Get over here and greet your new employee!"

Rafe Goodman turned toward us. He frowned at Fenn, but when he saw me, he grinned.

"Hang on just a second, Marvin! *Meh.*" He clasped the phone to his chest, right where the word *Mayor* was emblazoned in white. "Let him talk himself out, eh?"

He stepped forward with his hand outstretched and sighed with satisfaction. "Dr. Bloom. It's a pleasure to finally meet you in person."

"Mr. Goodman." I shook his hand but didn't return his smile. "I wish I could say the same, but we have some things to discuss."

"Of course! Yes! Of course we do!" Rafe nodded. "I'm sure you have many questions, and I'm happy to answer every single one of them. Just let me finish this call, alright? It's about the Whispering Key Labor Day Extravaganza. Can't be delayed!"

Fenn plopped on the sofa next to Gloria's seat, ignoring the way the springs protested. "We'll wait here."

"Nonsense." Rafe scowled. "You'll take Mason to my office while I finish up, Fenn. Explain the history of the island to him so he understands what makes Whispering Key so unique."

"Me? Explain what's unique about this place?" Fenn gave an exaggerated yawn. "*I* don't give a shit about the history of the island. Why would *he*?"

"Gloria, show the boys out." Rafe turned back to his conversation with a "Yes! I'm here, Marvin!" and I raked both hands through my hair, which had to look *amazing* at this point, but I couldn't find even one fuck to give.

I looked at Fenn, and he shrugged, daring me to speak up.

Fine.

"Mr. Goodman," I demanded loudly. "Mr. Goodman!"

Rafe barely glanced in my direction. He gave me a tight smile and made a shooing motion toward the back of the house.

"But Mr. Goodman, I insist that you—"

"Fenn Reardon! Doc Bloom!" Gloria chided, like we were a pair of seven-year-olds, though she'd known me less than three minutes. "Go on now, boys, and do what Mr. Goodman says!"

It was remarkably effective. I clenched my fists at my sides as steam escaped my ears.

"Ohhhh. Now I get it," Fenn said appreciatively. He twirled a finger in the air and pointed at my face. "Serial killer vibe. It's scary as fuck."

I inhaled sharply through my nose. I couldn't say what color my aura was just then, but it was sure as hell not white. "Where's this damn office?"

Fenn snorted. He got to his feet and stalked past me, bumping his shoulder into mine so I stumbled backward. He led me down a short hall past a bedroom and a small bathroom to a little mudroom.

"Once again, very mature," I said, chasing after him. "Where are we going?"

Fenn pushed open a screen door. "The office. Obvs."

"You keep the office in the backyard?" I scoffed. "Nice try."

Fenn rolled his eyes. "You caught me, Loafers. It's all a ploy. The gecko slipped me five bucks to get you out here alone. He's coming back to finish the job."

"Well!"

"Well, *what*? The only terrible thing I've done to you is bring you to this godforsaken island, and that's because you fucking insisted. Did it ever occur to you that you're pissed off about the wrong things?"

Was I?

I gaped at him for a minute, but when he swept a hand outside in a short, impatient motion, I stepped through.

Fenn followed, letting the door slam behind him, and then he stalked ahead of me through a tiny backyard of baked dirt, rocks, and empty flowerbeds. I could hear waves crashing somewhere on the other side of the fence, and I got excited when Fenn started fumbling with the back gate, thinking I was about to actually stand on the beach, but when he opened it, there was no water view, only a massive metal door set in the side of a miniature mountain. It was unreasonably disappointing, even after all the other disappointments of the day.

"What," I demanded, "is *that*?"

Fenn pushed open the door with a flick of his wrist. "*This* is an office."

Of course it was. The world's darkest, chilliest, most cave-like office *bunker*.

Did I mention it was *dark*?

Fenn held the door open for me, and I hesitated, my heart pounding in my ears and my palms gone clammy. I tried to make myself take a step forward, but I couldn't.

I was such an idiot sometimes. Maybe more than *sometimes*.

"Loafers." He sounded disgusted. "For the last *fucking* time, I am not a serial killer. I'm not going to harm you. My pure, white aura won't allow it."

"I know!" I said, sounding slightly panicked. I took a deep breath. "I know, Fenn."

"Then?"

"Then... nothing." I licked my lips, my eyes scanning the darkness inside. I couldn't make out a single shape, and there certainly wasn't another exit. "You go first."

"Why? Are you gonna try to lock me in?" He braced his hands on his hips and tried to stare me down. "Because all that would do is piss me off."

"No!" I said, horrified. "Of course not. I would literally *never* do that. I just... would prefer that you go first."

"And *I* would prefer you stopped acting like you were the second coming of Jesus and the rest of us had to do your bidding because the world doesn't *actually* revolve around *you*, Loafers. But we can't always get what we prefer, can we?"

"I just... I don't enjoy dark, enclosed spaces, okay?" I shot back, keeping my eyes trained on the side of the doorframe. "Is that alright with you?"

Fenn frowned. "Really?"

"Yes, really. It's a perfectly common... concern."

"You mean phobia."

"I mean *concern*. A phobia is an irrational fear, and I am not *irrationally* afraid."

In my opinion, it was very, *very* rational to not wish to be trapped below the earth. *God.*

"Ah." Fenn stepped inside the bunker and flipped on a light switch. "Better?"

I nodded once. "Marginally, yes." I hesitated, then added, "Thank you," before stepping in after him.

I can't say what I'd been expecting to see. Walls lined with canned goods, probably? Possibly a Dharma Initiative symbol? I definitely didn't expect to see a windowless room laid out like Lord Grantham's library at Downton, complete with Oriental rugs, leather furniture, glass display cases, a huge mahogany conference table, an oversized captain's desk, and dark green walls. The space was larger than the living room in the main house and twice as well appointed.

It was also *covered*, floor to ceiling, in maps and ancient tide charts, diagrams of boats and two-columned lists, bright yellow sticky notes and dull yellow newspaper clippings. The entire back wall was a bank of file cabinets and displays.

Fenn leaned against the giant table pretending to be relaxed while I studied the papers.

"June 25, 1803. Shipped by the Grace of God, in good Order by Willam Himmelhurst upon the ship called The Esmerelda, whereof is Captain under God for the present voyage Jacob Godfrey, and now riding anchor in the harbor at St. George's Caye and by God's grace bound for New York, were one thousand pieces gold, six barrels pork, forty-seven barrels rum..."

I traced my hand over the paper, which was clearly a copy of the original, but was so old and faded it had to have been decades old itself, and then I moved on to the next.

"New York, January 1804. By way of Charleston, we have the following account of damages sustained by a Hurricane which happened the 3rd of August, 1803. At the coast of Florida, a New York ship christened The Esmerelda, Captained by the Grace of God and Jacob Godfrey, drove against the rocks, and all her cargo and crew lost but two: Capt Godfrey and his Quartermaster..."

"Godfrey," I whispered. Like the name of every road and inn on the island.

Fenn made a noise like a sigh, and I turned toward him.

"What *is* all this?" I asked softly.

"Rafe's office. He has the most extensive collection of Gulf Coast shipwreck memorabilia in western Florida."

"Mr. Goodman collects this stuff?"

Fenn shrugged. "Some people collect Pez dispensers."

"And he keeps this collection in a bunker. On a *beach*."

"Why not?" Fenn shrugged again. "It's his office."

"They voluntarily work in a windowless bunker?" *Good God*, these people were monsters.

"Sure. It's nice and cool, for one thing. And to be fair, building the bunker wasn't Rafe's idea, he just took advantage of it when he inherited the property. It was built by the same guy who designed JFK's bunker over on Peanut Island back in the sixties during the Cold War. They built this thing out of shit tons of metal and concrete, probably sent five billion species of plants or birds spiraling into extinction along the way." He rolled his eyes. "But they made it watertight and humidity controlled, the perfect place for your loved ones and most important possessions to ride out the end of the world."

I looked around the room again. "There's so much stuff in here, you couldn't fit more than six or seven people unless you were sitting on each other. Four, if they were people your size."

"Uh-huh. But the *maps* would survive in climate-controlled comfort, and that's what's really important here."

I ran a finger over the laminated diagram of a sloop hanging on one of the walls. "And he studies these maps and diagrams?" I demanded, turning to look at Fenn. "Is he a historian in his spare time?"

"More like a gambler in his spare time." He sighed at my frown and settled himself more comfortably against the desk. "If Rafe Goodman has five dollars on his person, he'll use it to buy into a treasure hunt, sure as an alcoholic will find a drink. But he's been particularly obsessed with that one. The *Esmerelda*." He nodded toward the clippings I'd been reading.

"Why?"

"For one thing, it happened in our backyard, or pretty close. One night, back in eighteen-oh-something, a storm struck the area. If you ask Rafe—and Jesus, please do *not* get him started, okay?—there was something weird about the way it hit. It came in from the east, hit during an astronomically high tide, *blah blah*. A perfect storm. The waves were unbelievable—walls of water more than twenty feet tall, supposedly—and the *Esmerelda* went down somewhere out there. It's never been recovered. The only two survivors—Captain Jacob Godfrey and Resolute Goodman—clung to a piece of driftwood and washed up on shore half-drowned and feeling so incredibly lucky that later on, after they were found and rescued, they came back and brought their families to settle. They thought of this island as their fresh start."

"*Resolute* Goodman? As in..."

"As in Rafe Goodman? *Ding ding*. And that's another part of Rafe's obsession. He thinks the *Esmerelda* is his legacy or some shit. But more than that, there's a legend about a treasure."

I narrowed my eyes, my attention caught. "The one that went down with the ship."

Fenn shook his head. "The one that *didn't*. See, according to the legend, while the ship was being tossed around and the rest of the crew was saying their prayers and getting ready to meet their maker, Resolute Goodman, that crafty fucker, went down into the hold and stuffed bags with gold, then tied them to his waist. That's him, right there." He nodded at a print on the opposite wall, and I moved to look at it more closely.

"He doesn't look much like Rafe," I said, my eyes roaming over the guy's muttonchops, trying to find a likeness. "Maybe a little like your cousin, around the eyes."

"Big Rafe looks like the other side of his family, but believe me, the similarities of personality run *deep*. Everyone else on that crew just wanted to *live*, but Resolute Goodman wanted to live *well*. Sure, that much ballast tied to him should have almost guaranteed he sunk like the ship. Sure, he might've lost everything. But no point in living if you're not always trying to get something for yourself."

That sounded uncomfortably like what I'd been telling Micah just a few hours ago, and it put my back up. I turned to face Fenn with a frown. "There's nothing wrong with wanting something that's *yours*. There's nothing wrong with wanting financial stability for your family. Or even to find fame and fortune, if that's your thing."

"Why am I not surprised to hear you agree with him, Loafers? FYI, I think there's a lot wrong with it when you risk what you already *have* to get it. Goodman and Godfrey didn't get the treasure for their families. They didn't tell a soul about it until after Resolute died and they found his papers, in which he confessed to taking the money from the ship, splitting it with his captain, and *hiding it*, and provided a bunch of *clues* so fucking obscure that no one has figured it out yet. He died tormented and alone, and left his family with nothing but the land under their feet."

I swallowed, suddenly, intensely aware of just how small this room was, and just how many inches of steel and sand were poised above me. "I think I'll wait for Mr. Goodman outside."

Fenn moved to block me, the bulk of him obscuring my view of the daylight through the door. "Have I touched a nerve, Loafers?"

My heart beat triple time. "Excuse me, I'd like to leave."

"I think that's the smartest thing you've said." He stepped toward me. "Leave the bunker. Leave the *island*. Make better choices."

I stepped left, then shuffled right. He moved with me.

"Why do you care whether I stay or not?" I demanded. "It has nothing to do with you."

"I don't like you being here," he said bluntly. "Coming here in your fancy clothes with your fancy degrees, reminding everyone of how run-down this island is, and how sad and hopeless we are."

My jaw dropped. "I haven't uttered a single negative syllable about Whispering Key! *You* are the one who keeps saying negative things. And if you're so miserable in this place, why don't you take your shitty flip-flops and your... your... disgusting *T-shirt* and just *move away*?"

Fenn's eyes darkened like storm-tossed waves. "You have a real fixation with this shirt, Loafers. You keep eyeing it." He took another step toward me, and I darted around him, trying to make for the door, but he backed me against the wall and loomed over me.

"No, I have a fixation with *cleanliness*," I shot back, pushing up onto my toes and shoving uselessly at his chest. "With *hygiene*."

"Yeah? Then let me solve that problem for you." He reached down and grabbed the hem of his T-shirt, and in one smooth motion he dragged it off his body. "Done."

He tossed the cloth to the carpeted floor, where it landed with a whisper that echoed around the suddenly silent bunker like cannon fire.

Look, I'd seen many men's chests before.

Like, hundreds.

Hundreds of hundreds.

In locker rooms. On the beach. On my television. On Instagram. In my own damn bathroom mirror. And that wasn't even considering the plethora I saw in exam rooms *every single day*. I could catalog the muscles, and the bones beneath them. I could pinpoint each organ they protected. There was *nothing* remarkable about a chest. Nothing noteworthy about a guy taking off his shirt.

So it was absolutely not possible that Fenn Reardon taking his shirt off would cause my entire nervous system to short-circuit somehow... or make me view him with anything but clinical detachment... or stir up anything but increased disgust and annoyance.

I never had those kinds of uncontrolled, inappropriate feelings. Ever.

Except suddenly I did.

My brain stuttered, coughing up words like *smooth* and *tan* and *ohmyfuckinggod* before it flatlined completely. I swear there was a white noise buzzing in Rafe Goodman's bunker, like one of those giant seashells that sound like the ocean when you push it to your ear, except the bunker was the shell and the sound was coming from inside me.

His chest was broad and defined without being bulky. He had abs for days—*literally one for each day of the week and a spare for holidays*, I thought hysterically. He had a trail of hair leading down from his navel to the line of whiter skin peeking out of his low-slung cargo shorts. And on his right hip, he had a freckle just above the line of his muscle, like the North Star pointing toward a constellation I couldn't see.

My mouth went dry.

"You... you..." I nodded. Then shook my head. Then swallowed.

Transversus abdominus, Mason. *What the hell is your problem? It's a muscle. Everybody has them.*

But holy shit, not everyone had them *like that*.

"This better, Doctor? More hygienic?" Fenn's words danced on my skin like an ocean breeze, making me shiver.

"You're *ridiculous*," I said, but it came out more breathless than I'd hoped. I pushed at his shoulder. "Get dressed."

"What for?" he scoffed, leaning closer. "We're on Whispering Key. You're the one who's out of line." He tweaked at the waistband of my slim-fit chinos. "And that's my entire point. I live here. You *don't*. And your fancy clothes won't last a week in this heat."

My arms fluttered at my sides, wanting to push him away again but also somehow afraid to touch his skin, which was very, very *not* normal for me. I felt arousal arc through me like an electric current, like a literal *and* figurative shock.

What the fuck was that?

"Get. Dressed," I insisted.

"Make. Me."

"I'm not kidding. You need to back up." My hands clenched into fists, then relaxed again. *Clench, release. Clench, release.* I wanted to choke the life out of him.

Or something like that.

"You didn't seem to mind being this close when we were in the car earlier and you were all up in *my* business, inserting yourself where you didn't belong. Not fun, is it?"

"*What* exactly are you doing here, Fenn? Are you going to hit me? Or are you trying to intimidate me because you know I hate enclosed spaces? Or are you trying to fuck with me because I'm straight and you're gay? If it's the third, let me just say, that's probably one of the most insulting things anyone's ever done to me, so congratulations on that. What is *wrong* with you?"

Fenn blinked. He frowned. He swallowed. He looked vaguely stunned. Then he immediately stepped back.

"*Fenn Fisher Reardon.*" Rafe Goodman's voice boomed from

the doorway. "What in the holy hell are you doing without your shirt, boy?"

"I... I was, ah..." Fenn drew a deep breath and looked at his feet. His cheeks were pink, and his bad eye was still livid and swollen. He seemed absolutely miserable.

And he *ought to*, I reminded myself. There was no excuse for trying to intimidate someone the way he had been. And for what? What did he dislike about me so much?

But nearly as incomprehensible was my overwhelming urge to protect the idiot.

"Medical question," I lied. "Mr. Reardon was asking for my professional opinion on something."

Fenn looked up at me in surprise, his eyes searching mine.

"Fenn did?" Rafe frowned, looking between us. "Why? What's wrong with him?"

"Doctor-patient confidentiality," I lied again. "But not to worry. I was just assuring him that he seems to be in good health. Isn't that right, Fenn?"

"Yeah," Fenn confirmed gruffly. "That's what you said."

I nodded briskly and turned my attention to his uncle, trying not to notice that Fenn was still half-naked and radiating heat like my own personal sun. "Now, Mr. Goodman. You and I have several things to discuss."

Rafe crossed from the door to the rolling chair on the far side of the mahogany table and dropped into it heavily. "I suppose we do. Have you seen your room yet?" He looked from me to Fenn and back again. "I had Gloria go out and buy you a whole new bedding set—new pillows, sheets, bedcover thingy. The works!"

"I haven't seen it. I'm sure it's lovely. But the larger issue, Mr. Goodman—"

"Oh!" Rafe snapped his fingers. "Towels, too. Fenn, here, was always bitching about the towels when he first came to Whispering Key. Weren't you, Fenn?"

Fenn reached down, snatched his shirt up off the floor, and pulled it over his head. He didn't answer.

Rafe sighed. "That's my nephew for you. Never happy, that one. Living here on God's own island, at one with nature, blessed with the most beautiful views on this entire planet, and he complains about scratchy towels."

A muscle in Fenn's jaw ticked.

"You led me to believe that conditions on this island were far different than they actually are," I said, getting the conversation back on track before Fenn could reply. "For example, you said the majority of my patients would be guests, and there are none. You provided a list of amenities that don't exist. You..."

"Those things don't exist *yet*." Rafe leaned back in his chair and laced his fingers over his stomach, supremely unconcerned. "They will."

You were played, Loafers.

I clenched my hands into fists. "You lied, Mr. Goodman."

"I *anticipated*, Dr. Bloom. Your contract is for three years. By the end of those three years, this island will be turning people away." He nodded once, firmly. "And you can take that to the bank."

"And the grant I was offered to pay off my student loans? Was that something you anticipated, too?"

The man looked vaguely insulted. "Of course not! I have an investor who fronted the money for that. And your three years' salary, too. I'd never lie about that."

"No, just about everything else." Fenn shook his head and glared at the ceiling. "You never stop, do you?"

It was a rhetorical question, but Rafe leaned forward, making the chair's springs squeak in protest. "No, Fenn. I never do, and I never will. Not when it comes to improving the lives of the people on this island. To making things better for *my family*." He sat back in his chair and turned his attention to me. "*You* understand how the world works, Dr. Bloom. This island is a bit of a fixer-upper. A diamond in the rough. But for a man who can look past all the surface flaws, the rewards will be *unlimited*. I need to know... are you that man?"

Rafe's eyes were alight with the zeal of a true believer, and for a second, I was caught. Hypnotized. "I..."

"Stop! You're selling Loafers a pile of horseshit, Rafe, and I won't have it," Fenn insisted.

Rafe pointed at Fenn accusingly. "I'm offering him a *future*."

"You're offering him a *dream*."

"Yes." Rafe smiled smugly. "Yes, I am. And there is *nothing* wrong with having a dream, Fenn Reardon. You might try it sometime."

"Enough," I interrupted. "*Enough*. Look, Mr. Goodman—"

"The people of this island have gone for a long time without decent medical care," Rafe said sadly. "Do you know, Gloria hasn't had a checkup in years?"

I frowned.

"Don't let him guilt you, Loafers," Fenn warned. "He's a master manipulator."

I wasn't sure when Serial Killer Guy and I had ended up on the same team. I also wasn't sure why I liked it.

"Of course, I'll be happy to provide you with an excellent reference for your next employer," Rafe continued smoothly. "Or are you planning to go back to your old position?"

I cocked my head. He had to know my old position would have been filled already. "You really *are* a master."

Rafe spread his hands innocently.

"Fortunately for you, I've decided to stay—"

Fenn made a gurgling noise like he was being strangled, and I shot him a glare.

"—for exactly as long as it takes for me to find another job. And I'll stay because the people of this island deserve good medical care. But I already *have* dreams, Mr. Goodman." I gave him a half-smile. "And I will *not* sacrifice them for anyone else's."

He nodded slowly. "I can respect that."

"That means you'll need to start contacting the other candidates for this position *today* and find someone else to take over. And I'll get back on MedLister and hope someone else is as eager to help rush through my certifications as you were."

"I'm sure you will," Rafe said with a dismissive wave. "And in the meantime, you'll set up the clinic?" Rafe asked. "Get things in shape for the next person?"

"Of course. Yes."

Rafe nodded and came around the desk to shake my hand. "Good man. Just so you know, we've got a resident named Taffy Simmons who once did billing for a medical office on the mainland. Fenn'll drive you over to meet her tomorrow morning, and she can show you around the office we plan to set up as a clinic. She'll be handling your administrative work, and if you give her a list of supplies and equipment, I'll make sure you get them."

Fenn huffed out a breath, and Rafe's sharp-eyed brown gaze narrowed on him.

"And now Fenn, here, will show you to your room and bring up your luggage."

"Oh, will I?"

Rafe clapped his nephew on the shoulder and squeezed tight. "Of course you will. In fact, I expect you to be point man for Dr. Bloom here. Help him with whatever he needs over the next few weeks."

It was clear from the grim smile he shot me that Rafe intended this to be a reward for my attitude and a punishment for Fenn.

But looking at Fenn's face, I was pretty sure it was the other way around.

5

FENN

I finished unloading the last of Mason's suitcases from the Charger, slammed the trunk shut, and stared up at the motel where I was no longer the only resident. The heat of the day was radiating off the pavement and melting through my sandals, though the sun had dropped below the horizon line twenty minutes before.

Still, I was still reluctant to move. Dragging my feet, *literally*.

I'd gone to the Concha for dinner, which wasn't unusual, but for the first time in a while, the little restaurant with its sunshiny walls and tiny tables wasn't its quiet, homey self. The entire population of Whispering Key was *buzzing* with the news of Mason Bloom's arrival, and I was supposed to be the source of all information.

Lety's sister-in-law Juju, who'd heard about Loafers from Omar Abadi, who'd heard from Dale, had demanded to know if the new doctor was *handsome*.

Madeline McKetcham had twirled a lock of her blonde hair

and asked if he was *nice*, while her grandfather, George, had scathingly inquired if he was *young*.

Bubba, Lety's husband, had wanted to know where in the hell the new clinic was gonna be, and how he could get an appointment.

Mr. Wynott wondered if he should send over some books. Lety's sister Isobel had offered some decorations for his "apartment." Curt Ballinger wondered if he liked to fish. Gerry Twomey, predictably, had wanted to know if he liked *men*, and if so, was he attached?

I'd barely been able to eat two bites of my *pepian* without being harassed, and I'd grown increasingly pissed off as I ignored their questions.

Mason Bloom wasn't *handsome* or *nice*. Those were lame-ass words that in no way described the man. He was hot. He was a judgmental ass. I had no idea what he enjoyed doing, since I'd spent the entire ride from the airport wanting to fight him or fuck him or drive him away. I wanted him in my bed. I wanted him to go home.

And worst of *all*? I owed the man one hell of an apology.

I'd asked Lety for a second container of the chicken stew, figuring food was always a good peace offering, and Lety, who was more psychic than Beale and his mother put together, had looked me up and down and pursed her lips as she'd handed me the container.

"*El sabio cambia de opinion, el necio no,*" she'd said, and even though my Spanish was for shit, I'd understood that she'd read my guilt and issued me a stern warning. I imagined it meant something like, "Stop being a dumbass to the new doctor, Fenn Reardon, just because he's prissy and hates your ratty shirt and reminds you that you're sexually frustrated."

I took a deep breath and forced it out as I stared up at the building.

There wasn't really any excuse for my behavior earlier. I disliked Loafers—and, okay, *no*, that wasn't true. I didn't like that I *did* like him, in spite of his ridiculous shoes and his genuinely deplorable, snotty attitude—but that didn't matter. I *knew* better than to physically intimidate anyone or get in their personal space without a direct invitation. One minute we'd been talking about treasure, calm as you please, then suddenly we were arguing about life choices, and Mason's green eyes were looking at me like he knew my every secret weakness and I…

I'd Hulked out on him and ripped off my T-shirt in impotent rage.

Never a good idea. Especially not when you were a gay man, invading a straight man's space.

Yeah. So… not my finest hour. By a long shot.

And then having him come up with that story in front of Rafe? Saving my ass from a very awkward, fumbling explanation?

I recognized when I owed a debt, and I didn't enjoy the sensation, so I was going to attempt to repay it. Especially since the idiot was planning to stick around Whispering Key for a few weeks—likely *longer*, if I knew Rafe Goodman and his wheedling ways.

I hefted the bag of food higher on my hip and grabbed the handle of the suitcase, rolling it across the parking lot, up the stairs, and around the back side of the building.

The room Rafe had asked Gloria to prepare for Loafers was on the second floor facing the water, on the side of the property closest to the Goodmans' house, just down the walkway from my own place. Beale and I had hauled his other two suitcases up earlier, but I'd been too annoyed to apologize and Loafers hadn't seemed to expect me to, which was kind of lowering, when I thought about it.

I knocked loudly. "Loafers! Special delivery."

A seagull cried out, and I turned to watch it soar across the pink-and-scarlet horizon, its graceful arc reflected on the water below. There were seconds—or maybe fractions of seconds—when I could almost understand what Big Rafe saw in this place. It was beautiful and unspoiled, as familiar and constantly evolving as the waves themselves. I'd felt connected to the island the moment I'd set foot here, and I still did, in a way. But even all these years later, it didn't feel like *home* the way it did for Beale and Rafe. I wasn't sure it ever would.

I turned and pounded my fist against the door. "Loafers! You in there? I hauled your suitcase up here like a fucking bell-hop, dude. Least you could do is open the door."

I waited ten seconds. Twenty.

"Come *on*." I pounded again. "I brought you food! As a peace offering. And I... I'm sorry. Is that what you want to hear? I was way out of line earlier."

There was no response, and I sighed, resting my forehead against the door. For all I knew, Loafers had gone for a walk on the beach after Rafe had given him his key and pointed out his room. Or maybe he was chatting with Beale and Big Rafe, eating Hamburger Helper at the little Formica table in their mismatched kitchen.

I snorted. No, I couldn't quite picture Loafers doing that.

"Fine, whatever. I'm leaving the food here." I turned the suitcase on its side and set the food bag on top. And just in case he *was* inside, I added, "If you need anything—if you need *me*—I'm seven doors down on this—"

From inside the room came a shriek followed by a metallic clatter and a *thud* so loud I could almost feel the floor shake.

"Loafers?" *Fuck.* I kicked at the door. "Loafers! What's going on? It better not be another gecko!"

But there was no answer except another slightly garbled scream.

"*Shit*. I'm coming in, asshole! You'd better be decent!" I tried the door, but it was locked, so I pulled up on the knob and shoved my hip into the hollow metal. It opened with a *pop*, as I'd known it would, and my eyes darted around the darkened room.

Nothing seemed out of place. The room was ruthlessly clean and citrus fresh. The king-sized bed was covered with a tidy, and apparently *new*, white coverlet. A distinctive pair of brown loafers were lined up beside the bed. The world's saddest air conditioner chugged out an anemic stream of barely cool air. And from the closed bathroom came the sound of rushing water on tile along with a pained *groan*.

Shit.

Loafers was in the shower. And for all I knew, the cries I'd heard were not *unhappy* cries.

Thank God he hadn't seen me.

I pivoted to retreat, tiptoeing as much as a person could while wearing sandals, but just before I cleared the doorway, a tidal wave of water poured from under the bathroom door, soaking the threadbare carpet. Loafers gave another gurgling yell.

I stood for a second, undecided. I mean, what were the chances he was *getting off* on nearly drowning, versus the chances that he was *actually* drowning?

Loafers, who'd seemed shocked at the idea of rope play, was *probably* not into some kind of water-based autoerotic asphyxiation.

"*Fuck it*," I muttered. I pushed open the bathroom door and stepped into a fucking lake.

"*Mo-ther-fuck-ing-fuck!*" Loafers yelled, fortunately not at me but at the fire-hydrant-strength stream of water *gushing* out of a hole in the middle of the shower wall where the handle used to be.

Loafers was buck naked on his knees in the center of the tub, with his eyes screwed shut and his hands out in front of him, holding the broken shower handle like he was attempting to play a high-stakes game of pin the tail on the donkey *with the plumbing*. The drab gray shower curtain was halfway open like he'd debated escaping the shower before deciding to stand and fight. His hair was plastered to his head, and water sluiced down his surprisingly fit body in a way that was very, very...

Not the point, Reardon.

"Loafers!" I yelled. "Get out of there!"

He opened his eyes, and his head swung in my direction... and the stream of water smacked him in the side of the face, knocking him over. He floundered and it sounded like he hit his head against the bottom of the tub. *Shit.*

I waded through the puddled water, and nearly slipped and fell myself, until I ditched my flip-flops and surfed over to him.

"Loafers? Mason!" He was curled on his side, in the fetal position, covering his face. His fingers were still clenched around the stupid shower handle, and it sounded like he was saying, "It came off in my hands! It just... came off!" which meant he wasn't dead or dying... probably.

So I waded back out into the bedroom, ran to the empty closet, threw open the access panel in the lower back corner, and turned the shut-off valve until the sound of rushing water faded to a steady, hollow *drip-drip-drip.*

I heaved a shaky breath, then let it out.

"Mason?"

No response.

"Mason?" I stood and picked my way across the squelching carpet back to the bathroom. "Are you okay?"

The only reply was a wet, snuffling noise, and from the bathroom doorway I could see his shoulders shaking, like he was crying. Or maybe in shock. What did shock look like?

Damn it. What was the good of having a doctor around when *he* was the one hurt?

"Is it your head?" I demanded, rushing toward the tub with zero regard for the stupid flip-flops I'd abandoned earlier. I tripped and caught air, grabbing at the first thing I could find to break my fall, which happened to be the ancient shower curtain.

I landed directly on top of Mason in the tub, with the curtain tangled around my waist and one arm, while his shoulder lodged firmly into my opposite armpit. A second later, the curtain rod landed on my head.

"*Ow.* Piece of *shit!*"

I reached up and pushed the rod onto the floor, then balanced my weight on my one free hand, so I wasn't *entirely* suffocating the man beneath me, though I was pretty sure I wouldn't be able to extricate myself without assistance.

"Mason! Are you okay?"

He was still covering his face with his hands, clutching the stupid shower handle to his forehead, so I wriggled my trapped arm out of its plastic prison, grabbed the handle, and threw it on the floor next to the curtain rod where it landed with a splash.

Mason's shoulders shook harder than ever, and he made a sound like he was suppressing a sob.

My stomach twisted. I sucked at this *comforting* shit.

I pushed myself up further so he could maybe breathe better, and tried to pry his fingers away from his face, but I ended up slipping and falling on him more fully, because somehow this day kept getting *worse.*

"Christ, I'm sorry. Mason? *Fuck.* Please calm down. It's gonna be okay. Okay? It's gonna be... you know... *fine.*"

I shook his shoulder, but the sobbing continued, so I ran a hand over his wet hair instead. I was leagues out of my depth and sinking fast.

"I know you've had a lot happen today. And it's gotta seem overwhelming. But... just... don't cry. Did you concuss yourself?" I pulled at his fingers again. "Did you... Wait! *Motherfucker.* Are you *laughing*?"

Mason nodded, his eyes still squeezed shut. His whole body *trembled* as he sucked in a breath. "Oh, God! This day. I'm not a passionate *person*," he moaned. He let his forearm fall back over his face and shifted so he was lying on his back in the inch or so of water that remained in the tub. "Figures I want something that's *mine*, and it turns out what's *mine* is a situation that's fucked-up beyond all recognition."

"Are you... are you having a mental break right now?" I demanded as I tried to process his collection of unrelated sentences.

"All I wanted was respect and independence. Is this better or worse than being recruited by the mob, do you think?"

Shit. "How hard did you hit your head?" I pulled at his arm again. "Look at me, Mason. Can you focus? How many eyes do I have?"

He sniffed loudly and moved his arm just enough to look up at me.

"You have *one*," he said promptly. "At least, one that I can *see*, because the other is nearly swollen shut." He lifted a hand to my face, but I flinched away, and he shook his head disapprovingly. "You should've kept the ice on it," he chided softly.

"Yeah, well. I was a little busy playing chauffeur."

"And intimidating innocent doctors."

"Did not."

But he lifted an eyebrow, and all of a sudden, I remembered with a wince. Rafe's office. My shirt.

Right.

"You're not innocent. But I, ah… I definitely *do* owe you an apology for that scene earlier." I took a deep breath. "I'm truly sorry that I tried to intimidate you. I'm sorry I made things weird. I'm not that guy, I swear. Okay?"

Mason nodded slowly and wiped his eyes. "Okay."

"Just like that?" I mean, I wanted him to believe me. I just… didn't get why he would, after the day we'd had.

Mason smiled. "You're a jerk and possibly a serial killer, but I don't get the impression that you're a liar, and dealing with your uncle would make a saint commit a felony. Plus, I'm not sure if you noticed, but my own behavior today wasn't exactly impeccable. So, yeah. *Okay.*"

"*Okay*," I repeated, weirdly relieved. "So, I brought up your suitcases. And I bought you dinner." I hooked a thumb out the bathroom door, to where the room door was still hanging wide open and the darkening pink sky was just visible over the water. "Chicken stew and fried yucca. As a peace offering. And I, um... brought you an old plug-in night-light I found kicking around." Kicking around at Pickles' grocery store in the home goods section, to be precise. "Just in case the room got—" *Jesus, I sounded like an idiot.* "—dark."

"Wow." He smiled and turned my words from earlier back on me. "Well, as apologies go, I've had worse."

My throat went tight.

Mason's hair was a mass of damp, brown waves that made him look about twelve years old, all pushed back as they were. But right at the front, two or three silver threads glinted, and I couldn't help but stare. It was another chink in Mason Bloom's veneer of perfection—not that there was much of that left, to be honest, given where we were and why. A little crack that let the truth of him shine through.

My gaze tracked lower, and when our eyes met I saw that his were wide and watchful, a luminous green against his pale skin, and it might have just been my wishful thinking or whatever, but I'd have sworn he was waiting for something.

Waiting for *me*.

My eyes darted down to his lips, which were parted slightly, and I noticed the moment when his breathing hitched from something that was definitely *not* laughter. My gaze shifted back to his, but Mason didn't move, so neither did I, and the moment spun out. It lasted two seconds—then ten, then twenty—and for every second, there was an alternate universe in which one of us moved forward or back, committed or retreated, but in this one we were frozen. Staring. Daring each other with our eyes.

No misunderstandings. No place else to be. We might have stayed there forever.

But then a gust of salty air blew through the room, sending the bathroom door crashing into the wall and kicking up little goose bumps on every part of my skin that was damp —which was basically *all the parts*. I shivered back to reality and straight into an Adam-and-Steve-type moment of awareness, where I suddenly realized that—*Hey, now!*— Mason Bloom was all the way naked.

And lying under me.

In a pink bathtub.

Soaking wet.

With his body separated from my body by only a cheap plastic shower curtain and my damp, damp *cargo shorts.*

My dick went hard almost instantly.

I'll take Awkward Porn Scenarios for $2000, Alex?

But the weirdest part? Mason wasn't pushing me off him. He had to notice I was hard, the way my cock was pressed against his hip, but didn't say a word about it. In fact, he seemed pretty darn content to just stay there all night. A little smile played around his mouth, like he was... relaxed?

Just a couple of dudes, doing what dudes do on a Friday night. *In a tub.*

Mason even shifted his hips the tiniest bit like he was

getting comfortable, adjusting his position so the lower half of his body could better cradle mine.

You know, just one bro helping another, if the first bro was naked and the other was on top of him, fully erect and all wet. *No homo.*

The moment he shifted, though, we *both* noticed that wasn't the *only* issue at hand. Mason was hard, too. Undeniably, unequivocally, *rock*-fucking-*hard*.

I say we *both* noticed because yeah, Mason looked nearly as shocked as I was. I hadn't thought a guy could get that hard without noticing, but maybe the knock to the head had shaken him up or something.

His green eyes flared wide, and I could almost see him connecting the dots between "Oh, *gee*, I'm hard" and "Oh, *shit*, I'm hard and naked with *Fenn*."

I held my breath and waited for the fallout. For the freak-out. For the empty laugh that didn't cover the outraged anger. For the denial. For the *blame* that was 100 percent certainly gonna fall in my lap.

Instead, Mason blinked like a little owl, sank his teeth into his bottom lip, looking like all thirty-one flavors of fuckable in one annoying package. Then he *shifted again* so his erection rubbed against mine, and he sucked in a breath like it felt pretty damn good.

I was out of that tub in a nanosecond, on my knees on the floor in the cold water, struggling to remove the kraken-like shower curtain from around my ankles.

I didn't fuck around with straight guys, and I *definitely* didn't fuck around with guys who claimed to be straight but were willing to be corrupted.

"Listen, that thing in Rafe's office earlier?" I said, getting to my feet. "Me, getting in your space? That was my fault. A hundred percent. And I already apologized for it. But I'm not taking responsibility for... for... *this*." I waved a hand in the direction of his crotch. "You get me? This was *not* my fault, it was *yours*."

Mason's cheeks flamed red and he sat up, bunching the curtain over his groin like he was suddenly embarrassed—three minutes too late, in my opinion, 'cause I'd been *feeling* that hard length pressed against me until a second ago.

"Of course it wasn't your fault! It's not... it's not *anyone's* fault. It's not a fault *thing*. Stimulus is stimulus." He paused, like he was trying to digest his own bullshit.

"Really? You get stimulated around guys a lot?" I grabbed my sandals off the floor and jammed them on my feet. "'Cause there's a word for those of us who experience this regularly, and it's not *straight*."

"N-no, I never have. But we..." He waved his hand at the shower. "And you..." He waved a hand at the curtain on the floor. "And... it just happened. I don't know why." He sounded confused.

From a distant corner of my brain came a snippet of a conversation, playing like a picture-in-picture.

"It just happened, Fenn. I felt you wanting me from the minute you walked into my office, and I couldn't help it. You made me want you back."

"Why you gotta be so sexy, Fenn? I was doin' so good today, then you walk in here like a cool drink of water and I can't think right. Lock the door and get on your knees for me. Now."

"Come on, Fenn, me 'n' Misty have practically been engaged since the cradle. It don't mean a single thing to either of us. She's never made me feel the way you make me feel. Just one more kiss, Fenn. One more... that's it. God, Fenn, yes!"

"We need to make sure Dad never finds out. He wouldn't understand I'm still straight as I ever was. He wouldn't understand you made me weak for you."

I sucked in a deep breath and tried to focus on the shivering man in the bathtub.

"Yeah, well. My dick's usually a little more selective than yours seems to be. Stimulus is stimulus? *Please.*"

"What's *that* supposed to mean?"

"It means..." I stared down at him, trying to figure out what to say.

It meant... *I knew a guy like you, once.*

It meant... *Just about every gay man has known a* hundred *guys like you.*

It meant... *I am* done *with guys who are straight as an* arrow, *straight as a* line *while the lights are on but can't wait to get their dicks in my mouth the second we're alone.*

It meant... *I am* over *guys who let me fuck them, then end up fucking me over.*

"It means... nothing," I finally concluded, squeezing my eyes shut and turning around. "Not a damn thing. Enjoy your dinner in heterosexual tranquility."

"Wait, what?" Mason sputtered. "Don't be like that, Fenn! I'm sorry, okay? It was an accident. I couldn't *help* it!" His face got redder and redder. "I thought we were okay with each other now."

"God. Is there a script you people follow?"

"Us people?"

If he'd face-planted into the tub again, Mason couldn't have looked more bewildered, and on some level I *knew* I was being unfair. Mason wasn't Thad Chambers. Mason was Mason.

But also? I had One Life Rule for a reason.

"Never mind. Just..." I clenched my hands into fists. "Call Rafe. Tell him to get a plumber out here. Tell him to pay the guy a decent rate and not offer him a hunk of moon rock for the job."

"Okay, but—"

"And have him move you to another room. Immediately."

"Yeah, obviously. But—"

"And tell him *he* can take your ass to work in the morning."

"I can take my own ass!" he returned. "I'll call a cab."

I gave him a withering glance that I hoped conveyed his chances of finding a cab that would come all the way to Whispering Key and take him a mile down the road to work.

"And watch out, because there's a storm coming, and the door locks are shit," I warned. Turned out Beale and his motherfucking portents had been right, damn it all.

"Fenn!" I could hear the rustle of plastic as he shifted. "Can we please talk about—"

I shook my head. The last thing I wanted to do was talk. If I stayed one more minute, I was going to kiss him. I was going to do anything he'd *let* me do.

And then I'd hate myself even more than I already did.

"Have a good night, Loafers. Call me when you're ready to go back to the airport."

6

——————

MASON

I gritted my teeth and forced myself to type.

I shoved my phone facedown into the comforter and groaned up at the ceiling.

That was some bitter fucking irony right there. Micah thought I knew what I was doing? *Ha.* In my entire life—and I mean, even including the teenaged parts, when I did almost every harebrained thing my idiot friends ever dared me to do, complete with all the broken bones and community service that earned me—I had never, ever felt *less* like I knew what I was doing.

Taking control of my *one goddamn life* had ended up with me stranding myself on an island with spotty cell service, rotting plumbing, and the most insane collection of humans I'd ever seen assembled in one place.

Living *fearlessly* had resulted in me getting an erection under the worst, most humiliating circumstances possible, sending my serial killer slash new best friend fleeing into the night like my hard dick was a match that might light him on fire.

And now I was spending yet another night alone in my hotel room, which was way less comfortable than my old apartment, overthinking things, as usual, but now with the added bonus of sweating my ass off while I did it.

This morning being Monday, I'd officially opened the new medical center and seen my first Whispering Key patients... and if I hadn't been firmly committed to a career in medicine and firmly indebted to the bank that owned my student loans, I might have seriously reconsidered going back to my college barista gig, because these people were *certifiable.*

I'd trooped up the stairs to the old meeting rooms in the Whispering Key Rec Center where my new assistant Taffy and I had spent all weekend organizing a bunch of second-hand furniture and office supplies into something resembling a clinic, only to find thirty-four residents already crowding the makeshift waiting room, all insisting they'd gotten there first, and poor Taffy nearly in tears trying to corral them all.

It had only gone downhill from there.

Mrs. Lorenna McKetcham, aged seventy-eight, had started out the morning asking whether I planned to give out free condoms to advocate safe sex on Whispering Key, and if so, could she take some to share with her mahjong friends who'd be assembling down the hall later? "We get pretty wild after our game nights," she'd admitted with a terrifyingly girlish giggle. Then she'd bit her lip. "We're always looking for new members, Doc. You could stop by if you wanted to."

I'd thanked her politely and given her a large bag full of condoms, but I had *not* stopped by. If her group had found a way to make mahjong into foreplay, I did not possess the mental fortitude to know about it.

Gloria Frye had come in shortly after that, sporting a *different* floral dress and a pair of very bruised, heat-swollen feet stuffed, once again, into too-tight pumps. "Used to happen to my mother, too," she'd sighed. "Does this mean I'm getting... old?" She'd only come because Mr. Goodman had insisted, she said, but she'd been grimly satisfied when she'd stepped on the scale. "Lowest weight since I graduated high school, and it's all thanks to my miracle pineapple bread. Loaded with so many antioxidants that it improves your mood and *burns* calories while you chew it!"

I'd tried to explain that this was highly unlikely, but she'd just pinched her lips, looked me up and down, and told me in a cheerful voice that she'd bring me a loaf—*or maybe two* —which was so perfectly passive-aggressive, I couldn't feel anything but admiration.

Gerry Twomey, aged forty-seven, who had the most unnaturally smooth skin I'd seen in my entire life, stopped by to have me check out his hip, which he was fairly certain he'd injured by dancing. "It was all a blur once the party kicked in. I bet you know a thing or two about partying, Mason—do you mind if I call you Mason? I'm always up for a good time."

I'd prescribed rest, an anti-inflammatory, and a follow-up in a few weeks. I'd also kinda wanted to suggest he check out Mrs. McKetcham's group, down the hall... but then I'd thought better of it. Getting Gerry Twomey together with the Whispering Key Mahjong Society might create a public safety hazard.

Leticia Irvine, at least, had made no bones about why she'd *really* come to see me. After I'd examined her aching shoulder and prescribed some medication, she'd settled herself on the old couch at the front of the room and given me a searching look like she was assessing *my* vitals, rather than the other way around. "So, new doctor. You speak Spanish? No? Hmm. What brings you to the key, *patojo?*"

I'd stammered something about wanting a change and a fresh start, and she'd responded with a nod and a very long, very solemn, very sigh-filled string of Spanish.

"I'm sorry," I'd said, spreading my hands. "I didn't understand a word... or was that the point?"

She'd pushed herself to her feet, grabbed my chin, and

nodded firmly. "*Bien chispudo.* You'll do okay. Come to the Concha for your lunch. I'm making *tapado.* You'll love it."

I'd had no idea what that was either, but I'd nodded, because I was already getting that you didn't argue with Lety Irvine, and there was comfort in the idea that at least one of the incomprehensible things on this island didn't want or expect me to make sense of it.

And as it turned out, the seafood stew had been really fucking good.

But then Beale Goodman, who'd once again driven me the mile or so from the motel to the town center that morning and back home that evening, as sweet and good-natured as ever, had shown that he was a little bit *odd* as well. I'd noticed him favoring his shoulder, and he'd explained that he'd somehow sprained it while trapping a wild creature, which was... as valid a hobby as any, I supposed. But when I'd offered to treat it, he'd said he was *already* treating it by wearing a bracelet made of "white quartz crystals, which heal nearly *everything*, Doc."

Seriously, between the crystals and the *ferrymones*, it was amazing these people were still alive.

At least Beale had agreed to let me show him some stretches, proving he was odd but *reasonable*—

A door slammed outside, indicating that Fenn Reardon was home, after another day of successfully avoiding me.

—unlike his cousin, who remained provokingly *unreasonable.*

I was absolutely *not* going to chase the man. Hell, no. I'd tried to go after him the night he'd left, but he'd driven off in his stupid car. I'd spent an hour knocking on his door one day when I *knew* he was in there, and he hadn't answered. I had no clue why he'd overreacted the way he had, and if he didn't want to accept my apology for my... overenthusiasm, I wasn't going to humiliate myself further by obsessing over it.

That was that.

Over and done.

Moving on.

Except... I wasn't.

Because tonight, like the last three nights, I couldn't seem to *stop* myself from remembering every single moment of our interaction Friday, from the minute Fenn had appeared in the bathroom like a white knight who knew where the shutoff valve was, to the second he'd fallen on top of me—which should *not* have been amusing *or* comfortable given what a behemoth he was, but had actually been both until it was neither.

I... just... really... *liked* the guy.

There. I admitted it.

We had fuck all in common, he was a total asshole, and he wasn't *nearly* as amusing as he thought he was, but he'd bought me a freakin' night-light and some yummy dinner, so I was pissed at myself for ruining things.

And even weirder, how the fuck had I gotten aroused *for a man* when it fit precisely *zero* patterns?

Unassailable medical fact: most guys got erections *all the time*—doing sportsball things, or in the aftermath of danger, or when the fucking *breeze* blew too hard. And by the law of averages, sometimes other guys happened to be around when that happened. So, it could be *possible* that I hadn't been hard *for* Fenn, I'd just been hard *near* him—an accidental erection caused by endorphins, or adrenaline, or simple friction.

Correlation versus causation, right?

The only flaw in this logic was that I had never really been the sort of person who popped wood all over the place, not even as a teenager. I didn't have a problem getting an erection, with the right amount of effort, I just tended not to get them when I didn't need them, and I fucking did *not* need one last Friday.

You're not a passionate person, Mason, I heard Victoria saying, like it was incontrovertible fact.

So why, *why*, was I suddenly *passionate* about the man formerly known as Serial Killer Guy, of all people on earth? My whole body flushed with embarrassment.

Maybe I needed to try Beale's healing crystals on my *brain.*

I pushed myself off the bed and went to tinker with the air-conditioning unit under the window for the seven hundredth time in the past couple of days. The dial was set as cold as it could go, the blower was turned up to eleven, and the machine was making a racket like it was crushing ice for a margarita or preparing to launch the whole island into space, but exactly *nothing* happened, just like the other six hundred ninety-nine times I'd done this.

I turned around and sank down to the carpet with my back against the wall, resting my elbows on my bent knees and letting the thin stream of barely cool air wash over my sweaty skin. It had to be over a hundred degrees in the room, and I was roasting, even wearing nothing but boxer briefs. It didn't help that I had every incandescent bulb in the place glowing and the windows firmly shut, but there was another goddamn storm blowing over Whispering Key, whipping the palm trees next door around in the moonlight, and there were worse things than a little heatstroke.

Like thunderstorms. And darkness. And thunderstorms *in* the darkness.

It's not a phobia if you can handle it, I reminded myself. *It's a concern.*

But then a bead of sweat ran down my forehead, and suddenly I was right back in that shower with Fenn.

Fenn, who'd bought me a night-light that wasn't quite bright enough.

Fenn, who had well-formed abdominal muscles and nicely constructed shoulders.

Fenn, whose face had been poised above me, whose breath had mingled with mine, whose blue, blue eyes had been full of amusement and concern and just... *fuck*... appreciation...

Fenn, who wouldn't talk to me.

My stomach ached like I'd been whacked in the solar plexus.

I jumped up and straightened the brand-new coverlet on my bed, then lay down on top of it again, this time with my arms and legs spread wide to catch any hint of a breeze the AC might decide to spit out. It was too hot to unpack anymore, and I was wary of the shower after the first disaster. I was too amped to read, and too tired to concentrate on puzzles. The television got three channels, one of which was local cable news, and another a Spanish psychic who reminded me a lot of Lety, so I'd picked the program I could ignore most easily—a truly annoying infomercial about an oscillating dumbbell that promised to amp up my workouts. I considered turning it off entirely and going to sleep, but flashes of lightning still lit the sky through the thin curtains, making that a Very Bad Idea.

Really, what kind of idiot forgot Florida was the thunderstorm capital of America when he was making his life plans? *This fucking idiot right here.*

Thunder boomed outside, and I grabbed my phone to see if there were any new jobs on MedLister, because getting off this island was my top priority.

There was one near Atlanta, which could be nice, if it paid more. Another was for a town in Iowa, which sounded a lot like O'Leary: zero adventure and exponentially more corn. But the one with an international charity organization traveling to impoverished third-world countries was a little too *much* adventure for a guy who couldn't handle a broken shower knob. None of them seemed quite right.

Because you're Goldilocks all of a sudden and have the luxury of waiting for something just right?

I rolled my eyes at myself, forced myself to apply for all three jobs, and sent Rafe Goodman an email that he should be expecting some phone calls from these places *and* the others I'd already applied for over the weekend. I was sure any potential employer would want an explanation of my two-minute stay here on Whispering Key.

Sadly, none of that process took very long at all. Less time than it took for, say, the sky to stop flashing. Or for some muscle-bound idiot to sell me a vibrating dumbbell.

Definitely less time than it took for me to stop obsessing over Fenn Reardon.

What if... what *if*... it *had* actually been sexual attraction that had gotten me aroused? Occam's Razor, right? Shortest distance between two points was a straight line?

Except... *ha*... did that mean my line actually *wasn't* so straight?

It didn't seem possible.

Incontrovertible personal fact: I knew and loved dozens of gay and bisexual people, my own *brother* among them. I had a Human Rights Campaign shirt stuffed in one of my suitcases that said Proud Ally. I was not a late bloomer. I was not stuck in a closet. I didn't live a life where I'd never examined my sexuality.

Hell, I snorted to myself. My first kiss, back in high school? *With. A. Guy.* And the earth had not moved even a centimeter.

If I were bisexual, that kiss back in high school would have felt like puzzle pieces clicking together, the way Micah said his first kiss with a guy had felt. Or like the answer to a question I hadn't known to ask, as my friend Toby put it. I liked to imagine it would have felt like all the heavenly angels singing a hosanna as a light from heaven burst down. Something completely unsubtle like that. It definitely would *not* have felt fucking *weird* and unpleasant, which was how it *had* felt.

If Fenn had stuck around, I would have explained all this to him. I'd have told him that I'd run the tests years and years ago and the diagnosis was really fucking obvious: I was straight.

At least, I had been... until I'd landed on the Island of Misfit Toys, where bread burned calories, and snakes lived in clothes dryers, and straight people suddenly found they weren't.

And even now, when I thought about any other guy I knew, I got *zero* tingles. The thought of swapping saliva with Toby? *Blech.* The thought of fucking around with Constantine, even aside from the fact that Micah would beat me senseless if he knew I'd ever let the thought flash across my brain? *Gross.* The thought of Chris Pratt, who Victoria had always assured me was the hottest guy in Hollywood, doing anything on, around, or near my person? The thought of the muscle-bound guy from the Shake Weight infomercial right now on my television bringing his leering grin anywhere in my vicinity? *Distasteful in the extreme.*

But the thought of putting my lips near Fenn Reardon, with his knowing looks, and his busted eye, and his *childish* insistence on not calling me by my real name was... was...

I swallowed thickly, suddenly sucked into an image of me, rubbing my lips against Fenn's jaw, my cheek against his rough beard. My cock stirred in my underwear.

This was simply not right.

What was wrong with me?

Who the hell got all up in their feelings for someone not just *despite* the way they drove you crazy, but possibly *because* of it? Or possibly because there was honesty in their reactions, and they'd seen you at your worst, and you'd put zero effort into impressing them, but strangely enough, they'd seemed to like you anyway, for one brief, shining moment, even though you weren't the sort of person who inspired true passion in others.

I grabbed a pillow and pounded it several times before shoving it beneath my head.

Fenn and I had nothing in common. We were completely incompatible. He obviously had anger issues. He wore *cheap, plastic flip-flops.*

"Goddamn it!" I told the ceiling. "This is unacceptable!"

The ceiling remained impassively silent.

Maybe there was a third possibility. A possibility somewhere in between the two. I hadn't had sex with anyone since Victoria left over four months ago, and maybe I was suffering from some kind of sexual frustration that made my animal urges that much harder to ignore?

In layman's terms... I was *horny*. And lonely, too.

And it didn't take a medical degree to understand that the comorbidity of lonely and horny was only gonna make each condition worse, right?

Duh.

I closed my eyes and brushed a hand down my chest, toying with my nipple, and nearly snorted at the way blood *rushed* to my cock. One tiny motion and I was half-hard and tenting the front of my boxer briefs like I was sixteen again. Horny for *real.*

I spread my legs further, gliding my fingers along the edge of my waistband, letting the anticipation build, before I dragged them lower and gripped myself through the thin cotton.

Fuck. It had been too long since I'd done this. If two jerks through cloth got me fully hard, it was no wonder I was on a hair trigger and primed for *any* stimulus, no matter how ordinarily un-stimulating it might have been.

I slipped my free hand under my waistband to cup my balls and let my mind wander, enjoying the sensation, letting the moment spiral out, pondering abdominal muscles and tanned smooth skin, a challenging smile and eyes like deep water and...

Fuck.

I opened my eyes with a gasp and sat up.

This was ridiculous. When you tried too hard not to think of elephants, all you could think of was elephants, right? So, when I told myself not to think of Fenn Reardon, was it really so surprising that his naked chest sprang to mind?

I flipped the pillow over to find a cool spot, grabbed my phone, opened a private browser, typed in a random porn site, and immediately felt much, *much* better.

Porn wasn't always my thing—*Yes, really. No, I wasn't a prude. Much.*—but today the porn gods smiled on me, because when I clicked randomly on the first video that came up, the woman on the screen was really, *really* pretty, with long brown hair, big brown eyes, and perfectly proportioned, perfectly symmetrical breasts that worked for me in *all kinds of ways.*

I bit my lip, gripped myself through my underwear again, and found I was harder than ever. Yeah, this was *definitely* working for me. I arched my head back into the pillow and groaned as I worked myself over while the woman on the screen climbed atop her partner and threw her head back in desire.

I frowned and yanked out my headphones, since the brunette's fake sex noises were driving me crazy and not in a good way, then finally shut the phone off altogether. It was all too rehearsed. Too... *wrong.*

I spit in my palm and closed my eyes once more, conjuring an image of the woman from the video, her hair and her eyes and her beautiful breasts all poised above me. I stroked myself hard and fast, planting my feet flat on the bed and twisting my fist on the upstroke exactly the way I liked best.

Fuck. This was very, very good. Pure escapism. Pure release.

In my mind, the anonymous woman's hair hung down around us like a curtain, obscuring everything except her eyes. Her fingers threaded with mine, and she used them for leverage as she moved against me. My fist flew faster and faster on my spit-slicked dick, and I was so close, *so close,* caught up in that Gulf-blue gaze and the heavy, solid weight of her...

Wait, no.

The woman on the video had brown eyes. *Brown,* not Gulf blue. And she was probably light as a feather, not remotely solid. And she had breasts. Good Lord, the breasts!

But when I tried to picture them, to hold the thought in my mind... I couldn't.

Fuck.

I could *not.*

And Fenn Reardon grinned down at me, looking all kinds of smug and happy, as the annoying motherfucker hijacked my jerk session.

My brain screamed *abort, abort,* but it was way too late. I couldn't have, even if I'd wanted to and... okay, *fine,* I didn't want to. Those blue, blue, *blue* eyes were spurring me on, and his voice in my head was chanting *Mason, Mason, Mason* in time to my thrusts, and it was like a magic spell turning a key in a lock because I remembered that he *had* said my name in the bathroom Friday night. He'd said, "Look at me, Mason." *He'd said my name, and he'd looked at me like he knew me.*

And that, as they say, was that.

My orgasm hit me like a fucking *freight train*—head thrown back and spine stiffened all the way down to my toes, eyes squeezed so tight colors burst across my vision, as blast after blast of hot jizz spilled over my chest and stomach.

Then I jumped off the bed before my cock had stopped twitching and practically ran for the bathroom like the masturbation police might be after me, turning on the shower and resting my head against the powder-blue tile while all the evidence swirled down the drain.

So. *That* had happened.

But fuck if I knew what *that* was.

A bisexual awakening at thirty-five? *Shit.* No one would believe that. Hell, I wasn't sure *I* could believe it.

Demisexuality, maybe? But weren't you supposed to *like* the people you were aroused by? Did I have an annoyance kink?

Latent reverse-sapio-sexuality, where I was only into dudes who ignored me and acted like ignorant assholes?

Look, if I was bisexual, I was going to embrace the fuck out of it.

If I was.

But first I needed facts and data. I needed to diagnose the thing. I needed to figure out how to fit it inside my frame of reference, when it didn't track to anything I'd ever experienced, or even heard of.

What did you call it when a person whose very existence made you insane was also the person you connected with more instantly and completely than any other person?

Was idiot-sexual a thing?

Was *Fenn*-sexual?

Because evidence suggested that if it hadn't been before, maybe I'd just discovered it.

And I wasn't gonna be able to do a damn thing to fix it as long as the guy down the hall shut me out.

7

FENN

I was today years old when I learned that hotel room maintenance and guest satisfaction were part of my job description.

"Fenn, I need you to fix the air conditioner in a guest's room," Big Rafe had informed me this morning over the phone.

A guest. It hadn't taken me long to mentally flip through our extensive list of visitors and figure out who had complained.

"Busy," I'd informed him before hanging up and pulling my pillow back over my head.

He'd called back and started speaking like there'd been no interruption. "Mason's leaving for work in ten minutes. You know he's an early bird."

"I know nothing of the kind." In fact, I'd made it a point *not* to notice the way he'd left the motel before seven o'clock every morning in the week he'd been here. Or the way he'd come home by five o'clock in the evening. Or the way he kept his lights on each night until way late, like maybe the night-light I'd given him hadn't worked.

I also hadn't noticed him calling my name before I drove off last Friday night. And I most definitely hadn't noticed him knocking on my door for nearly an hour earlier in the week. In fact, it was surprisingly easy not to notice a person, when you put just a bit of effort into it.

Not thinking about that person, though… that was harder. In the case of Mason Bloom, it was fucking impossible. The fact that thinking about him got me hard slightly more often than it pissed me off was the icing on the cake. One more thing to blame the straight guy for.

"—and I promised him it'd be fixed today, since it's supposed to rain overnight."

"He can keep his window cracked open to catch the breeze like the rest of us. Come on."

"He shouldn't have to," Rafe shot back. "We take guest satisfaction seriously."

"Thought he was an employee."

"He's both."

Convenient. I sat up, dislodging the pillow. "And why is this *my* problem? Today's supposed to be my day off. Gotta change the oil in the Charger and buff her up. Have Beale do it."

Rafe sighed deeply, like the answer was obvious. "Beale *can't*. And if you spend any more time with that Charger, people are gonna start to talk. You're our mechanic, Fenn—"

"Still not a mechanic."

"—and air conditioners are mechanical, ergo this is your wheelhouse."

Rafe and his fucking *ergos* were gonna drive me demented.

But in the end, who'd levitated his sleepless ass off the bed, gotten in the shower, grabbed his screwdriver and Rafe's vacuum, and dragged himself down to Mason's room? Who'd pulled up a YouTube video on air conditioner repair and figured out how to remove the clogged air filter so he could wash it?

Yep. You know it.

So maybe "mechanic" was a thing one *did* as opposed to a thing one *was*.

"This is *disgusting*," I said to the empty room as I pulled out a flat, rectangular thing that could possibly have been alive at one point, based on the amount of fur covering it.

But per the instructions online, I just vacuumed the filter off, vacuumed the rest of the inside of the machine, too, for good measure, and reinserted it. Then, because I reasoned that a good mechanic would stick around to make sure it worked, *right?* I sat on the floor and allowed myself to do what I'd been dying to do since the moment I'd gotten into the room: I surveyed Mason's space.

Holy shit, the place was relentlessly, hopelessly, horrifyingly *tidy*.

The nightstand held a phone charger, a chunk of transparent rock that looked like something I could have found in Beale's room, and a dog-eared pirate thriller. The bed had been made without a single wrinkle, and I had the sudden urge to throw myself down and make snow angels.

The closet doors were open, and it was clear that Loafers had actually unpacked his bags—which was fucked-up, in my opinion, since I'd been here five years and still mostly lived out of a suitcase—and hung his many, many polos and button-downs in the closet *in precise rainbow order*. More than that, he'd clearly brought his own hangers, since they were all the exact same color and all faced the same direction. He'd put a couple of his big suitcases on the shelf at the top of the closet, and on the bottom he'd lined up his shoes like expensive little soldiers: six pairs of shiny leather ones in varying shades of brown and black, a single sand-covered pair of track shoes, and some high-end sandals.

And *which* of us supposedly gave off serial killer vibes, I ask you?

For a second, I wished he were there just so I could give him shit about that, because he was so fun when he was riled…

And then I remembered I'd been avoiding him for a week precisely *because* he was so fun to rile that *I* got easily riled, and I couldn't afford to be riled around him because he was so very, very, very, very *straight*.

And Life Rules were Life Rules, forever and ever. Amen.

"Fenn! Fenn Reardon!" a familiar voice bellowed from downstairs.

I stood and pulled back the curtains to find my uncle waving up at me. His T-shirt was orange today with the word *MAYOR* written in black across the front in shiny block letters, like we were celebrating Halloween five months early.

Jesus. How many of those shirts did he have?

"You done yet?" he yelled, hands on his hips.

I threw open the door and stepped out on the shared balcony.

"Nope."

"Yeah, ya are. Stop mooning over Mason's tighty-whiteys and get over to the house. I've got another job for ya and a big announcement!"

"Wait, what?" I had *not* been thinking about Mason's underwear.

Though, if I had been, I'd have pegged him as the type to wear tight, black boxer briefs. The plain kind that hugged every curve, and...

How the hell did Rafe know what kind of underwear he wore, anyway?

And what announcement?

By the time I thought about any of these excellent questions, it was too late to ask. Rafe had disappeared through the trees toward his house, whistling a peppy tune.

I rubbed a hand over my face and went back to Mason's room to collect my tools and vacuum, then—*under duress*, mind you—marched my ass next door.

I walked into the kitchen and found Young Rafe and Beale sitting silently, their bulky frames making the little table and chairs look like doll furniture. Rafe, who was just a fraction leaner than his younger brother with hair more black than brown, stared down at his phone and didn't acknowledge my arrival. He looked vaguely pissed off, but that was so common these days, the real shock would have been seeing him happy.

Beale gave me his usual cheery greeting. "Morning, Fenn. Eye looks way better today."

"Mmm. A week'll do that," I said sourly, heading for the coffeepot. "What's this announcement?"

"Dunno." Beale shrugged. "We were on the other side of the island, looking at the roof on Grandma Goodman's old place to get it fit for human habitation so Rafe can move in—"

I poured myself a cup of coffee from the pot on the counter. "Aw! Are you identifying as *human* now, Rafe? Congrats, bud!"

Rafe raised his middle finger in a salute but didn't otherwise look up from his phone.

"*Anyway.* We got a text from Dad, who told us to come home and wait in the kitchen. So here we are." Beale stretched his long arms toward the ceiling. "I bet it's about the Extravaganza, though. It's all he talks about."

I grunted in acknowledgement of this and grabbed an apple from the fruit bowl on the counter. "Rafe, you get your Jeep fixed yet?"

Rafe nodded absently. "You were right. Ignition coil." He lifted his head from his phone and speared me with a glance. "Two hundred American dollars later."

I winced. "Sucks."

"Mostly sucks because you called it, and I shouldn't have had to take it in at all. One of these days, you're gonna trust that you know what you're doing, rather than second-guessing every damn thing."

"Yeah, well." I sank into the seat opposite him and stretched out my long legs. "Last Friday was not that day. Today's not either."

Rafe snorted, but when he looked back down at his phone, a muscle in his jaw ticked.

"What's your phone done that makes you look even grumpier than usual?" I demanded.

"I might have a fairly good idea what my dad's announcement is about." He slid his phone across the table in my direction without meeting my eyes. "Gage sent me this a minute ago."

I took the phone and scrolled up, seeing the headline of the local paper.

"Jay Don Rollins returns to the Suncoast—" I read out loud, then paused. "Oooh, Jayd's gonna be pissed they used his real name."

Rafe huffed. "Good."

"—returns to the Suncoast this summer for a series of engagements." I glanced up. "He's coming back to Florida?"

"Keep reading," Rafe instructed.

"When asked about his plans following his sold-out North American tour, the singer-songwriter was quoted as saying he'd be spending time with family in the area, and he planned to play small shows in St. Pete Beach and Punta Gorda, before finishing with a... with a free public concert on the island of Whisper Key for the first annual Whisper

Key Labor Day Extravaganza." I slid the phone back to Rafe. "They didn't even get the island's name right."

"The very least of my concerns."

"So, your dad is inviting Jayd Rollins, even knowing that he's..."

"Aimee's brother. My ex-brother-in-law. My former friend. Yep."

"And he doesn't care that you're gonna be—"

Rafe pushed his chair back from the table with a squeal. "I'm not gonna be anything, Fenn, except *profoundly* annoyed that he tried to keep this a secret."

"Remember Dad's trying, you guys," Beale said softly. "Trying to bring life back to Whispering Key."

Rafe and I exchanged a look.

"Beale," Rafe began, "you realize Dad was the one who put the final nail in its coffin, right? You remember what happened last December, when we learned that Goodmen Outfitters had *zero* dollars left in its operating budget? When Dad told us the money was all tied up in his *assets*?"

"Of course I remember!" Beale said. "Gage stormed out and went back to campus. You stormed off and stayed off island all weekend, and it was just me and Fenn stuck here with Dad for the holiday. Fucking sucked."

"Love you too, buddy," I said dryly.

Beale flushed. "I just meant, it wasn't much of a Christmas with half the family gone."

"And that was on *Dad*. Because he lied, Beale, and of course we were mad! He wouldn't say where he'd spent the money or what his *assets* were." Rafe made air quotes. "But if past behavior is any prediction... Look, you were maybe too young to remember, but he and Mom used to argue about the *same* things back in the day. She'd need grocery money, but he'd've gone and bought shares in some expedition to find and raise the *Esmerelda*."

"I remember!" Beale repeated. "I'm not an idiot, Rafe, and I'm only three years younger than you. I remember it all went to shit. I remember he promised Mom he'd stop investing in salvage operations, too. And he did."

"Yeah, well." Rafe shrugged. "Mom's been gone for a couple years, bro. And this new money he's got? He *still* won't say where it's from, and we have no say in how he's spending it. Hell, the only reason Gage and I got involved with this concert was to try to hold him *back*. See how well that's working?"

"He's increasing tourism!" Beale argued a little desperately.

"Uh-huh. Because more tourists mean more people he can suck in with his ghost stories, which means more people interested in finding that fucking boat," Rafe said flatly. "And in the meantime..."

"In the meantime he's bringing Rafe's brother-in-law and the prissy doctor to Whispering Key." I rolled my eyes.

"*Former* brother-in-law," Rafe corrected, just a trifle bitterly.

"Right," I agreed. "That."

"Hey! Mason's not prissy," Beale said, blushing hotly. "He's... I dunno. Sweet."

"Sweet," I repeated, trying to reconcile that word with the guy I'd spent nearly an entire day with a week ago, and had been thinking about every day since. I couldn't get there. *Sexy*? Yup. *Distracting*? As fuck. *Intelligent*? Duh. A *smart-ass*? Hell, yeah. But... "Sweet? Really?"

"Yes, sweet! And *caring*," Beale said, blushing harder. "A really good doctor."

"Do tell." Rafe came back to the table with a fresh cup of coffee, spun his chair around to straddle it, and smiled just a bit too wide. "Maybe some good can come of this, after all. Have *you* been playing doctor with the doctor, little brother?"

"No!" Beale protested. "He just helped me out. Remember how I trapped that little opossum that's been getting in the garbage last Saturday night? I strained my shoulder tryna release him. I was fixing it up myself, but Mase offered to help. He helped me stretch it out."

"*Mase*, is he?" Rafe's voice was knowing. "And was that all? Just a little arm stretching? Or did he offer to let you stretch—"

"Hey!" I cut in, more annoyed than I had any reason to be. "Shut your mouth. The doctor's *straight*, Rafe." Or at least he claimed he was, I thought bitterly. I leaned my chair back to balance on two legs and studied the ragged edges of my nails.

"*Weeeeeell*," Beale told Rafe slowly, darting a look at me. "I may have driven Mase to and from work the last couple days and asked him to look at my shoulder again. Just to follow up?" He grinned. "And he maybe asked me more about crystals and how they worked..."

I remembered the hunk of selenite on the nightstand next door, right next to the bed where Loafers slept every night, and fought to keep my breathing even.

Rafe cackled. "And you blinked your big eyes at him…"

Beale ducked his head and bit his lip. "Maaaaybe."

I brought my chair forward with a *thump*. "Guys. He's off-limits. Jesus."

"And did you have him show you how to do the stretches again?" Rafe asked, wiggling his eyebrows and annoying me. "Did he have to put his big, strong hands on you to do it?"

Beale grinned innocently. "You know how bad my memory is, Rafe."

"The doctor is *straight*," I said, waving a hand between Rafe and Beale. "Hello? *Straight*. As in, not remotely attracted to a yahoo like you."

Beale blinked at me in astonishment. "So what?"

"So what? So he's not crawling into bed with you, that's what. You're barking up the wrong tree."

"He's pretty and he's funny. I like talking to him." Beale shrugged. "Plus, he smells good."

"But it won't *go* anywhere," I said a little more forcefully than necessary, since the last thing I needed after stewing over Mason for days and nights on end was a reminder of how good he smelled. Like salt water and something fancy—

"Not every flirtation has to go somewhere." Rafe sipped his coffee contemplatively. "Beale's acquiring fodder for his spank bank, since I'm pretty sure his personal kink is Really Nice Guys—"

"Hey!" Beale blushed crimson. "Fuck off!"

"—and the straight doctor's probably oblivious. No harm, no foul."

"But he's *straight*," I said for the seventy-seventh time, like a song stuck on repeat. I didn't want to think too closely about why Loafers being in Beale's spank bank pissed me off.

"You seem more concerned about that than Mase is," Beale said, eyeing me closely. "If he's cool, who cares?"

"I do! I care! Have you forgotten what happened last time I had a *harmless flirtation* with a *straight* guy?"

Beale and Rafe fell silent for a moment. They exchanged a look.

"That was different," Rafe said, his voice and his eyes gone hard. "That wasn't harmless, and Thad Chambers knew he wasn't straight."

"Thad's wife would beg to differ." I folded my arms over my chest. "Besides, smart money says Beale's 'cute and caring' doctor'll be gone by the end of the month. He's got an escape clause in his contract, you know. He's out of here as soon as he gets another job."

"I know. All the more reason to enjoy him while he's around," Beale said with a little smile. "Besides, his aura's *pink*."

I rolled my eyes. "I don't want to know what that means."

"I do," Rafe countered.

"It means Mason is open to new experiences."

Rafe's jaw dropped. "Your aura-reading is like... gaydar?"

"No, dumbass! *Jesus.* Mason asked that, too, when I told him!"

I rubbed my jaw. *I'd just bet he did.*

"It just means, maybe Mason'll surprise us," Beale said. "Maybe he'll decide to stay. I mean, we didn't think you'd last either, Fenn, but here you are!"

The two of them laughed. I did not.

"Hey, that was a *joke*." Beale kicked me under the table. "As in, *ha ha*? Funny? What crawled up your butt?"

"Your sense of humor," I said gruffly. "And it died there. Mason's not staying on Whispering Key."

Rafe snorted. "Why do you care? What'd this kid do to you?"

I shook my head. Mason Bloom had gotten under my skin like a freakin' burr, that's what he'd done. He'd made me jealous of my own cousin and his stupid, fake-injured shoulder. "Nothing. I just don't want you to get your hopes up. And he's not a kid. He's thirty-something anyway. Older than me, maybe even older than you."

"Ancient," Rafe said.

I opened my mouth to respond, when Gloria teetered into the kitchen from the back hall wearing a pair of purple high heels, a frilly lilac dress, and an enormous bow atop her head.

"Boys, it is hotter than the devil's backside out there! *Shoo.* You don't realize how nice and cool the bunker is until you get out in the yard." She crossed the room to lean on the counter by the coffeepot before looking at me. "You back already, Fenn, honey?"

"Back from where?"

I adamantly refused to fetch any more doctors from airports.

"Doc Mason's suitcase got delivered from the airline this morning! You're supposed to bring it to him."

"No, thank you," I said politely. "Today's my day off, and I already got conscripted into air conditioner repair. Loafers can haul it up the stairs himself."

"Whether Mason can or can't doesn't matter," Big Rafe said, coming in through the back door, a vision in fluorescent orange. "Deliver it to him at the clinic. And would it kill you to be friendly?"

There were so many things wrong with this, I wasn't sure where to begin. I decided to start with the basics. "We don't *have* a clinic."

"Sure we do! Second floor of the old rec center is now Whispering Key Medical Center." Gloria smiled as she handed Big Rafe a coffee. "I was just there yesterday, and it's looking just lovely."

"Yeah?" I frowned. "Everything okay?"

"Fine, Fenn, honey. Just prickly heat! Doc Mason was really attentive. And you wouldn't believe what he's done with the place. Working day and night, him and Taffy, to get everything set up."

Big Rafe eyed me over his coffee cup. "You were supposed to be helping him."

"He hasn't asked me for help."

"And have you offered?" Big Rafe countered. "*No.* So bring him his damn bag."

I sighed. "Do we even know that he wants the bag at the clinic? Do you know if it's medical supplies? Maybe it's just filled with his collection of second-best loafers, and after I cart the damn thing all the way up to the second floor of the rec center, I'll have to cart it *all the way* back down again." I was aware that I was whining. I just didn't care.

"You'll survive." Big Rafe smiled grimly. "Bringing him his bag is a thoughtful gesture. It's all part and parcel of *guest satisfaction.* And while you're there, you'll see what other kind of help he needs, and make sure he gets it."

"Why *me*? *Beale's* all friendly with Mason," I said sourly. "Send *him.*"

The fact that I absolutely did not want Beale getting any *more* friendly with him just proved that I needed to avoid Mason a little longer.

"Yeah!" Beale agreed. "I could go—"

"Beale's busy," Big Rafe interrupted.

"I am?" Beale's forehead wrinkled.

"You are," Big Rafe confirmed. "So's Young Rafe."

Rafe snorted and spoke for the first time since his father had come in the room. "Yeah? Doing what, Dad? Preparing for the Labor Day Extravaganza?" His voice was so cold I felt the chill from across the table.

"As a matter of fact." Big Rafe grinned, clearly pleased with himself. "That's my big announcement! You'll never guess who volunteered to come play—"

"Save it. It's already all over the papers." Young Rafe folded his arms across his chest.

Big Rafe frowned. "Is it? Damn. Wasn't supposed to go up until Saturday. Catch more readers that way!"

"Are you kidding me? You invited my ex-brother-in-law to play a show here and you think the outrage is that they published the article about it a day early? You know, a heads-up would've been nice."

"Agreed," Beale said, adopting his brother's cross-armed pose. "For all of us."

"You boys." Big Rafe sighed the sigh of a man who was perpetually misunderstood. "You know, this island is like our family—"

"Fucking ridiculous?" I supplied.

"Incredibly beautiful!" Gloria countered.

"Incredibly *dysfunctional*," Young Rafe bit out.

"In desperate need of an intervention," Beale said sadly.

"It's our *home*," Big Rafe continued, ignoring all of us. "It's our *refuge*. But it's not a prison. It's not a tomb to bury yourself in. You've gotta use it as a *foundation* and build yourself something better."

"That was lovely," I said, wiping a fake tear from my eye. "Somebody put that on a Hallmark card." I let my voice go hard. "Explain to me how hauling Mason Bloom's suitcase to his clinic is a *foundation* for any damn thing."

Young Rafe stood up, his face stony with anger. "And bringing Jayd here is supposed to, what? Help me *build something better* by reminding me Aimee was so fucking miserable on this island, she fled?" He laughed with zero humor, turned his chair back around and pushed it into the table with a clatter. "You take care, Gloria," he said, glaring at his father. Then he stormed out the front door.

"Rafe, wait!" Beale said. He shot his father an impatient glare. "This family's not gonna be able to *build* anything if you destroy it before we have a chance." He stalked out after his brother.

"Well," Gloria said cheerfully. "That went better than the last couple of times you were all together!"

Big Rafe rolled his eyes at her, then turned to me. "You need to skedaddle with that suitcase. Day's only getting hotter."

I stood from the table and clenched my hands into fists. "You know, I've been working for you for five years in March, Rafe. I captain your boat. I fix your cars. I run your errands."

Rafe's eyes met mine. "I know it."

"Don't you think I should get a say in what happens on Whispering Key? In the decisions that affect *my* life? Don't you think the others should?"

Rafe's chin went up. "I think you have *every* right to say what happens in your life, Fenn. I keep waiting for you to speak up." He shook his head sadly. Then he sucked in a breath and slapped his palm on the table. "Alrighty!

Moving on! What's first on the mayor's docket today, Gloria?"

"Are you kidding me?" I seethed. "We're not done talking! I don't know what that shit even means!"

Rafe acted like I hadn't spoken. Gloria, at least, gave me a sympathetic look, but then she turned her attention to Rafe, too. "You're meeting with Leonard Wilkins at eleven about permits for his food truck. He's already out back waiting."

"Lenny Wilkins?" I demanded. "Since when does he have a food truck?"

"Since eleven o'clock this morning," Rafe answered smugly. "He asked and he shall receive. *Some* people believe in the future of this island, Fenn. *Some* people have dreams. What else, Gloria?"

"Shannon Tate returned your call about holding an exclusive show, but—"

"Shannon Tate? From the gallery? What kind of show?"

"Fenn," Rafe chided. "Don't you have somewhere to be?"

For a second, I thought about telling him in graphic detail where he could shove Mason's fucking suitcase. I could almost hear myself saying the words. But in the end, I swallowed them down like poison, stalked out to the hall, and grabbed the bag.

The thing was heavy as fuck—of course it was. Why would this ever be *easy*?—and as I dragged it across the motel parking lot and shoved it in my trunk, I couldn't help but wonder: Did Rafe *want* me to leave Whispering Key? Sometimes, I almost deluded myself into thinking I was part of something here; that being a half-assed Goodman was better than nothing. Other days, like today, it was crystal clear he wanted me gone, and I was ready to take him up on his invitation. There were a billion other shitty jobs out there, a million shitty motel rooms to live in.

The drive to town took five minutes—five minutes that got me even more pissed, because it *was* hot as the devil's asshole out here and my radio had apparently decided to protest the working conditions since it wouldn't tune in to a station—but for the first and only time in the five years I'd lived on Whispering Key, there wasn't a parking spot in front of the rec center or even across the street. I had to park an entire block down Godfrey Pass and haul the fucking suit-case, which had somehow lost a *wheel* along the way, down the sidewalk to the white stucco building where block letters spelled out WHISPERING KEY RECREATION CENTER above the door.

Inside, the building smelled musty, like it hadn't been used in forever, but it was blessedly cool compared to the outside. The ground floor was covered in checkerboard linoleum, and a glass-covered signboard displayed a congratulatory list of the island's recent high school graduates.

Circa 1996.

Double doors straight ahead led to the auditorium and the elevator, but I had way too much energy to burn off, so I took the stairs on the left and followed the sound of voices to the second floor.

"Thought you were gonna make it better, Doc. Now it stings like a sumbitch!" Dale Jennings limped out of a room in the center of the hallway and stared forlornly down at his bandaged foot.

"I know, Dale," Mason soothed, following behind him. "Remember what I said? Rest it. Elevate it. Use ice. Take Tylenol. And—"

"No ferrymones," Dale recited sadly. "I know. Thanks, Doc."

Mason patted Dale's shoulder consolingly and gave him a little smile that didn't quite reach his green eyes. That smile made me stop in my tracks in the shadow of the stairwell, suitcase in hand, and stare at him.

Something about him had changed in the past week, but I couldn't figure out what.

"Come back to see me in a few days, okay? I had Taffy set up a time for you." Mason gestured to Taffy Simmons, who was sitting at a makeshift desk out in the wide hallway.

Last I'd heard, Taffy was working as a waitress at Blue Smoke, a bar over on Cooter where us locals sometimes hung out for lack of anywhere else to go. The waitresses and the guests at the Smoke—both male and female—tended to favor heavy denim, skimpy leather, eyeliner, and fuck-off attitudes. But now Taffy was wearing a short-sleeved blouse, a low bun, and a bright smile, clearly pretty damn pleased with her new job if the way she jumped to attention when Loafers said her name was anything to go by.

"Right here, Doc Mason?" She held up a small card and handed it to Dale, who gave her a wink.

"Thanks, Taff. Say hi to Orry and the boy," he said, shuffling toward the elevator at the other end of the hall. "See you next week, Doc."

"Um, Doc Mason?" Taffy asked hesitantly. "Would it be alright if I took my lunch now? Only, I need to pick up Max from school over on the mainland, 'cause Kono got a last-minute client at the salon, so I'm not sure how soon I'll be back? And do you mind if Max comes back with me?"

"You know I don't mind, Taffy. We talked about that. But take the afternoon. We've worked hard all week." Mason twisted his neck from one side to the other, stretching it. "I think I've seen every resident of the island, just about."

"You're a curiosity," Taffy said with a sweet smile, grabbing her purse from her desk drawer. "It'll die down soon."

Mason nodded and rubbed his shoulder, and it struck me that he was *tired*. Seriously tired, to the point of looking defeated. I wasn't sure why that bugged me so much, but it did.

None of your business, Reardon.

I took a step forward, ready to hand him the suitcase without a single word and get the hell out of there.

"But for now..." Taffy bit her lip hesitantly. "You've got one more patient in the waiting room for a follow-up?"

I paused where I was. Maybe I could just drop the bag on Taffy's desk while Mason was in his office, doing his thing, and no one needed to know I'd been here.

Mason dropped his hand and sighed. "Do I?"

"I can stay?" Taffy offered, clearly reluctant.

"Nah." Mason waved a hand. "Go on. I've got it."

Taffy grinned and headed for the elevator, herself. "Thanks, Doc Mason! You're a lifesaver!"

"Aren't I?" Mason said. He sighed again. "Who's the patient?"

"It's just—"

"Little old me!" Gerry Twomey rushed into the hall from some waiting room I couldn't see, grinning from ear to ear. He stuck out his hand. "Gerry Twomey. Remember me from the other day, Mason? I told you to call me Gerry?"

Gerry lifted a hand to push back his thick, spiky brown hair, and his short-sleeved button-down shirt gaped nearly to his navel, displaying his tan chest.

My eyes narrowed. Gerry needed to back the fuck up. Why was every guy on the key falling on Mason like hyenas on a fresh kill? And why the fuck was Mason allowing it *when he was straight*?

"I remember. And I said you could call me *Doctor*." Mason nodded as he shook Gerry's hand with polite interest. "How can I help you?"

Gerry looked momentarily crestfallen, and I felt a vicious satisfaction at that, but he rallied quickly.

"Well, you said to come back if my sore hip didn't get better. And, ah, it didn't." He massaged the back of his hip with one hand. "So here she is, ready to be examined again."

"I told you it could take a few *weeks* for it to get better, Mr. Twomey. I suggested that you make an appointment to follow up since I won't be doing walk-ins anymore."

"Oh, gosh!" Gerry shook his head and grinned wider. "Silly me! All that just went *zoom*! Right over my head." He stretched his hand up, miming a plane flying while also arching his back seductively. "I think I was a little distracted last time we were together. And so were you." He wagged a finger. "It's *Gerry*, remember?"

I gritted my teeth.

"But since I'm here now..." Gerry twisted so his right ass cheek was thrust in Mason's direction. "Maybe you could check it?"

"Not today, Mr. Twomey," Mason said firmly. "There'd be no point."

Gerry took this denial as encouragement, because that was how Gerry seemed to work.

"Real quick?" Gerry breathed. "*Please*?"

"I..." Mason let out a deep breath, and it looked like he was waffling. Like he was going to let Gerry into his office. Like *an idiot*. "I think..."

"Hey!" I said, strolling out of the staircase, carrying a suitcase, totally casually. "Hi. I need an emergency consultation."

Mason whirled to look at me in confusion. Gerry did, too.

"Fenn?" Mason said. He spied his bag. "Is that my—? What are you—?"

I grabbed his elbow, all but pushing him into his little office, then I turned to Gerry. "He's not your type, Gerry. Leave him be."

Gerry pouted. "You'd be surprised at how many people *think* they're not my type, then come a'knockin' in the end. You did." He grinned slyly. "In fact, my headboard still has the—"

"Goodbye, Gerry." I squeezed into Mason's office and closed the door behind me.

The room was half office, half exam room, with a large metal desk in one corner, a big, padded exam table in the center of the room, and an old, rattan sofa that had seen better days set against the opposite wall. It smelled like fresh paint and antiseptic. It also smelled like Mason Bloom and his fucking cologne.

Mason reached the exam table and whirled around, hands on his hips, eyes spitting green fire in my direction. "What *the hell* was that? How dare you!"

"Me?" I threw his suitcase onto the sofa. "You know what Gerry really wanted you to check out, right? Here's a hint: it was several inches *away* from his hip."

"No, Fenn, I had no idea!" Mason shot back. "For I am but an innocent doctor, untried in the ways of males—and *females*, for that matter—who mistake my office for the Happy Ending Massage Parlor. Christ, I've been propositioned by more people in the past week than in the past thirty years, and half of them were old enough to be my grandmother." He rolled his eyes and folded his arms over his chest, and I noticed that he was wearing another perfectly pressed button-down under his white coat, along with another pair of creased khakis and a fresh pair of loafers. "If you have an issue with your... *paramour* making a pass at me, kindly take it up with *him*, Mr. Reardon."

I squinted in confusion. "My paramour. You mean *Gerry*?"

"Who else? Apparently his headboard is still—" He frowned and waved a hand in the air. "—whatever the hell it is, from the last time you *came a'knocking*. At least now I understand what happened the other night when you ran away."

I had no fucking clue what he was talking about. "I didn't *run away*. Jesus. And FYI, Gerry and I fucked around once. *Once!* And I don't talk about it."

Mason's face flushed red, and he stalked around to the far side of his desk. "Of course! Because not talking about it means it didn't happen, right? Poor Gerry. Did you freak out when *he* got an erection?"

"Poor Gerry, my ass!" My gaze narrowed. "And I didn't *freak out*, Loafers. I didn't freak out *or* run away." If I kept saying it, maybe I'd start believing it. "I was pissed off, okay? And I saw no reason for us to continue our conversation. It was getting late. You were obviously tired."

"*Tired.*" Mason made air quotes. "The sun was barely setting, and you scurried out the door like I was physically attacking you—"

"*Scurried*," I scoffed. "No."

"—and you've avoided me all week. And I still don't understand why you were *so* annoyed!" Mason threw both hands in the air, then wrapped them both around the back of his neck, looking sad and defeated. "Just... go away, Fenn."

"Go away? Bullshit!" I countered, conveniently forgetting that I'd intended to do just that. "I just saved your ass—and I mean that literally—and that was *after* hauling your fucking suitcase all the way over here and up a flight of stairs! I've hauled caches of *rock* that weighed less, FYI. The least you could do is *thank* me."

"*Thanks*," Mason said coldly. "Should I tip you, too?"

There was literally nothing he could have said that would have pissed me off more, and the look in his eyes said he knew it, which had the perverse effect of deflating my temper completely.

"What's your problem?" I demanded.

Mason looked away and shook his head. "Nothing."

"Bullshit," I repeated. "You're not... *right*. There's something off, and I can't put my finger on it."

His eyes flew back to mine. "Because you know me so well, after spending a couple hours in my company? How about '*It's none of your fucking business*,' then. That more accurate?" He spread his hands. "I mean, Jesus, what could possibly be my problem, Fenn? Here I am, stuck on this fucking island until I find a new job, with no one to blame but myself because *I* signed the contract sight unseen, like God's own idiot child. I have no car down here, but hey, who cares, right? I'd have no place to go if I did, and my phone signal dies in at least three places between here and the clinic."

"I told you it was spotty—"

"I have no air-conditioning. No cable TV. It rains *every goddamn night*, with thunder and lightning fit to wake the dead. I haven't slept well in days because it's so hot—"

"I fixed your air conditioner this morning—"

"I have no one to talk to! The only creature on this island I've really bonded with is Topaz, Mr. Wynott's Pomeranian.

The only humans who *kinda* like me are Lety Irvine, who speaks mostly Spanish, and Taffy, who *has* to like me because it's her *job*, but who can't make a statement without turning it into a question. I will *not* talk about anything but the weather with my family or my best friend, because then I'd have to admit how *egregiously* I fucked myself by taking this job. And the one person I tried to talk to proved he might not be a serial killer *but is indeed an asshole*, because he's avoiding me like I'm diseased ever since I..." He broke off with a little hitch of breath and sank into his desk chair. "Seriously, Fenn. Just... leave me the hell alone, okay?"

I stood there, blinking down at him for a long minute.

I wished someone could explain to me why the sight of this one particular guy looking all dejected and tired and defeated did my head in. I was no Beale Goodman, going around rescuing strays, and there were many very compelling reasons why leaving Mason alone would be the best thing for both of us, the loafers on his feet being just the tip of that iceberg.

But I didn't need to have Aunt Mary's "sight" to know that wasn't gonna happen.

Mason Bloom in his fancy shoes was my polar opposite in almost every way—that was a given—but there were ways in which it seemed we were very, very much alike, too. We both knew what it felt like to be stuck in a place you didn't really choose, in a life you didn't really choose. We both knew what it felt like to blame yourself for it.

I didn't just want him badly, I actually *did* like him, I realized with something like a sigh. I liked him quite a bit. Enough that I wanted to be his friend. To make sure he was okay.

So in the end, it turned out Fenn Reardon's One and Only Life Rule *was* made to be broken, and it wasn't exactly a surprise when my mouth started talking before my brain had a hundred percent caught up.

"Sounds like you need a beer."

"Beer?" Mason snorted. "No. I need an exorcism, extensive therapy, and a good night's sleep."

"Potato, potahto, really."

Mason snorted again, then sobered. "Why do you do that?" he demanded. "Joke with me, and then... stop? Get all pissed off, and then... stop? Act like you give a shit, and then... stop? The hot and cold is really fucking confusing, Fenn."

I considered this. Strong irony, really, in the fact that *I* was the one leading the straight guy on, pissed at him for being confused when I was guilty of confusing him.

This wasn't something I wanted to think about at all. It was definitely not something I wanted to think about sober.

"Well, *I* need a beer," I said in place of an answer. I headed for the door.

"Does this place even *have* beer?" Mason demanded. "I swear I've tried to find some at the grocery store, Omar's Sundries, *and* the Concha. Why doesn't this island have a bar?"

I paused, startled, and turned to look at him. "I don't know. I've never really thought about it. I get beer from a brewery over on the mainland that's better than anything they'd have at Pickles', anyway. And," I added, "I share it with a fortunate few."

"Well, lucky you." Mason sounded peevish.

I took a deep breath, let it out, and said something incredibly fucking foolish—which seemed to be my MO whenever this guy was around.

"You wanna come with, Loafers? 'Cause if you wanna talk, I'll listen. I'm probably a better bet than the Pomeranian, at least."

Mason jumped up to follow me so fast, his rolling chair hit the wall behind him with a *crash*… which just proved he was no smarter than I was.

8

MASON

"I'm pretty sure," I said slowly, enunciating each word, "that hot beer and cold sunshine is..." I paused to burp delicately, like the civilized individual I was. "...the best medicine."

From the other side of the enormous checkered blanket he'd laid out across the cool sand, Fenn chuckled and turned on his side toward me.

"Pretty sure there's a flaw in that statement," he mused, his words mumbled and slow. "Not sure I care enough to figure out what it is right now, though."

I turned my head to face him and blinked my eyes open. The setting sun was kind to Fenn Reardon, settling into the dips and hollows of his muscular arms, glinting off his scruffy cheeks and messy hair, gilding him all-over gold.

I'd jerked off thinking of this guy.

Could he tell, just by looking at me? Could he scent it on the breeze, like Dale Jennings with his ridiculous pheromones?

Fenn was every bit as scruffy and unkempt as he'd been a week ago—I wasn't going blind—but he was objectively beautiful, too, with the artless, rugged appeal and grace of motion that, per Victoria, most guys on Instagram would kill for.

Since I was several beers deep in the cooler Fenn had provided, I was also perfectly comfortable admitting Fenn was *subjectively* beautiful, too. His blue, blue eyes and sleepy smile made my head spin and my pulse race in a way that had nothing to do with the alcohol.

I wasn't sure how it was possible for someone to drive me crazy and make me feel so damn comfortable and *safe* at the same time, but that was a conundrum for another time. A sober-er time.

A time when Fenn hadn't just brought me to his favorite spot on the whole island—a kind of natural cavern where some long-ago tide had scooped out the foundation of the rock bed, leaving an awning of rock hanging over the sand maybe two feet high, three feet deep, and six feet wide, under which the sand stayed cool despite the warm breeze and the late-day sun.

"You know, I walked this beach three mornings ago," I said, turning my face back up to the sky and enjoying the way the light burst in kaleidoscope sparkles across the inside of my eyelids. "I didn't even notice this spot was here, what with the overhang and that giant sort of treelike *thing* blocking the view from the shoreline." I waved at an enormous piece of driftwood that seemed to have washed up on the beach decades or centuries before, and now stuck out of the wall of tide-deposited rocks like a marvel of nature's architecture.

Fenn snorted. "*That giant treelike thing* is an actual tree, Loafers. A dead tree, but still a tree."

"I'm just *saying*. This place is like a secret fort. This is where I would—" I sat bolt upright. "Oh my God! This is where I would hide a treasure!" I squinted around at the rocks, hoping for a subtle-but-distinct X to suddenly become visible. "Maybe Resolute Goodman—"

Fenn laughed out loud and turned onto his back. "Ah, Loafers. You're about two hundred years and forty-five treasure hunters too late."

"Oh." I frowned. "Am I?"

"Yeah." He grabbed my elbow and tugged me so I was lying down again. "Resolute left instructions to find the treasure. I told you. If it ever existed, it was never around here."

"But you told me no one had found it!"

"Yeah, but not for lack of trying. According to Resolute's diary, the treasure 'lay in the garden of dreams' meaning the extensive garden he built to his wife's precise specifications up on what's now Margot Lane, near the mansions. But Sarah Goodman tore the gardens apart after he died and never found any treasure. I think Resolute and Jacob spent all the money. Maybe he meant the garden was the treasure because of the value of the land or something." He shrugged.

"And did Jacob Godfrey know what Resolute meant?"

Fenn shook his head. "Jacob passed a few months before Resolute, so he wasn't around to ask. But anyway, over the years, treasure hunters have given up on trying to solve the clue and just combed every beach on the island instead. Later on, they brought in metal detectors and ground-scanning equipment—none of which worked reliably, since the island has a high limestone composition."

"Oh, limestone. That makes sense." I nodded. Then I shook my head. "What's limestone?"

Fenn laughed again. "Seriously, I need to get you tipsy daily, Loafers, because it's a revelation. Limestone is a type of rock. It gets eaten away by the acid in rainwater and washed away."

"And turned into sand." I grabbed a handful from beside the blanket and let it filter through my fingers.

"Nope. That's a whole different thing."

"I'm not saying you're wrong." I couldn't help it if my smile was just the tiniest bit superior. "But I'm pretty sure sand comes from rocks, Fenn."

"Yep. And my geology degree says I have a pretty fair understanding of how rocks work, Loafers," he said mildly. "Different rocks, different types of erosion. Limestone erodes and leaves behind pockets that cause caverns and sometimes sinkholes, which is why it's really hard to narrow down a hole that's hiding a bag of gold, versus one that's full of nothing but air and water. *Quartz*, on the other hand, is the kind of rock that eroded into the sand we're sitting on. This stuff probably washed down from the Appalachians and into the Gulf."

"Wow. And ended up *here*. Right where it's supposed to be. Like destiny."

Fenn looked at me again, and light danced in his eyes like sunshine on water. "Deep Thoughts With Loafers. That deserves another beer." He sat up and took a dripping-wet bottle from the small cooler, then popped the top before handing it to me.

I hesitated before rolling up on an elbow to take it. "You know, I haven't had five beers at once since…"

"Ever?" Fenn suggested.

"Not *ever*, but a long time. High school." My eyes flickered to his, and I added darkly, "For good reason."

"Now that sounds like a story." He leaned his body toward me on the blanket, his legs crossed beneath him, and grabbed a beer for himself. "What happened? You puke? Confess your undying love for the cafeteria lady? Get a B+ on a test? What happens when Loafers *cuts loose* and has five beers?" he teased, lifting his bottle to his lips.

"I don't know where you get this idea of me." I sighed. "I jumped off a building."

Fenn choked, spraying beer all over both of us, and I laughed out loud.

"You did not."

"Did, too," I confessed. "Slid right down a construction chute from the top of my high school onto a blow-up mattress on the ground. Broke my elbow. Dislocated my shoulder."

"You?"

I sighed again. "I have done a *lot* of shit when dared to do it. It's kind of a personality failing. Stubbornness."

Fenn's lips twitched and his eyes gleamed in the fading light. "Is that *so*?" He drew out the last word tauntingly. "Let's test that."

"Let's not. I said it *was* so. *Was*. Past tense. When I was young and foolish. We're not testing it."

"Truth or dare, Loafers."

"No! Nope. I'm thirty-five, not seventeen, and I'm already gonna be feeling this beer until next week." Nevertheless, I took another long swallow of the dark brew. Fenn knew his stuff when it came to beer.

"If you play, I'll play, too," Fenn singsonged. "All my deep, dark secrets revealed."

I paused in my drinking and wiped my mouth with the back of my hand. "Really?"

"Cross my heart. You can even have the first question, and I'll give you a truth."

Oh, man. "Fine, I'll play," I agreed. "Why have you been avoiding me for the last week?"

"How did I know it would be this?" Fenn groaned. "You're so predictable."

"How did I know you weren't *really* gonna answer?" I retorted. "You're *so* predictable."

Fenn snorted and looked resolutely at the water. "I don't fuck straight men. I don't *fuck around* with straight men. It's as simple as that."

My cheeks burned. "I don't recall asking you to... to..."

"Is this like the Cooter Key thing? There are just words beyond your Loafery vocabulary?"

"I don't recall asking you to *fuck me*," I enunciated clearly. "Or fuck around with me."

"Not in so many words," he agreed. "But your dick did a lot of talking. Like a mime, pointing out a hole in your wall." He dropped an arm between us in a parody of my wall-building from a week ago and fluttered his lashes flirtatiously.

I blew out a breath. I'd known that was why, really. I wasn't sure why I'd expected there to be more to the story. I felt a little disappointed, like I'd wasted a truth.

"What, no comeback?" Fenn demanded. "No 'but I am innocent and straight, and my poor dick was confused by the jet lag, and stimulus is stimulus, and if you hadn't fallen on top of me that never would have happened'?"

I blinked at him, deciding how much to say. Every thought in my mind ended with a question mark. "Jet lag would be tricky to claim since New York is in this time zone."

He assessed me silently for a minute, then said, "Fine. My turn. Why the hell did you come here?"

He made it sound so personal, I had to laugh.

"It was all part of a master plan to destroy you, Fenn. I could tell you more, but..."

He nudged me with his elbow. "Truth, remember. What made you leave your cushy Loafers life and come down here?"

"My cushy Loafers life." I snorted. "It was not cushy. At first,"

I amended. He looked like he didn't believe me, which was annoying. "Not kidding."

"Hmm. I'm imagining you coming out of the womb with matching luggage full of shoes. Leading all the other high-fashion kindergarteners in your perfectly ironed clothing and fine *Italian* leather."

"Did you forget the part where I slid off a building?" I demanded.

"No! I just sort of assumed you were wearing those exact shoes while you did it." He nodded at the shoes I'd left on the edge of the blanket.

"I *definitely* wasn't." I shrugged. "I grew up in Upstate New York. We lived with my grandmother—my brother, two sisters, and me. I'm the baby."

"Of course you are."

"My grandmother wasn't... She was..." I cleared my throat and toyed with the collar of my polo shirt, trying to do the thing I usually did where I emphasized the cuteness of this story. The no-big-deal humor of it. "She was an odd duck. She legally changed her name to Moonflower Bloom and had a '68 VW bus she parked in the front yard. Total hippie. She grew marijuana in our vegetable garden and believed kids shouldn't have rules. And these, like, travelers who were friends of friends would stop by all the time and stay the night, or even for a couple months, and sometimes us kids would camp outside or sleep on the floor while they stayed in our rooms. It was kinda wild. You wouldn't know it to look at me, right?" I grinned and ran a hand through my hair, which had stopped responding to product the moment I touched down in Florida and had since gone feral.

Fenn didn't laugh. "Having strange people in your space all the time sounds like literal torture. And borderline scary, for a kid. Did you enjoy it?"

I shrugged and felt my grin fall. No one asked that. Ever. It was a cute story. Did he not see how cute it was?

"No. I didn't. When I was young, I thought it was all normal. I thought it was a game to hide your stash whenever anyone in authority stopped by. I thought it was common for brothers to spend their paper route money to buy bread. I was eleven or twelve the first time I realized it was *not*. That we were *that* family in town. That people looked at us and pitied us."

"Ahhh. So the loafers were a form of rebellion."

I snorted. "No. I tried *rebellion* as a form of rebellion. I painted graffiti on bridges and stole cigarettes from the corner store." I tipped back my beer and drank the remainder in one long swallow. "I just didn't care very much about anything."

"And then?" Fenn prompted.

I scrubbed at my hair. "Then I slid off the building and ended up at the hospital, where this doctor—Andrew Capon is his name. We keep in touch online still, from time to time—set my elbow. He talked to me like... like I was on his level. Like I could do more."

I cleared my throat and popped the top off my sixth beer myself, lost in memories. Fenn said nothing, he just watched me steadily.

"He *dared* me to do something better with my life. He helped me get into college and then medical school. My brother helped pay for it, along with a shit ton of loans." I shrugged. "And then I met a nice girl from a rich family who had a fondness for Italian leather, *lost* the girl when she got a better offer from another guy, and realized that somewhere along the way I'd tied my dreams with hers. Which made it kind of a double-bitch when she was gone. So I went looking for a dream that was *mine*, you know?"

Fenn nodded.

"I thought a fancy resort on a private island and a chance to get my med school loans paid off would be a good start. A way to impress my friends and relatives, earn their respect." I moved my hand in an arc that included the beach, the island, the whole shitshow I'd committed myself to. "Clearly, mission accomplished," I laughed.

Fenn did *not*. "That's... a much cooler story than I gave you credit for," he said, almost reluctantly.

I looked up at the darkening sky and smiled helplessly. "Thanks, I guess? Glad my childhood trauma endears me to you?"

Fenn poked me in the ribs. "I'm just saying, that wasn't easy."

I shifted my head to see him better. The wind was toying with his hair, and he was looking everywhere *besides* me, and I was suddenly a hundred percent certain with zero proof to back it up that Fenn had not said that as a throwaway comment. He meant it, and the idea made my stomach go hot.

"*Jesus*. Okay. Truth or dare?" I demanded.

Fenn sighed. "I feel like a dare would probably require me to move from this blanket—"

He shot me a look, and I nodded. "It would involve letting me drive your car."

"*God*." He shuddered. "So truth, then."

I grinned mischievously. "What's your favorite thing about Whispering Key?"

Fenn looked horrified. "Shit, I dunno. Nothing?"

"Truth, remember," I said, doing my best impression of his deep voice. "*One* thing. The beach? The fresh air? The scenery? Running a tour boat? Meeting me? Please, do be honest."

He shook his head. "Beach is fine. Boat is fine. You're *meh*. And there were plenty of fresh air and pretty views in the High Country. Ah... Western North Carolina. That's where I grew up," he offered when I gave him a puzzled frown. "Where my mom and stepfather still live." He chewed on his lip for a minute. "I dunno," he repeated at length. "I guess my favorite thing is... my family." He rolled his eyes, like his own sentimentality disgusted him. "Kinda sad, since they're destroying my brain cells on a daily basis just from interacting with them, but beggars can't be choosers."

"They're not your only family, though, right? If your mom and stepdad are still around?"

"Yep." He looked away, his eyes on the water again. It made the sunlight glint off his eyes, and I had to swallow when my mouth went dry.

Stop it, Mason.

"But the Goodmans, ah... you know. Did what family's meant to do. See, I didn't really spend time with my dad growing up, so I'd never laid eyes on my aunt Mary and her family until a few years ago. But when I ran into some trouble, my dad heard about it and invited me here and he —*they*—gave me a place to live. A job to do." He shrugged. "I'm grateful to them. They were there for me."

Which meant his *other* family *hadn't* been? That made me unreasonably pissed off.

"What kind of trouble? Legal? Financial?"

"Nope." Fenn's mouth twisted. "The kind of trouble that involved me being really, annoyingly, stubbornly *gay*, despite Mom and Neil's best efforts."

"What do you mean?" I demanded, outraged on his behalf. "What did they do?"

Fenn drew his spine straighter and cocked an eyebrow. "It's a boring-assed story, and besides, no two-for-one deals, Loafers. You got your truth. Your turn now. Truth or dare?"

I leaned up on one elbow. "Is that how we're playing this? I feel like I gave you a truth and a half, and got half a truth in return."

"That's the exchange rate, Loafers."

I narrowed my eyes. "I wasn't informed of this."

"Have you heard yourself talk? You easily use three times as many words as I do, on average, so to keep things equitable—"

"You're infuriating." I shoved at his arm.

"So you keep saying, yet here you are, drinking with me, sooo…" He tilted his head in my direction. "*Truth or dare*?"

"Fine." I sighed. "Make it an easy one. Truth."

Fenn looked at me for a minute like he was weighing multiple options. He shifted forward so he was nearly looming over me, and I felt like a bug under a microscope. I fought the urge to squirm.

"You have a side of this blanket," I informed him, putting up a wall with my arm. "Kindly stay on it."

He laughed out loud. In fact, his eyes were still dancing when he said, "So, tell me how you lost the girl," and I was so caught up in watching him that it took me a full two seconds to even process the question.

When I did, I sucked in a breath. "I asked for *easy*." I tried to make it sound less like a whine and more like a joke. I failed pretty hard.

"I know."

"I would really rather not talk about this," I said quietly.

"Ah." Fenn sat back a bit. "You're not over it."

"No, that's not it." I shook my head once. "I'm over *her*. I don't miss her or anything. It's just *embarrassing*." And it was true. I wasn't entirely sure I was over the way we'd broken up, but I was positive I was over *Victoria*.

I took a deep breath. "Her name is Victoria. She's very pretty. We were together for a year and a bit. Now we're not." I hesitated. "She left me for a globetrotting photographer we hired to take our pictures—"

Fenn's eyebrows shot up. "You're kidding."

"No, Fenn. Unlike you I understand that jokes are meant to be *funny*." I shoved his knee lightly. "The dude's name is *Gunner*. He's six five and built like a blond Jason Momoa. They first met on Instagram because he has a billion followers, he lives in a treehouse in Belize with a tame howler monkey when he's not traveling the world photographing shit, and he wanted her to be his *muse*. Whereas *I* am *me*—" I flicked my hand up and down myself. "I enjoy binge-watching period dramas. And *cuddling*." Not that she was ever into either. "Can't compete."

Fenn stared at me for a long minute. "No," he said finally. "No competition at all."

I nodded and looked out at the water, trying to convince myself that didn't sting.

"For one thing," Fenn said sadly, "no howler monkey."

I snorted and darted a look at Fenn, who was grinning, and then suddenly I was full-on laughing, too, flopping over on the blanket, gripping my stomach, even though it honestly wasn't that funny. I nearly spilled my beer until Fenn grabbed my hand and saved it.

I'd cried a little, after Victoria left. Then I'd gotten mad about it. Then I'd decided to take *action* about it. Then I'd tried not to think about it at all. But until this minute, I hadn't *laughed* about it, and now that I had, I felt something loosen inside me that I'd been holding really tight.

"The worst part was," I said, wiping my eyes, "I saw the whole thing happen right in front of me, like a slow-motion train wreck. Victoria and I were... okay. Happy enough, I thought. And then that guy walked into our apartment to take pictures and—" I shook my head. "That was that. It was like both of them lit up. My friend Toby says stuff like that just happens sometimes. Some kind of biochemical reaction."

"*Ferrymones,*" Fenn said in a hushed voice.

I snorted. "You think Gunner was taking the supplement? You think Dale has any more he could give me?"

"I don't think you need it," Fenn said. I couldn't see him clearly in the twilight, but his voice was soft and my lips opened in surprise.

Fenn cleared his throat. "Alright, one more truth. We're almost out of beer, and I'm almost out of words."

"So I should make it count, hmm? You said you got into trouble..."

"*God,*" Fenn groaned, throwing himself back down on the blanket. "*So* predictable."

"You hate my questions when they're predictable, you hate them when they're unpredictable. It's *almost* as though you're impossible to please."

"I can be pleased." He threw the words down like a challenge, and I nearly shivered.

"Answer."

Fenn sighed and pushed up on an elbow, those blue, blue eyes half-amused and half-exasperated in a way that did funny things to my stomach. "I have a geology degree. I mentioned that."

I nodded.

"I got it specifically because my stepfather's old Army buddy owed him a favor and offered to hook me up. And because I was a hick kid in a hick town and I thought it'd be great. I'd be able to travel the world."

He was silent for a minute.

"And you didn't?" I prompted.

"Well. I got as far as Texas. It was an okay job. Good money in hydrocarbon exploration. Lots of upward mobility. The boss liked me fine and took me under his wing. Took me to his house for Sunday barbecues with the family. I figured that was that, right? That was gonna be my life. Then I met a guy. A—how'd you put it earlier?—a nice guy from a rich family?"

"And you're not over him," I said, quoting Fenn from earlier.

One half of his mouth twisted up. "I'm over *him*. It's just *embarrassing*."

I grinned and flopped back down on the blanket. "If you tell me there was a photographer involved—"

"Ah, no. According to the employee records, I picked a fight with four guys because I was drunk and bored. I made lewd remarks to them. Sexually harassed them. So they had to defend themselves against my advances—"

"Against all four of them," I said, no longer amused. "You must have been *really* bored."

"—and I lost my job."

"And your nice guy?"

"Turned out to not be very nice. Or—" He shrugged. "—very mine." He cleared his throat before I could ask another follow-on question. "Okay, your turn. You pick *dare*."

"Do I?" I rolled my eyes. "I'm not getting naked. I'm not getting wet. I do not dance. I will not sing. I can't do gymnastics without hurting myself. Those are my hard limits. And if you get me sandy, you can expect that I will pay you back when it's your turn."

Fenn's eyes narrowed and his lips pursed. "You're zero fun."

"Prettier girls than you have confirmed this. I'm also incapable of passion, FYI, and possibly fundamentally broken thanks to my childhood." I laughed, but stopped when I caught Fenn looking at me funny. "What?"

"Nothing, just..." He hesitated. "That's someone trying to put the blame on you for something they did. You're a pain in the ass, and I mean that *sincerely*. But you're *never* boring or passionless. Okay?"

I nodded, and then I swallowed... or I tried to, anyway.

You know that expression "*his heart was in his throat*"? I thought I'd experienced it before, in times when my throat went thick with fear or anxiety. But when Fenn said those words, I could literally feel my heart beating in my throat—and my head, and my stomach, and the bottoms of my feet. Every *tha-thump* set off a Catherine wheel in my gut, which was exactly as thrilling and terrifying as it sounded.

He looked at the water for a minute, and when he turned back to me with a devilish look on his face, I couldn't come up with a single smart-ass remark.

"I dare you to take a picture or video of yourself doing something fun and a little crazy, then post it online to your Instagram."

"Like—" My voice cracked and I had to try again. "Like what? I can recite the alphabet backwards."

Fenn gave me a withering look. "This isn't a field sobriety test, Loafers. I said *crazy*. Something your high school self would be impressed by."

I spread my hands and tried to ignore the relentless *attraction* I felt pulling me toward him. "Sorry. I've got nothin'. I have actively repressed High School Mason. He has left the building. Besides, the whole point of this is for *you* to give me the specific thing I'm supposed to do, within the hard limits I've set. *Duh*."

"Unless the dare is to make you challenge *yourself* and push your *own* boundaries." He bopped me on the nose. "*Duh*."

I clapped a hand to my face. "I'll have you know, taking this job was daring. Look how that turned out."

Fenn smiled crookedly. "But what are your chances of rolling snake eyes twice?"

"At this rate?" I shrugged. "High."

"Do a dramatic recitation. Or do some yoga. Hashtag-marine-life!" he teased. "Hashtag-Loafers-in-the sand!"

"God no." I shook my head, imagining myself in downward dog. "My high school friends follow me on Instagram. My former colleagues. Dr. Capon. My *sister*. I want them to respect me, Fenn, not be forced to bleach their eyes."

"See, *this* is a great dare. Because *you* know what *you* find daring, so you have to make *yourself* uncomfortable. If I had a mustache, I would twirl it."

"If you had a mustache, I would shave it for my dare."

"Sure you would." He grinned, as wild as the breeze off the water. "Don't overthink it. That's the dare."

I swallowed. That was the dare, huh? What would I do if I didn't let myself think about it too much?

I dug my phone out of my pocket, sat up straight on the blanket next to Fenn. I turned the camera on, angled my face toward the pink light on the horizon.

My heart was still beating crazily, but indecision sat like lead in my stomach. Could I actually...?

It was crazy. Foolish. I was drunk off my ass... or I had been, until my adrenaline had started spiking, burning through the haze.

Mason Bloom Takes Charge of His One Goddamn Life and Lives Fearlessly, I reminded myself, when once again my stomach threatened to revolt.

What did I want to do? I wanted to kiss Fenn Reardon.

There. I'd captured the nebulous feelings that had been buzzing in my brain and translated them to actual words, forming an actual sentence.

I wanted to know why Fenn Reardon, who started out as everything I despised, had somehow caught my attention *and held it.* I wanted to know why this guy who gave me shit and had no plans for the future made me feel steadier than the sand beneath me. I desperately wanted to know why *his* face had been the one I'd been thinking of when I came the other night.

So I leaned over, pressed my lips to the stubble on Fenn's jaw, and clicked the shutter button.

9

FENN

One minute, I was sitting there, ass on the blanket and hands back in the sand, enjoying the moment—listening to the sound of the water, watching the line of pink cruising along the horizon, wondering if Loafers would surprise me and take the dare. The next thing I knew, his breath was hot on my cheek, his mouth was touching my skin, and the scent of him was all around me, just the two of us in this weird cocoon.

Danger, danger, danger.

I pulled away partly because I so badly wanted not to pull away at all.

"*That* was the wildest thing you could think of?" I demanded. My voice sounded all croaky.

Mason rubbed his lips together, and I wondered if he could still feel me there. My cheek burned where he'd kissed it.

"Hey! You said not to think too much!"

"Lame." I ran my fingertips over my face, touching the spot where his mouth had been. Every muscle in my body was gripped with sudden tension. "I could think of a thousand more exciting things without breaking a sweat. Pecking someone on the cheek isn't wild. I used to kiss my aunt that way."

"Kissing a *guy* on the cheek is not typical. Not for me," he said quietly.

My gaze followed his to the phone in his lap. In the photo on the screen, Mason's eyes were closed and his lips were pressed firmly against me, but he was smiling, too. Pleased with himself. Maybe pleased he'd taken this dare.

And me? My eyes were half-open, my lips parted in surprise, but though the image was still, I could feel my whole body leaning toward Mason, *wanting* him. Longing.

How fucking awkward.

When a peck on the cheek turned a guy like me into a yearning idiot, it was a sign I'd had enough beer... and enough trading confidences.

"Well, the dare was for you to challenge yourself," I said dubiously. I wiped my suddenly sweaty palms against my nylon shorts. "So I *guess* that counts. The real challenge will be posting it on Instagram where all your friends could see it. No hashtags. No apologies. No explanations."

I was almost positive he'd *never*, and maybe reminding myself of that would help me get over this infatuation.

Mason looked up, his eyes searching mine in the near darkness. "This was for me." He shut the phone off. "This is nobody's business but mine. And yours," he added.

"Let's be honest. It's mostly yours." I forced myself to speak dismissively, as though the image of him pecking me on the cheek wasn't indelibly inked in my brain. "Straight guy fun. Always amusing, until it's time to share the joke."

"That's not—" Mason's voice was small. Hurt.

I hated that. I hated this whole situation that *I'd* started by inviting him here tonight when I had really known better.

"Kidding, Loafers! I'm kidding. Hey, I'm hungry," I interrupted, clapping a hand to my stomach. "You hungry? I've got some chips upstairs, I think."

"No, I—"

"Yeah, just as well. Getting late anyway, huh?" I gestured to the skyline like maybe he hadn't noticed the sunset. "We should get back up there, otherwise we'll be stumbling around on the boardwalk with our flashlights in the dark, and I know you don't dig the dark." I waved at the forty-foot bridge over the sand dunes, which was less than ten feet from where we sat. "This was fun, Loafers!" I adopted a bright expression as I clambered to my knees. "You're a great guy, and I'm glad we cleared the air. We should grab a beer together again sometime." Just not this much beer. And not anytime soon.

"Stop!" Loafers commanded, pushing his hand firmly against my chest, preventing me from standing. "You're freaking out again. And you're running away again, too."

"Once again, not running. In fact, witness me, still *on my knees*."

He shook his head, his hand still poised above my heart. "*Tachycardia*," he murmured. "Racing heart. Dead giveaway.

Either there's a hungry T. Rex behind me and you're paralyzed with fear, or…"

"Or?" I shot back.

"Or." He licked his lips, and his cheeks blushed pink. "I don't know."

Except he did. That blush said he *did*.

Fuck.

"Illuminating, Dr. Loafers!" I wished like hell that he'd remove his hand from me, but felt like me forcibly removing it would be giving too much away. "Don't read anything into it. Some guy once told me stimulus is stimulus."

He swallowed and looked up, his green gaze slamming into mine. My breath hitched.

"That guy sounds like an idiot," he whispered. He bit his lip. "Hyperventilation, too, Fenn?"

"Don't do this, Loafers."

"Do what?" His fingers dug into the skin of my chest, but he sounded honestly curious, like he hadn't a clue what he was doing. Like maybe he hoped I'd tell him.

"You don't want my stimulus anywhere near your stimulus. Remember, Mason?"

"I wasn't the one who ran away like my dick was a cattle prod. Remember, Fenn?"

I laughed with no humor whatsoever. "You're *straight*."

"I'm… yes," Mason agreed. "It's probably very likely that I am."

"Probably very likely?" That was new. "So then what's this?" I nodded down at his hand, which was stuck to my T-shirt like a burr. I could feel each fingertip through the thin cotton like five tiny, fiery brands.

Mason swallowed so loudly I could hear him. "You were there in the bathroom the other night."

"I was," I agreed. "And I heard that *stimulus was stimulus*, which was the dumbest thing ever. That was more than just you getting a semi, Mason."

"And you left before I could process a fucking thing beyond that. And you avoided me for a solid week."

"During which, you processed it." I squeezed my hands tightly. "I'm dying to hear your conclusions."

"I… don't have any. I tried," he said in a small, bewildered voice. "I have. But I don't know *what* to conclude. If a person has believed himself to be straight for twelve thousand nine hundred eleven days, give or take, Fenn, and then realizes he's… having other ideas for *seven* days, what does that make him? Does the not-straightness erase the straightness, like all those years never happened? Or do you average the days of straightness and not-straightness and come up with something in between? Does it mean you've always been not-straight and just lying to yourself? Or can it just be something new you pick up? Something you start to feel for one person in one crazy scenario?" He sounded a little bit desperate and a whole lot confused.

He wasn't the only one. Was he talking about *him*? Was he talking about *me* and what happened last week?

"Is there, like, an algorithm, where the more recent days are weighted more?" he went on. "Does it matter how many people of each gender you've ever found attractive? Or, God, does it matter *how* attractive you've found the people of each gender? Is there a formula?"

"I... I have no idea."

"The internet assures me that sexual fluidity is *very* common. That people can become more or less sexually attracted to one gender over time—"

"Can they?" I shook my head. "Because as far as I know, you *can't* change your sexuality, Loafers, and no one can change it for you." It was the motto I'd repeated to myself over and over and over again, after what happened in Texas. It wasn't possible to make a person gay any more than it was possible for my mother to pray my gay away.

"Yeah, that's what *I* said!" Mason exclaimed. "To myself, I mean, when I was reading about this. I know it's a thing that exists, and if I'm sexually fluid or bi or pan or whatever, that's cool... but I still don't understand how it happens. Or what you call it. Or whether it's permanent. So that's why I'm saying, *probably very likely straight.* Okay?"

His fingers were clenching my pec, a nervous, unconscious motion. I grabbed his hand and held it tightly. "Loafers, breathe. It's fine, okay?"

It was *so* not fine. I was completely out of my depth with this. Knowing I was gay had been the easy part; accepting it had been harder; coming out to my family had been harder still. But it sounded like Mason could accept it just fine, if he could really *know* it. But how could you know it unless you...

Oh.

Oh.

"What are we doing here?" I whispered.

His fingers tightened in mine. "I want my last dare, Fenn."

I shook my head slowly. This was a capital *B* Bad Idea. Loafers was going to be on the island for weeks. We'd see each other all the time, and we'd never be able to unring this bell. And I had a rule about straight guys...

I had my *One and Only* Rule about straight guys.

Except maybe Loafers wasn't so straight.

And I'd already broken that rule, anyway.

"How do you know what a thing *is* until you've classified it, Fenn? Until you've looked at the symptoms and run the tests and diagnosed it? Last week I... I thought about you." His confession came out squeaky and breathless.

I nodded. "Sure. Yeah. It was a weird encounter. I thought about you, too. But that doesn't—"

"No." Mason clenched his eyes shut, and I could feel the heat radiating off his face. "No, Fenn, I mean I *thought about you* while I..." He squeezed my hands tight, and I suddenly understood.

Oh.

Motherfucker.

"You have really *got* to learn to say some words, Loafers," I said roughly, but my fingers had tightened on his, too, holding him in place.

"While I *masturbated*," he whispered.

My mouth went dry, and my brain went blank.

"So... I'd really like you to kiss me," Mason blurted. "That's my dare."

"Like you kissed me?" I croaked. I leaned over and pecked his cheek, making sure I didn't linger over it or inhale his scent... much.

"No, *kiss* me," Mason said again, his voice lower this time and more urgent. He scooted several inches in my direction. "A real kiss this time. A... lip kiss."

"A lip kiss." I couldn't decide if his grade school innocence was the best or worst thing ever. Hell, I was pretty sure I'd stopped comprehending English somewhere in the last ten seconds, once all the blood had started rushing to my cock.

"A *tongue* kiss." Mason pushed our joined hands against my knee, leaning toward me. "A *french* kiss."

"You sound like you're twelve," I told him, and it was supposed to be an insult, but it came out all fond and amused. *Fuck*.

I closed my eyes, trying to remember all the reasons I'd totally disliked this guy a week ago. His stupid perfect hair. His stupid shiny shoes. His unnatural confidence. The way he'd sneered at me. The way he'd looked all shocked and aroused in the bathroom.

But it was hard to reconcile that guy from the airport with *this* man on *this* beach, smelling unbearably familiar and delicious, playing with my fingers like we'd been holding hands forever. And if everything he was saying now was true, Mason's shock last Friday night had been really *real*.

Which meant maybe I'd been the one who'd reacted shittily.

"Your fingers are way bigger than mine," he said curiously. He held them up and inspected them in the thin moonlight. "Hairier. And your skin's all calloused."

I fought the urge to snatch my hand away and hide it behind my back, but Mason didn't seem bothered by it. He seemed fascinated. And with every stroke of his hand against mine, my cock jumped.

"I like it." Mason sounded like he was confessing something, and *shit*, I really hated feeling like the sin on someone's conscience.

"Mason. We don't need to do—"

"I kissed a guy once. On a dare. It was *awful*," Mason whispered in a rush. "I never wanted to repeat it. Why bother? But then this week I started thinking, what if the kiss was bad because I wasn't into *Rory*? Or what if I wasn't attracted to guys at all back then and I evolved? Or what if I'm only attracted to *certain* people regardless of sex?"

He meant *me*. He meant, he was attracted to *me*. I clenched my hands into fists to keep myself from grabbing him and pushing him down to the blanket.

"It's not a big deal to me if I'm bisexual, or whatever I am," he repeated. "But the idea that there's this huge thing about myself that I got wrong, that I didn't *know*? That's just..." He huffed out a laugh and ran his hands through his hair, mussing the waves beyond all recognition. I wanted to replace his hands with mine. "What else have I gotten wrong? How much have I just not seen?"

"Mason." I grabbed his jaw—just to steady him, I told myself. To comfort him. Definitely not so I could enjoy the feel of his light stubble under my thumbs as I stroked his cheek. "Chill out, okay?"

He nodded mechanically, his eyes studying the neckline of my shirt like it was a code he had to break. "I'm chill. Very chill. But—" He licked his lips. "I know I'm probably not your usual kind of guy. You probably like men who at least know how to kiss another man, right?" He laughed shortly. "Like, how to maneuver to avoid beard burn and who goes left and who goes right? But..." He looked up, his face flaming like a beacon in the fading light. "You're someone I feel passionate about. So, please kiss me, just this once?"

My chest squeezed. My hands flexed against his jaw, and my fingers threaded into the short, brown waves by his ears.

"Okay," I agreed. "Just this once." Then I crossed the six inches that separated us and took his mouth with mine.

There was nothing else for it, really, was there? It had been bound to happen since the moment I'd laid eyes on him at the airport, all perfectly pressed and horribly out of his element, and there was a kind of relief in just letting it fucking *happen*.

Mason Bloom was an asteroid, and I was the earth, and Bruce Willis wasn't conveniently around to save the day and avert the collision, so I might as well surrender to the impact.

And mother of *God*, the impact.

Mason tasted like salty tears and sweet surprise. He smelled like his fucking intoxicating cologne. His hair was silky soft, but not a single other thing about him was—not the lightly muscled body under my roving hands nor the press of his lips against mine. He went to my head like strong liquor, making me light-headed and brave all at once.

The entire world shifted on its axis as Mason pushed me down, and I didn't even notice until my back hit the sand behind me and Mason's shoes landed somewhere by my head with a soft plop. He climbed on top of me, barely breaking the kiss, all lean limbs and enthusiasm, saying my name in this little animal growl that was the least Loafery thing I'd ever heard.

This was *not* my first kiss with a guy by a long shot, but I'd had full-on orgasms that didn't get me as worked up as kissing Mason Bloom did. I wrapped my arms around him and slid my hands down to cup his ass.

Mason moaned, a filthy sound that made my cock jump to life like my mom's old border collie hearing the rattle of keys. *Wanna go for a ride, Charlie?* Fuck yes, I did.

And it occurred to me that for all that this was Mason's first time, his experimental kiss, I was as much a newbie here as he was.

"Now what?" Mason demanded, pulling away with a gasp, only to rub his lips against my chin, like he was enjoying the scruff there. "What comes next?"

I swallowed. "Mason, maybe we should—"

"*Fenn*," he begged. "Fenn. Please." Then he did the same thing he'd done the other night—a tiny little undulation of his hips, the world's most tentative fucking motion as he rubbed himself against my stomach—and my cock reacted to that tiny movement like he'd stripped naked and started dancing. One hundred percent, immediate commitment; zero to sixty in 0.6 seconds.

"*Fuck.*" A broken rule was a broken rule, right? If you were gonna rob a bank, you might as well take *all* the money? If you were gonna speed, you might as well fucking *speed*?

This was the distorted logic in my fevered brain, anyway. And that logic told me that when the guy who'd pissed me off and invaded my mind for the past six days was on top of me, whimpering my name, I was damn well gonna make him come so hard it obliterated every question in his mind... and maybe every question in mine.

We'd fuck this out of our systems—he'd get his answers, I'd get an orgasm, and then maybe this connection would end.

Mason's face hovered over mine, a giant shadow in the darkness with the moon behind him, and I wanted so badly to see his eyes, to know that they were wide open and he was seeing me.

I speared a hand into the hair at the back of his head and dragged him down for another fierce kiss, and then I rolled us so his back was against the blanket.

I was prepared for him to try to stop me, to have to wrestle him just a little, since he always seemed to give as good as he got. I was *not* prepared for him to go boneless underneath me, and I was *definitely* not ready for him to start moaning like a porn star.

"Oh my God. Yes. It happened exactly like this when I thought of you." He bucked up from underneath me, as frantic for friction as I was. "*Fenn.*"

"Yeah," I croaked, rolling my hips down against him. "I'm right here, Mason."

And I *was*, literally and figuratively, because I'd never had an experience like this before, not ever. Not the kind of sexual encounter that felt less like a choice and more like an inevitability, like a point we'd been driving toward for an entire week, even in the hours we were apart. I'd never gotten off in a way that made me want to watch every emotion play out on the expressive face of the man beneath me, like that was more important than getting off *myself*. I was two seconds from coming just from his throaty groans and the friction of shorts on shorts. I hadn't even gotten a hand on him yet.

I pulled back, just slightly, and Mason whined until I leaned in and bit his bottom lip.

"Get these off," I commanded. My voice was rough even to my own ears, but that was apparently what happened when my dick was hard enough to bend steel and my balls were more primed to explode than C4 with the cap attached.

Not that Mason seemed to expect anything fancier than that. This was in no way a seduction—it was pure, primal need.

I dug my toes in the cool sand and lifted my weight off him for a second in plank position, while he pushed his heavy cotton shorts out of the way. My own shorts were the thin nylon kind that—

Oh. My. Fucking. God.

—were almost like wearing nothing, when Mason bucked up under me again.

My head snapped back, spine going taut. "*Mason.*"

He ran his hands over my abs and down to my shorts. "Yours, too?" he panted against my lips, like he was asking permission or something.

Like I was about to say no. "Yeah. Yes."

Mason dragged my shorts down over my hips to my thighs, then started to repeat the motion with my underwear... but he froze with his hands on my waistband.

Big, green eyes stared up at me, almost a little fearful, like in that one moment, his brain had caught up to his body and he realized just how far this dare had gotten out of hand.

"You good, ba—Mason?" I lifted one hand to brush his wavy hair off his forehead. His skin was damp with sweat, even though the air was chilly.

Mason hesitated for a second, like he was really thinking about it, then nodded slowly, almost solemnly. "I'm really, *really* good."

"Yeah? You want more?" *Please*, I begged a Universe that probably didn't exist. *Make the man want more.*

Mason's tongue darted out to wet his lips, and his eyes crossed like he could taste me there and I tasted delicious. "*Yeah*," he breathed.

Fuck. Yeah, this moment was seriously, seriously *inevitable*. And I was also gonna make damn sure it was *perfect*.

I lowered myself back down so our dicks were flush against each other, separated only by two layers of thin cotton, and balanced myself on my elbows so I hovered above him. Then I kissed him, slow and hard and messy.

I shifted to one hip without breaking the kiss and ran my hand up under his shirt. His skin was smooth and hot, and my fingertips traced what I thought were soothing patterns on his stomach, though the way his muscles flexed and jumped under my hand made me think maybe it was more arousing than anything.

Good.

I ran my fingertips under the top of his boxer briefs—I was *so* right about his underwear—at the same time I licked into his mouth, and Mason groaned louder than ever. I swallowed the sound and molded the length of him through the cotton.

Mason broke the kiss and sucked in a huge gulp of air, oxygen starved. He turned toward me just a little and traced his fingers up my stomach, too, eyes wide.

"Now what?"

It was cute. I'd never been an expert guide at anything before, and I kinda liked it.

"Now... *this.*" Within two seconds, I'd peeled our underwear down and introduced our cocks to one another. I licked my palm, wrapped my fingers around both of us, and started jacking us together slowly.

With the first tug, Mason's eyes rolled back in his head. With the second, he started praying to saints I was pretty sure even my mom had never heard of. Something like, *"Jesus fucking Christ and all the sweet baby bunnies, fuck fuck fuck fuck fuck."*

I would have given him shit for finding religion all of a sudden, except I was thinking just about the same thing, and I couldn't help kissing his swollen lips again.

He started writhing against me—long, sinuous movements in perfect rhythm with my strokes—and I knew he was close when he reached down and grabbed my wrist, not to move me away or control the rhythm, but like he wanted to be an active part of the process. My stomach, which was already soaring and dipping like a kite on a breeze, flipped over entirely.

"Stay with me, Fenn," he said, the way other guys might yell *don't stop* or something. "Stay with me." And the look in his eyes as they locked on mine was...

Shit.

In that moment, there was nothing I didn't like about Mason Bloom.

"Mason," I breathed—just that one single sound—and I came all over both of us. Half a second later, Mason shouted my name as he came, too.

It was one second of utter bliss—powerful and life changing.

And then it was all completely over.

I hadn't even moved my hand away before Mason stiffened and sucked in a breath, and I could almost *hear* the vacuum-sucking sound of rational thought rushing into Mason's head, replacing the lust we'd burned off.

What have I done? And why with Fenn? What the fuck was I thinking?

I wiped my hand on the blanket and turned on my back with a sigh.

"Good?" I said lightly.

Mason's chest heaved and his gaze latched onto my mouth, but he blinked in confusion like I'd started speaking Swahili. "Huh?"

"Are. You. Good?"

"Oh. Yes," he croaked. "I think..." He touched his fingers to his lips and frowned. "I think *very* good?"

I smiled. "Agreed. Really good. High five. Good job, Loafers. Experiment was a success."

I needed to stop talking. I needed a shower.

I pulled off my shirt and used it to mop at my stomach, then offered the fabric to Loafers. I pulled up my shorts, sat up with a groan, and ran my clean hand over my head to shake out the sand.

"I can't decide if rolling off the blanket means we lose points or get bonus points," I teased. I organized a bunch of the empty bottles in the cooler and put the lid on it. "We should coordinate showers when we get back. I'd hate to overload the system." I pushed to my feet.

"Right." Mason was still lying on the ground, clenching my shirt, his lower half resting on the blanket so I couldn't shake it out. "Fenn? Are we okay?"

"Duh. Why wouldn't we be?" I busied myself dusting sand off my ass.

"Did I sorta guilt you into—?"

"No! Don't do that. We both just agreed that was *really good*, right? If no one's told you this before, lemme clue you in: you're hot. The hair. The *eyes*." I shrugged. "Definitely not a hardship."

"But then why... I mean. This has the feeling of you running away again," he said darkly, sitting up and mopping off with my shirt at last. "Is this a *you* thing? Because it's really annoying, if so."

"Hey!" I scowled. "I'm not *running* away. I never have." I licked my lips and honesty compelled me to add, "But you might say I'm... walking. At a sedate and moderate pace. Totally different."

He frowned. "But why?"

I sighed and raked both hands through my hair. "Loafers, it's important that you take your time with all this stuff and wrap your head around it with zero pressure from some random guy who wants to hook up with you. You don't owe anybody anything. Nobody else's expectations matter, even mine. You with me?"

"I'm with you."

"Good. But I... I *do* have expectations." I shrugged apologetically. "Of the guys I'm with, I mean. I usually don't do hookups—"

"You did with Gerry."

"I was feeling sentimental," I said defensively. "They played 'Auld Lang Syne.'"

"Oh."

"Yeah, *oh*. I want someone I can hang out with. Someone I can date. *Openly*. I don't need to take out a billboard on Route 75, but I'm not into being someone's hush-hush experiment or their gay test, either." I tried to say it kindly. I was pretty sure from his expression I'd missed the mark. "I've tried that in the past, Loafers, and the experiment didn't go well. Safe to say we, ah, blew up the lab." I licked my lips and went all in on the honesty. "Which is why it's time to pull back and be friends while I still can. Okay? We stop now, it's a hand job between buds, and that's *nothing*."

Mason nodded slowly. "You think it'll be that easy?"

It had better fucking be. "Yeah. Trust me. Happens all the time. I mean, I'm hot, but I'm not *that* hot."

Mason's face heated. "Right. Okay, then."

"Good."

And it was. Very good. Even if I hadn't expected him to agree quite that quickly. Even if I hadn't left him much room to *disagree* unless he was about to pull a rose from his pocket like this was some hidden-camera episode of *The Bachelor* and make an insincere public declaration of his undying love.

Instead, he just stood up and dusted off, and we worked together in silence to fold the blanket. It wasn't uncomfortable, exactly, but all of our earlier closeness had fled, and I found that I missed it.

A lot.

Not enough to take back what I'd said, though.

It's okay to set boundaries, I told myself. *It's okay not to take every risk.* But I didn't quite manage to convince myself of that either.

Thunder boomed in the distance, and Loafers jumped.

"Another storm. Third or fourth night this week."

Loafers nodded jerkily. "Fifth, actually. We should hurry."

"We've got a few minutes before it hits," I reassured him. "Thunder another one of your not-irrational concerns?"

"Maybe." He bit his lip and forced a smile.

I wanted to take his hand, but I couldn't.

And in the end, Loafers and I left our little cocoon and walked back along the shore to the boardwalk, letting the tide erase our footprints like they'd never existed at all.

10

MASON

That night, I dealt with my thunder *absolutely-not-a-phobia* by barricading myself in the bathroom with the door closed and my headphones in, praying the rain would fuck off soon.

According to Kono, the pint-sized brunette married to Taffy's boyfriend Orry's brother Tim, nighttime thunderstorms were pretty rare this time of year.

Marius Wynott, on the other hand, who had about fifty-seven books on the subject of weather on the Gulf Coast, told me this kind of storm pattern came around every ten years or so. "They call it shipwreck weather!" he'd said, which was just super, super comforting.

But when Juju Irvine, Lety's sister-in-law, who worked the cash register at the Concha, had started complaining, Lety had waved a giant spoon in the air like a magic wand, and solemnly declared, *"Cuando lluve, deja que llueva,"* like this was the final word on the matter.

"Just means, 'When it rains, let it rain,' Doc," Bubba had said mildly, like he was used to his wife making pronouncements he thought were mostly nonsense. But as far as I was concerned, Lety's words had power.

Bad things were gonna happen. You could sit around trying to predict them, or dissecting what had caused them, or wishing them away—for example, while lying flat on your cold bathroom tiles as an infomercial blared in the other room, subliminally convincing you to get a home gym that folded under your bed—but ultimately, you couldn't control it, so why bother. Why not just accept what you couldn't change and move on?

I mean, let's be honest, I would literally *never* be able to live that way, but I admired people who could be all Zen and not overthink shit and have it work out for them. When *I* didn't overthink things, I ended up stranded on Crazy Island, making out with a guy.

I shifted onto my stomach and elbows on the hard tiles and stared down at my phone screen. Not sure why I was staring since I'd more or less memorized the picture already. My lips were pressed to Fenn's cheek, and he looked a little startled, but not unhappy, I didn't think. Meanwhile, *I* was grinning like a fool because I was a little drunk from the beer, a little drunk on my own boldness, and a whole lot drunk on just being with Fenn. That fact was far easier to accept than it would have been even a couple of days ago.

I wanted Fenn Reardon. Simple as that.

I wanted him the way I wanted my next breath—the kind of wanting where it physically hurt and made my heart pound in fear to consider *not* having it.

And I'd been right that I'd needed to kiss him again to prove it to myself. When I could close my eyes and remember the exact feeling of his bicep against my chest when I'd leaned in to kiss him, or the way his fingers had felt sliding down my back, or how his big, calloused hand had fit perfectly around my cock, or how every movement of his lips on mine made electric sparks zing through my bloodstream, it was pretty hard to pass off the attraction as loneliness or adrenaline.

That was how someone else's hands on you were *supposed* to feel. *That* was the answer to the question I'd never thought to ask. *There* was the heavenly chorus, the puzzle pieces clicking, the feeling people fought wars over... and possibly the feeling people abandoned their fiancées and jetted off to Belize for. That was the passion Victoria said I'd been missing, but which Fenn seemed to have no problem unearthing.

It was very, very real.

But when symptoms came on as fast as my attraction to Fenn had, who knew if or when they'd resolve? Maybe I'd wake up in the morning, or next Tuesday, or sometime in November, and my feelings for Fenn would have faded back to normal friendship. Wouldn't I feel foolish if I'd rushed to acknowledge my new sexual orientation publicly, only to have to change it back again? "Poor Mason. He's been so confused since Victoria left," people would say to themselves. "How gross that Mason Bloom's jumping on a trend and trying to get social cred," they'd think. "What kind of idiot doesn't *know* who he's attracted to after thirty-five years?" they'd wonder. "Isn't he supposed to be a *doctor*?"

And they'd be right.

I'd never suggest a patient change his future plans based on a condition he could *maybe* have. Every day in my practice, I weighed the risks of action versus the risks of inaction. I remembered to first do no harm. And yet, I'd forgotten every fucking part of that back down on the beach. I'd gotten so caught up in how good it felt, how *right* it felt, that I hadn't considered any of these important, responsible things. Fenn had been right to pull back and protect himself from the quivering mass of anxious uncertainty that was *me*.

Mason Bloom Takes Control and Lives Fearlessly was doomed before it began, really. I might have changed my job and my wardrobe and my state of residency and even who I found attractive, but ultimately, I was the same person I'd ever been.

Still unsure. Still afraid. Still paralyzed by thinking, thinking, thinking.

The phone rang while I was holding it, and a picture of my best friend's grinning face appeared where the image of Fenn and I had been.

After a heart-pounding second of completely forgetting how technology worked, wondering whether Toby could see what I'd been looking at, and how the hell I would explain it if he could, I remembered that this wasn't science fiction.

Besides, it was only Toby, who'd probably understand better than anyone.

Maybe even better than me.

I swiped the screen to accept the call.

"Chubby baby Jesus and all the heavenly angels, he lives!" Toby said, before I had a chance to even say hello. "Are they keeping you *prisoner* down in that resort, Mason, sweetness? Cough once for yes, twice for no. Cough *three* times if your captors are adorable and I should change into something devastating before I fly down to rescue you."

I snorted. "Hello, Toby."

"Do not *Hello, Toby* me, Mason Bloom! How many times have I called you in the past week? Hmm? Two? *No.* Four? *No.* It's been *eight times*, Mason. Eight times, these poor little fingers had to dial your number, not knowing if you were dead or, worse, alive but with a new best friend! I even wondered if somehow I'd gotten your number wrong, and I had to call Yiannis to see if he had a better one!"

"Yiannis? Who in the world is Yiannis?"

"Who's—" He made a disbelieving noise. "You *wound* me, Mason. You really do. Yiannis is the host from *Davio!* Remember, last time you visited, when Yiannis got us the patio table and later that evening I, ah, compensated him appropriately for his kindness? Thirty-inch neck, adorable Greek accent, hung like a horse?"

I wrinkled my nose. "Tall guy? Dark, curly hair?"

"Mason." Toby gave a long-suffering sigh. "Your descriptions are deplorable."

"Yes, I'm a constant disappointment to you," I agreed sadly. "And after you made the huge sacrifice of calling Yanny just to try to track me down and everything."

"*Yiannis.* And I'll have you know, we conducted an extensive search for you, Mason. Up and down. *Ngh.* High and low. We went All. Night. Long. And we *did not rest.*"

I shifted to sit against the bathtub with my knees up and found myself grinning. "Why do our conversations always become X-rated, Tobias?"

"It's your punishment for running out on me and leaving me to suffer in the frozen tundras of New York on my own." Toby sniffed.

"It's spring. Hardly frozen."

"And then *compounding* your sins by failing to answer a single call or text for a solid *week*."

"I've been busy—"

"Mason, sweetness, *'busy'* is a sham," he said darkly. "You weren't too busy to eat, were you? Or shower? Or cavort on the beach and work on your tan? One would think I'd be *at least* that important, after decades of friendship." He sighed again. "Gone a week, and I'm already forgotten."

"Hardly," I told him honestly. "You are utterly unforgettable."

Toby *hmphed*. "Make it up to me. Tell me every detail *right now* and I might decide that our friendship can continue. Remember to describe things *properly*."

I laughed weakly. "Hard to know where to begin, really." Which was why I hadn't answered any of his calls or increasingly demanding texts for pictures and updates. I didn't want to lie, but I couldn't bring myself to tell the truth.

Toby was momentarily silent—a minor miracle—and when he spoke again, his voice was serious. "Alright, what's up? The island not as amazing as you thought it would be?"

"No. Not exactly." I sucked in a breath and felt tears prick behind my eyes. More like, *nothing* like I thought it would be. And *I* was nothing like I thought I would be.

"Tell me!" he insisted.

Well, Toby, the plumbing is trying to kill me.

I've watched thirteen infomercials in a week, and I'm considering turning my motel room into an As Seen on TV showroom.

One of my patients ingests pheromones to increase his sexual potency, and has a possibly cancerous mole that he swears grows and shrinks according to the tide schedule on Whispering Key Beach.

My boss is a treasure-hunting con man.

Geckos are fucking terrifying Satan-spawn, and the way they dart around on their disgusting gecko-feet makes me want to burn the entire earth just to eradicate them.

I'm thirty minutes from a laundromat that doesn't contain reptiles, and I'm sweating through my clothing at an alarming rate.

There's a man on Whispering Key who looks like a GI Joe doll who rescues kittens and tells me my aura is pink.

There's a lady here who makes the world's tastiest pineapple bread as a weight-loss supplement and has very concerning petechiae on her feet, but refuses to stop wearing her too-tight shoes.

And there's this guy... this one, amazing guy... and he kissed me... and then we... and then we...

"The job's not what I expected," I choked out. "I'm leaving as soon as I can find a new one."

"Ah, shit. I'm sorry, boo." But I noticed Toby didn't sound all that upset. "I'm sure you'll find something else soon. Maybe back here? Closer to the city? We could be roommates, just like the olden days."

"Also, I... I have a patient," I lied. "He's, uh... he's having a hard time. With his sexuality. Potentially coming out? It's concerning." I folded the edge of the shower curtain into a triangle and smoothed the line with my fingernail.

"Oh," Toby said, all sympathy. "That's rough. A kid?"

"No, he's older, actually. Around our age. Which is part of the trouble."

"Yeah, more complications that way sometimes," Toby agreed. "He have children? A wife?"

"No, no. Nothing like that! Just, you know. It's a little odd, right?" I forced a slight laugh as I folded my fabric triangle into ever-smaller triangles. "He's that old, and he's only just *now* figuring his shit out?"

Toby was silent for a long minute. "No, Mason. Not odd at all. Come on, baby, this is Gay 101. You know better. Sexuality evolves."

I did. I really did. Except... not as it applied to *me*.

"Well, the thing is, he doesn't know exactly how to label himself. What if it turns out that his feelings go away, and he needs to take it back? Imagine if he goes around saying, 'Oh, hey, I'm bisexual.' Except then he realizes it was just a fluke?" I swallowed. "A mistake."

"Except, if it's the way he's feeling now, it's *not* a mistake because, again, sexuality evolves. It's complex and not black and white. And *you know this*." He paused, and I could picture him trying to peer through the phone. "Mason, are you okay?"

"Yes, peachy! Just thinking how you lose credibility when you keep changing your mind about things, though, you know? How do you respect a person who doesn't recognize something integral like that? It's probably best for him to be... cautious... since coming out might be useless."

"Mmmmkay. I mean, it's true that no one can tell you when it's the right time—"

"You mean *him*. My patient. Edgar."

Toby sighed. "Yes, obviously. I meant *Edgar*. If *Edgar* chooses to come out, it should be a thing he does for himself, and other people's opinions have fuck all to do with it."

I snorted. "I mean, it's easy to *say* that—"

"Mason, do you hear yourself? It is *not* easy to say that. At all." Toby laughed a little bitterly. "You remember my coming out, right?"

I felt instantly ashamed. "Yeah, I remember."

"But coming out might be empowering for, ah... Eddie."

"Edgar."

"Right. Because coming out's not a one-shot deal *anyway*. It's not like sending an 'I've Moved!' card to your friends and neighbors to let them know they can now find you amongst the Super Queers. It's hard doing it over and over, especially since there *will* be negative reactions. It's easier knowing there are a whole bunch of people who get you."

"That's not a concern for Edgar. The... the acceptance."

"It's the idea that he might be wrong?"

I cleared my throat. "Yeah."

"Jesus H. Christ on a gondola. I don't suppose Eddie—"

"Edgar!"

Toby nearly growled. "*Right*," he said impatiently. "I don't suppose he recently rescued himself from indentured servitude to a blonde who exploited his perfectionism and never deserved his noble, self-sacrificing ass?"

"Wha—"

"Maybe *Edgar* is totes fine accepting he's gay, but he needs to *come out* as an actual, fallible, evolving human being, not a perfect Instagram image."

"I don't—"

"Oh, by the wigs of Lovey Bricknell. What's his name, sweetness?"

I clenched the shower curtain in my fist. "Whose?" I asked faintly.

"The guy Edgar's hot for."

I made a noise that was half laugh, half sob. The guy I was hot for. It should have sounded weirder than it did.

"It's Fenn," I admitted miserably. "He's fucking gorgeous, Toby. And so completely wrong for... *Edgar*."

"Wrong because he's a dude."

"No! No, even aside from that." I took a deep breath, and everything I'd been feeling and not saying tumbled out of me in a rush. "Fenn's sarcastic—you would love him—and when you give him shit, he dishes it right back. And he makes nonviolent people want to do violent, violent things, because he gets this smirk and this look in his eyes that... *gah*."

"Oh, boy."

"And he wears these horrible flip-flops literally everywhere —the thin, plastic kind that make those rude, slappy noises. Any sane person would want to chuck them into the Gulf, no matter how environmentally irresponsible that would be, they're *that* annoying—except somehow, after walking beside him for a minute, you become really aware of how silent your steps are when he's not there. And then you realize you're having fond thoughts about dollar-store footwear and you start to get concerned about your own mental state."

"Mason."

"And he's sometimes insulting or eye-rolly when you tell him things, like there's something inherently wrong with having your future planned out, but... he also makes you feel like he *gets it*, even if he doesn't *get it* get it, and like you could tell him any random, insane thought or doubt or worry that jumps into your brain and it wouldn't even faze him. And he makes you laugh about things you didn't think would ever be funny."

"Sweetness."

"And he... he has this soap-clean smell. A stomach-flipping manly smell." I sighed. "And he has a scruffy chin that's softer than you'd think and makes you wanna rub your face against it. And... he's like poison ivy and a weighted blanket all rolled into one."

"Motherfucker. Where is Yiannis when I need him?"

I snorted. "And he... he has a real aversion to dating anyone who's not out. He's been someone's experiment before, and I think he got hurt."

"Ohhhh." Toby was silent for a second. "That can't be your... *Edgar's* problem. You know that, right? Edgar can't come out for Perfect Fenn."

"Fenn's not perfect. And I know you're right. Edgar knows. Fenn knows, too. He said that himself, earlier tonight. After he and Edgar, um..."

"Um? *Finish that sentence immediately.*"

"I can't! I don't have the vocabulary for what it was! Hands and *rocking* and kissing and... *rocking.*"

"*Hhhhngh.*"

"You okay?"

"The vocabulary word you're searching for is *frotting,*" Toby said in a strangled voice. "And if your Fenn doesn't get off on having you be all innocent and untutored, he's a fucking idiot."

"He's not my Fenn."

"Jesus fucking Christ. *Edgar's* Fenn, then."

"That's not what I meant! I mean, Fenn wants to be friends. No more... hooking up. Because he wants someone he can date, and I..." I took a deep breath. "I'm not out. I don't know what I am." I swallowed and curled up on the cold bathroom floor. "And it's better that way. I'm not an idiot. There's no future for me on Whispering Key. I'm leaving as soon as possible. This island is a tiny blip on my path. I'm not getting tied down here or anywhere."

Why, *why* did that simple, obvious truth make me want to cry, and/or rush down the balcony to Fenn's door and force him to hug me until I felt less shitty?

"Mason, I have total faith that you'll get where you need to be eventually."

"Yeah? Well. That makes one of us."

"What does Micah say?"

"Micah? Please. He'd fly down here and wouldn't leave until he'd sorted me out. And if I thought he could do it, I'd let him, but he can't, so I'm not telling him shit." I pushed a hand through my hair. "I hate feeling this way, you know? Like I don't know what I'm supposed to be doing. Tell me what to do."

"You're gonna hate this advice," Toby said gleefully. "You ready? You need to give it time. Stop spiraling on this. Let your lizard brain catch up to your frontal lobe, or vice versa. Live your life. Let the seeds you planted germinate. Let Fenn's caveman instincts overwhelm his reason. Then we'll see."

"*Then we'll see*? That's the worst advice ever," I grumbled. That was the *exact opposite* of what I was trying to do with my life. "I want a *plan*, Tobias. I want steps. I want to take action. 'Seeing what happens' is what fucked things up with Victoria."

"No, sweetness, that was not the issue. *Settling* was the issue. So, you want to take action? Don't settle. Be honest with yourself about what you want. Be honest with Fenn. But don't overthink your way into a tiny box and pretend that's you taking control of your life."

"I take it back. *That* is the worst advice ever." If I were honest with Fenn about the things I was feeling, I was pretty sure he'd take out a restraining order against me. With good reason.

But once Toby laughed and said goodbye, I was left staring at the picture of Fenn and me again.

Was Toby right? Was I really so scared of making a mistake that I couldn't be honest about who I was and what I wanted right in this moment? I'd decided, back in my New York loft, that I wanted a life that was truly *mine*... and being real about myself was part of that. Even if Fenn and I were never together again, that moment on the beach earlier had been the truest, most honest experience of my entire life. Something *I'd* made happen. Something that was, therefore, inherently *mine*, even if it never happened again. Even if I never wanted it to.

I stared at that picture for an hour before opening my Instagram, then another hour trying to think up a caption, before I realized I didn't have to. Fenn had already given me the perfect one.

"I dare you, Mason Bloom," I whispered to myself from the tile floor of the tiny bathroom.

I hit Post, and immediately fell asleep with the phone in my hands.

11

FENN

Factually speaking, my room at the Five Star was the same size it ever was. Same industrial carpet, same sand-colored walls, same artwork I'd hung haphazardly over the years. At some point last night, though, during the hour or so when the thunder had been loud enough to shake the world, I'd lain on my bed in the dark and thought about Mason, who couldn't sleep in the thunder, and the walls had seemed to close in on me.

Which, yeah, was fucking pathetic.

I'd finally drifted off to sleep, and when I'd blinked my gritty eyes open to the sound of my stupid alarm at 5:00 a.m., the room had been klieg-light bright again in the Florida sun, but I'd felt weirdly dissatisfied. The room had gotten bigger while I'd slept. Too big. Too sterile and impersonal. Too empty.

Which was arguably *more* pathetic.

So, before I could trace those lonely thoughts back to their source, I'd jumped in the shower. For the first time in a while, I was actually eager to get to work, because in the grand scheme of bullshit ways to spend my time, running Rafe's boat ranked somewhere above pining for the straight guy down the hall when I'd fucking *sworn* I would never do that again.

I was so pissed at myself, I wasn't paying attention when I passed Mason's door... which was how I came to find myself with two arms full of stammering, shower-damp, sexy-as-fuck man.

"Whoa!" I grabbed Mason by his upper arms to steady him before he hit his head on the doorjamb. He smelled like salt and woodsmoke and everything cozy. I wanted to cuddle him, so I pushed him away. And it took *effort*.

But we were *friends*. So.

"Shit, sorry!" He took one look at my face and moved back another half step as he removed his earbuds. "Sorry, Fenn, I didn't—"

"Have psychic powers to detect that I'd be walking by just now?" I said, forcing an unconcerned smile. "It's fine. My fault, too."

It was absolutely not fine. His wet hair curled on his forehead and waved around his ears. He was wearing a thin cotton T-shirt that highlighted his lean muscles and the dip of his collarbone, a body part that had never before and would never again be as sexy as it was in that frustrated moment.

Just friends. Whose fucked-up idea was this?

Oh. Right.

Mason chuckled and looked down at the sandy sneakers I'd noticed in his closet when I was playing super-stalker the day before. "Yeah, no. No psychic powers. I'll leave that to Beale." He smiled and it looked pained.

My own smile faltered. "Beale told you about that?" I didn't know he talked much about his portents and shit outside the family.

"What? Oh. Yeah. He's been driving me to work. Gave me a crystal to cleanse the air in my room." He rubbed the back of his neck. "Supposed to help me sleep."

"Did it work?"

He shook his head and gave me a look that so clearly said, *What the hell do you think, dumbass?* that I could almost hear his voice in my head. "But it was sweet of him."

There were a lot of directions my brain could have gone from there. Like, pondering how Mason hadn't slept any better than I had. Like, forcing my feet to keep walking down the balcony to the stairs and then out to my car. Instead, it snagged on the word *sweet* and hung there.

Beale thought Mason was sweet. *Mason* thought Beale was sweet.

Nobody thought *I* was sweet, and all the sugar in the air was a little nauseating.

I set my jaw.

On paper, Beale would be a much better choice for Mason. He didn't have the same baggage I did. He might be more than open to a little experimentation with the cute and friendly doctor for as long as he was stranded on Whispering Key.

Nauseous-er and nauseous-er.

"Yeah, well. Beale..." I hesitated. I hated lying. I especially hated people who lied for their own gain. Was I really going to lie about *Beale* of all people? Just because I was jealous?

No. I'd hate myself.

"I don't know anything about auras," Mason continued, a little smile playing on his lips, "but whatever color means adorable and honorable, that's Beale's color." He beamed. "And he's been *so* patient with me this week, too, helping me get acclimated to the island. Poor guy can't remember how to stretch his shoulder to save his life, but I don't mind showing him—"

"He's in love with someone," I blurted.

Mason and I stared at each other, both wide-eyed with shock.

"Please forget you heard that." I closed my eyes and rubbed at the spot between my brows. "That's... not a thing I should be talking about."

"No, of course." Mason mimed zipping his lips together. "But... who?"

My mouth opened and closed like the world's largest, most dishonest fish.

"Fenn... we're friends, right? Isn't that what we decided?"

I nodded woodenly. We'd decided. Or possibly Beale's Universe had decided for us, because it was capricious as fuck and loved to taunt me with things I couldn't have. One or the other.

"So you know I'm not going to say a word. You can tell me." He stepped closer like he was worried about being overheard. Of course he wanted to know.

My punishment for lying was immediate and totally disproportionate to my crime. Having Mason in my space, close enough that his scent filled my lungs and his green eyes filled my vision, felt like being on fire.

"I... I can't say," I croaked. "Jesus, I shouldn't have said even that much. It's a, um... complicated situation."

Mason sank his teeth into his lower lip, looking so sexy I nearly groaned. "The poor guy."

Beale was going to kill me. And at this rate, it would be a mercy killing.

"Loafers, stick to doctoring. Don't worry about Beale."

"Right." Mason pursed his lips and gave me a knowing look. "Say no more."

"I'm serious."

Mason stepped away and blinked in feigned innocence. "Of course you are. Me too!" He grabbed his doorknob and pulled his door closed, which was when I put together exactly how he was dressed, in a plain T-shirt and shorts that didn't even look ironed.

"Fenn! Get your ass down here!" Beale yelled good-naturedly. "Dad wants us."

Mason and I both stepped forward to peer over the railing, our shoulders brushing.

We looked at each other guiltily and each took a step away.

"Yeah, coming," I called down.

"Doc!" Beale's smile was like the sun emerging from a cloud. "Hey! How's your Saturday going?"

"It's about an hour old, but so far so good. Just going for a walk on the beach now," he called down to Beale.

Beale grinned, eager as a fucking puppy. "Nice! I just finished a run, myself!"

I rolled my eyes.

"Fenn and I are working today, but I should be back around lunchtime, if you want me to drive you anywhere," Beale offered.

Mason shot me a look I couldn't decipher. "Nah, I can walk myself down to town if I need to go. That's fine. But thanks."

"Let me know if you change your mind!" Beale's good cheer was disgusting, and absolutely sincere. I should have felt worse about lying.

"Seriously, he's *so sweet*," Mason cooed, too low for Beale to hear.

Okay, yup, *now* I felt worse. But not about lying.

"Anyway. I guess I'll run into you later. Hopefully not literally. *Ha*." Mason aimed a smile somewhere over my shoulder.

It was all I could do not to answer the same happy-puppy way Beale had, tongue hanging out of my mouth and all.

"Loafers, we can't seem to help it," I said wryly.

Mason's smile turned rueful, and he shook his head as he walked away, clearly taking it as a joke, but as he disappeared around the side of the building, I was uncomfortably sure I'd spoken nothing less than the truth.

Saturdays on the boat were the ultimate distraction—the water was packed with boats, the boats were packed with tourists, and there were a thousand and one tiny tasks that required my attention, even during the parts of the tour I wasn't narrating. Nothing like salt air, sunshine, and hard work to keep my mind off... anything I'd rather not think about. Right?

Yeah, not so much.

"Let me tell you a story about the *Esmerelda*," I'd said into my microphone as we rounded the southern end of Whispering Key—an action I performed literally six times a week —but *this* time, I'd remembered Mason's excited face when he thought he was the first guy to wonder if Resolute Goodman had hidden his half of the treasure near the rocks.

After the tour was over, a lady in a pink visor and sensible shoes had passed me a folded-up twenty, patted my hand as she disembarked, and said, "You have a gift for storytelling, young man. And such youthful enthusiasm!" and I fought the sudden urge to text Loafers that I was *youthfully enthusiastic*, not *childlike or ridiculous*, just because I knew he'd roll his eyes at me.

"Do you do private parties?" a middle-aged man in a cute polo shirt and boat shoes had asked, handing me a business card, and I'd smiled hard and tried *not* to think about when and how I'd begun finding polo shirts cute.

The wind kicked up and caught the flag above the cockpit, twisting it around the pole, and I'd pictured wavy brown hair blowing around laughing green eyes.

In short, I. Was. *Sprung*.

It was horrible. And I didn't know how to stop it, or even if I wanted to.

"Yo, Fenn." An enormous hand waved in front of my face, and I jumped away from the clear plastic I'd been tying down over the open window, instinctively sinking into a fighter's stance.

"Jesus Christ, Beale! Don't fucking sneak up on a person!"

"Sneak up? I've called your name sixty-seven times."

I shook my head and stretched my neck from one side to the other.

"Dad called your name twice, too," Beale continued smugly. "But I think he just assumed you were ignoring him, 'cause he muttered something under his breath and left."

I looked around. "Left. But didn't he—"

"We finished locking everything down at least ten minutes ago." Beale smirked. "While you stood here in your own little world, thinking about... what, exactly?"

"I wasn't... I didn't sleep well last night," I told him honestly. "I'm zoned out because I'm tired."

"Gotcha." Beale knocked me out of the way, took the plastic from my fingers, and deftly finished my task. "So, what were you and Mason chatting about this morning?"

"Chatting?" I snorted. "We weren't *chatting*. He came out of his door the same minute I was walking past it. Coincidence."

"Ah."

"What's that mean?"

Beale shrugged his enormous shoulders and shoved his hands in the pockets of his cargo shorts. "I thought he was a *snob*, that's all. Or, no, *prissy*, wasn't that the word? Aura as brown as his shoes? Thought you were a serial killer? *Loafers*?"

I brushed my hair out of my eyes. "Your dad told me to be nice to him."

"Oh!" Beale nodded vigorously. "Of course! Of course. Silly me. You're always so great about backing Dad's plays. Obviously you're being friendly with the doctor because Dad told you to! Because you're a team player."

I cleared my throat. "Yep. So, where'd your dad disappear to, anyway? Gosh, I feel like we spend hardly any time together."

"Your changed attitude toward Mason is most definitely not because he's got a tight body," Beale persisted. "Or pretty eyes. Or because he's so smart. Or because he doesn't take your shit, and you find that irresistible. Those things are just incidental."

"Mmmm. Smells like lunch." I patted my stomach. "Wonder what Lety's got cooking?"

"And this attitude change has nothing whatsoever to do with you spending the evening at the rocks last night, drinking."

I stopped in my tracks, heart racing. Of everyone on this island, Beale was the only one who knew how much I loved the rocks. As far as I knew, he was the only one who even remembered that spot was there. Had Beale seen us? I hadn't even considered that last night, and *fuck*, Mason would *not* be happy if this got out.

"I don't know what you thought you saw, but you keep your mouth *shut*, get it?" I took a threatening step in his direction and lowered my voice. "I'm being very, *very* serious here, Beale. Do *not* tell your father, do *not* tell your brothers. Tell *no one*. Mason's sorting through some shit, and he doesn't need anyone up in his business."

A slow smile dawned on Beale's face. "I didn't see a damn thing last night, Fenn. But this morning, when I was running on the beach, I saw an empty bottle of your schmancy beer and two sets of footprints. In fact, *at first*, I was gonna give you shit about picking things up with Gerry—"

I made a disgusted noise. "How many times do I have to tell you, that is a thing that will *never* be picked up? I can't manage to have a conversation with the man while sober, Beale. Okay?"

Beale held his palms up. "Yeah. Okay! Chill." He rocked on the soles of his boots. "So, when you say Mason doesn't need anyone up in his business, I take it you mean besides *you*?"

"No." I resumed walking. "I'm not up in his business either. Not like that. We're *friends*. We decided."

"You realize that saying you *decided* to be friends implies that there were other choices *besides* friendship."

Fuck, fuck, fuck. I was digging myself into a hole, so I tried keeping my mouth shut.

It didn't work.

"So is Mason into you? Did you hook up?" Beale didn't look *nearly* as surprised by this development as I would have expected him to be.

"What happened between us was *none* of your goddamn business." I felt my face go hot. "Anyway, we're *friends*. And he's leaving here the second he gets another job, which could be tomorrow for all I know. It's better if we just... don't... discuss any non-friendship options that might exist."

Beale tilted his head to one side and assessed me for a moment. "Ahhh." He nodded in understanding. "Yeah, no, I feel you, Fenn. If Mason is... how'd you put it? 'Sorting through some shit'? That's probably not a good situation for you. After Texas Thad fucked you over, it's better if you stick to guys who've been out and proud a while, huh?"

I scowled. "It's not like that—"

"But since *you're* not interested, and Mason *might* be, I might as well up my flirting game! Set blasters to *kill* instead of *stun*." He rubbed his hands together and wiggled his eyebrows.

I whirled to face him. "No. You should *not*. Just leave Mason be."

"But why? *If* Mason's taking some fledgling steps into figuring out his sexuality, he'll need a guide," Beale said mildly. "And I'm a great guide. Really gentle and patient—"

Red mist covered my vision, and I thumped Beale's shoulder, *hard*. "He doesn't need you to be his gay sherpa!"

Beale's tongue traced the inside of his cheek as he regarded me, no trace of his customary smile in place.

A new, disturbing thought occurred to me. "Wait. Beale, do you have *feelings* for Mason?"

The air was heavy and close in the boat with the plastic down, which was obviously why I was sweating.

Obviously.

"Would it matter to you if I did?" Beale asked at length. "Would you be okay if I made a play for him, then?"

"Ye—" I broke off with a cough. There was only one right answer to that question, but somehow, I couldn't make myself give it. "I mean..."

"Uh-huh." Beale's face split in a shit-eating grin. "Your aura is so freakin' red right now, I can't even handle it. I do *not* have feelings for Mason, Fenn. But *you* do."

"Do not."

"Jealousy is a feeling, buddy."

"I..." I opened my mouth and closed it again. *Fuck.*

"Question is, what you plan to do about it—"

"I already told you. *Friends.*"

"—because if you don't want him—"

"I don't." Not... an unreasonable amount. Not an insurmountable... amount.

"—that's cool, but someone else will. Either on this island or elsewhere. So, like, he's gonna do what he's gonna do. Eventually. With someone. Who's not you."

I rubbed at the back of my neck, angry at the world. "What do you want from me, Beale? This isn't easy, you know?"

"Right? I know. So imagine how hard it is for Mason." Beale pursed his lips. "And just to say, and then I really will drop it forever before your talking-about-feelings allergy kicks in and you go into anaphylactic shock—"

"*Jesus*—"

"—one of the things that hurt you most about Thad when he fucked you over was that he made you think he was really into you, but every time he had a chance to prove it, pushed you away, right?"

I swallowed. I hadn't pushed Mason away. "Mason and I agreed." It sounded lame, even to my own ears.

"You know, Mason and I were talking the other day—"

"Yeah, I heard all about your *talks*." I made air quotes, even though I hated making air quotes, just on general principle.

Beale didn't even bother concealing his amusement anymore. "Anyway, he mentioned something about his Instagram account, so I've been checking it every morning after my beach run, while I eat my oatmeal—"

"I'm aware he has an Instagram account, Beale." I was *very* aware. I also knew exactly which pictures made the cut and which did not.

"Hmm. Maybe you should check it out. I have to say, I found his most recent post... highly educational."

Educational? "What the fuck would I want to do that for? Last thing I need is endless pictures of his stupid loafers, or the hashtag-mating habits of whatever hashtag-wildlife he thinks he's seen."

Beale literally doubled over with laughter.

"Have you finally lost your mind?" I demanded. "Is this how it ends?"

Beale sobered somewhat. "Sorry! Sorry. Just... *mating habits.* That's a good one." He sniffed loudly like he was trying to compose himself and clapped my shoulder with one giant paw. "Anyway, I'm just saying, if you could see what Mason looks like when he's looking at you... if you could see what *you* look like when you look at him... you might remember that he is *not* Texas Thad. And you might rethink your decisions."

He turned and strolled off, whistling.

I narrowed my eyes and watched him walk, wondering what the hell he meant. How did Mason look at me? How did I look at Mason? What was so educational about Mason's Instagram?

Well played, Beale.

I hurried after him.

12

———

MASON

Per Toby's advice, I'd woken up Saturday determined to be *patient*, to give things time, to not overthink. I had *not* checked my Instagram to see the fallout of posting my picture with Fenn, because that post had been an accurate representation of where I was for that one moment in time, and it shouldn't matter what anyone else thought. I didn't let myself replay the kiss over and over in my mind, because Fenn and I were going to be *friends*, and thinking about him sexually was counterproductive. I congratulated myself for evolving and maturing to the point where I'd mastered my own thoughts and regarded self-knowledge as its own beautiful reward.

In short, it was maybe the most peaceful nineteen minutes of my life.

And it had ended the literal *second* I'd crashed into Fenn on the balcony.

I could *not* be friends with Fenn Reardon. What the hell had I been thinking to ever agree to such a stupid plan? It was adorable that Fenn wanted friendship, it really was. But that friendship was meant for some alternate-universe Mason and Fenn. An innocent universe. A universe where Fenn's hand had never been on my cock and I'd never screamed his name while I orgasmed my spleen onto the Florida sand.

Sadly, in *this* world, I was fairly certain that if I ever got close enough to breathe his air again, like I had this morning, I was going to molest the fuck out of him, despite him explaining very logically last night why that would not be good for either of us, and despite the fact that I very logically agreed with him.

Mason Bloom Takes Charge of His One Goddamn Life was never meant to be a romance.

So, therefore, I was putting a restraining order on myself. If I saw Fenn coming, I was going to walk away. If I knew Fenn was going to be hanging around the motel, working on his car, I would be elsewhere.

If the man had managed to avoid me for an entire week, surely I could avoid him just as easily, right? *Pfft*. Of course I could.

Which was why I found myself walking into town along the Godfrey Pass about half a mile north of the Five Star, sweating off all the water in my body as the midday sun beat down on me, just when the younger Rafe Goodman happened along in his Jeep, headed for the motel.

"Morning, Doc." Young Rafe rolled down his window and slowed his Jeep to a crawl. "Out exploring?"

I took a step closer to the car, only because it would have been rude to stay away, and not at all because of the blasts of beautifully cool air-conditioning wafting through the window. I hadn't spoken to the oldest Goodman brother very much, and I got the impression he didn't approve of me, somehow, though I wasn't sure if that was because I was new in town, or because I was a doctor, or because I was part of his father's plan for Whispering Key. Or maybe, as Fenn would have said, *"Smart money says a little of each."*

Except, I wasn't thinking about what Fenn would have said anymore.

"Uh. No. Not sure there's much here to explore?" I side-eyed the columns of palms lining each side of the road. "For me, I mean. I'm not much of a... tree person." Trees meant bugs, and bugs likely meant geckos. Thus ended any desire I had to walk into the Florida woods.

Rafe snorted. "Yeah, me neither. Beale's the tree-hugger of the family. I'm happier on the water. And Gage... His natural habitat is air-conditioning."

"Hey! Nothing wrong with that!" I exclaimed, and we both laughed.

Part of me was dying to ask what Fenn's habitat was, but I would *not*.

I was quitting him cold turkey.

"You ever hear the story of Resolute Goodman, my great-great-times-a-billion-grandfather?" Rafe asked, eyeing me curiously.

I nodded. "Of course. He was a quartermaster who took gold from the *Esmerelda* before it sank and wound up founding Whispering Key along with Jacob Godfrey, the captain." I'd heard the story from... *he who would not be named*... and then

I'd gotten several more earfuls from people in town. Every person had their own piece of Godfrey memorabilia and their own ideas about where the treasure was most likely hidden.

"Jeez, we indoctrinate folks fast around here." Rafe smiled ruefully. "Well, if you're really hard up for something to do, the remains of the place the men stayed when they first came ashore after the shipwreck are right through those woods." He pointed out his window. "We call it the Original Homestead. Not sure why, since it wasn't much of a homestead and there's hardly any of the original building left anyway, but that's neither here nor there. See where the road dips and there's a break in the trees? Walk back about two feet, and you'll see the world's densest, *thorniest* patch of blackberries, in a big ol' rectangle marked off with white seashells, like they were attempting to cultivate them. Very domestic. Walk ten feet back from *that* and you'll see hatch marks on a tree that mean… who the hell knows what? Probably communicating with aliens. Five feet back from *that*, a big stone fire pit where they'd roast their Sunday possum. Be sure to take pictures to share with your friends."

"Wow! Does the path dump me out at a gift shop where I can buy a book of traditional possum recipes and my very own hatchmark-making kit?"

Rafe's face split in a grin that made him look ten years younger and infinitely more handsome. "I'm gonna suggest that at the next Whispering Key town meeting."

"Please make sure you credit me."

He chuckled and his eyes softened in appreciation. "Oh, you bet I will. Can I give you a lift somewhere?"

I was tempted for a second, because it was really quite, *quite* warm for a walk, but I shook my head. "Thanks anyway, but I'm going in the opposite direction. Heading to town. Gonna treat myself to some lunch."

Beale had said he and Fenn would be back at the motel in the early afternoon. Therefore, I was resolved to spend the early afternoon *elsewhere*.

"Yeah? Going to the Concha?" Rafe sounded surprised.

"Yep. I love it there. Besides, not a lot of choice unless a new restaurant has opened in the last two days!"

Rafe snorted. "Not that I know of. Though, to hear my dad talk about it…" He broke off and shook his head. "You know, he was telling me and Beale last night that he's gonna be trialing food trucks next month for the Labor Day Extravaganza? You heard about the Extravaganza, right?"

I nodded. "Hard to exist in this town and *not*. Literally everyone who comes by the clinic has had something to say. What do you mean trialing the trucks?"

"Starting in a couple weeks, every Saturday, they're gonna park in town down by the pier. The ones we all like best will get asked back." He shook his head, more bewildered than excited. "People are *competing* for spots. On Whispering Key."

"That's a good thing, right?"

Rafe shook himself. "I guess. Dad's been talking about the revival of Whispering Key for a *long* time. I didn't take him seriously this time around." His lips twisted up. "Anyway, enjoy your lunch. Beale and Fenn should be finishing up their tour in a half hour or so, so you might catch them on their way back if you want a ride home."

I waved a hand in goodbye as he drove off, very much hoping I did *not* catch Fenn… at all.

My phone chimed with an incoming text, and I pulled it from my pocket.

UNKNOWN

Hey.

It was from a Florida number I didn't recognize, which was weird since I'd only given my number to Big Rafe, Beale, and Taffy. I ignored it.

UNKNOWN

It's Fenn. Can we talk?

Shit. I wished I could ignore the way my stomach jumped, just reading that.

That feeling—that weird, jittery, fluttery feeling—had never happened to me before. *Ever.* Not in high school, when I took Celeste Nustlebaum to prom, or when I'd kissed Rory. Not when I'd dated the gorgeous Emily Lu in college, or sweet, funny Becky in med school. Not even in the earliest early days with Victoria, who I'd planned to marry. Apparently I *was* capable of feeling passion, I'd just been looking for it in the wrong people.

This would have been a more comforting revelation if the *one* person I felt this way about had been capable of returning my feelings, but he wasn't. And this overcaffeinated, anxiety-attack feeling was not compatible with friendship.

I stuck my phone back in my pocket and decided it wasn't *hiding* if you refused to acknowledge someone was *looking* for you.

I also fervently hoped that one of the fourteen MedLister jobs I'd applied for would call me back soon.

"Morning, Dr. Bloom!" a voice called from across the street.

I blinked out of my daze and realized that I'd nearly reached the curve in the road where the town center began. It was a good thing there was hardly any traffic—Fenn Reardon was dangerous to my senses in more ways than one.

"Mr. Wynott!" I lifted a hand in a wave at the short, starchy man in his fedora, holding his tiny dog on a leash. "How are you?"

Marius Wynott was the owner of Wynott's Books, a second-hand bookshop located on the ground floor of his gorgeous Victorian home. Taffy had said the house had been in his family for ages, and the two upper floors were even grander than the first. Gloria had told me I *needed* to see Mr. Wynott's collection of local memorabilia. But when I'd stopped by Wednesday, the man had barely started showing me around when his Pomeranian attacked me with love, literally *trembling* in excitement as she licked my chin, so I'd been *forced* to sit and pet her instead. I'd left with a book on pirates and a smile on my face.

Mr. Wynott crossed the street, led by a white-brown-and-black blur of barking excitement.

"Topaz!" I bent down to caress her furry face. "Really, more people ought to display this level of excitement at seeing me."

"She's usually very reserved and dignified," Mr. Wynott said, bewildered. "But she's taken to you immediately."

"Have you? Have you, baby girl?"

She yapped excitedly, and I hadn't thought I was a fan of tiny dogs, but I decided this one was an exception.

"That reminds me," Mr. Wynott said. He hesitated. "I'm going to a writing conference for two weeks in early July, and I wonder... could you watch Topaz for me? My friend Chrissy is coming to mind the shop while I'm gone, and she does an excellent job, but she's a cat person." He wrinkled his nose like this was an embarrassing flaw to confess about his friend. "She and Topaz have almost nothing to say to one another."

I grinned. "Sure. Let me give you my number and you can text me the dates, and I'll..." I blinked. Wait. *July.* Would I still be here then? I mean, probably, right? That was weeks away.

I grabbed my phone to check my calendar again and saw that I'd gotten two more texts from Fenn.

Seriously, Loafers. Can we talk?

Are you avoiding me? Who's running now?

Okay, that one stung.

Topaz licked my face, and I resumed petting her. "Sorry," I told Mr. Wynott. "Just give Taffy the dates and I'll put them on my calendar later, okay?"

"You're a treasure, Doctor!" Mr. Wynott tipped his fedora. "Come, Topaz. It's nearly nap time. Mason, you're welcome to stop by later and visit your betrothed." He winked.

I barely had time to be amused by this before Taffy and her son, Max, pulled into a parking space near me, and Taffy waved.

"Max, you remember Doc Mason, right?" Taffy said. She ruffled her son's reddish hair.

Max gave a long-suffering sigh, then shot me a very solemn, Fenn-like chin lift. "Yep. Hey."

"Hey," I agreed, giving him a chin-lift in reply. I remembered what it was like to be ten *way* too clearly. "What are you two doing today?"

"Arcade," Max said effusively, hooking a thumb over his shoulder.

"Jeremy Mickell is opening Mickell's Arcade on the weekends again, starting this morning," Taffy explained, grinning broadly. "He got some kind of small-business grant through Big Rafe Goodman! I don't know what magic he's working, but *man*, is it exciting."

I understood what she meant. All around, the little town center was buzzing, even on a Saturday. The whine of saws and crack of hammers filled the air. People stood chatting and laughing on the sidewalks, despite the heat of the day. The place felt cautiously optimistic, like a crocus in the spring, and I found myself absorbing the vibe.

"Mom! Bean Me Up is open." Max pointed toward the coffee shop I'd walked by several times while it was closed, but which now had a couple of small tables and chairs arranged on the sidewalk. "Can we get donuts before we game?"

Taffy grinned. "Sure. Just this once."

Max ran off without another word, and Taffy bit her lip.

"It's been so hard for him." She shook her head once. "I mean, first-world problems, right? But all his friends are off-Key and we only have the one car, and he's getting to an age where he's starting to feel like he's missing out on things?" She sighed. "He wants me to leave him with his grandmother, Orry's mom, on the mainland during the week, but I... I'd miss him, you know? So it's nice that there'll be things for him to do here?"

I swallowed. "Taffy, you're a great mom. And Max will appreciate that when he's older."

"You think?" She looked deeply skeptical, but pleased nevertheless. "Just how old?"

"Eh. By thirty-five, for sure."

She laughed and smacked me lightly on the upper arm as she went to join Max. "You're welcome to join us, if video games are your thing."

"Oh, I..." I noticed that the *Mary Anna* was docked at the pier and Fenn's Charger was parked in a spot over by Goodmen Outfitters. *Shit.* "Rain check, Taffy! And if anyone asks, you haven't seen me."

"Um." Taffy frowned. "Okay, I guess? See you Monday?"

I didn't return the goodbye. I ran across the street as fast as I could and threw open the door to the Concha.

"Doc Mason!" Juju called out when I stepped into the blessedly cold air. "How are ya?"

I really wished she'd kept her voice down.

Lety's place was tiny and homey. But this meant every time Juju greeted someone—which she did literally every time the door opened—the entire restaurant turned and greeted them, too.

"Dr. Mason!" Lety wiped her hands on the plain apron covering her brightly patterned dress and gave me a smile as I slid onto a stool in front of the counter. "You come for me to decide what you need for lunch?"

I grinned back, feeling some of my anxiety slip away. If you'd asked me, a month ago, whether I could fall in love with a restaurant so tiny it didn't even have a menu, I'd have said it was impossible. But I'd lived on Whispering Key for a week and a bit now, and already this had become routine. I walked into Lety's place every afternoon, she'd look me up and down like she was making a diagnosis, and then she'd prescribe me exactly what I needed. "I think the *pulique* today," she'd say. Or, "Ahhh, today is for *chile rellenos*."

It was mostly for show, really, because I knew she only had a couple of items cooking on any given day, but it felt nice to have someone looking out for me. And every single time, the food was *amazing*. Some of the best I'd ever eaten. Complex and richly flavored, not nearly as spicy as I'd expected, just... comforting.

"Today I made you something extra special," she told me. "I woke up this morning and my shoulder was *perfect*. Must be the medicine you gave me. I'm like a young lady again! So I said, I need to make *caldo de gallina* for Doc Mason. And I made it with extra love in there for you. Okay?"

"*Caldo de gallina*," I repeated carefully. "Soup of... something."

"Hen." She nodded. "You're getting better, *mijo*. Nothing better for a hot day than hot soup. And this is a lucky soup, too. *Justo lo que se necesita para dar la vuelta a la tortilla.* Okay?"

I nodded sagely. I didn't understand a word she'd said, except the part about tortillas, and I was 97 percent sure whatever she'd said had nothing to do with *actual* tortillas. But Lety never translated her wise words to me, and I never asked either. Sometimes it was enough to know that someone cared enough to offer life advice, without expecting you to actually take it.

"That sounds delicious. But, um." I eyed the door. "Maybe could I take it to go?"

Lety pursed her lips and studied me again. One side of her mouth twisted up in a smile. "Sure, *mijo*. Two minutes."

Gloria Frye got up from her table and tottered over to slide onto the stool beside mine, wobbly as a newborn foal in her high heels.

"Doc Mason," she said. "How are you?"

"I'm doing okay. Gloria, we talked about those shoes."

"I know," she said. "I know we did." She bit her lip. "They're just so darn *pretty*. And they make *me* feel pretty. I'm weak that way."

I shook my head but laughed, too. I mean, not that I knew a damn thing about enjoying something that was bad for you, right?

"How've you been feeling?" I asked.

"Oh, alright! Just the heat takes it out of me, same as ever. Might be alright if I lost a few more pounds, too." She winked. "Think I'm on the right track, though. Down another pound and a half this week."

I blinked, my attention completely diverted. "Gloria, maybe you should come see me again. I'd like to run a couple more tests."

"I'd love to, sweetie, but I can't this week. Big Rafe's got me running all over creation, helping him put together the Extravaganza. He says I'm his right-hand woman." She blushed in a way I'd bet had nothing to do with the weather, though she laughed and fanned her face anyway before toying with the bow on the front of her short-sleeved pink sweater.

Really. Big Rafe and Gloria? Stranger things had happened. But I wondered if Fenn...

I stopped the thought in its tracks. "I wonder if Fenn" was no longer gonna be a song on my playlist.

"But I'd really like it if you did." I gave her what I hoped was a winning smile. "I'll even squeeze you in today, if you could. In, say, an hour?"

"Anything for you, Doc." She blushed deeper. "Maybe two hours? I'm meeting with Big Rafe in a minute."

"Sure," I agreed. "See you then."

The little bell over the front door jangled. "Heya, everyone!" Beale called.

Gloria, Juju, Lety, and I all sang back, "Heya, Beale!" and waved at the exact same moment. I froze.

It was bad enough that the rest of the town was synchronized. When had I suddenly joined the chorus?

Beale strolled over and took the stool on my other side. "Heya, Mason."

I kept one anxious eye focused on the door, expecting Fenn to walk through any minute, but really, there was no way to avoid him if he did unless I was prepared to do a barrel roll over the counter and beg Lety to hide me, which I wasn't. Quite.

I forced my attention to Beale. "Hey. How's the shoulder?"

"Better."

"You doing the stretches? Or do you need me to show them to you again?"

"*Welllll*." Beale cast his eyes to the ceiling. "I feel like that wouldn't be the best idea for my health."

I frowned. "The stretches won't hurt you."

He grinned. "Yeah, but somebody else might," he said incomprehensibly. "So, um, what are you doing with your afternoon?"

"Oh. Gonna put in a few hours at the office, I think. *Super* busy," I added just in case Fenn asked him later. "Like, *so* busy. No time for socializing *at all*. Why, what's going on with you? You and, um, Fenn were working today, right? You have plans for later?" So I could avoid them.

"Me?" The corners of Beale's mouth turned down in an exaggerated frown. "Nope. And I definitely don't know what Fenn is doing either! Everyone thinks I'm a shit secret-keeper, so no one tells me anything!"

I blinked. What did *that* mean? Did Fenn think I was gonna be pumping Beale for information? *Pfft.* Fenn was the one texting *me*, for goodness' sake!

I was tempted to reply just to tell him to fuck off.

"I'll refrain from asking about Fenn," I said stiffly. "Shouldn't be hard. He's not that interesting."

Beale rubbed one giant hand over his mouth. "Do you believe in karma, Mase?" Beale asked, apropos of nothing. "Because I'm concerned that I'm enjoying a certain situation just a little too much. The backlash might be brutal."

"Enjoying... *Oh.*" I recalled what Fenn had said earlier about Beale being in love. I leaned toward him. "Let me guess. Are you enjoying a certain *romantic situation*?" I gave him an encouraging smile.

Beale looked surprised. "Actually... yeah. That's exactly it."

"Don't be upset, but Fenn let something slip earlier today. About you being in love with someone," I explained, when Beale frowned.

Beale's head went back, and he folded his arms over his enormous chest. "Did he now?"

I nodded and laid a hand on his arm. "Look, he only shared it because I told him I liked you a lot, and I thought you were a really great person. *Sweet.*"

"You said that?" Beale grinned. "Yep. That'd do it, alright."

"I won't tell another soul, but I'm so glad things are working out for you. And this romance... it's definitely *love*?" It wasn't that I was nosy, per se, I just hated not knowing anything. Ever.

"Oh, yup. I definitely love one of the guys," Beale agreed. "Even though he's a lying sack of shit, I'd take a bullet for him."

I blinked. There were many things to focus on here.

"One of them?" I repeated. "There's more than one guy?"

Beale sucked his top lip between his teeth and nodded, his blue eyes shining. "The other guy's really nice, too. I like him a lot. Great style. Braver than he looks. I think things are gonna work out just fine."

"Well... good." I blinked some more. "That's... good, Beale. Look, if you need to talk—"

"Soup is ready, Dr. Mason!" Lety said from behind me.

Beale winked. "You'd best go get to work, hmm?"

"I... I guess, yeah." I recalled suddenly that I was supposed to be avoiding Fenn, anyway. "Catch you later?"

"You know it."

Huh. First Rafe and Gloria. Now Beale in a poly relationship. I wondered if Fenn...

Gah. I needed to stop.

I took a breath and blew it out, then gave Juju some cash and walked outside. Fenn's car was still parked in the lot by Goodmen Outfitters, but I didn't see him on the street. I checked my phone, but he hadn't texted me again, which was probably for the best, and not the sort of thing I should be irrationally disappointed about.

Jesus, Mason, make up your mind.

I scurried across the street to the rec center, ran up the stairs, unlocked the door, darted into my office, and quickly closed the door behind me.

Safe.

For now, anyway.

From behind me came the sound of rustling paper, and I whirled around, clapping a hand to my chest and nearly dropping my bag of food in the process.

There, sprawled out on the exam table with one hand stacked behind his head, one hand on his chest, and his booted feet crossed at the ankles, lay Fenn Reardon.

"What the *hell* are you doing here?"

Fenn's eyes widened like *I* was the crazy one in the room. "Uh. This is the doctor's office, isn't it? I'm here to see the doctor. Obviously."

My heart beat crazy-fast, and only part of that was from shock. He was wearing the same threadbare T-shirt he'd been wearing last week.

I had distinctly fonder feelings about it now.

"How did you get in when the door was locked?"

"*Was* it locked? Hmm. I can't really remember. I might have been in a fugue state. Which is why I need a doctor."

"It's a Saturday," I informed him, setting my bag of food on the desk. "I only work Saturdays in emergencies."

Fenn's blue, blue eyes met mine, and though he didn't smile, they crinkled at the corners with amusement and something hotter. Something that made my stomach swoop. "This is definitely an emergency."

I forced myself to look away. "You'd better tell me about your symptoms, then. You look okay, to me."

"Look closer," he invited.

I bit my lip. My fucking hands were shaking. What *was* this thing between us? Lust? Attraction?

Stimulus was sure as fuck not stimulus. What an idiot I'd been.

What an idiot I *continued* to be.

I grabbed my stethoscope from my desk and looped it around my neck, then turned toward him. He didn't move a muscle. Even his breathing was shallow.

I laid my palm lightly against his forehead. Our skin was the same temperature, but Fenn shivered anyway and his eyes blinked shut.

"No sign of fever," I said softly.

I brushed a lock of hair off his forehead, then trailed my fingers down the sides of his face to the hinge of his stubbled jaw, and lower still, until I could feel his Adam's apple jerking convulsively as he swallowed.

"Everything feels normal." My voice was loud in the silent room, and my hand came to rest near his on his chest. "Why don't you tell me what you've been experiencing."

Fenn's eyes met mine. "Well. For one thing, I can't concentrate for shit. I've been hallucinating. I'm hungry, but not for food. And I've had… tachy-things. In my heart."

I pursed my lips. *Fuck*, he could be adorable. "How long have you been experiencing these symptoms?"

"To be honest, it hasn't really gone away since last night, Mason. But certain things have made it worse."

Mason.

I slid the stethoscope into my ears and pressed the chest-piece to his T-shirt with one palm, while I slid the other along the hard plane of his abs. The quick, steady *lub-dub, lub-dub, lub-dub* in my ears did funny things to my own heartbeat.

I took my stethoscope off and inhaled sharply. I could almost taste the soap-clean scent of him. "What sorts of things have made it worse?"

He moved his hand from behind his head to thread with mine atop his chest. "Thinking about you. Trying *not* to think about you. Seeing you earlier. Seeing you now. Hearing your voice."

"B-but—"

"Then there was this…" His fingers held on to mine when I tried to pull away, to get a little space, and I saw that he was holding his phone in his other hand. He swiped it open with his thumb. "'*No hashtags. No apologies. No explanations.*' That's a heck of a caption."

I swallowed, looking from the picture of us on his screen— the picture I'd posted—to his eyes, to our joined hands. "You gave me the words. Accidentally."

"I know."

"But I didn't post that for *you*. It wasn't because of the dare."

"I know."

"I didn't expect you to ever see it."

"I know."

"I didn't even know you had Instagram."

"I didn't, until about two hours ago, when Beale suggested I look at your account."

I blinked. "Beale saw the picture?"

"Yes. Is that a problem?"

"N-no. Not at all. He just didn't say anything to me about it." Probably because it wasn't nearly as remarkable to anyone else as it was to me. I blew out a breath. "I posted that picture because it was true and honest. But I'm still a work in progress. For the first time I can remember, I don't know exactly what my future is going to look like. And I know you want someone who's got their shit figured out. You deserve that. But I... I don't know how to just be friends with you, so—"

Fenn swung his legs over the side of the table toward me and used our joined hands to pull me between his spread knees. "You wanna hear my truth, Mason?"

I nodded.

He smiled, just a little. "I didn't want to stop holding you last night."

"Yeah?" I sucked in a breath, lost in the blue-blue.

I didn't think anyone had ever wanted to hold me before, or even wanted me to hold them. I felt like when Fenn looked at me, he saw a different Mason from the rest of the world—

not a fuckup or a passionless, emotionally stunted person, but something closer to the real me. Something closer to the person I wanted to be, anyway.

"I could have stayed on that blanket for hours, and I would have given you truth after truth to keep you there. And it scared me how much I wanted that. I put it on you, for not having your shit figured out, when the truth is that none of us have our shit figured out." His mouth twisted into a rueful smile. "Sure as fuck not *me*." He hesitated. "So, look. You're here for a couple more weeks, right? If you want—no pressure—we could spend that time together, and—"

I pressed my lips to his, cutting off the rest of his words. His arms wrapped around my back, pulling me in closer as our breaths mingled.

No part of it was weird, no part of it felt *wrong*, and all the tension I'd been holding in all day leached out through the kiss, only to be replaced by a different kind of tension.

My hands trailed up from his waist beneath his shirt, and he moaned, fingers flexing against my spine. I pulled back slightly.

"We have a problem," I informed him. "This T-shirt is absolutely disgusting."

Fenn raised one eyebrow. "It's my favorite shirt."

I shook my head. "Its existence is an insult to high-quality T-shirts everywhere." I tugged at the sleeve of my own shirt in demonstration. "Your shirt goes, right now, or I do."

"Wow. You drive a hard bargain." Fenn's lips were red and damp from our kisses as he smiled hugely. He pulled his shirt off and threw it across the room to land on the sofa. "Done."

"Much better," I said delightedly, sliding both hands over those abs that had been taunting me for days.

"Not so fast." Fenn grabbed my hands and pulled them away, flashing me a challenging look. "Those shoes are not Loafers-approved footwear." He nodded down at the ratty, old sneakers I'd pulled on that morning. "We have standards in Whispering Key."

"Is that right?"

"We're very big on Italian leather."

I whistled through my teeth to hide the wellspring of joy that had sprung up in my stomach. "Far be it from me to disregard your local customs." I toed off my shoes and kicked them in the general area of my desk.

"Better?" I asked.

"Much," he whispered.

I wrapped one hand around the back of his neck and pulled his smiling mouth to mine.

As it turned out, Fenn also objected strongly to my T-shirt (too tight) and shorts (too loose), which was fine, because I had strong objections to his boots (too large), and his underwear (too small).

"You can't possibly have a problem with my underwear," he argued, dragging his teeth over my bottom lip in a way that made me shiver. "You can't even *see* them under my shorts."

"That just makes it worse," I informed him. "The shorts are accomplices. They have to go, too."

He shook his head, grinning. "Who the hell are you, Loafers? Where did you come from?"

The question made me pause for a second. Who *was* I? A week ago, I'd been... very, very certain about a lot of things. Now, I had more questions than answers. But it felt like my time on Whispering Key was a step removed from reality—like, the second I'd passed over the Cooter Key Bridge, I'd entered an alternate universe where the old rules didn't apply. So, for as long as I was here... maybe I didn't need answers. Maybe I could just take Toby's advice and see how things went.

"Delaying the process won't go well for you. Or the underwear," I assured him.

"You sure about this?" Fenn cupped the side of my neck with one large hand and stroked his thumb over my cheekbone. "We can take things slow. I'd be more than fine with that."

"I'm very sure."

"Committed to acquiring data, hmm?" His thumb moved to trace the corner of my lips, and his voice said he was kinda teasing, but not. "Gotta have an adequate sampling? For scientific accuracy? To test your hypothesis?"

I moved my tongue to trace the tip of his thumb. "No, um. That portion of the experiment concluded last night, as far as I'm concerned. Overwhelming clinical evidence outweighs theoretical every time. I just... really, really wanna see you naked."

Fenn laughed out loud. "Well, hot damn, Loafers. Why didn't you say so?"

He unzipped his shorts and let them drop, then kicked them over by my desk to join my shoes.

He hooked his thumbs in the waistband of his underwear and started to drag them off, but I pushed his hands away. I didn't want to be a passive observer here.

"Let me," I said. I knelt in front of him to pull them off slowly and toss them to one side, then stayed there on the hard floor, staring at everything I'd unwrapped. I traced my splayed fingers down the center of his stomach, over his high navel, and his happy trail, and the place where his tanned chest gave way to whiter skin.

Fenn leaned back against the exam table, and his fingers clenched the padding at the edge.

It felt almost unbearably intimate, looking at him like this, getting to touch him like this. Like something I hadn't known I'd wanted until I'd almost lost the opportunity to have it.

Fenn's cock was half-hard, and his blue eyes stared down at me, daring me, but I didn't need a dare to do what I wanted to in that moment. I slid my hands up his thighs slowly and wrapped them both around the base of his cock.

"Mason. Fucking *fuck*."

I laughed, but it came out more like a gust of breath.

"So, what I'm hearing you say is that you have some sensitivity here?" I asked in my best doctor voice. "I'm thinking I'll need to do more tests."

I leaned forward and bit the freckle on his right hip. Fenn banged his palm against the table and made a strangled noise.

"Mmm hmm. Very interesting," I said, but it came out slurred because my lips were already busy mouthing a damp path to his navel. I moved one hand off his cock to hold his hip in place.

I'd received plenty of blow jobs in my lifetime, so I had a vague idea of what I was supposed to do, but the buildup was so much better and more distracting than I could have imagined.

Fenn smelled musky and soapy, which was incredibly arousing. He was trying to play it casual, but his fingers were clench-releasing the table every time my breath hit him.

"Trying to be patient here, Loafers, but you're gonna wanna move this along. However you're moving it along."

I snorted. "I've been waiting thirty-five years for this, Mr. Reardon. So you're gonna wanna work harder on your patience."

He laughed helplessly and threaded his fingers into my hair, tugging slightly. "If you're gonna do something, do— Oh, *fu-hu-ck.*" He broke off as I ran my tongue up the underside of his dick.

"You were saying?" I breathed against his damp skin.

"*Nothing.*"

"No thoughts or opinions to share?" I swirled my tongue over the tip, knowing it would taste bitter and salty but completely surprised to find I *liked* it.

"I'll say this," Fenn croaked. "You're way better at blow jobs than you were at truth or dare."

"You just couldn't keep your mouth shut, could you?" I demanded.

And then I wrapped my lips around him, just to shut him up.

It was objectively not the best blow job ever given. I had a very well-developed gag reflex, and I choked every time I tried to take him deep, but Fenn didn't seem to give a shit. He was breathing like he'd been running for hours, stomach muscles rippling beneath my hand, like I was making him lose his mind and he *liked it*, which was basically how I'd felt about Fenn since the first day we met.

The whole thing was a mindfuck of sensation. All the things I would have thought I'd hate—the pain of the hard floor under my knees, having him stare down at me, the discomfort of stretching my mouth wide around his cock. I wanted those bruises on my knees, I wanted the stretch, because they meant I'd earned every second of the look he was giving me, the pure blue fire in his eyes.

Fenn's hand tightened in my hair, pulling me off. "Enough. Not yet. Come up here."

"Hurry up. Slow down." I licked my lips as he helped me stand. "You're impossible to pl—"

He cut off my teasing by thrusting his tongue between my lips, and the heat of it made my knees weak.

"I promise you..." He stood and turned us so my ass was against the table. "I am very, *very* pleased." He knelt and pulled my tented boxers down. "This was not how I saw today going." He looked up at me. "Which means I'm kind of an idiot."

"Are you?" I had no idea what we were talking about. "That's... *Hahaholy shit!*" I laughed in disbelief as he put his mouth on me. *That was impossibly good.*

Fenn snorted and pulled off me. "Did you just *laugh* during a blow job?"

"Shhh." I tugged at his overlong hair. "Back to work, buddy."

He snorted again, but his eyes met mine and... fuck. It was better than the blow job—okay, total lie, but *almost*. His gaze held mine as his mouth slid up and down my length, and his eyes were full of lust and appreciation. In that second, I knew every single molecule of his attention was focused on me, and it made me more turned on than I'd ever been in my entire life.

"Fenn," I whimpered, reaching one hand back to the table and one hand forward to Fenn's jaw.

Fenn's blue eyes went cloudy with lust, and I watched him stroke himself with one hand while the other held the base of my erection as he sucked me.

I stroked a finger over his cheek, loving the way his stubble felt against my skin. I could *feel myself* in his mouth, and an overwhelming wave of arousal had me punching my hips forward, something I'd never let myself do during oral sex before. I'd always sort of felt absurdly grateful that someone was doing this for me, and I'd never wanted to be rude or presumptuous. I'd never before felt like doing something for *me* was doing something for someone *else*. But Fenn moaned and pulled at my hip, encouraging me to thrust into his mouth again and again.

"Christ, Fenn." I cradled his head in both hands, never breaking eye contact as I moved against him. "*Fuck, baby.*"

The word slipped out, startling both of us, but the look in his eyes said he *liked* it. His hand clenched around my hip hard enough to bruise, and it felt like he was saying it back.

That was it for me. My release took me by surprise, rushing over me like a tidal wave, and I clung to Fenn for support as he swallowed me down.

Then, before I could even process what was happening, I was bent backward over the table and he was standing over me, jerking himself while his hand ran possessively up and down my flank.

"*Yeah,*" he breathed, and then he came all over my stomach.

Well, hot *damn.*

I blinked up at him, utterly stupefied. "That was..."

"I know."

"I never..."

"Me neither."

I surged up and kissed him, and he laughed.

A little while later, we were cleaned up and sitting on the sofa eating Lety's lucky soup. She'd packed up *two* containers and wrapped them both in foil to keep warm.

"Do you think she's psychic?" I demanded, leaning back against the arm of the chair and nudging Fenn's leg with my foot. I was so relaxed, I couldn't bring myself to obsess over how weird it was that I was so relaxed.

Fenn grabbed my foot and trapped it under his thigh before going back to his soup. "No such thing. She's just very observant and very nosy. And very kind."

"Hmmm."

"Come on, Mason, you're a doctor. You know better. No such thing as mystical woo-woo."

I shrugged. "I know enough to know there are things we can't explain."

"What, like Beale's auras and crystals? Nope. I believe what I can see with my own two eyes." He slid his hand up my thigh, and my breath hitched. "For example, I can see that..."

"Mason?" a high-pitched voice called before there was a tentative knock on the door. "Doc Mason?"

Fuck. "Gloria!" I stared at Fenn in horror. "I forgot she was coming by this afternoon."

"Did you lock the door?" Fenn demanded.

"I... don't..."

Fenn jumped up and vaulted over me, reaching over to flip the lock just before someone tried the door handle.

"Be right there, Gloria!" I called. "Just finishing up with a patient!"

Fenn dropped his chin to his chest and laughed silently.

"Get *dressed*!" I hissed, barely able to keep from laughing, though this was, by far, the least professional moment of my entire life.

Turned out, having your clothes strewn around the room made it difficult to dress quickly, and somehow when we were nearly done, I found myself holding Fenn's disgusting shirt in my hand and watching him pull my size-too-small-shirt down over his abs.

I bit my lip.

Fenn kissed me briefly on the cheek. "You ready?"

"Wait, no! You're wearing my shirt."

"Mmm." He ran a hand down his stomach. "You're right! It really *is* high-quality."

"I hate you." I pulled his shirt over my head, not nearly as upset as I was pretending to be. In fact, not upset *at all*.

He grinned and moved toward the door. "You can show me how much. Later."

"Gloria!" Fenn opened the door with a wide smile. "Sorry about that. Hey, thanks for seeing me, Dr. Bloom. I'm feeling much better." He pressed a hand to his diaphragm, took a deep breath, and let it out with a grin. "You're a miracle worker."

I leaned against the doorjamb. I needed to focus on Gloria, but I couldn't quite get there while this demented life force was staring at me like he wanted to laugh at me and devour me at the same time. "Anytime, Mr. Reardon. Really."

Fenn grinned. "I'll be back in an hour with your town car."

I snorted. "Thought you weren't a livery driver."

"We can all learn to enjoy new things, can't we?" He gave me a jaunty salute and Gloria a bright smile before strolling away.

"That boy," Gloria said fondly. "Doesn't half know his worth."

I grinned. I was pretty sure I did. And I was gonna enjoy every minute I got to spend with him.

Fenn was right. My plan for the day hadn't looked a damn thing like this either... But I was getting really comfortable with going off plan.

13

———

FENN

"You really wanna do this?" I demanded, pulling Mason against my chest the second he cleared the walkway to the *Mary Anna*. The sun brought his brown hair to life, teasing out glints of red and gold as he grinned up at me.

"I really, definitely wanna do this. Why wouldn't I?" He pressed his free hand to my T-shirt, pushing back just far enough that he could look up at me.

I rolled my eyes. "Because you already know all about the treasure, and I could think of a hundred things more fun than spending your day off on this boat?"

"I can't! Not when *you* are on the boat." He blushed, like he couldn't believe the shit that came out of his mouth, but he didn't take it back.

Oh, man. That blush. That little smile. The sweet shit he said. *Fucking temptation.*

If you'd told me three weeks ago the lengths I would go to

for those things, I would not have believed you. I would not have *wanted* to believe you.

But here we were, three weeks into this fling of ours—three weeks of Mason kissing me goodbye in the Charger when I dropped him off for work, Mason sitting beside me at the town meetings about the Extravaganza, and Mason going bright red when Lety called me Mason's *novio* like he knew the word meant *boyfriend*, but not correcting her. Three weeks of nights where I'd brought my tablet with its hot spot to his room so we could "watch movies," but mostly just so I could lie on his bed, watch him putter around his room, put things away *just so*, hang up his clothes, and brush his teeth, before giving me a big smile and climbing into bed beside me like I was the reward for his work. Three weeks where my sandals had gotten their own spot near his door, and where he'd bought me coffee in exchange for me washing his clothes, since he hated the dark, tomb-like laundry room on the first floor. Three weeks where we'd missed almost every episode of whatever-the-fuck British period drama Mason had chosen for us to watch, because we were too busy making out or trading blow jobs.

And now I got why Big Rafe kept sinking money into finding treasures, and why my own dad had never given up the bottle for long. If you had this happiness once, what wouldn't you do to keep it? What lies wouldn't you tell yourself? What risks wouldn't you take?

"Besides," Mason continued, leaning back against the boat's rail, "I don't know *all* about the treasure. I know the bits and pieces you told me when we were in Rafe's office, and I know a little from spending a day at Wynott's Books last weekend, but I would not say I have a comprehensive picture. So I'm gonna play tourist and sit there with all the blue-haired ladies—" He waved a hand toward the bench seats in the rear of the boat. "—and ask the handsome tour guide lots of questions." He wiggled his eyebrows.

"Wow. Pretty presumptuous of you to assume I'll answer them." I moved my hands to Mason's hips, and my thumbs stroked the skin under his polo, just above the waistband of his shorts. "You know, most of those ladies give me tips when the tour is over. Just sayin'."

"Ah, darnity *darn*." Mason bit his lip. "Now you tell me! And here I am with no small bills in my wallet!"

"That's too bad. But for you, I could consider accepting alternate forms of *incentivizing*." I drew him even closer so I could run my nose along the bottom of his jaw and feel him shiver in the hot sun.

"Incentivizing?" he said roughly. "Is that a real word?"

"Mmhmm. Like I'm gonna *incentivize* you to go skinny-dipping with me by taking you out to dinner off island next weekend. And remember when you *incentivized* me to watch that stupid show of yours?"

"Excuse you. *Downton Abbey* is *not* stupid. You *love Downton Abbey* nights!"

"You're right," I agreed, though I was pretty sure I'd never seen an entire episode and didn't care to. "I do love *Downton Abbey* nights."

His answering grin held a tinge of relief that made me shake my head and press a soft kiss to his lips. How the guy could doubt I loved our time together was beyond me. Little known, seriously disgusting, and highly scary fact? I would have incentivized *him* for the privilege of being there.

"Heya, boys!" Big Rafe called from down on the dock and my head turned in his direction. He was sporting yet another *MAYOR* shirt. This one, a vision in highlighter pink.

Mason straightened and took half a step back, like he'd forgotten we were in public. His hand didn't move from my chest, though, and he didn't pull away.

I wasn't sure why I kept expecting him to.

Mason hadn't spoken to his family about his sexuality yet, since he wanted to do that in person, but he was "out" on Whispering Key, and he was sure as fuck out in his bedroom late at night. After the evening on the beach and the next day in his office, he hadn't hesitated to embrace this thing between us in private *or* in public. Not once. All of which was so very, *very* different from anything that had ever happened with Thad Chambers back in Texas, it didn't bear comparison.

So why the fuck did I keep comparing them?

"Heya, Mr. Goodman!" Mason called to Big Rafe.

"It's *Rafe*, son. Did you get that message I left with Taffy? About the places that called me for references?"

Oh, *right*. I kept comparing them because Thad had hurt me and Mason…

Mason was gonna fucking crush me when he left. It was inevitable.

And I'd known the score from the start—this was only ever meant to be short-term, fun while it lasted, so I had no one to blame but myself for letting things go further than that, for letting him burrow deeper into my chest than that.

Mason nodded stiffly. "Ah, yeah. Got it. Thanks."

"I told 'em you were the second coming of Jesus, more or less, so I'd be shocked if you don't get a call back—"

"Yeah, we'll see," Mason interrupted hurriedly, closing that half step between us again. "Thank you."

Rafe looked back and forth between Mason and me curiously. "Boy oh boy, you applied for a lot of jobs, huh? Something's bound to come through for you soon!"

Mason smiled tightly. "Maybe. I'll let you know."

"I mean, with so many great opportunities—"

"Rafe, did you just stop by to chat about this? I've gotta get the boat ready and see where Beale is."

"Ah. About that. Good news and bad news!" Big Rafe tapped his fingers against the dock railing. "Tour group canceled. I guess one of the ladies got heatstroke. So I told Beale he's not needed here. But, the group paid their cancellation fee, so you might as well take Mason out anyway."

"Nah, we could—" I began.

"A private tour," Mason said, low enough so only I could hear. "Would inspire much *incentivization*."

"—we could definitely go out," I agreed. "Good call."

"Good! Good, good," Rafe said. He patted the top rail of the dock again and darted a look at Mason. "So. Shame about that tour group. I guess the heat can be real bad for ladies of a certain age?"

"Heat can be dangerous to lots of people," Mason agreed.

"Like, Gloria," Big Rafe said. "She's been struggling with this an awful lot. She's gone to see you a few times, right?"

Mason's fingers flexed slightly against my chest, but his smile never faltered. "You know I can't tell you that, Rafe. You'll need to ask her."

Rafe scratched at his nose. "Already done that, but the woman won't tell me a damn thing." He shook his head. "Don't tell me anything personal about her, just tell me... is she okay?"

Mason shook his head. "*Ask her.*"

Rafe blew out a breath. "I know. I know. Alright, get along with you." He rubbed his jaw. "I've got some planning to do."

"I'd ask what kind of plans, but I'm scared to know."

Rafe shot me a look, then darted a glance at Mason. "Oh, you'll find out soon enough, Fenn Reardon, don't you worry. Enjoy your tour."

"I think that man has finally lost his last marble," I said, watching Rafe's back as he retreated up the dock. "What the heck is he planning *now*?"

Mason stepped closer. "I think he and Gloria have a romance going on."

"Gloria?" I snorted. "*Gloria* Gloria? No. No way. They've known each other for decades. She was friends with my aunt Mary."

Mason made a noncommittal noise. "On this island, everyone is somebody's friend. Pretty sure that doesn't preclude people from having sex, Fenn. Or caring about each other."

"Okay, I never want to hear you talking about Rafe and sex at the same time," I warned him. "Besides, if they're together, why wouldn't she tell him if she was sick?"

Mason opened his mouth, then shut it again. He laughed shortly. "Right. Because people who are *together* always talk about hard things?"

I frowned. "So there *is* something wrong with Gloria?"

"I—" Mason shook his head. "You know, I have never had this problem before."

"What problem?"

"Having to struggle not to share confidential information. In the past, my patients and my personal life never intersected." He thumped me lightly in the abs. "But I'm not sliding down that slippery slope, so we're changing the subject." He took a step back and spread his hands. "You know, I boarded this vessel thinking I was going for a tour, but we haven't even... kicked off, or whatever you call it. What am I paying you for?"

I folded my arms over my chest. *Shit.* I never got tired of looking at him, especially when he looked back at me like that.

"I wasn't aware you were paying me at all?"

"*Pfft.* Not with that attitude." He set his hands on his hips and waved a hand imperiously, looking just like the guy I'd picked up from the airport back in April. "I want my ghost stories."

I grabbed Mason roughly by the front of his red polo shirt, dragged him a couple paces to the tiny cockpit, and pushed him against the back wall. His green eyes flared wide, and his mouth parted in surprise, but he didn't object at all to the manhandling. In fact, the way his gaze kept darting to my mouth said he was very much into it.

"Who's the captain of this boat, Loafers?"

He arched an eyebrow and bit his lip. "Oooh. Are we playing captain and naughty quartermaster now? *I promise I didn't mean to steal the treasure, Captain Godfrey.* I'll be good and share."

I made a vomiting noise and pushed away from him while he cackled. "Why would you do that, when I have to tell that story six times a week? *Why*?"

Mason sat in the side chair looking all prim and proper in his ironed shorts and polo... until you saw his eyes, which were still filled with laughter.

I couldn't remember the last time I'd liked someone this much. When I thought about it too much, it scared the shit out of me.

"Alright, troublemaker. I'm casting off."

Mason sat there, mostly quiet, until I'd steered us out into the water just south of the island. He propped his feet underneath the front window and leaned back in his chair, his eyes roaming over the boats and the island with undis-guised curiosity that made me try to see things through his eyes, just the way he had since the day we met. It made my heart melt, and—

Okay. Seriously. I needed to stop.

"Right, so!" I began.

His eyes swung to me. "Oh! Treasure story time?"

"Uh-huh. During the dark and quiet of a summer evening in 1803, a merchant ship called the *Esmerelda*, laden with goods from Belize, having passed between Cancún and the island of Cuba made its way across the Gulf of Mexico…"

Mason watched me intently as I recounted the story of the hurricane and the shipwreck, most of which he already knew.

"They were injured and weary, half-drowned when they washed up here, on the rocky point at the southern tip of the key." I pointed to the island, where we could see the Five Star Resort and the walkway to the beach over the sand dunes. "Resolute Goodman had a badly broken leg and Jacob Godfrey, his dutiful captain, refused to leave his quartermaster."

Mason smirked at me, and I shook my head sternly. I was never going to get through that part of the tour again without thinking of sex, damn it.

"They remained on the island for nearly eight months, healing, before they swam to the mainland. No longer desiring a merchant life after their brush with death, the men resolved to move their families down to the island where they'd washed up—the island that Jacob Godfrey swore had *whispered* to him in the depths of the storm." I glanced in

Mason's direction. "This is the part where you're supposed to *oooh*, FYI."

Mason wrinkled his nose. "Dude, I'm still back on him taking eight *months* to heal from a broken leg."

I rolled my eyes. "Their X-ray machine was down, Loafers."

He shook his head. "Yeah, but that's a *really* long time. Like, if it was set properly, it would get well in a matter of weeks. If it wasn't set properly, it—"

"Who's telling this story, Loafers?"

He pinched his lips together. "You are—"

"Damn straight."

"—*Captain*," he added breathlessly.

"I'm gonna make you walk the plank," I informed him. "You wanted to hear this, remember?"

He mimed zipping his lips shut.

"Now. Where was I?"

"The island was whispering," Mason said in an appropriately hushed voice.

I resisted the urge to laugh. "Right! So, the Goodman and Godfrey families settled on the island. Resolute and Sarah Goodman built a large home on the northern half of the island, while Jacob and Daisy Godfrey built a home in what's now the town center, just a mile and a half north of the spot where Goodman and Godfrey came ashore."

"Reeeeally."

"Marius Wynott never told you that his bookstore was the original Godfrey house?"

"No! And wait, and where did they land? On the beach near where we, um... live in the motel?"

That was *so* not what he was going to say. "Yeah, they landed by the rocks. Haven't we discussed this already?"

"Did we?" He lifted a shoulder in a way that would have seemed casual if his face hadn't flushed pink. "One beach on the island was the same as the other until, you know... recently."

"Ah, until I kissed you on that particular stretch of beach, you mean?" I said smugly. "Yeah, then the two of them went about half a mile inland and cleared a spot in the woods we call the Original Homestead. They built a temporary shelter out of driftwood and palm trees. Made a fire pit. Even..."

"Grew little plots of blackberries," he said impatiently. "Yes, I've heard. But back up the bus. *I* totally kissed *you*, Mr. Reardon. Check Instagram if you don't recall."

"I haven't checked Instagram since... the one and only time I ever checked Instagram weeks ago," I informed him. "Unlike some people, I don't need to follow anyone, let alone have them following *me*."

The very idea was horrifying.

Mason's nose wrinkled. "So, you haven't seen all the pictures I've posted of us?"

"What *all the pictures*?"

"Never mind. Not important. Back to your story. What happened after they moved their families here? They had a bunch of babies and populated the place? When did people start hunting the treasure?"

"Jacob and Resolute each had three children before the day they boarded the *Esmerelda*." I set the engine to idle, and the boat rolled gently in the chop. "The first recorded mention of the treasure came when Resolute Goodman died in 1850 and his family examined his papers—"

Mason laughed and folded his hands under his chin.

"What?"

"Nothing! Sorry! Just… I understand why you don't talk a lot because holy shit, you must get so tired of talking. But also? I'm gonna need you to use this tour-guide voice on all kinds of things now. It's really hot. Please narrate the way you change the oil in the Charger, and how Dale Jennings eats his dinner, and how Beale's cat hates everyone, including Beale, and—"

"*Ahem.* I don't require your commentary. Do I tell you how to doctor people, Loafers?"

"No." He pushed his lips together. "I beg your pardon. Pray continue."

I rolled my eyes but dropped my tour-guide narration voice. "I mean, looking back, how fucking stupid were their families not to realize Jacob and Resolute had to have *some* source of income? The soil here is shit for farming, and they didn't have enough land cleared to make money anyway, but every once in a while, according to Resolute's diary, they'd take a trip off island and 'trade for supplies.' He just never mentioned *what* they were trading. Plus, they arrived long after the time when you could just stick a flag down and say '*mine.*' Florida was a Spanish territory at the time, and they had to have paid some serious bribes to someone in order to stay. And then paid again, when it became a US territory. And probably again when it became a state. There's no record of any of that, but it just makes sense."

Mason nodded, a little frown between his eyes.

"Anyway." I propped my foot up on the arm of the chair and sat sideways, facing him. "Kids grew up. All but one stayed on the island, and they subdivided the land. Jacob's wife died young, but he never remarried. He lived to be seventy-something, which was nice and old back then, and died in his sleep, easy peasy. And that's when the story starts getting *interesting.*"

"It's already interesting."

"Yeah, but this is the part with..." I paused dramatically. "The ghost."

"Of course." Mason nodded slowly. "I mean, it needed only this, really. I'm assuming this is the malevolent spirit you mentioned the day I met you?"

"Did I?" I ran a hand over my forehead. "Wow, I really wanted you to get off this island, huh?"

"Yeah, and why was that?"

I dropped my hand and eyed him. "Why did I want the hot, straight guy to leave the island, instead of staying and making me insane with lust? I don't know, Loafers. Guess."

Mason grinned. "Awww. But now you're so glad I stayed."

I pursed my lips. "Marginally."

"Entirely!"

"Occasionally. Mostly when I'm getting my dick sucked."

"Always! Even when I change the radio station in the car." Mason stood and leaned over my seat, and his mouth was *right there*, so I took it, wrapping my hand in his shirt and yanking him forward to sprawl awkwardly on my lap.

"You are determined to destroy this polo," he said. He moved his leg slightly so he was facing me and nuzzled my neck. "Go on, then. Malevolent spirits?"

"Seriously? Now?" I ran my hands up his thighs to cup his ass. "With you distracting me? Nuh-uh."

We hadn't explored much sexually beyond oral sex, which was fine—seriously, who *wouldn't* be satisfied with blow jobs?—but that didn't mean I hadn't thought about it. I was committed to taking things *slow*, but when I'd run slick fingers over his taint the last couple of times I'd blown him, his eyes had glazed over with want, which made keeping my promise really difficult. I wanted to show the man *everything*... especially when he planted his dick this close to my dick.

"Not sure why you're so distracted," he teased. He mouthed at the tendon between my neck and shoulder.

"Really?" I squeezed the ass I held with both hands. "You can't imagine?"

He pulled back slightly. "Okay, fine. New plan. Spirits, then more distractions. Go."

"I enjoy your plans."

He cocked his head to one side, waiting.

"Spirits. *Right*. So, Jacob Godfrey died with very little money to his name. He left a will with his best buddy, Resolute, as the executor. He left his land to his kids, with the stipulation that he didn't want any of it to be sold off. He wanted Whispering Key to stay within the two families. And he told Resolute Goodman to make sure his family was cared for."

"Fair enough." Mason's fingers played with the hair at the nape of my neck, and I pulled him tighter.

"By all accounts, Resolute went a little crazy not long after that. Started walking the island at all hours of the day and night, according to some letters his wife wrote. Claimed Jacob visited him in his sleep. Talked with anyone who'd listen about how Jacob was the best of men and deserved a better friend than Resolute had been to him."

"Hmm." Mason's brow furrowed, and I felt the urge to kiss the wrinkle away, but I manfully resisted it.

This thing between me and Mason was not *that*. It was time to start instituting some boundaries I should have put in place weeks ago.

"Resolute died of a fever just a few months later, and in his ranting period near the end, he was obsessed with Jacob Godfrey. Named every rock and tree on this island after him. Wrote a whole long confession in his diary about stealing the treasure from the *Esmerelda* and how he and his BFF Jacob had split it." I toyed with the hem of Mason's shirt, lifting it just a few inches so I could feel his skin under my palms. "A treasure he claimed he'd hidden in—"

"His wife's garden."

"Yep."

"But it wasn't there."

"Nope. And when Jacob's relatives heard this tale of missing money, and looked around at the zero dollars they had in the bank and the fact that many of their father's personal papers were missing, they put two and two together and got twenty-two. They concluded that Resolute had stiffed them. They even claimed that Jacob's ghost had *haunted* Resolute and driven him to his death for stealing their father's part of the treasure."

Mason looked oddly outraged on behalf of a man he'd never met. "Based on nothing?"

I shrugged. "Sometimes people need someone to blame when they're unhappy with their lot in life, right? I personally think it's ironic that Resolute nearly died to get that treasure, and in the end, it drove him crazy." My hands moved lower, my pinkies coasting beneath his waistband. "Anyway, most of the Godfrey heirs were capital *N Not* gonna keep living on an island with the Goodmans after that, so they spread the legend of the treasure far and wide, sold off their land—"

"In direct violation of their father's wishes! *Pfft*. What a bunch of hypocrites."

"You're catching on. And the new owners by and large were speculators or folks who leased the rights for treasure hunters to come in and turn the island into swiss cheese to find the treasure anywhere it might remotely be hidden and lots of places where it couldn't possibly be. It was a huge draw for tourists, which started up a whole secondary business for the island. You know how some people want to stay in haunted hotels and that kind of thing?" I traced patterns up Mason's spine, making him shiver.

Mason nodded.

"I guess it was sort of like that. Families would come on vacation because of the beaches, and the concerts in the park, and the carousel, but they'd also have fun watching whoever was heading up the salvage operation that particular year and trying to put the clues together." I shrugged. "They'd tell ghost stories about Jacob Godfrey haunting the island, looking for his lost treasure. Harmless fun."

"And then?"

"Then... the speculators drilled too much, too incautiously. It was irresponsible and fucking *stupid*. They're supposed to have oversight for these things, you know? The state, the local government, they're supposed to approve permits." I shook my head. "This was sixty, seventy years ago, so who knows what the hell was going on? What I *do* know is that a six-foot sinkhole opened on the upper part of the island, near Godfrey Promontory, and a tourist died."

Mason gasped. "The ground *opened*?"

"Caved in, kinda. Yeah. But, of course, the legend said that Jacob Godfrey's pissed-off ghost caused the sinkhole and killed the man... and then the ghost story wasn't so harmless or fun anymore."

Mason froze, his muscles tense. "He just... fell in? It collapsed on top of him?"

Too late, I remembered Mason's not-irrational *concern* about dark, enclosed spaces.

Damn it.

"Remember, I explained about erosion?" I soothed, rubbing circles into his upper back. "It's rare to have a sinkhole large enough to hurt someone, Mason. Data confirms this. We should look up the statistics later so you can see. I think you'll find them really comforting."

Mason pulled back to look at me. His mouth twitched at one corner, and his green eyes went soft. "I find *you* really comforting," he said... and then he *blushed* again.

God. How the fuck could I establish boundaries when the man kept saying stuff like that? I couldn't even manage a cogent response.

"So." Mason cleared his throat, deliberately attempting to change the subject. "What would you do? If you ever found the treasure?"

"The treasure that probably doesn't exist?" I kept my voice gentle.

"Play the game," he insisted. "Would you travel? Buy a sports car? End world hunger? Write a novel? Go back to geology? Mess around with the Charger all day? What?"

"You realize that the first question, if you found the treasure, would be who it belonged to, right? Unless you've been buying up land on Whispering Key without telling me, the owner of the land is the one who'd own anything you found on it, and you wouldn't get more than a small percentage as a thank-you. And *then*, you'd have to establish how much the treasure is worth. Big Rafe thinks it could be as much as *thirteen* million, but my dad used to say it was probably closer to *three*, which means you're not coming away with more than 1.3 million at the most, assuming the owner is generous and gives you a ten percent cut. And yeah, that's a *very* tidy sum, don't get me wrong, but hardly the kind of money that—"

"*You realize* that you have no clue how to play this game, right?" Mason shook my shoulders, plainly annoyed. "Daydream, for God's sake. Be *happy*, Fenn. Be unrealistic. *Yeesh*. No one's gonna smite you down for it."

"Smite me." I rolled my eyes. Where did the man get his ideas? "I'm trying to be *accurate* since some people appreciate facts and figures." I smacked Mason's ass lightly and he yelped. "Fine. I'd... yeah, maybe I'd mess around with the Charger. When I was younger, I wanted to work on cars. Restoring them." I scratched at my beard. "I think I got the idea because I knew my dad—my biological dad—was into it, and I thought it'd be something we'd have in common, but I ended up really liking it. I was never into geology. That was just a means to an end and a way to placate my stepfather. There's something satisfying about making things work the way they're supposed to, though. So, I guess if I didn't have to worry about bills and keeping Goodmen Outfitters running... that's what I'd do. Mess around with old cars and bring them back to life." Mason was watching me intently, and I resisted the urge to squirm. "Probably sounds kinda stupid. Not *quite* on the level of practicing medicine, huh?"

"Practicing medicine, the business of making *people* work the way they're supposed to? Yeah, no, I totally wouldn't understand why you'd find that satisfying."

I snorted. *When he put it that way...*

"So why don't you do it?" He shook my shoulder again. "Why not open a shop, or a restoration company, or whatever it's called?"

"Just like that, huh?" I smirked. "First, I don't have the *money*. Second, no *money*. Third, I'm kind of a hack. I know a lot about a *few* cars, but I'm hardly an expert in everything. And fourth, and most importantly, there's the small issue of *money*. So, unless Resolute's treasure falls out of a tree and lands on my head..."

"In which case, knowing you, you'd have to figure out who owned the tree..."

I dug my fingers into Mason's ribs.

"Hey!" He grabbed my hands and held them. "Being serious, though! You could save up the money. Get a loan. Hell, Rafe is handing out money like it's trick-or-treat and he forgot to buy a bag of Raisinets. Why not ask him—"

"Ask my uncle?" I snorted. "Fuck no. Under no circumstances. It would have to be a matter of life and death. I came here five years ago with nothing, and he helped me out, but he's made it pretty clear I'm not really a part of his family. I'm his wife's nephew, the son of a deadbeat brother-in-law he never had much use for. Doesn't matter how much I work or..." I took a deep breath and stopped my fucking mouth from running. "Besides which, haven't you noticed that making plans only leads to misery? I had a really nice *plan* for my life in Texas and got it paid back to me *with interest*. Planning is like asking for disappointment. If there's some sentient being out there, some Universe like Beale says —" I waved a hand toward the roof of the cockpit and the sky beyond. "—it loves nothing more than fucking with people's plans. Otherwise—" I grinned evilly. "—you'd be sipping mai tais at an actual five-star resort with some hot blonde named Tiffani-with-an-*i*, and not here with me."

"Huh." Mason's expression grew thoughtful.

"What about you, then? Just how many loafers would you buy?"

"Oh. Hmm." Mason stacked his hands on my chest and rested his chin there. "None. I'd pay off my med school loans. I'd move someplace beautiful where the taxes were low and property values were stable, and I'd find a job with lots of growth potential. Then… I don't know. Invest the rest of the money, maybe? Something high yield and low risk?"

I laughed out loud. "Of course you would, Loafers."

"What? What's wrong with that?"

"I thought we were daydreaming here? I thought we were supposed to be unrealistic and happy?"

"That *would* make me happy." He licked his lips. "And I'd bring my Mercedes to you for you to fix, but I wouldn't let you *drive* it. Ever." He raised one eyebrow. "So you'd know how this lack of trust between us feels and finally let me drive the Charger."

"Oooh. I take it back, you do know how to be unrealistic," I laughed, and then I kissed the outraged look off Mason's face. When I finally pulled back, the look in his eyes gave me the courage to ask something I'd been wanting to ask for a while now.

"Can I ask you a question?" I held him firmly, just in case he said no and decided to swim for shore.

"Yeah. Anything."

"How are you so okay with this? With us? That night on the beach, you wanted answers and data. You talked about your dreams and not settling. But everything changed for you all at once, and that's gotta be a big deal for someone who wants all his ducks in a row."

"I just... I feel like things are different on Whispering Key," he said finally. He frowned a little and ran his fingers along the front of my T-shirt collar, thinking. "Like *I'm* different. Out there, in the real world, I know it's important to be successful so I never have to worry about money. I know I need to look before I leap and make responsible choices. I know I can't afford to make mistakes the way I did when I was a kid, and that it'd be selfish to make my family worry. I think, and I think, and I think again. But while I'm here..." He traced the edge of my lips with his finger. "I'm so far removed from all of that. I can do my job and take care of people, and make myself happy, and make *you* happy... and that's enough. For right now, that's enough."

For right now. That should *not* have made my gut clench the way it did. It should not have made me want to steer this boat out into the open water and just keep drifting forever.

I tugged at the back of his hair. "What I hear you saying is that you want to make me happy, Loafers."

Mason snorted. "That *would* be what you took from all that."

"What I hear is, I can have whatever I want." I bit his bottom lip firmly.

"You heard that?" His breathing grew erratic. "How long have you suffered from these delusions?"

"What I hear is... I'm the captain of this boat, and you do what I say."

Mason laughed out loud. "Oh. My. God. And what is it you want me to do, my captain?"

I bit that laughing mouth, then pushed him off my lap and onto his knees.

"*Incentivize* me."

14

MASON

"Hello, Taffy! How are you this fine morning?" I strode down the hall of the rec center, coffee in one hand, a pair of white paper bakery bags in the other. "How was your weekend? How's Max?"

Taffy, who was already sitting at her desk looking way too cool and collected, lifted her head and smiled. "Well. Don't you look happy for a Monday, Doc!"

"Do I?" I unlocked the door to my office and deposited my coffee and bakery bag on my desk, then turned to hand the other bag to Taffy. "Must be because Bean Me Up is open every morning now."

It definitely was *not* because I'd spent the weekend with my boyfriend, including an actual off-island *date* at a brew pub called the Barrel House, which was owned by Fenn's friend Luke, where they had an *actual* menu and where I'd gotten to meet Fenn's youngest cousin, Gage, for the first time. It was not because Luke had made eyes at Fenn just long enough for me to truly understand the value of public displays of affection, or because I'd then whispered lots of very innocent questions about the anatomical possibility of certain sex acts very hotly in Fenn's ear, or because Fenn had then kissed me right in the middle of the restaurant, called me a "troublemaker," and sat with his arm over my shoulders for the rest of the night.

It was certainly not because I was getting blown or jerked off every single evening and most mornings, too, and each time was better than the time before.

It was not because I'd taken Toby's advice to heart, stopped overthinking, and let myself be happy.

I picked up my coffee and took an appreciative sip. "Don't tell Lety I said this, but Scotty at the Bean does a better skinny latte than she does, and he remembers I like it with the poison sugar in the colored pack."

Taffy blinked down at the bag in her hands. "*Does* Lety do a skinny latte?"

I snorted. "Uh, *no*. She only serves instant coffee. But the first morning I went in there, that's what I asked for, so then *every* morning after that, she'd laugh and hand me a cup of instant and say, 'I got your skinny latte, Dr. Mason.'" I rolled my eyes as I took my white coat down from the hook on the back of the office door. "I don't feel too bad about deserting her since Lety was behind me in line at the Bean today, herself."

"And what's this?" Taffy asked, looking in the bag.

"That's a Florida Sunrise Muffin, with oranges, pineapple, pecans, and coconut."

"In a muffin?" She took a cautious sniff.

"It's either going to be glorious or horrifying, Taff. Either way, I decided we should experience it together."

Taffy laughed and shook her head, folding the bag closed. "Mr. Goodman called a few minutes ago to see if you could squeeze him in this morning. You've got Ms. Beecham coming at 9:30, but you might just have time now. Or, if not, you could see him after Ms. Frye comes at 10:00."

I hesitated. Over the past couple of weeks, I'd gotten even more convinced that Gloria and Big Rafe were a *thing*, but it was also pretty clear she wasn't sharing her health concerns with him for whatever reason.

"Better make it now, Taff, if he can get here fast. Is he coming for a checkup?"

Big Rafe seemed like the sort of person who'd rather die than admit to his own mortality by visiting a doctor.

"Don't think so. He said a *consultation*." She shrugged. "Whatever that means. If I were a betting woman, I'd say he was coming to ask you to do something for the Labor Day Extravaganza."

"Oh." I nodded. "Like, being on call or running a medical tent?"

"Maybe that, too. But you know there's gonna be a talent show the Friday night before the big concert, right?"

"This sounds vaguely familiar from one of the planning meetings Fenn dragged me to. It's still months and months away, though!"

Time on Whispering Key moved fast and slow all at once. July had seemed ages away when Mr. Wynott first asked me to watch Topaz, and now it was just over the horizon. I didn't want to think about Labor Day in September and where I might be by then. Leaving the island was becoming harder and harder to think about, yet staying here seemed impossible, and thinking about any kind of change made me vaguely jittery.

"I know, but it's the most exciting thing to happen here this millennium, so folks are pretty excited, and they're having a time trying to find an impartial judge. Bubba Irvine wanted to do it, but he and Scott Blanchard had words a couple years back over a dog Scott wanted to buy—"

"Wait, Scotty who makes my coffee?"

"You're so cute, Doc." She laughed. "Yeah, that Scotty. He and Bubba are friendly enough these days, but you can bet if one of them says the sky is blue, the other's gonna say it's purple. So, last night at the Concha, *Scotty* said he didn't trust *Bubba* to judge impartially. And *Bubba* said good luck finding someone *more* impartial, and he wasn't gonna be okay with any of *Scotty*'s friends doing the judging." Her head ticked from side to side like a metronome as she recounted each side of the conversation. "And *Scotty* said what about Dr. Bloom, and *Bubba* couldn't think of a darn thing to say because he trusts you, too." She shrugged. "So, you're it."

"Ah. Because I don't know anyone and haven't heard about their feuds, so I'm impartial."

"No, silly! Because you know *everyone*, and you're friendly with them all. All of them think you like them *best*. You're good at that."

I frowned. Was I? The idea made my chest feel warm.

"Anyway! I'll let Mr. Goodman know. And I'll try to get him to fill out a new patient form when he gets here."

Taffy strode out of the office, and I grinned at her retreating back as I took a bite of my surprisingly yummy muffin. After a couple of weeks where the woman couldn't speak without ending everything as a question, she'd settled down into one of the most competent, intuitive medical office managers I'd ever worked with.

My phone buzzed in my pocket, and I pulled it out, already smiling because I knew who it would be. My *boyfriend*—and yeah, that was still a mindfuck to think about—must have just gotten back into a cell service area.

FENN

Loafers, what the hell is this list you sent me?

I grinned and bit my lip.

ME

Hey! How's your fishing trip?

FENN

Fine. The tourists are enjoying themselves. Now answer the question.

ME

Missed you this morning.

The three dots on the bottom of my phone appeared and disappeared for a long while. I'd noticed he had the most conflicted reaction whenever I said stuff like that—pleased, but mistrustful, but *pleased*—and I could just picture him trying to figure out how to respond to honest, straightforward emotion. It was kind of adorable.

FENN

You seemed perfectly fine when I left last
night.

I snorted. When in doubt, bring it back to sex. The Fenn
Reardon philosophy of relationships. Not that I was much
better.

ME

I seemed perfectly passed out because I
WAS. That tongue thing should be illegal.

FENN

Tongue thing? We're gonna work on your
vocabulary, Loafers. RIMMING. Say it.

I giggled, then clapped a hand over my mouth before Taffy
heard me.

FENN

You just did that awkward giggle,
didn't you?

I gaped at the phone. How did he always know? *Fucker.*

ME

Busy now. Patient. Can't chat.

FENN

Liar. Your office doesn't open for twenty
more minutes.

You're blushing, aren't you?

I rolled my eyes. It was annoying to have someone know me
that well.

It was also really, really hot. Hot enough to make me wish the man was on dry land and we were both back in my room. Hot enough to make me wish I hadn't agreed with Fenn's proposal to "take things slow," since slow for Fenn apparently meant *glacial.* I was very, very interested in moving faster, and I was pretty sure he was, too, so I wasn't sure what the hell was holding us back.

Yeah, Fenn was definitely not the only one who defaulted to sex these days. And *that* was a mindfuck too... but I liked it.

FENN

So, the list?

Oh, right.

ME

It's obvs a list of TV shows! Pick one to watch now that we've finished Downton.

FENN

Pick from this list? Hell, no. Is this revenge for me not being around to drive you to work today?

I couldn't say why his grumpy attitude filled me with such giddy happiness. Just one of life's little mysteries.

ME

Revenge? Pfft. I'm letting YOU pick.

FENN

This list includes Buffy the Vampire Slayer. Mason, baby, take your own temperature right now. Report back.

Baby. I sighed deeply and clutched the phone to my chest, well aware I looked and sounded like a lovesick idiot.

It was just a word. A joking word. Toby called me *honey* and *sweetness* all the time and it didn't make me clench the phone harder, I reminded myself. I needed to calm the fuck down.

Except I sorta felt like there was meaning in everything Fenn said, so it meant *something*, and... okay, maybe he wasn't the only one who had a hard time processing emotions. *Shit.*

"Dr. Bloom!"

Big Rafe strode into the office, wreathed in smiles, wearing a bright red shirt with white letters that spelled out MAYOR. I tucked my phone away like a guilty secret and gave him a cheerful smile.

"Mr. Goodman." I stood to shake his hand and gestured toward the seat in front of the desk. "What brings you by?"

"You, as a matter of fact!"

"Me?" I took my seat behind the desk and gave him a knowing look. "Is this about the Labor Day Extravaganza?"

"Oh." Rafe's forehead furrowed. "No."

"Oh." I tilted my head to one side. "It's not about Gloria is it?"

"No, no." Rafe waved his hand. "Of course not. I know why you can't tell me." He pressed his lips together and looked at me beneath lowered brows. "Thing is, Doc, I've got a lead on a doctor who's interested in coming to work here."

I blinked in confusion, but my stomach swoop-dived like a seabird, apparently getting the message before my conscious brain could process it. The only thing I could think to say was "Oh."

Rafe shook his dark, shaggy head. "Now, thing is, Mason, there's *nothing* I'd like better than for you to stay. *Nothing.* If it were a matter of getting you a signing bonus or a better housing situation, I'd see what I could do. But it's not those things, is it?"

"I—" I shook my head. "No."

"You're a man after my own heart," Rafe said with a grim smile. "Ambitious. Determined. I wish it weren't so, but like recognizes like. You've got big dreams. Big plans. You don't just wanna be a cog in the wheel, you want to be the motor that turns the cogs. You want the fancy title and the penthouse suite." He winked. "I get it."

I frowned. It felt like a long time since I'd thought about it like that, and it sounded strange hearing it spoken aloud now, like a choice I dimly remembered was the *right* thing, though I couldn't quite remember why anymore.

"Now! I know you said you were gonna stay until we found your replacement and you found a new job, but I know you." He wagged a finger at me. "You're putting it off."

"Me? I don't know what you're talking about."

"Mason, the lady I spoke to at the big hospital in Minneapolis was so impressed, she wanted to interview you online that same day. Didn't she call you?"

"Um." I made a show of straightening the perfectly straight blotter on my desk and tidying the pens Taffy had stuck in an *I Heart Cooter Key* mug for me. "I believe she did, yes."

"And?"

"I thought better of it. I mean, Minnesota? In the winter?" I shuddered. "Worse than Upstate, and I left there for a reason."

"Mmmm. And the folks in Greensboro? Got a cousin up there who says it's real pretty country and the winters are nice and mild."

"I'm sure that's true. But Greensboro's smallish—"

He snorted. "'Bout a hundred times bigger than here."

"—and there are no beaches."

"Ah. So that means those folks who called me from Des Moines and Sonoma are out of luck, too?"

I frowned. "It was Davenport, not Des Moines, and yeah, neither of them were the right fit."

"And what does Fenn say about all this?"

I waved a hand airily and lied through my teeth. "I have no idea, because it has nothing to do with him."

Rafe was silent for a long moment. "Mason, you're as transparent as that window."

I winced. "Am I?" I was afraid of that. I mean, not that I'd consciously been turning down *amazing* jobs, of course, but I'd definitely gotten more selective.

Much, *much* more selective.

"You're gonna find fault with every job you apply for, aren't you?"

"I—" Possibly.

"Because you're staying here out of a misplaced sense of obligation to the town."

To the town. I blinked. "Oh. Um..." *Sure. Let's go with that.*

"You need to stop. We all care about you, Mason. You've made a lot of friends here in a short time."

Had I?

"But you don't owe us anything. And I'm sure that Aaron will do *nearly* as good a job as you'd do yourself."

"Aaron."

"Aaron Smith, your potential replacement! Nice guy. Real down-to-earth. Good-looking. Tall. Blond. Not nearly as well qualified as you, if I'm being honest, but he'll do. Bit of a talker. Likes sports cars. Big Bucs fan. Gay, too! And before you yell at me, he volunteered that." Rafe nodded firmly. "I know better than to ask."

I sucked in a breath. Rafe was going to replace me with a tall, blond, out-and-proud, *sports car enthusiast*?

I was being replaced with the anti-me?

With Fenn Reardon's paper-perfect match?

I stared at Rafe for half a minute without blinking, utterly paralyzed.

"I mean," Rafe said, clearly uncomfortable, "if you're interested in staying, all you have to do is say so, Mason. As I said, you're our first choice. You just need to decide that you'll stay for the length of the contract."

Just decide.

Easy as that.

I felt the little hamsters in my brain, which had been quiet and docile for weeks, begin to rise, and stretch, and jump back on their wheel.

It wasn't like I hadn't considered staying on Whispering Key and serving out my contract. Jeez, of *course* I had. I'd been here for weeks already, and I'd enjoyed almost all of it. When I looked out the window of this office, over the low buildings across the street, I saw endless sunshine and water, and it made me happy. The people on this island were weird but relentlessly kind, and I wouldn't have traded the reality of this place for the five-star resort I'd imagined it to be.

Hell, I'd even learned to tolerate the geckos.

Mostly.

The problem was, if I went to that window and looked out at the water view, my mind would conjure Fenn Reardon's blue, blue eyes. My gaze would track all the way to the right *every single time*, so I could see whether the *Mary Anna* was back at the dock yet. If it was, my heart would give a crazy, joyful thump. If it *wasn't* there, like now, my mind would wander to where Fenn was and what he might be doing.

Victoria had said I wasn't capable of loving someone fully... but clearly I could obsess with the best of them.

I could come up with a thousand and one really *compelling* reasons to stay on Whispering Key for three years—I hated leaving before I fulfilled a commitment. I worried that Aaron, who sounded *very* poorly qualified in my professional opinion, wouldn't be as concerned as I was about

Lety's shoulder as he should be, or about Gloria's strange symptoms that really needed to be monitored, or about Dale's mole, which needed to be biopsied *again* since the lab had fucked up the first sample, but which I'd had a devil of a time pinning him down to get done—but if I stayed, it wouldn't be for any of that. It would be because I'd gotten addicted to the hot almost-mechanic down the hall.

A man who'd changed the entire trajectory of my life just by existing and being so wholly himself that I couldn't help but want him.

A man who lit me up just by looking at me.

A man who was so allergic to planning for the future, he didn't even have an if-I-found-the-treasure bucket list kicking around.

A man who wouldn't just throw me off course when he ran off to Belize (or whatever the Fenn-appropriate equivalent was) but might capsize my ship entirely and drown me forever.

I knew what my heart wanted.

I knew what logic and good sense demanded.

And I had no idea how to triage those conflicting needs.

"Well!" Rafe slapped his thighs, then got to his feet. "Gotta go help Fenn run the afternoon tour. Lots of folks rescheduling for earlier this week since the weather's gonna get rough just before the weekend. How about you take a couple days to think about it? I promised Aaron I'd get him a contract by Monday morning."

"And you told him the truth, right?" I demanded. "You didn't lie or *anticipate*, did you?"

Rafe clasped a hand to his heart and shook his head ruefully. "Mason, you wound me, you really do."

It wasn't until much later that I realized he hadn't entirely answered the question.

———

"Doc Mason?"

I looked up from my deep contemplation of my pen drumming against my blotter to find Taffy standing by my desk, looking uncertain.

"Hey! Sorry. How was your lunch?" I put my pen away. "Everything okay?"

"Yeah. Fine. Lety asked for you."

My heart gave a little lurch. "I'll go by tomorrow and see her."

"Listen, it's none of my business, but um…" She sank into the seat in front of my desk, worrying her lip. "Juju said Isobel said Gloria said Rafe said he was coming to talk to you today about whether you were gonna stay here. Is that why he came this morning?"

I rubbed my eyebrow. "Yeah. He's, um, found a replacement for me." I pasted on a smile. "So, I guess I need to stop messing around and find a job, huh?"

"Well, I—that is to say, *we*—really hope you'll stay." Taffy's whole face scrunched up. "It's prob'ly not my place to say. I know we're not really friends, and you've got your plans—"

I chuckled once without humor. I hadn't had a clear plan in weeks. I'd gotten used to not having one. I'd started to *like* not having one.

"—but you fit here," Taffy said quietly. "I mean, you could probably fit *anywhere*, but why not here, you know? Stay where you're appreciated."

"That's very kind of you—"

"Not being kind. And I'm not just saying it just because this is the best job I've ever had either." She smiled brightly. "I really mean it. Everyone at the Concha meant it."

I snorted. I stood and came around to the front of the desk, leaned a hip back against it, and folded my arms. "You're amazing at your job, Taffy. Whoever runs this office next will be lucky to have you. And I'm sure you'll appreciate them, too." My chest felt hollow just saying the words.

"Yeah, but would whoever comes next be able to convince Barbara Patenaude to let Emmaline Young drive her around town, and somehow make Barbara think she was doing a favor for a poor widow while *also* convincing Emmaline she was keeping the streets of Whispering Key safer? Would they be able to finally get Gloria Frye to stop wearing those dang high heels?"

I laughed. "Noticed that, did you?"

"Turns out she's not much taller than I am!" Taffy giggled. "Think that'll help her?"

I shook my head. "Wish I knew for sure." I bit the inside of my lip and admitted, "I'm worried it might not be her shoes at all, but something with her heart. I want her to get some tests done. Things I can't do here." I spread my hands wide. "I told her I'd set it up. Even offered to go with her."

"And no dice?"

"Nope. Big Rafe can't function without her for a morning, or so she claims."

"More like she doesn't want him to have to," Taffy said indulgently. "She's got a bit of a crush on him."

"Right?" I said, widening my eyes. "I completely agree. Which is probably why she's not telling him anything about her symptoms. She wants to be superwoman in high heels, helping him preside over Whispering Key."

"Yep." Taffy grinned. "See? You get it. *You fit.*"

I hesitated. "I love it here, Taffy. I really do. Way, *way* more than I thought I could even a few weeks ago. But—" I broke off and shook my head. "I don't know."

"But you want an important job in a big city."

I slid my tongue over my teeth. "There's a lot more stability in a job like that," I said, quoting Mason-from-months-ago. "Financial security."

"Right. Well, if you're on the fence at all, try asking yourself if it's better to be a *little* important to a *lot* of people or to be really, *really* important to a *few* people. Like, basically everyone on Whispering Key." She smiled broadly and stood to leave. "And specifically to Fenn, of course."

I forced an answering smile. Yeah, there was no *of course* about it. Fenn liked me *a lot*. I was as confident of that as I was of my own name. But what would Fenn-the-unplanner say if he heard I was thinking about staying on Whispering Key? Would he be excited? Or would he be annoyed that the terms had changed for this short-term thing we'd started? Would the idea of us being together long-term seem a little too much like planning for the future?

Besides which, I'd promised myself I wasn't going to let someone else dictate my future ever again. Would I choose Whispering Key if it didn't come with Fenn Reardon?

My phone buzzed in my pocket like the man had heard me.

FENN

Hey, I'm taking Beale on a grocery run off island after Big Rafe and I finish our afternoon tour. Anything you need?

I chewed on my bottom lip. Whether I was ready or not, Rafe's visit meant *something* was about to change. The crazy, beautiful thing Fenn and I had would either morph into something better and more secure, or... or it might cease to be at all.

I knew in my heart that I'd never feel as much for anyone else as I felt for him. I didn't want to miss a single second of the time we had together. I didn't want to regret *anything*. So in the end, I took a page from Fenn's book.

When in doubt...

ME

Yeah. Get condoms and lube.

The three dots appeared and disappeared on the screen for so long I nearly called him.

ME

> Ordinarily I'd have some here at the office
>
> But I gave them all to Mrs. McKetcham
>
> And I'll be damned if I go and ask her for some just so I can have sex with my boyfriend

The dots disappeared altogether for a long moment.

ME

> Unless you'd rather not. We haven't talked about this recently. That's fine!
>
> I know you wanted to take things slow.
>
> You could reply anytime now!
>
> Yes, no? Maybe?

Those fucking dots circled and spun for another ten seconds, then finally...

FENN

Yeah, baby. Got it.

I held the phone against my chest like that might stop my heart from pounding out of my rib cage.

Then I closed the door, locked it, and called my best friend.

"Tobias," I said the second the call engaged. "I need you to tell me everything you know about anal sex."

15

FENN

There were times when I almost liked my job.

"I just have to tell you, that was so fun!" A brunette teenager with braided hair grinned up at me as I waved goodbye to her family after our afternoon tour. "Thank you for making this incredibly boring day a little more exciting."

I met the eyes of the girl's mom over her head, and the corners of her lips quirked up.

"Jessica's been researching this island and the treasure since she heard we were coming here," she said, hands bracketing her daughter's shoulders. "She was *not* excited about spending spring break here when she could've been home with her friends, but her dad and I overruled her."

"Families," Jessica said crisply, "are annoying."

Wasn't that the damn truth?

I smiled back. "Thank *you* for asking some good questions about Jacob and Resolute's history. You're very insightful."

"Did you know, there're, like, hardly *any* books on the Whispering Key treasure at all? It's odd. But there was a website with all kinds of theories and scanned images of documents and stuff. And when I read about Resolute and Jacob saving each other's lives, and surviving together for so long I, like, totally shipped them." She flushed pink. "So, you know, I choose not to believe Resolute did Jacob wrong in the end."

I raised an eyebrow. "You *shipped* them?"

"As in *relation*ship?"

"Okay?"

"I mean, like, I think they could have been *together*. In love."

"Oh. That's..." *Bizarre. Fantastical. Disturbing.* "Interesting."

She grinned. "It's a thing. And yeah, probably not very likely given how society was back then, but wouldn't it be cool if it was true? Two guys stranded on an island. They fall in love and decide to stay. They're best friends for the whole rest of their lives—"

"With their wives and kids."

She shrugged, not remotely troubled by this. "Neither of them has the courage to really say how he feels, but—"

"Alrighty!" Jessica's mom shook her shoulders slightly. "We need to go, sweets. Your dad's looking impatient."

Jessica sighed and gave me a lopsided grin. "Anyway. Nice meeting you."

Jessica's mom smiled apologetically as Jessica departed. "She has a wild imagination. She reads a lot of romance novels."

"Oh, I'm hard to shock," I lied. "I've heard some pretty crazy theories over the years. You guys have a great day."

I chuckled to myself as I grabbed the broom from the little supply closet next to the cockpit and started sweeping. I wished everyone on my tours was as genuinely excited as Jessica. She reminded me a little of Mason that way. *But she probably had better taste in television shows.*

I snorted. There was no way I was gonna share her *shipping* ideas with Mason, or the man's Captain-and-the-Naughty-Quartermaster shtick was gonna get worse than ever.

I paused in my sweeping, feeling my blood thrum in anticipation.

On second thought, considering the text he sent me earlier... that might be a good thing.

"Would you look at that?" Big Rafe walked out of the cockpit, sporting a neon blue MAYOR tee.

"Look at what? I can't see anything but your shirt." I squinted and held up a hand to protect myself from the glare.

"Pretty eye-catching, isn't it?" Rafe smoothed the cotton down his barrel chest fondly. "I think Gloria got a deal on them. She did the lettering herself."

Huh. Maybe Mason was right about Rafe and Gloria after all.

Poor Gloria.

I collected the ropes from around the cleats attached to the pilings and prepared to cast off and head back to the key.

"Ready to go?" I had shit to do, and some seriously exciting plans to get home for.

"In a minute." Rafe stood by the cockpit door, hands on his hips, rocking on the balls of his feet, watching me.

"Problem?" I demanded.

"You enjoyed talking to those folks," he accused.

I peered at him. "Uh, yeah. So?"

"So, you don't hate working with people."

"Hardly a secret. Who said I did?"

"What is it that you dislike so much about this job, then?"

I blinked. "Does it matter?"

"I'm asking, Fenn. Ergo, it *must*."

Ergo. I took a deep breath and begged a Universe I didn't believe in for patience. "I don't know, Rafe. Nothing and everything, I guess." I shrugged and stowed the broom in the cupboard by the cabin. "Ready *now*?" I demanded.

"Yeah." Rafe heaved a sigh and rolled his eyes. "Ready."

But as he walked back into the cockpit to take the wheel, I found myself thinking about his question honestly for once.

"It's not the people," I said, following him a few minutes later and slumping down in the seat beside his. "It's never been the people I minded. I like working with customers."

Rafe nodded. He kept his gaze on the water and held his tongue for once. The only sound was the hum of the motor and the call of the seagulls.

"It's not the boat either," I said at length. "I like the variety in my days. I never enjoyed working a desk."

"I'm the same," Rafe agreed, pursing his lips. "Couldn't do a nine-to-five. Never bothered to try one. Breathing recycled air in some office? Pure misery. You were smart to get out of that corporate life while you still could."

I laughed. In the five years since I'd left Texas, I'd gotten raked over the coals by my stepfather and prayed over by my mother for being fool enough to get involved with Thad Chambers. Even my dad had laughed and said I was a chip off the old block—he'd gotten into trouble for sticking his dick where it didn't belong, too, except in that case he'd ended up with me. At no time had anyone, including myself, ever called me *smart*.

"It wasn't actually a choice," I reminded Rafe. "Mr. Chambers terminated my employment." I rubbed a hand over my ribs, though they hadn't twinged in years.

"There's things you plan for, Fenn, and the things you do to roll with the punches you've been dealt. You've done a real good job of rolling."

"Uh." I frowned, completely unsure how to handle this. I couldn't recall Rafe ever complimenting me before, and I wondered if I'd slipped and hit my head or something. If so, I was enjoying the hallucination. "Thanks?"

Rafe's mouth quirked up in a smile, and he darted me a quick glance. "Trouble is, you're not doing much of the planning."

Ah, there we go. That was more like it.

"I plan for plenty, Rafe," I said mildly. "I planned to get up this morning, I planned to do my work, I plan to meet up with Mason tonight."

"Yeah? And what about tomorrow?" Rafe pressed. "What about the day after? What about this time next year? You still gonna be doing a job you don't really love, working as a tour guide and mechanic—"

"Not a mechanic."

"—and laying around the resort for the rest of your days?"

I bristled. "I work hard. I earn my keep as much as any of the guys."

Rafe *hmphed*. "My boys know not to expect a free ride."

And so do I, I wanted to say, but I bit my tongue.

"What's the point of this conversation?" I demanded.

Rafe sighed. "You gotta think about your future. Where do you wanna be in ten years? You wanna go back to your rocks, that's fine. Or maybe you wanna do something else instead. Forge a new path. But you're not gonna be running this boat forever, Fenn. So what comes next for you? *That's* the point."

I folded my arms over my chest. "Who's gonna be running it, then? You?"

He shook his head. "You don't see it yet, but Whispering Key's growing by leaps and bounds. I have plans in place that are going to set the Goodman family up for the future, and they're already starting to take shape. The Whispering Key Extravaganza is only the beginning. Renovating the Five-

Star? Tip of the iceberg. I'm talking investing in restaurants and renting out vacation homes. I'm talking creating an industry that gives us passive income! And when the island is back in fighting form? When the carousel is running again, and the inn is full, and there are restaurants all up and down the Pass?" He sucked in a breath and smiled, like he could picture it all in his mind. "I'm gonna repurpose the *Mary Anna*. Might sail her down to Key West for a bit. Might trick her out for all the grandchildren my boys will be giving me." He shrugged. "All the things Mary and I always wanted to do. All the things I'm gonna do for *both* of us."

I rolled my eyes to hide the sting of this. Must be nice for *the Goodman family* to have so much to look forward to.

"Fine." I set my teeth. "You wanna get rid of me that bad? Let me know when I need to look for another job."

"Prickly as a porcupine." Rafe shook his head sadly. "I don't get you, Fenn. You're young and healthy. Don't you want to make something of your life? How long are you gonna let what happened in Texas hold you back?"

I sucked in a breath, because that stung, too.

"Hold me back from *what*? Christ, Rafe. Until a few weeks ago, you were the mayor of a bankrupt island no one had ever heard of! Then you lied and you *cheated* to get money to fix things up on the island. And it looks like it's paying off for you, so *great*! Lucky you! But please do not act like you're therefore qualified to deliver a sermon to me on how I'm not doing enough with my life, okay? You were no better off than I was two months ago. Probably worse."

Rafe puffed out his chest. "You couldn't miss my point any harder if you tried. And I have *never* been worse off than you, Fenn. Because I never believed for a second that what I had was all I deserved."

"The fuck is that supposed to mean?"

"It means I know what I want, and I believe I can get it if I work hard enough. If I *fight* hard enough. I know you boys think I'm a selfish asshole. Not without reason," Rafe admitted. "And I know Whispering Key thinks I'm twelve donuts shy of a dozen. That doesn't bother me in the slightest. Because I can see the future I'm dreaming of, Fenn. A future for everyone I love, so close I can taste it. And I'm not gonna let anything hold me back from getting it for them, even if it means I need to pull a few strings and bruise a few egos to get it."

I set my teeth. "You don't care if you have to *manipulate* people, the way you manipulated Mason—"

Rafe snorted. "Mason's gotten over it well enough and enjoyed his time here. A month from now, when he's working at his next big job, he'll look back on us fondly."

"Please. He's not—" I scowled. "What do you mean, a month from now?"

"I mean, when he finally accepts one of the job offers he's gotten and leaves!" Rafe searched my face for something, then said sadly, "Oh, I see. You didn't know. Well! Mason must've been offered half a dozen jobs by now. Minnesota, North Carolina, Arizona... He's turned down a bunch already, probably for the wrong reasons. Not sure which one he's gonna pick, but it's only a matter of time, really. I'm sure he'll do well wherever he ends up." He sighed. "I'd love for him to stay, but it's not fair to tie him someplace unless we can give him what he wants. What he *deserves*." He turned his shrewd gaze in my direction. "Can you give him what he deserves, Fenn?"

I breathed through my nose, nostrils flaring, while the bottom fell out of my stomach and my thoughts tangled together like fishing line.

You think you know what he deserves?

You think you know how I feel about him?

And winding through it all with a sound like the clanging of a cell door... *a month from now.*

"I need some air," I said, pushing up from the chair and striding through the door. "I'm suddenly feeling seasick."

When Rafe docked the *Mary Anna*, I didn't stick around to help him clean up. I blew off Beale and our plans to go shopping, too. Instead, I jumped in the Charger and headed directly to the motel, consumed by the need to see Mason *immediately*. Honestly, it was a little pathetic, but there wasn't a specific thought in my head beyond that.

I needed Mason Bloom. Do not pass Go, do not collect $200.

I ran up the concrete steps on the outside of the building two at a time. There'd been painters there that afternoon, freshening up the stucco and tidying the trim, and I could smell chlorine in the air from the pool and hot tub Rafe had paid to have fixed. I'd been trying to coax Mason into skinny-dipping in that hot tub, and now... I couldn't find it in me to give a shit.

I strode down the balcony and banged his door with the side of my fist. "Mase?"

Nothing.

I banged louder. "Mason!"

Fuck.

He was *always* home by five. *Always.*

I ran a hand through my hair, too frantic to think straight. I pulled up on the knob and popped the door open with my hip...

It was a weird sort of déjà vu, stepping into Mason's room and hearing the shower running, just like the first day we'd met. Except this time, instead of screaming, Mason was singing some song I'd never heard of. And instead of me trying real hard *not* to picture Mason naked in the shower, now I knew exactly what he looked like, a sight that would be seared in my memory banks until I died.

I slipped off my sandals, taking a second to put them in their spot, and locked the door behind me. The sun still shone brightly outside, but when I closed the curtains, the room was shadowy and cool. I threw my wallet and keys on the little table by the window, then draped my shirt and shorts on top of them. When I was down to only my boxers, I turned toward the bathroom door...

And that was when I noticed the world's tiniest bottle of lube and at least four *packages* of condoms sitting on the nightstand.

Fuck.

I closed my eyes while I exhaled a shaky breath. In my haste, I'd forgotten the supplies, but Mason hadn't. There were definite upsides to dating a planner.

The shower turned off while I was still standing there, and the next thing I knew, Mason was walking out with a towel around his waist.

"Holy... *Fenn!*" He clasped a hand to his naked chest, but the sides of his mouth turned up in a smile and he sounded more excited than outraged. "What are you—?"

I crossed the distance between us in two long strides. One more step had him back against the bathroom doorjamb with my chest pressed against his. His hands settled on my back above the line of my underwear.

"Wow." His smile lit up all the dark and anxious parts of me like a sunbeam. "Somebody's excited about—"

I kissed him—a hard, claiming kiss, cradling the back of his head with both hands as my tongue invaded his mouth. *Hell, yes.*

His hands were cool from the shower as they trailed up my naked back, and I shivered against him, breaking our kiss so I could suck at his neck, lick at his earlobe, paint his Adam's apple with my tongue.

"*Shit*, Fenn. *Shit.*" Mason's green eyes glowed warm in the dimness of the room, and I vaguely remembered thinking he was *cold* when we'd first met. *I was such a fucking idiot.* I'd wasted so much time. Days and *days* when he could have been mine, but hadn't been. My hands tightened on the back of his neck.

"Are you okay?" Mason asked, cupping my cheek with one hand. "Fenn... *baby*... are you—"

He said the word tentatively, gauging my reaction, and I pressed my forehead to his. *Oh, yeah, I liked it.* I reached one hand up to grasp his wrist, and the fucking thing *shook*.

Get it together, Reardon.

"Yeah. Yeah, I'm good. I'm fine. I'm just—"

"Fenn, we don't have to do anything you don't want to do," Mason said, his face anxious but his words calm and slow, like I was one of Beale's feral cats and he didn't wanna scare me off. I almost laughed out loud. Like *that* was what terrified me right now? "We haven't talked a whole lot about this, but I really wanted—"

I cut him off with another swift kiss. "I want *you*, Mason Bloom. Any way you want. Okay?"

His anxious frown melted into something warmer. "Yeah." He bit his bottom lip, clearly pleased. "Yeah, good."

I pushed his damp hair back from his forehead. "So, tell me how you want this to go."

"Oh, I. Um. I mean." He turned bright red, so I *had* to lean in and press my lips to his cheek in an openmouthed kiss, just to taste that blush. "I'm pretty open-minded but I..."

"But you?"

"I've been thinking about this for a while."

"Have you now?"

"And I thought, just for the sake of trying all the new experiences, that I might like to try..." He nodded at the bed and somehow managed to flush harder. "You know. That... thing."

He was gonna kill me with this shit, he really was. And I was gonna love every second of it.

"Say the words, Mason. Ask for what you want."

I trailed my lips down his throat and *felt* him swallow.

"I'd like to *bottom*."

Well, fuck. I hadn't realized how much I wanted that until he said it out loud. I was vers and I'd never minded bottoming in the past, but in that moment, with Mason, I wanted to top more than I ever had before. I wanted to be inside him. I wanted to stay there forever.

I kissed him again, harder, and slid my hands to his shoulders, pulling his chest into mine.

I felt him hesitate, just the tiniest bit of resistance against the embrace before he gave in. I pulled back. "Mason?"

He shook his head and pulled against my hips. "No, don't stop. It's fine. Never mind. Come back."

I would not be moved. "What? If we're going to do this, you need to be a hundred percent honest with me about what's going on in that brain, starting now."

"I just—" He rolled his eyes. "It's stupid. I stopped at Pickles' and got snacks. And I have the beer from the Barrel House. And I thought maybe we could make it, like..." He waved a hand in the air.

"Words, Mason," I prompted gently.

"A date. Or a date-like, date-type *thing* with, um... drinking, and talking, like last weekend." He darted a look up at me, green eyes behind dark lashes. "But I like your idea better. Less talking, more kissing. The talking can wait."

Fuck. This was Mason's first time having anal sex—which, let's face it, was really *not* a huge deal in the grand scheme of life or a thing to get precious about, considering I barely remembered my first time, and there'd sure as hell been no hearts and flowers—but also *was* a huge deal, because I'd gone and fallen for an overthinker, and all kinds of unimportant shit took on deep significance for him.

Plus, why shouldn't Mason get the hearts and flowers? Or in this case, beers and conversation? He damn well deserved them, and it wasn't a huge sacrifice on my part. It wasn't any sacrifice at all.

"That's too bad, because now I like your idea better," I informed him. I slapped him lightly on his towel-covered ass and crossed the room to pull two beers from the minifridge.

"You're annoying." He scowled as he sat on the edge of the bed. "I reserve the right to change my mind when I feel like it."

I crossed the room and nudged him over to sit in the middle of the bed and handed him a beer. "But why, when you have such good ideas the first time around?" I nodded at the many, many boxes of condoms on the nightstand. "Although, unless we're having a water balloon fight later, your condom-to-lube ratio is off, baby." I leaned back against the pillow, and an instant later, Mason leaned over to put his beer on the nightstand and curl against my side.

Yeah, definitely not a sacrifice.

"'Pickles' is not the best place to buy sex accouterments, FYI."

"No? Surprising."

"This was their entire supply of lube, and I refused to ask Jim if he had more out back, especially since I thought you'd be buying some, and I didn't have a car to go—"

"I have some already. In my room."

"Oh." He flushed. "That's right, because you've... *right*." He buried his face in my armpit.

I snorted. *This guy*. "You know, lube is useful for other things besides anal sex. Like, jerking off in the morning when I've had to spend the night in my own bed the night before, the way I did last night."

Mason's face emerged and he looked somewhat mollified. "Yeah?"

"Definitely, yeah. And you know, you *could* drive my car if you had a non-lube emergency. As long as you understand that the Charger is my most precious possession, vow to never drive her over the speed limit, park her at the very back of every lot, and put her back exactly where you found her. Big Rafe has a spare key." Then I added grimly. "For now, anyway."

Mason's eyes widened. "I can drive your car? Oh my God. Does this mean we're going steady? Are you giving me your letterman-jacket-thing, Danny Zuko?"

I set my beer next to his on the nightstand.

"You. Are a dork." I rolled on top of him, bracing on my forearms, and dropped a kiss on his lips.

Mason laced his fingers behind my neck and grinned. "So. Why will Big Rafe only have a key *for now*?" He mimicked my deeper voice on the last two words.

"Because he pissed me off." I sighed. "Worse than usual."

"Yeah? He had a banner day today. What did he say?"

I focused on the wall behind Mason's bed. "That I need to stop letting the past hold me back and start planning a brighter future. Total bullshit."

Mason's fingers tangled in the hair at the back of my neck. "Why's that bullshit?"

"Because I'm fine with the life I've got now. I don't want more. I don't *want* to want more."

Mason stared at me steadily for a minute. "This is about that guy in Texas."

"No, *Uncle Rafe*, it's really not." Not a hundred percent.

"Oooh, Big Rafe caught that, too, huh? No wonder you're pissy." Mason's fingers tugged on my hair. "*If we're going to do this, you need to be a hundred percent honest with me about what's going on in that brain.*"

"I'm not pissy. And your Fenn-voice needs so much work."

He grinned. "I'll keep practicing. Now start talking."

I rolled my eyes. "Not sure if you noticed, but I have a hot guy nearly *naked* underneath me, a beer cracked open, and a plentiful—" I eyed the nightstand. "—okay, *adequate* supply of lube waiting for us to get to it. I do *not* wanna talk about Thad Chambers right now, Mason."

"Thad Chambers." Mason bit my jaw. "Now we're getting somewhere. He even *sounds* evil. How'd you meet?"

I huffed out a breath and pulled back to press a kiss to the center of his chest.

I didn't talk about this stuff at *all*. Even my family only knew the bare bones of the story. There was a *reason* for that—no one liked to be reminded they'd been a fucking idiot. But there was something about Mason's bright eyes and the quiet room, the slivers of sunshine peeking through the curtains and the way his fingers smoothed down the back of my neck—gentling me again—that made it feel okay.

I propped my chin on my hands just above his breastbone.

"I told you my stepdad got me the job at an oil company in Texas, right? It was a whole thing Neil worked out with his buddy Paul back when I was in high school, and Paul came through. He was the head of the whole Texas division, and he treated me like a second son." I bit my lip. "*Thad* was his first son. He was a lawyer for the same company."

"Ah." Mason's fingers didn't stop their stroking. "Was he cute?"

I nodded. "Had a chin dimple like Henry Cavill."

He whistled appreciatively. "This does nothing for me, mind you, but I get the appeal."

"Uh-huh. I had a crush on him the first moment I met him, but office gossip said he had quite a reputation with the ladies, so I figured that was that. Then Paul invited me to the family ranch for dinner, and Thad took me on a tour of the grounds... And he blew me against the door of the pool house." My lips twisted. "Thus proving that every porn has some basis in reality."

"Shit," Mason said ruefully. "So many things about the way you first thought of me make sense now."

"Yeah, but that's on *me*, Mason. You've never been like him." I tweaked his nipple with my thumb, just to ground us both in the here and now. "I figured out pretty fast that you're honest."

"I try to be."

"Whereas Thad got off on the lies," I admitted. "At the time, I didn't get that. I'd been out in college, but quietly. My mom and Neil very much hoped it was just a phase—still do, I think—so I was used to not talking about my sexuality. When things started with Thad, it seemed natural to not flaunt it. I was twenty-two and he was ten years older than me, and the shit he said—that I made him weak, that I was too hard to resist, that I tempted him—I thought it was all compliments. It wasn't until a lot later that I realized how fucked-up it was. In the moment, I thought it was *fun* that he'd ignore me all day at work, or when his parents had me over for barbecues, and then show up at my apartment at night. It was a game. A competition to hide from the idiots we worked with."

"I get it," Mason said. "A little bit taboo, a little bit the two of you against the world." His fingers carded through my hair, and something inside me settled.

I hated this story. The idiot in this story wasn't the person I wanted to be. But it didn't seem to faze Mason in the slightest, and that helped me keep going. To tell him the whole fucked-up thing.

"Thad said it wouldn't be like that forever, though. Once he got a promotion, he'd come out. We talked about the kind of house we wanted to live in, and how many kids we wanted to adopt. He told me he loved me. And I believed him."

"Why wouldn't you?" Mason sighed, and his hands clenched my hair. The light from outside grew dimmer, and I figured if Beale's Universe was real, it appreciated some good mood lighting.

"But then he got the promotion. And he didn't come out. He *couldn't*. Not yet. His dad was still in charge of the division, you know? We'd both lose our jobs. We just needed to plan better. Save up. His dad would be retiring in a year, two at the most. We could hold out that long, right? I loved him that much, right?"

I winced. "I went on a site visit a few months later, and when I came back, I heard Paul had made a company-wide announcement that Thad was engaged to Misty Bowles, his high school sweetheart."

"*Baby*."

I shook my head. I didn't want sympathy or pity, and he needed to hear this part so he'd *really* understand who he was sleeping with.

"I called it off. I did. Told him we were *done.* But he came over that night and I... *fuck.* I just wanted to believe him so badly. He said Misty meant nothing. He planned to break it off before the wedding, he just had to play the game a little longer. I want to tell you I saw through it, but... I didn't. I was so fucking *naive*. I told Thad I was gonna talk to his dad. He liked me, right? He wouldn't love that Thad was gay, but he'd accept it eventually. I wouldn't let Thad talk me out of it."

I kept my eyes on the center of Mason's chest, where I traced a random pattern with my fingertip. Outside, I could hear the wind picking up, sending raindrops skittering against the windowpane.

"That night, Thad didn't show up, but a bunch of his buddies did. They beat the crap out of me. Broke two ribs. Then they went to Paul Chambers and told their lies to him and to the police." I shrugged. "Paul came to see me in the hospital, and I... There's no way he actually believed what I was accused of, you know? Not a chance. But it didn't matter. Everyone else believed what he told them to believe, including my mom and Neil." I shrugged again. "So I called my dad for the first time in *years*. And for once in my life, he stepped up. He brought me here."

Mason's voice was unbearably kind. "Then he left you, too."

"Well, no. He died," I corrected. "Heart attack."

"As a wiseass once told me, '*Potato, potahto, really*.'" He sat up and rolled us over so we were sideways across the bed and he was on top, and then he pressed a hundred tiny kisses onto my cheeks, my lips, and my chest.

"I don't need pity, Mason."

Mason snorted. "I'm not pitying you, I'm fucking pissed for you. That should *never* have happened. And if those guys ever come to Whispering Key, I will kick their asses. In medical school they teach us ways to kill a man without leaving a mark."

I snorted and felt my mouth stretch into a smile that shouldn't have been possible with the air in the room as heavy as it was. "Is that so?"

"Hell, no," he admitted. "But I watched a lot of Wrestle-Mania when I was a kid and I could figure something out."

I laughed out loud and curled my abs so I could lift up to kiss him.

"And this explains why you don't plan for the future at all, huh?"

I sighed wearily. "Yes, Mason! Every time I put an appointment on the calendar, my deep, psychological man pain overwhelms me. Every time the dentist sends an appointment reminder, I take to my bed for a week—" I broke off with a laugh as Mason jabbed his fingers in my ribs.

"I'm being serious, Fenn!"

"I know. But it's *not* that serious or that... conscious. I just don't see the benefit of planning when *everything* in life gets fucked around anyway. What's that expression? 'Man plans, God laughs?' All good things end? Why put your energy into something that might never be?"

Outside, thunder *boomed* and Mason's eyes went unfocused for a second before he refocused on me.

"You okay?" I asked.

"Yeah, I'm fine."

"You wanna tell me why you're so scared of storms?"

"Uh, *no*. We've already covered *my* past psychological trauma, Fenn. Today's about *your* man pain, m'kay?"

"Have we, though?" I demanded. I sat up, taking him with me, forcing him to straddle my lap. "I think it's your turn. I shared a truth…"

"Oh, we're playing truth or dare again?"

"No, baby. On the first day we met, you told me this is how friendship works, remember? *I* share something, *you* share something…"

Mason laughed.

"Besides, haven't we gotten past the point where we have to dare each other?"

16

MASON

Yeah. Yeah, we were definitely past that point.

For all that I'd studied the human body for years, the way the human brain worked was still a total mystery to me. Sometimes I couldn't stop myself from overthinking the dumbest shit, and other times, like right that minute, I *knew* something with 100 percent certainty, and no way of explaining how I knew, since I'd never experienced it before.

I was in love with Fenn Reardon.

It was a hot coal in the center of my chest that I could hold without burning, a light that radiated outward and made me look at everything and everyone around me with a little more joy and a little more empathy... except for a bunch of assholes in Texas I would happily maim on sight.

This was *not* an emotion I'd ever felt for Victoria, nor for anyone else. It was nothing like the way I felt for my family or for Toby. And I didn't believe for a second that it meant I was guaranteed a happy ending or anything like that, because this was not one of those cheesy TV movies Constantine liked to watch, and because, from what I'd seen, love wasn't like a life preserver that kept you from drowning, anyway. It was more like a reason you kept swimming long after any sane person would have given up.

"Mason?" His fingers ghosted up my back. "You gonna tell me?"

"Nah. It's a really dumb story," I croaked.

He frowned in concern, and I knew it was because I was all choked up over my fucking *lurve* revelations while *he* thought I was suffering through some horrible memory. *Figured*.

"No, seriously. It's a stupid story," I repeated. "In a whole line of stupid stories about my childhood. Not any worse than any others, I swear."

When his jaw set like he wasn't going to be appeased, I sighed and relented. "My grandmother had a root cellar on her property where she stored vegetables. Sorta like Rafe's office bunker, except the floor was dirt, not cement, and the door was wood, and there was nothing climate-controlled. It was cold in there and full of spiders, so we all sort of avoided it, but once when I was seven, I played hide-and-seek with my sisters and some of the kids staying with us, and I hid there." I rolled my eyes at myself. "I thought it would be fine, since the door wasn't really fitted well, and there was plenty of light coming through. But then someone—I never figured out who—thought it would be really funny to lock me in, and it took flipping forever for them to find me, so I ended up spending the night there."

"No one noticed you were gone?"

"Ah, nope. Everyone figured I was with someone else. And it wasn't like we had mealtimes or bedtimes, people just did what they did. No rules at all. And then it *rained*, just to make the story sadder, and the floor got all muddy. Oh, and I was forced to eat jars of peaches for dinner. Like, five jars all to myself." I grinned. "I was scared to death at the time, but now it just pisses me off that I have this reaction I can't figure out how to get rid of."

"Why does this not surprise me?"

"I feel like it's getting better recently, though!" I defended. "Accidental exposure therapy." *And also possibly because I'd spent many nights sleeping next to Fenn.*

"And maybe also because you're strong as fuck, and you know the past can't hurt you anymore?"

I kissed him softly. "I like the sound of that." Then I pulled back. "Anyway, that was probably why I am *too broken to fall in love*," I said, lifting my hand to my forehead dramatically. "Boy, we are a *pair*, hmm?"

"Too broken to fall in love?" He lifted one dark eyebrow.

I waved this away. "Just something Victoria once said."

Fenn's eyes narrowed. "After hearing that story, *that* is what she said? And do you believe it?"

"Are you kidding? I never told her that story. *Pfft*. Don't be silly. And no, I don't believe it. Victoria said I was passionless, too..." I rubbed my nose lightly against Fenn's, which happened to put my mouth in proximity to his, so of course I had to suck his bottom lip between my teeth and bite down lightly, like that was the kind of thing I'd been doing all my life when it absolutely wasn't a thing I'd ever wanted to do until Fenn. "So clearly she wasn't right about everything."

Part of me wanted to tell Fenn exactly how I knew she was wrong, because I'd accidentally found myself in love with *him*, but after the story he'd told me... I wasn't sure how. That jerk in Texas had dangled love in front of Fenn with no possibility of a future. And it seemed really cheap to give Fenn promises of love now when I had no idea whether a future would be possible for us either, or whether he'd want that.

I remembered Fenn telling me, the first day we met, that people shouldn't do things because someone gave them pretty words. That people should care about how you treated them when you had nothing to gain from the interaction. And I wanted that, right now, with Fenn.

"You feeling passionate, Mason?" Fenn demanded, but the smile on his face said he knew.

Thunder rolled outside the window and rain lashed against the walls, but in here, I had everything I needed to feel safe.

"Very," I said, rubbing the tented bath towel against his stomach as proof.

I pushed Fenn down onto his back again, and he let me, sliding his hands down my thighs as he went, and he even lay there patiently while I examined him like one of the puzzle boxes they had in the tourist shops on Cooter Key, looking for the hidden mechanism that would crack him open completely and reveal all his secrets.

"I'm suddenly feeling like I'm a helpless gecko and you're a snake waiting to pounce," Fenn said.

I shuddered just a little. "If you continue to compare yourself to a gecko, this is going to end very quickly and unsatisfactorily for both of us."

I grabbed his hands in mine and leaned forward, pushing his wrists against the mattress. "Now just lie there," I whispered hotly in his ear, "and take what you've got coming to you." Then I proceeded to tell Fenn exactly how I felt about him without words.

That place just under his jawline where his pulse beat fast? It was beautiful, so I kissed it. His nipples were hard and waiting for me, so I flicked them with my tongue. That navel with the happy trail that led down past the band of his boxers needed attention, so I licked it. That freckle on his hip was begging for my mouth, so I bit it lightly, wishing I could mark it for good. Claim his body like a new continent, wash up on his shore, and just decide to stay forever. And the whole time he writhed and moaned beneath me, I thought *mine, mine, mine, mine, mine.*

I stripped his boxers in two seconds and took him in my mouth, lavishing all the love on him that I couldn't give him in words. My skills had improved quite a bit over the past few weeks, if I said so myself, and I pulled out every trick he'd taught me, holding him by the root, taking him all the way to the back of my throat, bobbing my head and working my tongue, though my eyes watered and my nose ran, because none of that mattered. All that mattered was making him feel what I felt, for as long as I—

"Mason." Fenn's voice was barely above a growl. "Get up on the bed."

It wasn't a polite suggestion.

I crawled up beside him on all fours while he slid to one side. "Like this?"

Fenn crawled behind me and ran his hands over my ass in a proprietary way. It made me shiver. "Yeah, baby. Just like that. *Fuck*. I'm gonna take my time stretching you, okay? It's gonna feel so good."

"I know it will," I whispered. How could it not, when I was with him?

Fenn took his time reacquainting himself with me, like my body had become something different in the twenty-four hours since we'd last been together. He kissed a damp trail up my spine and over the back of my neck, then back down again, just to make me crazy. He pumped my cock like he had some kind of direct connection between my dick and his hand that bypassed my brain. And then he got started on the... the *rimming*, alternating long, slow sweeps of his tongue with hard thrusts that made me bite the blanket and moan into the mattress because the pleasure of it was so sharp it was nearly pain.

Finally, when I was rocking my ass against him shamelessly, he sat back.

"Mason? Baby, turn over."

It took me entire seconds to process his words and turn those words into action, and by the time I'd done it, he'd retrieved the lube and a condom and was staring down at me with 100 percent concentrated attention that lit me up almost as much as his tongue had a minute before.

Fuck, fuck, fuck.

"Wanna see your face when I do this. You ready?" He poured the lube on his fingers, then poured more over the heat of my erection. I sucked in a breath at the sensation, my mouth open in a reverse scream, and then he spread the lube around my hole with one blunt finger.

"Yeah," I whimpered. "Shit, Fenn."

Earlier, when I'd talked to Toby, he'd been only too happy to share all his anal sex tips and tricks, the asshole, and he'd managed to sound like RuPaul narrating a D-Day invasion documentary. I needed to prepare myself for *invaaaay-sion.* I needed to let my walls down so my fortifications could be *buh-reached.*

If I'd been even one percent less committed to the endeavor than I had been, I'd have run for the fucking hills.

But the experience with Fenn was not a damn thing like Toby had described. Nothing felt strange, there was absolutely no pain or discomfort, or *invasion.* I was floating, and blissful, and...

"Oh! Okay, wait. Hold the phone!" I sucked in a breath, and my eyes, which had somehow fallen closed, popped *wide* as soon as his first finger passed inside me. *That burned.* It wasn't terrible, exactly, just... unusual. It was hard to overcome my instincts to squirm away, even though I understood the mechanics.

"Shhhh," Fenn said, his eyes hot on mine. "Relax. Stop thinking and feel it, Mason. Feel me."

Looking in those eyes made everything better. From the first moment we'd met, Fenn Reardon had hypnotized me, made me feel things I didn't want to feel, allowed me to want things I hadn't known I could want, so it was no real shock that he made this good, too.

One finger became two and then three. My legs were spread wide, and I was rocking and keening and biting my lip, loving the way he felt sliding in and out of me. He twisted his fingers to touch my prostate and—*hallelujah!*—my entire body lit up from the inside.

"H-h-holy *fuck*, Fenn."

He withdrew his fingers slowly, then pushed my legs back to my chest.

"You are—" He broke off with a sharp inhale. "The sexiest thing I've ever seen."

The look in his eyes was so intense I felt drunk with it. Euphoric. I smiled, and he smiled back in perfect understanding. Then he pushed my legs back further and leaned in to bite down on my ass.

"Hey!" I said with as much outrage as I could muster, which was to say none at all. "Why'd you stop?"

"I didn't." Fenn grabbed a condom box at random from the side table and rolled one on. "I'm just getting started."

He poured more lube on his cock, then pushed my right knee back even further with one hand while the other gripped the base of his dick, guiding it to my opening. He lifted his face, harsh with tension, and our eyes met.

"Oh, hell, yes," I said, just in case he was waiting for permission, and my eyes fluttered shut as he began to push and I pushed back...

And, okay... mother*fucker*. I blew out a breath. That was unpleasant. "This isn't gonna—*fuck*. Fenn, I don't think—"

"Baby," Fenn said, voice tight as he leaned forward, opening me further. "*Stop* thinking. Just for now. Look at me."

Looking at him was always my favorite thing to do. His face was absolutely *contorted* with pleasure, which made *me* feel pleasure. His cheeks were pink beneath his stubble, his lips bright red from kissing, and every muscle in his arms strained as he held himself over me.

And those *eyes*... Blue as the sky. Blue as the *ocean*. Deep, drowning blue. Fenn's eyes had captivated me from the first day we'd met in a way I knew would never change. Right then, those eyes were glued to me like I was the single most important thing in the universe, and I thought if I drowned in him right then, I wouldn't mind at all.

I felt myself relaxing into the stretch, into *Fenn*, letting it happen, letting *go*, enjoying every second of the ride as he started to move inside me.

"Oh, God," I moaned as he tagged my prostate again, making my cock jump against my torso. "There, *there! Fuck me*. Jesus. Harder, Fenn. Harder!"

"*Shit*," Fenn moaned, snapping his hips with brutal force that felt so much better inside me than I'd ever imagined. "*Now* you start with the dirty talk? Christ, Mason. What happened to *you know*? What happened to *that thing*?"

I pushed my head back into the mattress and tried to lift my legs even higher. "I need you to do *that thing*, Fenn, exactly the way you're doing it—" I broke off in a low whine as he tagged my prostate *one-two-three* times at just the right angle. "And then I'm gonna *you know* all over both of us."

"God," he said. "You are un-fucking-believable. Touch yourself, Mason. Come on! Let me see you come."

I *felt* unbelievable. Completely myself, totally confident, and... *fuck*. It was so incredibly *right* that Fenn was the only person who'd ever been like this with me, I had to bite my lip against all the promises that wanted to come spewing out of my mouth with every jerk of my hand.

I loved Fenn Reardon. Loved him. And if this wasn't the kind of love that poets rhymed about, then I didn't wanna know what more there was than this. My heart would be unable to hold it.

I screamed his name as I came all over *both* of our stomachs in lava-hot splashes.

"So hot," Fenn chanted. "So perfect." He snarled and came down on his forearms over me, and I wrapped my legs around him as he moved faster and faster and then chased me over the edge.

"Is it weird to think," I panted sometime later, my arms and legs spread-eagle on the bed, my eyes on the ceiling, and a pleasant throb in my ass, "that if your uncle wasn't a manipulative asshole, this would never have happened?"

Fenn, who hadn't had energy to do more than tie off the condom and drop it to the floor, groaned from his sprawl half beside and half on top of me. He turned his head to the side so he could murmur against my ear. "Please. We have nothing to do with him. He was a manipulative asshole and it *still* almost didn't happen. Not sure if you're aware, but you *kinda* gave me the impression you didn't like me when we first met."

I laughed freely, enjoying the way it made us rub up against one another. "Did I? Whereas you had nothing but positive thoughts about me from the very beginning?"

"Obviously. But don't beat yourself up over it, Mase. You can't be the best at everything." He yawned and tucked his face into my neck.

I lifted my hand to his ribs threateningly, though I was too tired to even tickle him. "You lie like a rug on the floor."

"Listen to those baseless accusations, all because I happen to be a better judge of character. *Tsk, tsk.*" Fenn kissed the underside of my jaw. "Stick with me, baby. I'll train you up right."

I sucked in a tiny breath and held it.

I could hardly believe how much I'd changed since Micah had said that to Con a few weeks back.

I'd learned I was strong and adaptable, that I was brave enough to live my life openly, and lucky enough to have a lot of friends. I also learned it was *definitely* possible for me to be jealous of Micah and Con and their relationship which was steady and solid and real.

"You're younger than I am, you realize? By a solid five years?" I croaked.

Fenn shrugged one shoulder. "So?"

So… I swallowed.

"I'll stick with you," I agreed. But as Fenn's breathing evened out and the sweet weight of him grew heavier against my chest, I wondered how long we'd have.

17

FENN

"No, what I'm saying is David Tennant brings a certain gravitas to the portrayal—"

"And I'm saying Matt Smith's hotter," I proclaimed, crossing my feet at the ankles and stacking my hands behind my head on the bed. "So bite me."

Mason turned from the closet, where he was hanging his clean laundry, and glared. "'*So bite me*' is *not* a compelling argument as to why we should start binging *Dr. Who* on season five."

Unfortunately for Mason, his glare wasn't quite as impressive when he was wearing nothing but his boxers and he was still damp from our post-sex, post-nap shower. I had to crush my lip with my teeth to stop myself from smiling.

Outside the open curtains, the sky was still bright. The humidity haze had caught the glow of the sinking sun and turned everything liquid gold, and tiny water droplets from the passing thunderstorm still clung to everything, but I had no desire to be out there, and apparently neither did Mason.

We were doing our usual evening routine, where he bustled around the room tidying shit that was already tidy while I spread out on the bed and watched him, chatting about stupid stuff. It was comfortable. It *should* have been reassuring. Hell, after the mind-blowing sex we'd had just a couple of hours ago, there shouldn't even have been a *need* for reassurance.

But there was a strange tension in the air I couldn't identify or dispel. If Beale had been around, he would have said it was a portent or some shit... but he fucking *wasn't*, so we were not calling it that.

Mason paused in his tidying and looked over at me. He opened his mouth and took a breath like he was about to speak. Then he hesitated, shut his lips, cleared his throat, gave me an anemic smile, and resumed his task. For the fourth time in fifteen minutes.

He clearly had something to say but didn't want to say it.

I ran a hand through my hair, smiled back half-heartedly, and watched the shadows shift as the sun sank, deliberately not calling Mason out on whatever words were stuck in his throat. Also for the fourth time in fifteen minutes.

Because whatever he didn't want to say, I sure as fuck didn't want to hear, and so the tension in the room ratcheted up another notch.

Mason's phone chimed from the table in front of the window, and he glanced in that direction but didn't move.

"Want me to check it?" I asked, eager for distraction. "Might be about a patient."

Mason shrugged. "If you want. But the answering service doesn't text, they call. It's probably Toby wanting to know, ah —" He cleared his throat. "—how I'm doing. You know, on second thought, don't bother—"

But it was too late. I was already up and off the bed, grabbing his phone from the charger.

"It's Toby," I confirmed, checking the screen. "He says '*I need a status update! Has Edgar been invaded? Have the barricades been breached? Were there casualties? Report, soldier!*' Followed by an eggplant emoji, a bomb emoji, a peach emoji, a volcano emoji, a fire emoji, and a Red Cross emoji." I lifted an eyebrow toward the suspiciously frozen man in front of the closet. "Baby, who or what is Edgar?"

Mason closed his eyes, flattened his lips together, and shook his head very minutely. "That's not... It doesn't..." He inhaled sharply. "I refuse to answer on the grounds I may incriminate myself."

"Incriminate yourself?"

"Yes. And then you will mock me relentlessly until the end of time. No. Nope. Suffice it to say, I hate Tobias and we are no longer friends. Therefore, it's as though that text was never sent."

"Hmm. Don't think it works that way. Weren't you the one who told me—"

I broke off as an Instagram notification appeared on his screen.

"Who told you what?" Mason demanded. He moved into the bathroom and turned on the faucet. "No doubt, whatever I said was absolutely accurate as it applied to *you* but should never be applied to me. Fenn? What's up? Did Toby write more?"

"Huh?" I glanced up. "Oh, no. You, um. You got an Instagram notification. You received a direct message from Victorious626."

Mason's head went back an inch, and his forehead creased. "Really? What's Victoria want?"

"I can't read it. You have to unlock your phone."

"Huh." He shut the water off and strode toward me, all lean and firm and mouthwatering, grabbed the phone from my hand and unlocked it. "Vic wants to *talk*." He rolled his eyes and handed the phone back to me. "I'll get right on that."

I looked down at the screen as he walked away.

VICTORIOUS626

Hey, Mase! Really excited to see you posting so much. Um, this is so awks but could we talk at some point? You probs already know I'm back in the States for now, so just call whenever, k? Love you!

Love you. I sucked in a breath. That was... totally normal. They'd dated for a long time, so of course she loved him. Or thought she did.

Bitch.

"Why does she think you *probs already know* she's back in the States?" I asked, trying to keep my voice casual.

"Oh, she probably posted about it and thought I'd seen it," Mason said dismissively. He opened a bottle on the vanity and began to massage some goop into his face. "I haven't been on much recently, and I haven't done anything but post. It's kinda freeing, not seeing anyone else's pics or even reading the comments on mine."

"Yeah? You don't mind if I look, do you?"

Mason shot me a questioning look. "At the comments? What for?"

"No, I mean... last week you mentioned you'd posted pictures of us. I was... curious." I shrugged.

"*Ohhh!* Yeah. Of course you can! Have at it. Mi Instagram es su Instagram."

I gave him a half-smile and backed up a couple of paces so I was sitting on Mason's side of the bed—which was to say, the side of the bed Mason usually lay on, not that we had official sides of the bed, because that would imply... *Whatever.*

"So, um. Taffy was talking about the Labor Day Extravaganza earlier," Mason said.

"Yeah?"

"She said they might want me to judge a talent contest? Which would be... fun? I think? If I'm still here then, obviously. But by then, I'd be past my probationary period, so I'd be agreeing to stay here for three years. So, what do you think?"

"Uh-huh," I said, distracted by the pretty pictures. "Sounds fun."

Mason snorted. "I see now how social media destroys relationships."

I glanced up. "What?"

"Nothing," he said dismissively, a smile playing on his lips as he focused on his reflection. "Not a conversation for now, anyway."

I frowned down at the phone in my hands.

The most recent picture on his feed was one of us from this past weekend at the Barrel Brewhouse, my buddy Luke's place over on the mainland. We were sitting in the lobby in front of the plate-glass window at the front of the restaurant, waiting for my cousin to show up, and Mason had wanted to take a selfie, so I'd rolled my eyes, pretending to be annoyed, and leaned in. Mason looked gorgeous in the picture, all artfully tousled hair, crisply collared shirt, and bright eyes. I sported two days' worth of beard growth and hair that curled around my ears because it should've been trimmed months ago. But I could still remember how he'd smelled when his temple was resting against mine. *Hashtag-Barrel-Brewhouse. Hashtag date.*

I ran a hand over my jaw.

Next back was a picture from the week before that, when I'd taken him out for his private boat tour. Once again, Mason was tidy perfection—happy, positive—and I looked vaguely menacing and rumpled and totally besotted. *Hashtag-My-Captain.*

Damn.

The next one was a shot of me, from the rear, standing in flip-flops, baggy shorts, and an ancient T-shirt with the sleeves cut off, watching the sun set over the water. *Hashtag-Never-Gets-Old.*

And then before that, the shot of us on the beach and Mason planting one on my cheek.

Smiling to myself, I scrolled back further. A shot of a cute little kid wearing a dance costume and a unicorn horn. *Hashtag-niece, hashtag-favorite-uncle.*

A reminder that February was National Heart Month and people should get *hashtag-screened.*

A little kid drawing of Santa Claus on the beach. *Hashtag-Christmas-Magic-in-January.*

A casual picture taken in front of a Christmas tree. Identical twin women who looked remarkably like Mason squeezed his shoulders, and a guy who looked like a younger, lankier version of me stood behind Mason, photo-bombing him with devil horns. *Hashtag-why-Constantine-why.*

A family picture taken behind a Thanksgiving table *packed* with food. Mason sat to one side of the image, the two twins sat in the center, and an older, less-refined version of Mason sat at the far end, which I knew had to be his brother, Micah. The goofball—Constantine?—had his arms wrapped around Micah from behind. Each of the twins had a smiling guy behind them. And Mason...

I sucked in a breath.

The woman behind him looked like a blonde Jessica Rabbit, with huge doe eyes and a trim figure tucked into a fitted cream dress. She pouted dreamily into the camera, blonde hair perfectly curled and one red-taloned hand propped on Mason's shoulder sporting...

Record scratch.

I enlarged the picture to get a better look at the diamond ring on her finger.

They'd been *engaged*? How had I not known this? He'd had the girl, he'd lost the girl. I definitely did not remember him saying he'd planned to make a lifetime commitment to the girl.

"Hey!" Mason called from the bathroom, toothbrush hanging out of his mouth. "Whatcha doin'?"

"Oh, uh... scrolling your feed."

"Really?" Mason rolled his eyes and rinsed his brush. "You looked like you wanted to blow something up. Someone making political posts again?"

I shook my head, scrolling back further.

Mason and Victoria at a *hashtag-farmers-market* wearing coordinating sweaters.

Mason and Victoria dressed in red, white, and blue for a Fourth of July *hashtag-fun-run,* surrounded by a bunch of similarly dressed prepsters on Long Island.

Mason and Victoria looking like fucking Barbie-and-Ken-go-to-prom, all dressed up in a tuxedo and a long, pink dress for some *hashtag-charity* gala.

I felt a curl of something dark and noxious rise up in my chest like a kraken, ready to choke me.

Look, I hadn't had some instantaneous personality transplant that made me give a shit how I dressed or how I looked, and I didn't suddenly imagine Mason gave a shit what I looked like either—my bed head hadn't stopped him from orgasming with the force of a rip current earlier, right?

But I couldn't help noticing that, just like in that song from the kids' show said, one of these things was not like the others. And it wasn't just because it looked like I didn't own a piece of clothing without holes. He had a bunch of friends I'd never met. An entire *family* I'd never met. A whole life he'd led before he'd ever set foot on this island...

A life he would go back to as soon as he left.

Whispering Key was my world. I'd chosen it, five years ago. But for Mason, the key was a stopover, the tiny airport where he'd catch his connecting flight to the big, bright future he deserved.

And the only thing that would hurt worse than losing him would be having him stay when he shouldn't.

"Mason must've been offered half a dozen jobs by now ... He's turned down a bunch already, probably for the wrong reasons ... It's not fair to tie him someplace unless we can give him what he wants. What he deserves. *Can you give him what he deserves, Fenn?"*

Fucking Rafe. He'd recognized this before I had.

My finger hovered over the picture of Mason in his tuxedo, his hair ruthlessly tidy, his green eyes clear and confident, his shoes perfectly *shiny*. I huffed out a laugh and blinked moisture out of my eyes, then closed the app and tossed his phone in the center of the bed.

What an idiot I was. I had *known* this would happen, and I'd let myself fall for him anyway.

"M'kay." Mason padded back out of the bathroom on bare feet and moved to shut the curtains, the muscles in his back and ass flexing as he walked. "Time to meet your fate, Fenn

Reardon. Will it be *Dr. Who* season two or season five?" He turned toward me with a bright smile.

My gut cramped. I wanted more time with him. Another night, another *week*, where I could commit every facet of him to memory. His smell, the texture of his hair between my fingers, the sound of his voice when he laughed, and when he teased, and when he talked about his past.

And how the hell remembering any of that was gonna help me let go of him more easily, I couldn't fucking tell you. The best thing for both of us would be to forget as soon as possible.

"Actually, Loafers, I'm not feeling great." I stood and walked around him to retrieve my shorts from the table by the window. "Probably better if I sleep in my own bed."

"Yeah?" Mason's smile fell and his forehead creased. "What's going on?"

Fuck. Right. Don't fake illness when dating a doctor.

"Just tired. Up early, remember? Long-ass day, even before you wore me out." I tossed him a wink. "Got another one tomorrow. Big storm coming this weekend, so we've rescheduled some stuff for tomorrow, and then we've got to prep the boat and the office later in the week."

"Aw, babe, you should have said! We don't have to watch TV." He laid a hand on my jaw. "We can go to sleep if you—"

"It's, like, 7:30 p.m." I stepped away from his hand and grabbed my shirt from the table to drop it over my head. "You're not gonna go to sleep at seven thirty just 'cause the guy you're fucking has a job that means he has to go out before the ass-crack of dawn. Don't be ridiculous."

His mouth snapped shut, and his eyes flared with hurt. I couldn't handle it. I needed to get away.

"Sleep well, okay?" I leaned in and kissed his smooth cheek, letting myself get one last big lungful of his scent before I moved away.

But Mason's fingers clenched in my shirt, a little panicky, holding me in place. "What's going on, Fenn? What did I do?"

"You haven't done a damn thing, Loafers. You're great. You're *perfect*."

He shook his head. "Yet you're running away again." He took a step away and ran two hands through his hair. "Jesus Christ, Fenn. Why? It's like every time we take a step forward—"

"I'm not running. I'm *not*. I'm right here on Whispering Key, where I've always been." I spread my arms wide. "Tomorrow, I'll be on Whispering Key. Come June or September or next year, when you're long gone, still on Whispering Key."

"I don't care where your feet are," Mason said in a dull, flat voice I'd never heard from him before. "Right now you're emotionally light-years away from me."

"That's not—"

"Do *not* lie to me. This morning, you called me *baby*. When you broke into my room, you called me *baby*. When you had your cock in my ass two hours ago, I was definitely—" His voice broke and he seemed to crumple in on himself. "—*baby*. Now, I'm Loafers again, and you're 'the guy I'm fucking.' So I'm asking, what changed? Was it something I did?"

Oh, man. Oh, *man*. In my entire Universe-forsaken life, I hadn't had that much raw emotion leveled in my direction *ever*. I was not worthy of that much emotion.

I grabbed his chin with my hand. "You didn't do *anything* wrong, Mason. You hear me? Not a damn thing. You are brilliant. You're gorgeous."

He frowned, his eyes red-rimmed and shiny. "Right. Sure, I am. So tell me you're not breaking up with me right now."

"Come on, Lo—*Mason*. Don't be dramatic. *Breaking up*? This thing with you and me, it was always going to end when you left! It's been amazing. *You* are amazing. But it's not serious. Don't turn it into something it's not, okay?"

"Right. And you came to this revelation *after* we had sex."

"Hey! That was *your* idea." I winced. "No, I mean, I wanted it, too! *Clearly*. It's just that I wouldn't have—"

Mason held up a hand to cut me off and drew himself straighter. "Being with you, Fenn Reardon, is like being strapped unwillingly to the front of a roller coaster. What happens next? Do you want me? Do you not? Are you pulling me close? Are you pushing me away? I have no say in any of it. All I can do is ride the track you've laid down, and I *promised* myself I wouldn't do this shit again, Fenn. So, I'm done. I want off the ride. I could never tie myself permanently to a guy like you."

I wanted to hold him so badly I had to clench my hands into fists. "I would *never* ask you to tie yourself to me, Mason."

"No," he said softly. "You wouldn't. And that's the trouble." He strode to the door and held it open for me. "You take care of yourself, Fenn Reardon."

This was better, I told myself. So much better. No bitter tears this way. No guilt.

I hesitated by the door, desperately wanting to kiss him again, but if I did, I might break down and beg him to never leave me, and then where would we be?

So instead, I said, "Sleep well, Mason Bloom." Then I headed out into the gathering darkness and heard Mason's door shut firmly behind me.

"You're a fucking idiot," I whispered to myself.

But as I lay in bed that night, I wasn't sure whether the truly stupid thing was letting Mason into my life... or letting him go.

18

MASON

"Mason! Hey, Mase! Doc Bloom!"

Beale's boots clomped down the sidewalk after me as I left Bean Me Up two days after Fenn and I had very reasonably, very logically ended our *thing*, and I was coping just fine. In fact, I'd hardly noticed the lack of Fenn Reardon in my life at all, which was pretty darn spectacular for a guy who'd spent months on the couch after his last breakup.

I mean, I might possibly not have slept perfectly. Or felt like eating. I might have had to delete Fenn's number from my phone to prevent myself from angrily texting him once or thrice, and I very pettily had not returned his shirt or the phone charger he'd left in my room. But other than those tiny, minor things, I was going about my business, living my life on Whispering Key the same as I ever had... and the more I thought about it, the *finer* I felt.

Fine, fine, fine. So much fine! Veritable *rivers* of fine. Entire *oceans* of fine. A Mariana Trench of total, absolute... *fine*.

But that didn't mean I was ready for a one-on-one with Fenn's cousin.

I gripped my iced coffee and walk-jogged a little faster, though the sun was turned up to eleventy billion and the humidity had little rivulets of sweat rolling down my temples.

"Mason! Hey!" Beale ran up and gave me a gigantic smile, looking dry and fresh as a daisy despite his heavy boots and long pants. It was fucking *unnatural*. He slowed to walk beside me. "Couldn't you hear me calling you?"

"Oh, were you? Sorry! No. I was just, um... enjoying my coffee so much—" I took a giant sip of the brew in my hand and nearly spat it out. *The fuck was this shit*? "Mmmm."

"Wow, really? 'Cause I'm pretty sure that's my drink, and Scotty gave me your drink instead!" He held a plastic cup in his enormous hand clearly labeled with my name, and his smile intensified. "Hardly anyone enjoys my yerba mate and hemp milk!"

"How weird," I said, yanking the correct drink out of Beale's hand and shoving the devil juice back at him. "Thanks for sorting it out." I arranged my face into an approximation of a smile and kept walking.

"Wait!" Beale said, and I rolled my eyes before he could see me. "Hey, so, I wanted to chat with you for other reasons, too."

"Really?" I asked politely. "Medical reasons?"

"Well. Not exactly. It's actually about, um... Fenn."

I nodded and resumed walking. "Does Fenn have a medical condition?"

"No? Sort of." Beale stepped in front of me and started walking backward. "Isn't mental health a part of overall health?" he asked earnestly.

"It definitely is. You should contact someone who specializes in that and ask them about your concerns."

"Mason, please. He's been a wreck and you—"

I held up a hand, gauging the distance between where we stood at the edge of the town center, and the clinic, which was four blocks away, and the length of Beale's stride compared to mine. *Too far to outrun him.*

Yeah, okay, four *feet* would have been too far to outrun him.

"I'd love to chat with you more, Beale, but I have to..." My gaze shifted around us, and I caught sight of the white fence just beside us and the little, white Victorian house-turned-bookstore beyond. "I have to go to Wynott's right now. It's urgent. I'll talk to you later!" I pushed open the fence and started up the white pea gravel pathway.

"Mason, please! Just hear me out." Beale followed me up the path, and only at that moment did it occur to me that he was actually allowed to follow me into the bookstore.

Okay, so maybe my river of *fine* was running just a wee bit low.

"I would, Beale!" I called over my shoulder as I hurried up the porch steps. "I would, but... I need to check something vital."

"In the bookstore?" Beale demanded. "But—"

I paused with my hand on the knob of the red front door and pressed a finger to my lips. "Shhhhh, Beale! No talking! You need to be quiet in a bookstore! It's disrespectful."

"Mason, that's librar—"

I cut him off with a wide-eyed glare.

"Fine!" He threw his hands in the air in frustration, spilling several drops of his drink in the process, and scrubbed at his brown hair. He lowered his voice to a whisper. "Fine."

I forced a little smile. "Thank you. I'll see you later."

But just when I thought Beale would turn around, he made a sweeping motion toward the door like he'd follow me inside.

Damn it.

I opened the door to a jingle of bells and the sound of running water from Mr. Wynott's indoor water feature—a three-foot circle of rocks and gurgling water set into the marble floor in one corner of the store's entryway that I found ostentatious but adorable, rather like Mr. Wynott himself. Directly in front of us, a roped-off staircase led to the private floors of the house, and to either side of the entry, gingerbread-topped archways led into shelf-lined rooms. I headed left, and once again, Beale followed me.

Marius Wynott, kitted out in an immaculate three-piece suit, materialized from a back room somewhere, and smiled when he saw me. "Ah, Dr. Bloom!" He glanced at Beale, and his smile fell just a fraction. "Mr. Goodman. Can I help you?"

"No," I said with false cheer. "Just poking around."

Beale frowned. "Thought you needed to do something urgent."

"Yes." I pressed my lips together firmly. "I'm poking *urgently*. You're distracting me."

"Were you looking for a book?" Mr. Wynott asked. "Or a chat?"

With my luck, Beale would stay and chat *with* us. "A book," I said. "I was so fascinated by the last book you recommended, I wondered if there was a sequel!"

Mr. Wynott's wrinkled face fell somewhat. "But Doctor, they all died at the end."

"Oh! Right, yes," I agreed. "Silly me! So they did." I wouldn't know, since I'd been too busy to read more than the first chapter so far. "I meant more of a, um… a similar story?"

"Ah!" Mr. Wynott's smile was restored. "I have a selection of them I can show you! Would you prefer—?" In some dark recess of the house, a phone began to ring. "Would you excuse me just a moment while I get that? Feel free to look around! I'm not sure you saw all of my collection last time you were here."

"Sure! I'll do that." *Shit.* Shit, shit, shit. I was now officially Beale's captive audience.

I strode purposefully to the other side of the entryway, to the small room where Mr. Wynott kept his glass cases full of Whispering Key memorabilia, and pretended to be fascinated.

"Well, look at that! Jacob Godfrey was a poet! *Ode to Blackberry Season!*"

"Mase—"

"Don't you just love how he rhymes *tart* and *heart*? And how he says he wants to lick the juice and spread the seeds on…" I peered more closely. "Oh, ew. This is vaguely pornographic. The man really loved his fruit, huh?"

"Mason. Please just hear me out. Two minutes and then I'll shut up, okay?"

I clenched my iced coffee straw between my teeth. "Would you look at that! A *sextant*. I've always wondered how to use one of those."

Beale grabbed my forearm and gently turned me from the case. "You point it at the horizon line, rotate the mirror until whatever celestial body you're using to navigate by appears to hover over the horizon, then use that angle to figure out distance or time of day, depending."

I blinked at him in surprise. "Oh."

He sighed. "I'm actually not an idiot, Mason. And Fenn would kill me *dead* if he knew I was talking to you, so could you just listen really fast?"

"Beale." I sighed and dragged him into the front room so we could sit side by side on the scroll-backed sofa by the window. Beale took up two seats to my one. "I *know* you're not an idiot. You know I consider you a friend. I just don't want to talk about this."

"Exactly what Fenn said." Beale shook his head. "You're both ridiculous. Fenn's a mess. You're a mess. And—"

"That's crazy. I'm not a mess! I'm dealing with this whole situation perfectly fine."

"Right." He folded his enormous arms over his chest and looked pointedly at my outfit. "You're fine."

I glanced down at myself. Light blue polo shirt. Fitted slacks. *Oh.* One black loafer and one brown. I tucked my feet beneath the edge of the sofa.

"I'm trying out a new trend," I informed him, lifting my chin defiantly. "It's a *look*."

Beale burst out laughing. "Uh-huh. You know, Fenn took a wrong turn yesterday while he was manning the wheel on our morning tour. Wanna know what he told me when I called him on it?"

I stared at him and shook my head slightly.

"That he was just looking for a *shortcut*." He chuckled to himself. "The tour goes in a fucking circle around the island, Mason."

I rubbed a hand over my forehead. "That's…" I cleared my throat. It was actually really fucking nice to hear I wasn't the only one having trouble, even if it didn't change anything. "It could be totally unrelated."

"Nope. He hasn't slept in days. If someone says your name, he looks vaguely like he's gotten kicked in the nads." Beale tilted his head to one side. "He's got a broken heart."

"Well, I'm not sure how much he told you, Beale, but if he's got a broken heart, he's broken it himself." I jumped up from the couch and slurped the last dregs of my coffee. "It was his idea to proactively not be together since I'm… I'm leaving the island."

"Right. Yeah. So that's the thing." Beale rubbed his hands on his pants. "It's like this, Mason... Has Fenn told you anything about his past?"

"Some." Angry as I was at Fenn, if Thad Chambers ever appeared in my vicinity...

"Right. So you know, then, that Fenn's never been good enough for anyone, right?"

I squinted at him. "Are you insane?"

Beale shrugged. "I mean, Thad—"

"Was a closeted asshole who led him on and then literally got him beaten! That's not on Fenn. God."

"Right. But you know, his mom and stepdad—"

"Are *homophobic* assholes who abandoned him when he was at his lowest point. Also not on Fenn."

"Yeeeees," Beale allowed. "But you know, his dad—my uncle Jared—left his mom before he was born—"

"And then abandoned his responsibilities for years and left Fenn at the mercy of his mother and stepfather. Again, Beale, not seeing how this is about Fenn."

Beale gave me a lopsided smile. "You're so good for him, Mason Bloom, and you don't even know it."

I shook my head. "That's not—"

"To Fenn, Mason, every single one of those incidents, plus a hundred more besides, have been him not being *worthy* of being chosen."

I frowned. "What?"

"Come on," he chided softly. "You're a smart guy. Fenn's mom wanted a nice, straight Christian boy. His stepfather wanted a man's man, whatever the fuck that means. Thad wanted someone who would stay his dirty secret for as long as possible. Uncle Jared wanted someone who'd take care of him, in the end, and that's what Fenn did for the first couple years he lived here, until Jared died. Even my dad, who loves Fenn to death and wants the world for him, has never bothered to try to understand what *Fenn* wants. It's like they speak different dialects of the same language, and they have entire conversations at cross-purposes. It'd be funny if it weren't so damn sad." He sighed. "Nobody's ever looked at Fenn and wanted *him*. Can you imagine what it's like to have everyone you've ever loved turn you away or hold you at arm's length?"

My stomach inverted and filled with lead. I had to press a hand under my ribs. "Strong coffee," I told Beale.

"Sure." The sympathetic look in his eyes said he knew better.

"But," I said, attempting to rally, "that has nothing to do with me, you know? Fenn doesn't *love* me. This was a short-term thing—"

"But it doesn't have to be. You could stay here. My dad would *shit* himself."

"Charming."

Beale smiled affably and shrugged, unbothered. "Point is, you have a job here. You're *needed* here. And not just any doctor—*you* specifically. *Take the job.*"

I blew out a breath. "There are reasons why I can't just take the job here, Beale. I need stability. I need... I need to not tie my entire life to a person who doesn't want me. Every time our relationship gets the tiniest bit real, he gets scared off. He's not all in with me. Which is fine! You know? Totally... very... *understandable.* That he doesn't feel that way about me." I tightened my free hand into a fist and shoved it in my pocket. "I've been down this road before. I was dating someone for a long time, and we broke up in January—"

"A *fiancée*," Beale said, nodding. "Yes, I know. You were going to spend your whole life with her, and no wonder! She's perfect, and lovely, and blonde, and female, and everything you deserve in your life."

I stared at Beale in disbelief. "She what? Are you seeing visions now, Beale?"

"Uh, no. Sadly. Did I forget to mention that I got Fenn drunk last night so I could figure out what the fuck was going on? Because I did. Sorry, not sorry." He lifted one shoulder. "I heard a lot about how brilliant you are, how you make people feel good." He ticked the items off on his fingers. "How he should never have gotten involved with you because he'll never be truly happy now, but how you *deserve* a better life than you'll ever have on Whispering Key. How *fucking* hot and *passionate* you are—heard that *multiple* times." He ticked off four fingers, and I felt my face flame. "And how, after scrolling your Instagram, he cares enough about you to let you go."

My jaw dropped open. "Are you kidding me?"

Beale shook his head.

"That... that... giant *asshole.*"

"No!" Beale's eyes widened. "No, wait, you don't under—"

"He was doing the whole '*if I love something I'll set it free*' bullshit? On *me*? And after I tried to oh-so-casually bring up the idea of me *staying* on this freakin' island and everything?" I shoved my empty cup in Beale's direction, and he took it mutely. "He's a dead man."

"Sure," Beale agreed, nodding. "You can kill him. That's fair. But maybe remember that with Fenn you have to be super explicit. Because he's always going to default to the worst possible interpretation of whatever you said."

Like when I said I could never tie myself to someone like him?

"Fuck." I ran both hands through my hair. "Where is he?"

"Fenn?" Beale's face split in a grin. "He's over on the *Mary Anna*." He hooked a thumb over his shoulder in the direction of the town center. "You heard about the storm, right? Gonna be a bad one tonight, so they're battening down everything on the boat and at the Goodmen Outfitters office. But that means it'll be the perfect night to stay in and *make up*." He wiggled his eyebrows. "Getcha plenty of supplies."

My cheeks went hot. "We'll see about that. Still not entirely sure this will work out exactly how you hope it will."

"So... does this mean you're taking the job?"

From the back of the house came a joyous bark, followed by the clack of feet against Mr. Wynott's pristine, wide pine floors, and then ten pounds of fur was launching itself against my midsection. I caught Topaz in my arms and lifted her to lick my face with her rough tongue.

Mr. Wynott followed, shaking his head and grinning. "Topaz jumped the dog fence! She would *not* be restrained, Dr. Bloom! True love sees no barriers, only possibilities!"

I snorted. These crazy people—Beale and Mr. Wynott, Big Rafe and Gloria, Young Rafe and Lety—had become really important to me in just a short period of time. I thought of Taffy, asking me if it were better to be a little important to a lot of people or really important to just a few, and I could now say unequivocally which I wanted.

"Yeah," I told Beale. "I'll take it." I was going to stay on Whispering Key.

And I would be happy here even if Fenn and I didn't work out. Hell, I would *thrive*... but I'd really prefer to thrive with Fenn, and I was beginning to think he'd prefer to thrive with me, too. So maybe... maybe it was time someone stuck around and fought for Fenn.

"Then it will work out *exactly* the way I think," Beale said with preternatural confidence. "And don't tell Fenn, but I have a *feeling* about this." He winked. "A really good feeling."

My lips twitched as I wrestled the furball in my arms. "So do I." My phone rang and I dug it out of my pocket, full-on grinning when I read the display.

"Mr. Goodman!" I said, my eyes on Beale's encouraging ones as I accepted the call. "I have good news. Well, for me anyway. I'm afraid you'll have to tell Dr. Aaron Smith that—"

"Mason." Rafe cut me off, his voice low and strained. "I need you to get out to the bunker right now. Gloria is... Her chest is tight, she says. She's having trouble catching her breath. It's like heatstroke, but worse."

Fuck. I'd been so worried about this. But clearly, not worried *enough.*

"Sorry, Mr. Wynott. I can't stay." I set Topaz on the floor, caught Beale's eye, and nodded toward the door. "You have a car?" Beale nodded. "I need a ride off the island. Now," I whispered. To Rafe, I said, "Call for an ambulance, and Beale and I will—"

"Would take a hundred years to get an ambulance out here over Cooter Key!" Rafe said. "Need you to get here now, Mason."

Shit.

Beale drove his father's pickup down Godfrey Pass like we were setting land speed records, going around the big curve in the road on two wheels. He hit a huge pothole in the center of the road, and the impact made the truck jump. My teeth clacked together when we landed again, and all the things in the bed of the truck—floating bumper-things and other boat-type accessories—crashed against one another.

"Damn it," Beale muttered as the car started making a rhythmic *tat tat tat tat* noise. "Tire's blown, but we'll get there."

He drove past the unmarked turnoff to the Goodman house and pulled into the motel parking lot instead. "Easier for Fenn to fix her up this way," he said, though I hadn't asked.

I jumped out of the truck, pulling my keys from my pocket. "Beale, go up to my room and grab my first aid kit from under the table by the window, just in case. Meet me in the bunker."

I tore through the tree break and around the side of the Goodmans' yard, through the market path and past the sign that said Mayor's Office, to Rafe's office bunker, which was standing wide open... and I skidded to a halt.

The entry to the bunker was so fucking dark. Dark as a *tomb*. And whatever I'd told Fenn about how stupid the story was, my fear of the dark and being entombed was very, *very* real. How fucked-up was it that I was more afraid of a *man-made dwelling* than the woman struggling to breathe inside?

Fenn's words from the other night came back to me. *"You're strong as fuck, and you know the past can't hurt you anymore..."*

I swallowed, huffed out a breath, and ducked inside.

Gloria was lying on the big mahogany table in the middle of the room with Big Rafe standing next to her, wearing one of his goofy *MAYOR* T-shirts, holding her small hand in both of his. Her other hand was clasped to her chest as she labored to draw erratic breaths.

"Doc!" Gloria said, trying to summon a smile when she saw me. "H-hey. I'm. Fine. Just. H-hurts. A bit. To. Breathe?"

"Help me sit her up, Rafe," I instructed, feeling for her pulse, which was steady but weak. "Beale's bringing my bag, and then we're gonna help you out to the car, okay? Gonna get you to the hospital."

Gloria shook her head as she swung her legs to one side of the table. "N-no! No. Hospital. I'm..." She heaved a breath. "Fine!"

"Gloria, you remember those important tests I wanted you to get? There's no delay now. You need them immediately."

"Tests?" Rafe scowled at both of us. "What tests?"

"I. S-stopped. Wearing the. H-heels. It h-helped!"

"Your feet were symptoms of the problem, Gloria, not the whole problem. Whatever's going on with you is serious—"

"R-rafe. Needs me. H-here!"

Rafe's forehead drew down in an impressive frown. "Christ alive, woman! I need you *well*."

She shook her head again, sending her red curls bobbing around her ghostly pale face. "Y-you have plans! F-for the." Another deep breath. "*Extravaganza*. You said. No time to delay. You'll. Be damned. If. You miss. This. *Chance*."

Rafe's expression was stricken. "But not at the expense of the people I *love*. Damn it, Gloria, if you knew you needed tests, why wouldn't you—"

"Mr. Goodman." I caught his eye and shook my head slightly. "There'll be time for that later, okay? For now, we're going to the hospital, and we'll focus on getting you well."

Beale arrived and handed me the black backpack where I kept my supplies. I removed my stethoscope and listened to Gloria's heart. There was a murmur there I hadn't heard before.

"We need a car," I said, removing the earpieces. "The pickup has a flat. Who can we call?"

"Fenn's Charger's in the lot," Beale said. "He and Young Rafe took the Jeep to the dock today."

"That's it," Big Rafe agreed. "Keys are hanging in the utility closet off the kitchen, Mason. The keychain shaped like an alligator."

"You grab them," I instructed. "Beale and I will get Gloria to the car. Grab her purse, too."

Rafe nodded and left.

"Gloria," I said, leaning down to speak to her. "This is the smart thing. I promise you."

She nodded mutely and focused on her breathing.

Beale lifted Gloria in his arms as easily as I'd lifted Topaz and strode out of the bunker while I trailed behind them. Big Rafe met us halfway to the parking lot.

Beale laid Gloria in the back seat of the Charger and pressed a kiss to her forehead. "You feel better now, alright?"

Gloria patted his hand weakly.

"I'll drive while you sit in the back with her, Mason," Big Rafe instructed, rushing to open the doors. "Beale, you ride shotgun."

Beale shook his head. "Nah. Someone needs to stay here to make sure the house gets locked down for the storm. I'm on it. And I've got my bike, so I'll ride up and make sure Rafe's place is all battened down, too."

I slid into the open back door. "If you see Fenn..." I bit my lip. "Tell him I'm sorry and I'll catch him later, okay?"

Beale saluted, then Big Rafe backed out of the parking space and screamed out of the lot.

19

FENN

"Fuck." My cousin Rafe threw his phone onto the captain's chair in the cockpit and grabbed his water bottle. "Where the fuck is my dad? He was supposed to be back with the rest of the fenders and the extra tarps for the shack by midafternoon and it's nearly *four*. Now he's not even answering his damn phone."

I wrapped duct tape around the waterproof material that protected the navigation system just in case one of the windows broke and shrugged half-heartedly. "He'll get here when he gets here, I guess. I'm sure he's doing the best he can."

Rafe's head went forward. "You realize you're talking about my father, right? Rafe Goodman? Tall guy? Looks weirdly like me but hasn't lifted a weight in ten years? You're saying *he's* doing the best he can?"

I shrugged again.

"Ohhh, I get it. This is a dead giveaway that you've been

replaced by your evil twin, isn't it? Who are you and what have you done with Fenn?"

"Ha. Pass me the utility knife, please?"

Rafe handed it over, but his gaze stayed fixed on my face. "You know, I might leave you here and go see where Dad got to."

"Sure."

"I might go get your Charger and take it for a spin."

"Uh-huh."

"Might go sell her to someone who isn't a total punk when it comes to fixing cars and has the balls to actually say what he thinks and stand behind it."

"Gee." I winced. "Thanks."

"All right, fuck off," Rafe said, leaning against the console right where I was working and effectively blocking me in. "What's going on with you?"

A shit ton of things, but exactly two I'd cop to. "Tired and hungover. Could you move?"

"Could. *Won't.* Since when do you get drunk on a work night?"

"On a work night, Principal Goodman?" I rolled my eyes. "Since your brother invited himself over and started pouring me shots with beer chasers." I shuddered. "I haven't been that wasted in a while."

"Beale poured you shots?" Rafe's brow puckered. "*Beale* did?"

"Beale Goodman," I confirmed. "Tall guy. Looks weirdly like you, except attractive?"

"Well, damn! Whose wake was it, and why wasn't I informed?"

"Nobody died." I sighed deeply. No sense keeping secrets on an island like Whispering Key. "Mason and I ended things, and Beale was trying to be nosy and get details."

And he'd succeeded, the fucker. Before he'd forced me to drink three bottles of water and some Tylenol and tucked me in bed.

Rafe snorted, then frowned more deeply. "Wait, you're serious? You ended things with the doctor?" Rafe sounded annoyed.

"Yep."

"Well, fuck, Fenn."

I rolled my eyes. "Since when do you care?"

"Since..." He shook his head. "I dunno. He's a good guy. What'd you do?"

"Me?" I stood and closed the knife, then threw it on the chair next to Rafe's phone. "I don't know why you assume it was my fault."

"You're saying *he* dumped *you*?"

"I'm saying it was inevitable. He's leaving Whispering Key, remember? He's got a whole big fucking life to get back to. You know how this song goes better than anyone."

Of all the people in the world, or at least on this island, Rafe should get just how hard it sucked when someone you cared about left you behind.

"I see," Rafe said, nodding solemnly. "You see some similarities between me and Aimee, and you and Mason?"

I shrugged. "Somewhat."

"Ah, Fenn." Rafe clapped me on the shoulder as he headed out of the cockpit. "You're such a fucking idiot."

Wait, what?

"Uh, no, asshole." I chased him out onto the rear deck. "I'm being *smart.*"

Rafe laughed out loud and headed to check the slip line tied to the cleat closest to the dock. "Are you, sad panda? Doesn't look like it. You're being a little bitch, and I have no sympathy for you."

"Fuck *you.* I'm trying to have the courage to make the hard decisions *now* before Mason ties himself here and gets miserable. Maybe then I won't end up like *you* did, all mopey and gross."

Rafe spun to face me. "Yeah, well, I *earned* the right to be mopey and gross! Aimee left despite *all* my best efforts to keep her here. She blew off the key in the middle of the night and left me a goddamn letter, and I *still* went after her. I hired a private investigator. Jayd almost took out a restraining order against me because I beat his ass. Remember all *that*?"

I ground my molars together.

"Meanwhile *you* are all, 'Boo hoo! I cannot allow my beloved to stay here and live perfectly happily forever under the weight of my love! I must let him go, because I'm so fucking wise that I know what's best for both of us, even though I can't find my own ass with two hands and a headlamp!"

"Who said I loved him?" I demanded. "I didn't say *love*."

"You didn't have to. It's as obvious as the clouds on the horizon." He pointed southwest, toward the roiling gray mass heading in our direction. "Stop being a baby and go tell him you lurve him. If you keep taking my insults, I'm gonna have to start dishing them out to Beale instead of you, and then no one will be happy."

"Why the *hell* would I tell Mason how I feel? *God*. How long's he gonna be happy here, Rafe? How long 'til he realizes he can do more and be more? Until he decides he doesn't wanna be tied to a half-assed, grumpy tour boat operator?"

"How long until *you* do?"

"What?"

"Fenn, you've been mostly miserable here for years. And you know what? I understood that, more or less. You had a shit hand dealt you in Texas. *That* was like me and Aimee. You tried your best, and it ended anyway. Now, since you hooked up with Mason, you've come alive again. You *smile*. I mean, not at me, thank fuck, but at other people who actually like that stupid mug of yours." He grabbed my chin, holding me immobile, and gave me two insolent cheek pats before laughing and twisting out of my reach. "You've got Dad ready to do *literally* anything you asked of him that he's capable of doing. You have a guy who cares about you, and you're pushing him away. I dunno, man. I think this—" He waved a hand from my head to my feet. "—is on *you*."

"Oh my God." I widened my eyes. "What is life like in your reality?" I wrapped my arms around him tight. "Please, Rafe, take me back to Narnia with you when you go!"

Rafe drove an elbow into my stomach, sending me back a pace. "I'm serious."

"You're *delirious*. Your dad is willing to do anything for me? Ha!"

"Did you ever notice you and my dad have these conversations that are in mirror writing? He writes the message left to right, you read it right to left? Every damn time." He broke off with a shake of his head. "Anyway, trust me when I tell you, he wants you to be happy, and to stop living half a life."

"No. No, you're—"

"I know this because he *told me so*. In those words." Rafe pursed his lips. "The man is an asshole, a liar, and a manipulator. Half the time, Fenn, I don't even know if I love him or I hate him, because he never *thinks* and he never fucking *listens*. But... I don't doubt that he cares. He's just very, *very* wrong in the ways he shows that."

Rafe made *zero sense*. "Your dad calls me *Mary's nephew*, Rafe. Not even *his own* nephew, mind you." He rolled his eyes. "I'm..."

Rafe's entire face cracked into a wild grin, the kind I rarely saw on him anymore and realized I'd *missed*. "Fenn. What's the name of this boat?"

"What?"

"The boat." He shimmied side to side. "This piece of shit flotation device we're standing on, which also happens to be the most expensive thing my dad owns, and the source of his livelihood. His life's work, Fenn. *What. Is. It. Called?*"

"The *Mary Anna*. So?"

"So, Fenn, you utter, utter *fool*, if he named the most important thing in his world after my mom, didn't you ever think that him calling you Mary's nephew makes you *more* important, not less?"

I gaped at him. *No.* No, that had literally never occurred to me, any more than believing in Beale's portents had occurred to me, or believing the treasure was real had occurred to me, or thinking I could morph into a unicorn had occurred to me.

"For fuck's sake, cousin, stop psyching yourself out about what'll happen if life goes wrong. Start thinking what might happen if it all goes *right*. I promise you from experience, if it goes to shit and you're sad later, it won't make you feel better knowing you wasted your chance to be happy."

"Is this a pep talk?" I demanded. "Because I've never had one of these, and I need to know if we're supposed to hug it out after, or if that's weird because we're related or..."

"Asshole," Rafe said without heat. "And look, it causes me physical pain to say this, but you're a good guy. A hard worker. A talented mechanic. Why don't you let Dad invest in *you*? Take one of his small-business loans. Open a garage."

"Uh, because I don't know how to—"

"Then *find out*. Jesus. Kids today! Want every damn thing handed to them."

"But what if I fuck up—"

"What if you don't?"

I frowned. *What if I didn't?*

"And while you're at it, why not call the hot doctor? A man could do worse than spending his life with you, that's all I'm saying." He tilted his head from side to side lightly. "I mean, not a *lot* worse, but…"

I snorted as a kind of wild hope started spreading inside me. "Hey! Who's the asshole now?"

"Still you." Rafe grinned that full-on version of his smile just as a crack of purple lightning rent the sky, and then neither of us was smiling.

"Well, that was rude," Rafe yelled at the sky. He rolled his eyes. "Especially since I still need to go climb on the fucking roof of the office to secure the rest of the tarps."

I shook my head. "Can't do that when your *dad* has the rest of the tarps, remember? Let's just lock it down as best we can and figure out where he is."

We finished securing the boat and the Goodmen Outfitters office, then ran up the dock to Rafe's Jeep. We climbed inside and shut the doors just as the sky opened and rain began to pour down.

"Hot damn," Rafe said. "Been a minute since we've had one like this. Makes all the other storms this season seem like a warmup." His windshield wipers could barely handle the onslaught as he crept down the road toward the motel.

Meanwhile, I grabbed my phone from my pocket and texted.

ME

Mason, I...

Fuck. This was harder than I'd thought. I felt like I'd been apologizing to him since almost the first minute we'd met. I'd gotten *him* wrong, I'd gotten his *situation* wrong, I'd gotten my *responses* wrong, over and over. And every damn time, I'd apologized and Mason had accepted it. Accepted that I was flawed and human and really fucking scared.

In exchange, he'd made me feel... incredible. Happy. Important. Simultaneously relaxed and ready to take on the world. His faith in me, in *us*, hadn't wavered once, despite all the times I'd pushed him away.

So, yeah, a fucking apology text was not gonna cut it. I was gonna need to do something bigger. Something *more*. Something that might convince him to accept just one more apology from me and give me one more chance.

But first I decided to start with the most pressing thing. I sent off a text:

ME

Mason, stay at the clinic. Don't try to get home in this. I'll pick you up.

"Well, shit." Rafe pointed up ahead, at the pickup parked in the lot by the motel. "Found the tarps. No Dad, though."

"He got a flat." I pointed at the passenger's front tire. "Looks like he dented the rim."

"Bet I know how. While you were texting your honey bunch, I was navigating around a huge-ass pothole in the Pass 'bout a half a mile up from here."

Texting my honey bunch. I snorted. I resisted the urge to tell Rafe what I'd actually been thinking.

"It's the rain," I said instead. "All these storms over the past month mean a ton of standing water eroding the rock under the asphalt."

"Can you fix it?"

"Fix... erosion?" I blinked. "Uh, no, Rafe. How about I fix the tire on the truck instead?"

"In this rain? No way. And I don't have Dad's keys, so it'd be a waste of time. I'm grabbing the tarps just in case. Text him for me, would you? Find out where the hell he is."

But when Rafe got back in the car a minute later, Big Rafe hadn't answered.

"Let's stop by his office," I suggested, hooking a thumb toward the house.

So Rafe pulled the car in next door, and the two of us bolted up the porch stairs... only to find the front door locked.

"You have your key?" I demanded.

Rafe shook his head. "Took a little too much delight in handing it back to Dad a couple weeks ago when I moved into Grandma Goodman's old house."

"Great. Well, I have a key, but it's over in my..." I squinted through the tree break. "Fuck. Rafe borrowed my car!"

"Let's see if Gloria's out back."

I followed Rafe around the side of the house, and both of us were drenched to the skin before we reached the bunker door... which happened to be firmly shut and locked.

"*Shit,*" Rafe said, ducking under the small overhang to bang on the door anyway.

"I'm checking the back door of the house." I went back the way we came but detoured up the wooden stairs to the back entrance. That door was locked also. The storm windows were down, and everything looked secure.

I took my phone from my pocket and hit Redial.

"Hey! Dad's phone's ringing in there!" Rafe yelled from the bunker. "I hear it echoing!"

He came running through the yard a second later and stood beside me on the porch, dripping.

"Well, wherever Rafe and Gloria are, Rafe got shit sorted for the storm before he left." I gestured to the storm windows. "But forgot his phone."

"I guess so," Rafe muttered. He tapped a couple of buttons on his own device. "I'm calling Beale to see what the hell is going on. It's starting to feel like an episode of that apocalyptic show where everyone goes missing and— Hey! Hey, Beale! Beale, you're breaking up! Where are y—? *Double fuck.* Call dropped." Rafe clicked his phone off and kicked at the porch railing. "Lightning must've hit the tower on the north side of the island. *Again.*"

Which meant Mason probably hadn't received my text either.

Lightning speared the sky, and thunder *boomed* so hard the world shook. The rain was like a living curtain hanging over the edges of the porch, obscuring everything beyond it.

"So what now?" Rafe demanded.

"Now I'm running up to the motel to get a change of clothes and my rain gear. Then we get back in your car and head for town to find Mason and Rafe and Beale, because I'll be damned if I'm spending the apocalypse with you."

"But Fenn!" Rafe called as he hurried down the stairs after me. "My favorite cousin! We could be apocalypse buddies!"

I snorted and ran off the porch, through the tree break, and up the concrete stairs to my room at a pace that was probably not smart given the level of standing water on the ground. I purposely took the closer stairs, just to give me an excuse to go past Mason's room and make sure all was well. His curtains were closed and it was dark inside, which meant he wasn't there, because I couldn't imagine him being inside without the lights on when the storm was this bad. My stomach twisted, wondering if he was scared, wherever he was.

I took a second to call him while I was throwing on some dry clothes, but the phone clicked to voicemail immediately.

"Mason, if you get this... call me or text me, okay? Let me know you're alright? I'll come to you, wherever you are." And as I hit the red button to disconnect, I realized it was true. I'd go wherever he was, on the island or off... and not just today, but in the future. I could leave Whispering Key anytime I wanted, and I'd be willing to leave for him.

This was way more of a revelation than it should have been.

I remembered Big Rafe telling us a few weeks ago that the island wasn't a prison or a tomb, and… okay, when Big Rafe started making sense, you had to wonder if maybe Beale was right about portents or if Young Rafe was right and the apocalypse *was* coming.

By the time we got back to town, after white-knuckling the drive even at fifteen miles an hour, our humor had fled once more, because the apocalypse thing wasn't as funny when the streets of town looked literally deserted. I reminded myself that—*duh!*—the rain was coming down in buckets and no one was going to be standing outside in this, but I was still more relieved than I wanted to admit when Rafe pulled the Jeep into the lot behind the Concha and found it full of cars. I didn't see my Charger anywhere in the lot or on the street.

I wrenched open the door to the little restaurant and immediately scanned the tables, even as everyone turned around to say, "Heya, Fenn! Heya, Rafe!"

Kono Cuddins and her husband were sitting at one table. Marius Wynott sat alone at another. Lorenna McKetcham and her granddaughter were at a third. Pete Blumenthal and his girlfriend, Marlie Coblet, at a fourth. Dale Jennings and Omar Abadi at a fifth. Juju Irvine was sitting on a stool beside Gerry Twomey, leaning back against the bar, and her brother Bubba sat on her other side. Lety was behind the counter cooking something, as usual.

No Big Rafe. No Beale…

Most importantly (and disappointingly), no Mason.

"Hey," Rafe said. "Have any of you guys seen my dad or Beale?"

"Or Dr. Bloom?" I added.

"Saw Rafe this morning at the Bean!" Marlie said. "Said to let anyone know if they needed help with storm preparations. He could be helping out!"

Right. That made sense.

"And I saw Dr. Bloom earlier today!" Marius Wynott volunteered. "Came by my shop with your *Beale*." Mr. Wynott looked vaguely disapproving. "Had a bit of a kerfuffle, alas."

"Beale and Mason? What happened?" I demanded.

Mr. Wynott sniffed. "I'm not sure I should say."

I narrowed my eyes and leaned forward, but Rafe put a restraining hand on my arm.

"Marius, you answer Fenn's question," Lety ordered, and Mr. Wynott pursed his lips and rolled his eyes, but complied.

"*Well*. I was about to help Dr. Bloom select a new book to read when I got called away momentarily. When I came back, I heard him speaking quite *heatedly* with young Mr. Goodman. Dr. Bloom was on the phone and said he was going to '*take the job.*' He told *me* he couldn't stay. And then he told Beale he required a ride off the island." He sighed. "I wonder if this means he won't be able to take care of Topaz while I'm gone in July?"

"Yeah, that's really the most important concern here," Maddie McKetcham muttered before her grandmother shot her a quelling look.

"That's ridiculous," I informed Marius. "Mason's not leaving yet. He's still looking for a job." And he wouldn't be leaving at all, if I could convince him to stay.

Juju exchanged a dubious glance with Maddie. "Last I heard, Big Rafe already found someone to replace Doc Bloom."

"What?" I scowled. "No. Not a chance—"

"Yep. That's what I heard, too," Bubba said worriedly. "Told Mason about it the other day. And Gloria said *Big Rafe* said he had a *million* job offers. She's shocked he hasn't taken one. So it's only a matter of time before he leaves, I'm afraid."

"Does this mean there's trouble in paradise?" Gerry asked slyly. "If you need a friend in your hour of need, Fenn—"

"Not now, Gerry," Lorenna said.

I ran a hand through my hair, remembering I hadn't gone inside Mason's room at all. I'd *assumed* he was at the clinic...

"Maybe Mason's at work!" I almost smacked my forehead at this obvious explanation. "I'll go check—"

"I doubt it," Kono piped up. "Taffy called me half an hour ago and said Mason told her to close up at lunch 'cause they had no appointments. She ended up staying until Orry could pick her up, and Mason never came back from lunch. She figured he was caught in the rain and went home."

This got weirder and weirder. And I was really fucking annoyed that I couldn't make a damn phone call.

There was *no* chance that Mason had left this island for good. *None.* Not without saying goodbye to everyone. Worst-case scenario, he'd gone for an interview off island.

No, I reminded myself, worst case, he'd actually taken a job off island.

But I wasn't going to give up. I'd done that too many times already.

"I'm gonna miss him a lot," Juju said with a sniff. "Mason, I mean."

Lorenna nodded sadly. "I was *thisclose* to getting him to join the Mahjong Society."

"He was a trustworthy guy," Bubba said.

"He was hot as fuck," Gerry said mournfully.

"Not *now*, Gerry!" Rafe, Kono, and Maddie said at once.

"You guys are talking about him like he's leaving," I said angrily. "He's not. He's gonna be back, you know. Tonight. And once he is, it's up to *us* to convince him to stay."

"On Whispering Key?" Kono shook her head. "What would he wanna stay here for?"

"Because this is where he's *needed*," I said, realizing the truth of my statement as I said it. All the eyes in the place shot to my face simultaneously.

"But, Christmas Eve three years ago, didn't you call Whispering Key a Universe-forsaken hunk of rock inhabited by a bunch of shit-for-brains dumbasses?" Dale wanted to know.

And holy shit, if his *ferrymones* gave him a memory like that, he shouldn't let Mason make him give them up.

"I... I *might* have," I allowed. "It's all a blur. But the point is, maybe it *is* a forsaken hunk of rock, but it's *our* forsaken hunk of rock! And we might be a bunch of shit-for-brains dumbasses, but we're *lovable* shit-for-brains dumbasses—"

"I certainly find *you* lovable," Gerry began, and the entire room shouted, "Not *now*, Gerry."

"Big Rafe is right when he says this island is changing," I told them. "It's growing already. Waking up. Coming alive. Even *I* can feel it. It's like that scene at the end of *Beauty and the Beast*, when all the talking clocks come back to life—"

"Dibs on being the dancing teapot!" Maddie said.

"Things are getting better here," I concluded. "But honestly? Some things were already pretty fucking great, and I don't think I saw them until Mason came here and *made* me see them. Like, the way we all look out for each other. The way when one of us has a problem, we *all* share that problem. The way we've made each other crazy, and kept each other safe, and stuck together through all the bad times like... like *family*." Like my own crazy, ridiculous, lovable family. "So why *wouldn't* Mason want to stay here, when we all want him to? You want him to stay, don't you, Lorenna? Gerry? Maddie?"

All of them nodded.

"Then... maybe it's time we stop just *accepting* the shit that happens to us around here." I looked at each one of them in turn. "Maybe it's time we decide what we want for ourselves. What we want this island to be. And then we go out and *get* it. Starting with Mason Bloom."

"Fuck yeah!" Maddie said, standing up. "Alright, Fenn Reardon. What do we do?"

"Well." I swallowed. "I have an idea."

Then I went on to sketch out the lamest, hokiest, cheesiest plan ever. But it just might work.

"You know," Rafe said, clapping me on the shoulder. "For a guy who had no experience with pep talks, you gave a damn good one. I credit myself, really, for teaching you how it's done."

I snorted. "Now we just need to get back out there, find your dad so we can figure out where the fuck Mason is, and get him back."

"Easy peasy," Rafe said, and I grinned just as Rafe's phone rang in his pocket.

"Beale," he crowed as he checked the display. "Ha! Now we'll get to the bottom of this mystery, Shaggy."

"Does that make you Scooby, Rafael?"

"Fuck you, I'm *Fred*. The handsome one."

"Sure you are."

Lety bustled around the counter and smiled at me approvingly. "*Ese chico te ama, Fenn. Encuéntralo y tráemelo de regreso. Es pan comido.* Okay?"

Something about bread and eating? Sounded just about right.

"Okay," I agreed solemnly, pretty sure in that one shining moment that I could achieve just about anything.

Then I turned and saw Rafe's wide-eyed, stricken expression.

"There's been an accident," he whispered.

"Oh fuck. Beale? Is he..."

Rafe shook his head. "Not Beale, Fenn. *Mason.*"

20

MASON

Searching for service...

Searching for service...

Searching for service...

No service found.

"Motherfucker," I grumbled at the phone I'd propped on the dashboard, aware I sounded like Fenn. "Search *harder*, damn it."

The sky was sloshing down rain like I was at a car wash, and the sky was pitch-black. I could barely see a hand in front of me, and I'd turned the radio off to concentrate, so the only sounds were the swish of the wiper blades as they flew across the windshield and the pounding of rain on the hood of the car.

I took the exit for Cooter Key Bridge, and the traffic lights and glowing signs looked like watercolor images, hazy and surreal. I touched my brakes—Fenn's brakes—as the traffic light turned red, and the Charger fishtailed just a little in the standing water before coming to rest in the perfect spot in front of the white line.

Figures he has the best brakes in the world, I thought with a relieved sigh, and I refreshed my phone to see if it could catch a fucking signal *finally*.

To say that I was in a hurry to get home was an understatement and...

Whoa. Huh. Apparently Whispering Key had become home?

But the more I thought about it, the more right it felt. I just needed to talk to Fenn. Like, really, *really* needed to talk to him.

Taking Gloria to the hospital had been an eye-opening experience. Up in New York, I'd gotten spoiled by how close things were. Even growing up in a small town where folks complained about how it took twenty-five minutes to get to a decent mall, we had access to EMTs who'd arrive within ten minutes—as I had reason to find out on more than one occasion. So while I'd always enjoyed my job and found it fulfilling, I'd never had a visceral understanding of how important I could be to someone, just by being in the right place at the right time.

I'd gotten it that afternoon.

Keeping Gloria (and Rafe) calm in the car, explaining her condition to the ER doctors—including the elevated white blood cell count on her last test and my concerns about the petechiae in her feet—had helped her get diagnosed with pericarditis, an infection of the lining around her heart, and put on a powerful antibiotic that much faster. I felt accomplished and *needed* in a way I'd never felt while working at my suburban practice.

Taffy had asked how many people I needed to be important to, and sitting in that emergency room, I'd known the answer: exactly *one*. One patient I could help, one patient I could comfort, one patient I could someday save. That was exactly as important as I wanted or needed to be.

And of course, as soon as I'd realized that, I'd wanted to call Fenn and share this revelation, the same way I wanted to share all my happy and sad things with him. Except, some idiot (yeah, it was me) had deleted his number from my phone. And it was Murphy's Law that Rafe had left *his* phone at home. And none of my calls to Beale or Taffy had gone through *either*. And every moment that passed where I couldn't get in touch with Fenn was fucking excruciating, because he'd become that important to me that fast.

For once, I wasn't concerned about whether it was *okay* or *normal* to care about Fenn that much. I wasn't spiraling over whether the feeling had come on too fast to be trusted or would all go away tomorrow. I wasn't overthinking *any* of that. Watching Gloria's eyes fixed on Rafe's above her oxygen mask, seeing Rafe consciously synchronize his breathing with hers, was the very best kind of gut check, and it was startlingly easy to see how *none* of the shit I worried about was important in the grand scheme of things.

It occurred to me that *normal* and *too fast* weren't words we used to talk about our *own* realizations and decisions, anyway; they were the words we used to judge *other* people's. Deep inside, I *knew* how I felt about Fenn—that he'd been the truest thing in my life from the very second we'd met, breaking down all my damn walls faster than I could throw them up, and that loving him was very, spectacularly *real*. I was done giving headspace to how other people viewed *my* life. I was done avoiding risks.

Now, I just needed to find Fenn and convince him to take a risk on me, which I would do as soon as...

The ring of my phone was startlingly loud as I drove down the dark and quiet streets of Cooter Key.

Unknown caller. Could be Rafe at the hospital. Could be *Fenn*.

I quickly accepted the call and put it on speaker.

"Dr. Mason Bloom."

"Um, hey? Mase?"

Jesus. I huffed out a breath. "Victoria. Hey. Now's not really—"

"I'm so excited you answered! I wasn't sure if you would, since I'd changed my number, and um, I sent you flowers from that florist I love that does those ultramodern arrangements? But they couldn't be delivered because you're still in Florida or whatever, and I tried to DM you on Insta, but you didn't answer, and I couldn't call your family for your new address, because you know I have *never* been a favorite of theirs, so I wondered how you were."

I almost snorted. *I, I, I...* How had I never noticed that Victoria talked this way?

"I'm great," I said. "Thanks. Not a vacation, I live in Florida now. But now's not an awesome time to chat, honestly, Vic. I'm driving and the rain is pouring, so... was there something you needed?"

"Oh. Well." She cleared her throat. "I just wanted to say that I'm sorry about the way things ended, Mase."

For half a second I wondered if she was going to want to get back together, and I couldn't restrain my shudder at the idea. The Mason who'd been so content with her was a completely different person than the man I was now, and I had no desire to go back to that.

"Gunner and I were talking. I, um, told him I regretted some of the things I said, and he reminded me that it wasn't too late to tell you the things I *should* have said instead." The affection in her voice was clear, and I actually smiled in the darkness. I was *glad* she was happy.

And Gunner was *still* a stupid name.

"Vic, I don't expect—"

"No, I know. This is for me." She took a deep breath. "I'm sorry that I made this out to be your fault, Mason. It wasn't. You're a very passionate person. You're passionate about your family, and about medicine. You just weren't very passionate about... *me*. And it hurt. But until I met Gunner, I didn't have the... the *strength*, I guess... to be honest with myself about that. About wanting *more*."

"I get it," I said quietly. "And *thank you*. Because if you hadn't been the one to make that break, I don't know that I would have. I was sleepwalking."

"And now you're not."

"Now neither of us is, sounds like." Definitely *not* asleep. Not when the mere fact that I'd passed over the bridge and was now on Whispering Key made my stomach flip.

"Yeah." She paused. "The guy on your Insta…"

"Fenn. My boyfriend." *I think. If he'll let me be.*

"He's cute," she said, and I could hear the smile in her voice. "What did your family say about him?"

I snorted. "Nothing yet. None of them are Instagram regulars, and I figured this was a conversation I wanted to have in person, anyway."

"Yeah. For what it's worth, I'm really happy you're happy, Mason. You deserve that. Take care."

I clicked the disconnect button and lifted my ass to shove my phone in my pocket.

As I drove through the center of town, which appeared completely deserted in the dark and lashing water, I marveled that today was officially the most surreal day of my life. Except that this *was* my life. And I was pretty fucking happy about—

It hit without warning as I went around the curve in the road by the motel. The pothole I'd forgotten from earlier was suddenly no longer a pothole but a *crater* in the center of the road, nearly ten feet wide, three or four feet across, and God only knew how deep.

I knew immediately that it was too big and I was going too fast to avoid it, even as I slammed on the brakes and steered into the left lane, and then suddenly I was on a roller coaster, flipping ass over head, *falling falling falling…* And all I could think was that I couldn't let this be the end because I hadn't gotten to tell Fenn I loved him.

"Mason! Mason! Ah, *fuck fuck fuck*. Fenn is gonna *freak* when he gets here. Mason! It's Beale! Help is on the way! I called Rafe and I called the police. I'm going to get something to get you out of there, okay? If you can hear me, *hang on!*"

I groaned and opened my eyes to the darkness—absolute, unrelenting darkness. No headlights. No flashlight. No moonlight. *Nothing.*

Think, Mason, think.

My ribs felt bruised, and my shoulder was a little numb and probably sprained. I could feel an abrasion throbbing on my hand. My knees were smushed underneath the dashboard and ached. All in all, not as bad as it could be...

But it also felt like the weight of the entire earth was pushing *down* on the back of the driver's seat, and the seat was forcing my diaphragm into the steering wheel, making it harder and harder to breathe. I pushed back experimentally and the seat moved, but so did the car, and I suddenly realized the steering wheel was the only thing preventing me from falling into the yawning crevasse into the earth's core in the middle of Godfrey Pass. Breathing suddenly didn't seem *that* important.

I forced myself to swallow. Okay, *yawning crevasse* was probably a bit dramatic. It was likely more of a very wide pothole. Of unknown depth.

Maybe.

Or maybe it was exactly as bad as I imagined, *because I couldn't see.*

Don't panic. Panic helps nothing, I reminded myself. Unsurprisingly, this didn't help.

Water poured in the busted windshield, soaking me to the skin, and I could feel it pooling up around my feet.

Oh my God. How was this happening?

I pinched myself, foolishly, wondering if I'd somehow fallen asleep, possibly on my bed back in New York, and I'd dreamed up my entire life on Whispering Key, both the beautiful dream that was Fenn and the horrible nightmare that was *this right now*.

And then the nightmare and the dream were one and the same because there in the cold, wet darkness, deep inside the earth, I heard Fenn's voice.

"Mason! Mase! For fuck's sake, you'd better be alive down there!"

I sucked in the biggest breath I could, which was not very big, and managed to squeak out, "Fenn!" There was no way he could hear it over the pounding rain...

Except he did.

"He's alive. He's conscious! Fuck, Rafe, give me the rope. Oh, yes I fucking can! You stay back and— *Listen to me!* I know what I'm talking about here, okay? This whole area is unstable, and you need to stay *back* or it could collapse further. No more weight. Just hold the rope, and when Beale gets back with the ladder, you push it over to me, okay?"

I couldn't hear a damn thing Rafe said, if he replied; the only thing I was capable of hearing—the only thing I wanted to hear—was Fenn's voice.

"Mason! I'm coming down, okay? Can you talk to me, baby?"

I was pretty sure I could do a whole lot of things if he kept calling me *baby*, but I didn't say that. Instead, I managed a pitiful, "*Yeah.*"

"Good! Okay, so what we have here is a sinkhole. Remember we talked about those, Mase?"

Yeah. I remembered him saying they were super rare, the lying liar. "Yeah," I managed, a little more strongly this time.

Suddenly, there was light shining down from above, illuminating my hands on the steering wheel and the crumpled front end of the car. It was only the weak light of someone's phone flashlight, but it was better than nothing and it calmed me slightly... at least until the beam swung toward the nose of the car, which was hanging over *empty space*.

"This is good, Mase!" Fenn said, as calmly as if we were talking about television shows.

I was glad one of us thought so. But it was hard not to respond to the overwhelming confidence in Fenn's voice, hard not to feel like, as long as he was with me, everything wasn't just *going* to be fine, it already was.

"This side hasn't collapsed entirely, so I'm sliding down to get you, baby. It's slow going. Can you do me a favor and open the car door?"

I felt for the handle and found it easily, but before I pulled it, I hesitated. "Safe?" I croaked.

"Of course! It'll be fine. Just push that door open gently, okay? Try not to rock the car too much."

Oh, sure. Just open the door without rocking the car. *No prob.*

I did exactly as I was told and... *shit*. The water poured into the car even faster.

"Fenn!"

"Yeah, baby! Right here." His voice was closer now. Almost right next to me.

"I'm stuck." *No shit, Mason.*

"It's okay. I'm coming!" His hand flew in the open door and smacked me in the face.

"Hey!" I said, but I grabbed at that hand anyway and clasped it with bruising force like the lifeline it was.

"Okay. *Okay*," Fenn breathed, like he was reassuring himself more than me. "I've got you. I've got you, and I'm not letting go."

That sounded seriously fucking perfect.

"Fenn! Got the ladder!" Beale's voice called from somewhere above. "You sure this will work?"

Fenn edged closer. "Absolutely *positive*. I've seen cave-ins like this before. This is standard procedure. It's going to be *fine*. Lower the ladder down to me, just don't come close to the edge, Beale. I'm gonna attach the rope to it, then you and Rafe are gonna pull the rope to get us out."

And that's exactly what happened. Fenn helped push the seat back so I could squeeze out of the car, and then he positioned me flat on the ladder, which he used almost like an EMT's spinal board. He laid himself on top of me, holding on to the ladder while I held on to *him*. And then Beale and Rafe, with much groaning, managed to haul us up onto the pavement where the headlights from Rafe's Jeep *and* Beale's motorcycle lit the place up nearly as bright as day.

With the last dregs of my adrenaline rush, I rolled off the ladder, taking Fenn with me. The two of us landed in a puddle on the ground—well, more me than him, really, since he was on top of me, braced on his forearms.

I stared up at him, at his shadowed eyes and his concerned expression, and my brain finally computed that I was *okay* —that *we* were okay—and maybe even *more* than okay, because Fenn had once again called me *baby*. Then my arms were around him for reasons that had nothing to do with being rescued and everything to do with the man who'd rescued me.

Who'd rescued me *in so many ways*.

"You came! You came, you came, you came." I ran my hands through Fenn's hair, tugging him closer, and kissed him over and over.

"Mason," he breathed. "I will *always* come for you, okay? Always, *always*. And if you doubted that for a second, I—"

Because this was *my* life, of course I started *crying* at that point, hot tears mixing with the cold rain, one tear for every second that I'd been *so fucking scared* not just after the accident, but earlier, too. I draped my arm over my eyes and let it happen with no shame.

"Mason? It's okay! Fuck. Are you hurt?" He lifted his torso up just enough to pry my arm away from my eyes and peer down at me, running the beam of his phone light over my face just to be sure... and blinding me in the process.

"Ack! I'm okay! Shut it off, Fenn! Shut it off!" I closed my eyes and wriggled beneath him...

And just like that, I felt like I was back in the stupid bathtub at the motel the first night we'd met: soaking wet and inappropriately aroused, with eyes only for the man above me. Unlike that night, though I knew *exactly* what I wanted from Fenn Reardon now. So I lifted my hips slightly, deliberately rubbing myself against him.

I wasn't quite insane enough to be *hard* under these circumstances, but still, Fenn froze, and I could almost feel his mind tracking backward, replaying the memory of the last time we'd been like this, under circumstances that were totally different and incredibly similar at the same time. We'd fought it for a minute, the two of us, but he and I had always been inevitable.

I sniffled a little and ran a hand over my wet face. "Fenn Reardon," I said. "We have *got* to stop meeting like this."

Fenn shook his head, shocked and amused and vaguely disapproving. "I'm not taking an ounce of responsibility. I'll have you know, *nothing* like this happened to me until you wandered into my life, Mason Bloom."

"Wandered?"

"Flew, then." He settled against me more firmly. "Slid off a building and—"

"Crash-landed?" We both snorted and stared at each other, giddy with adrenaline and relief and *love*.

I bit my lip. "I wrecked your car."

He huffed out a startled laugh. "You did. I'm going to be very annoyed about that."

"Are you?"

"Definitely." He dropped a kiss on my nose. "As soon as I stop being really fucking grateful you're okay." He kissed me deeply, then pulled back. "Okay, done." He pretended to move off me, but I locked my arms and legs around his back to hold him exactly where he was.

"Are you guys having sex in the rain right now?" Beale demanded, reminding me that we weren't alone.

"Beale, stop perving on the idiots! Crawl over here and check this out!" Rafe yelled. "What's that by the front wheel—"

Fenn and I ignored both of them.

"Gloria's in the hospital," I told him. "She's gonna be *fine*, but your uncle's staying—"

"I know," he cut me off. "Beale gave Rafe the rundown when he called to say you'd been in an accident. I have never been so scared in my entire life."

"Me neither." My hands tightened on the back of his neck. "It was fucking dark, and I was so scared... and then you called my name and were grumpy at me." I licked my lips, tasting the rain and Fenn. "That's how I knew it was really you."

Fenn snorted. "Giving me shit in the middle of the street, in a tropical downpour? Really?"

I nodded. "Always. That's how *you* know it's really *me*."

Fenn braced his weight on his forearms and leaned over me. "I love you, Mason Bloom. I don't care if you wanna live here or New York or... wherever. I just wanna live with you. With no walls between us."

It was probably the sappiest thing Fenn Reardon had ever said or ever would say. And sometime when we *weren't* lying in the road in a tropical downpour, I was going to tease him about it mercilessly. But in that moment, all I wanted was to kiss him, so I lifted my neck and did just that. "I love you, too. And I don't think I knew what that meant before. Which is why we're staying on Whispering Key."

"Yeah?" Fenn grinned broadly, then pressed his smiling lips to mine, the taste and texture and hard reality of him reminding me that beauty could be found in the weirdest, *wettest* places.

"Fenn! Holy fucking shitballs. *Fenn*! Stop kissing your boyfriend in the fucking monsoon and come see this!" Beale called.

"I'm taking you home and putting you to bed," Fenn said mildly, ignoring his cousin. "Unless you think you need a hospital?"

I shook my head, knowing I was going to be sore the next day no matter what, but that I needed rest more than a hospital. Rest, and... "I really need to be with you," I admitted. Letting him hold me and ground me in the safety I only ever felt with him.

"Handy, Loafers. Because that's exactly what I need, too." He kissed me again, with his forearms under my shoulders and his fingers supporting my head.

I sighed.

"For the love of Jacob Godfrey's ghost! Fenn and Mason! Stop dry humping... uh? Wet humping? Whatever. Get your asses over here!"

I darted a glance toward the edge of the sinkhole and shuddered. Yeah, I had *zero* desire to crawl back over there. But Fenn was already levering himself off me and offering me both of his hands to help pull me up.

Once I was on my feet, though, he didn't drag me toward the hellmouth; he pulled me into his arms like he was as reluctant to let go as I was, and he kissed me *again*. I could get very, very used to this.

I was thankful I was *alive* to get used to this.

"Shower," I mumbled. "Beer. Bed."

"Baby, you have seriously good plans—"

"*Jesus Christ!*" Beale yelled. "There's a fucking *box* in this hole, boys! A very old, very heavy *box*. Are you hearing me? Blink once for yes, twice for no!"

But Fenn and I just stared at each other without blinking at all.

"You need me to spell it out? I'm pretty sure this means Mason just crashed your Charger into the Whispering Key treasure, Fenn!" Beale yelled. "So stop your *canoodling* and come fucking *see it*."

"There is no way," Fenn said, shaking his head slowly. "Not possible. In *what universe* would a person have a car accident and find a treasure people have hunted for centuries?"

As it turned out, the answer to that question was... this one.

21

FENN

Two mornings later, I stepped out the back door of the Goodmans' house into somewhat-organized chaos. The sun was shining, the ground was boggy, and the air was thick with humidity.

Young Rafe and Beale were manning a chain saw—never a good idea—to hack a storm-downed tree into tiny pieces for yard cleanup.

Beale's cat, Marjorie, whose delusions of being a pit bull grew more and more pronounced each day, stood on the porch steps hissing at the noise.

Big Rafe manned the barbecue smoker just out of sight, sending giant white plumes wafting across the covered patio where an enormous picnic table covered in a red-and-white-checked cloth stood ready and waiting for food.

Gage waved at the smoke from his spot on the porch stairs, where he chatted with Mason, who was sprawled across the lounge chair I'd threatened to strap him to if he attempted to move.

Just a typical family Sunday, right?

Except it hadn't really been typical for any of us up to now. Not even a little. There was a feeling of happiness and anticipation hanging in the air, along with the smoke and the humidity. A sense of camaraderie. I feeling that we were... I dunno. Actually *family*.

A lot of the happy buzz had to do with the contents of the safe in the floor of Uncle Rafe's bunker—a wooden chest banded with iron containing several gold bars, gold coins, pouches filled with gold dust, and a pair of gold rings, one inscribed with the initials *JG*, the other *RG*, like the original owners wanted to be *extra* sure we knew just who it had belonged to.

But I think even more of it had to do with how close we'd come to losing Gloria (who was still in the hospital, but feeling fit enough to video chat with Gage and walk him through her pineapple bread recipe) and Mason (who was bruised to hell and back but was, in his professional opinion, "Perfectly fine, for fuck's sake, Fenn, but if we don't have makeup sex soon, I won't be responsible for my actions"). There was something to be said for remembering that no matter how much we pissed each other off—*and we did*—we really loved one another, too.

"Hey," I said, approaching Mason's lounge chair. I ruffled Gage's hair and pushed at his head when he muttered, "Dick."

To Mason, I said, "You relaxing, baby?"

Mason pushed his sunglasses up through his wavy, dark hair and narrowed his eyes in annoyance. "Clearly, yes. I had no idea you had this relaxation kink. I offered to help Beale and Rafe with the tree, and Beale threatened to sit on me if I tried, which is counterproductive to my bruised ribs healing, FYI."

"Yeah, but the threat worked, didn't it. You're still lying here?" I braced my hands on the arms of his chair and leaned down to give him a long, thorough kiss.

"I feel if you want me lying down, there are better ways to accomplish it, that's all I'm saying," Mason whispered against my mouth when I pulled back. "That's all I *keep* saying."

I grinned and knocked his feet out of the way so I could sit on the end of his lounger.

"Fine," I agreed. "Fine. If that's *really* what you want to do… you've convinced me."

"Wait, really?" His green eyes were so damn beautiful. "Because I could fake being tired right now and we could be up in my room in minutes, and I could do that thing where—"

"You know I can hear you, right?" Gage demanded. "My young, impressionable ears are *bleeding*."

"Sure," I said, shrugging. "If you really want to, let's go. In fact! Hey, why don't we *all* go?"

Mason's eyes widened and his lip curled. "*All*?"

"Yeah, the whole family! Might be crowded, but I think they'd love to watch."

"*What*?"

"You don't think Uncle Rafe and the boys would enjoy season two of *Dr. Who*? That *was* what you were suggesting, right? No? Otherwise, I don't—"

Mason grabbed my shirt, and I laughed out loud as he drew me toward him.

Someone really had to tell the man his "threatening" face was *so* not threatening, but that person was *not* going to be me.

"I hate you," he said.

"Too late," I sang. "You already told me you loved me. No take-backsies."

"I said it after a traumatic incident! That shit doesn't count."

"You said it after a traumatic incident, so it counts *more*."

"I should have taken a cab from the airport that first day," he groaned.

I leaned over him and looked seriously into those eyes I loved, eyes I never wanted to go a single day without seeing. "No, baby, you shouldn't have."

His green eyes went soft on mine. He put his hand on my jaw and leaned up to kiss the corner of my mouth. "No," he said seriously. "You're right. I shouldn't have."

"Aaand *still* hearing you!" Gage interrupted. "Come *on*, guys, give me a break. I haven't gotten laid in *months*, and the tension between you is so thick I could cut it."

"It's my *ferrymones*," I said solemnly. "They make me irresistible."

Mason laughed, my favorite sound ever, and Gage shook his head. "You guys are so weird."

Young Rafe and Beale wandered over and sat down on chairs under the patio cover.

"Who's weird? Fenn?" Rafe said. "This is not new information, little brother. And poor Mason has a coordinating aura."

"A *compatible* aura," Beale corrected, rolling his eyes. "Coordinating is for paint chips. And you know, the funniest thing about you is that *your* aura is—"

Rafe held up a hand. "None of my business. I let you worry about my aura, Beale."

"Hey, Dad!" Gage called. "Are you done burning the steaks yet? This is fun and whatever, but I have plans tonight, so I've gotta get back to campus, and we haven't talked about the treasure *at all* except when that reporter knocked on the door and you yelled '*No comment*' through the peephole."

Big Rafe leaned around the side of the house and scowled. "Gage Spence Goodman, you can't head off island yet. The Pass is still an unholy mess, with all those work crews all over the place."

"Yeah, I know," he said patiently. "I'm the one who drove here and had to park my car more than half a mile up the road, remember? And lemme just tell you, walking around the crater brought me past the Original Homestead, which totally gave me the heebie-jeebies." He leaned closer to Mason. "*Ghosts*, you know?"

Mason snorted... but held me tighter anyway. I suppressed a smile.

"*Ergo*, if you go back to campus, the reporters will *hound* you," Big Rafe warned.

Gage shook his head. "Nope. Not a soul knows who I am there. It's you guys I feel bad for, especially Fenn and Mason. The second y'all alerted the state about the treasure, you became sitting ducks, and once they heard about Mason's near miss? Story's total clickbait."

Big Rafe came and took a seat next to the picnic table. I waited for him to say something about this being exactly what he'd hoped for—good publicity for the island! Instead he gave Mason a stern look.

"Mason, you'd best tell me if it gets to be too much, you hear? If they want an official statement, you direct them to the mayor's office. And that goes for you, too, Fenn."

Huh.

But Mason nodded, taking it all in stride. "I will. I haven't gotten a single call yet." He shook me gently. "Though this might be partly because someone hid my phone yesterday and didn't give it back until this morning."

"You needed the rest," I said. And more than that, I'd needed *him*. We'd spent the day mostly alone, dozing in bed for long hours, calling to check on Gloria, taking a short walk on the beach, soaking in the idea that the two of us were a package deal now, talking about places we wanted to travel, debating the dog Mason wanted to adopt... and absolutely *not* doing more than kissing, because I refused to even contemplate hurting him by being too enthusiastic. "It's what your doctor would prescribe, if your doctor wasn't *you*."

Mason snorted and admitted, "You're not entirely wrong," which was as close to an endorsement as I was going to get.

"Cancel your plans," Big Rafe said again, eyeing his youngest. "Stay here. Spend time with the family."

"Can't. Got tickets to a concert." Gage shrugged apologetically.

"Yeah? Who's playing?" Young Rafe demanded.

Gage shrugged again and got very busy toying with his watch band. "Nobody you'd know."

"Ohhh, I do believe our Gage-let has a *date*," Beale said with a smile. "It's not so much about the music as it is about the hot guy waiting for him if you catch my drift, Rafe. How's my intuition, little brother?"

"Nonexistent." Gage cleared his throat. "*So*. As I was saying. Small matter of a treasure?"

Big Rafe shrugged, clearly subdued, and Mason poked me, as if to say this was not the Rafe Goodman he knew.

I knew that was what he meant because I was thinking it, too.

"I'm assuming you four guys are going to split it since you were all there when it was found?" Gage continued. "That's fair. But I expect one of you assholes to get me a decent car, okay?"

Rafe snorted. "Yeah, right. Not buying my brother some bougie vehicle just to help him get laid. When Jayd Rollins comes to the island this summer, you can drive him around just fine in your Civic, and then tell whichever asshole you date next that if your car was good enough for the likes of Jayd, it's plenty good enough for them."

"I'm not driving Jayd around! He's *your* ex-brother-in-law." Gage blushed, all out of proportion to his brother's teasing. "And no one said anything about *bougie*, Rafael. First, because I don't *use* the word *bougie*, and second because I'm not talking about buying me a Vanquish or what-the-fuck-ever. I'm just saying, you guys finding a multimillion-dollar treasure justifies a slight upgrade from my 1982 Civic, okay? I'd like a car where I don't have to actually *crank* the windows down." He pushed his shaggy, sun-shot hair away from his brown eyes and mimed turning a window crank.

"Hey! As a person who happens to drive a car with windows that need to be cranked..." I stopped, remembered, and winced.

Mason sat forward so he could wrap strong arms around me from behind and prop his chin on my shoulder. "Moment of silence," he whispered. "May the Charger rest in peace."

"Actually." I twisted slightly to look at him. "About that. I think I know what I want to do with any treasure money that comes my way." I twisted my lips up into a hopeful smile and waited for him to catch on.

It took 2.4 seconds for Mason to get it, but when he did, his face broke out in the happiest smile I'd ever seen on him yet... and just to say, his post-orgasm smile wasn't exactly *low-voltage*. "A car restoration shop," he said triumphantly. "Hell, yes."

"And it's fitting that my baby should be my first patient, right?"

"Absolutely." But Mason's smile dimmed to a frown, and he bit his lip. "You know, not to be Debbie Downer here, but this way-smart guy I know once told me that step one after finding the treasure is figuring out who owns it." He darted a look from me to Big Rafe. "And the best you could do would be to get a *portion* of the money as a reward?"

I shrugged, totally unconcerned. "It'll be enough for a down payment. And then I thought I could talk to the mayor of Whispering Key about getting a small-business loan for the rest."

Big Rafe looked up, startled, and his eyes narrowed on me. "You serious? You wanna open a garage?"

I nodded slowly. "I really do."

"Yeah?" His smile dawned slowly. "So you're staying, then? The both of you?"

Mason's arms tightened around me. "Yeah. I'm waiving my probationary period. You guys are stuck with me. And you'll have to tell Aaron Smith to look elsewhere."

I squeezed his knee, more than happy with this idea.

Big Rafe nodded. "Good," he whispered, quietly pleased. "That's real good. I'll make sure you get what you need, Fenn."

And, look, not that I wasn't glad that he was glad, but... I'd sort of expected something *more*.

"Uncle Rafe, is there an issue with the treasure?" I demanded. "Because if there's some legal question where, like, the state might own it all because it was under a road or some shit, just tell us now."

Big Rafe shook his head, looking pained. He clenched and unclenched his hands. "It's not that," he said. "Treasure's yours. Ours. The whole thing."

Five sets of eyes stared at one another and then at Big Rafe, but Beale was the one who finally demanded, "How's that possible?"

"You remember I told you boys I was making investments? That's why Goodmen Outfitters went under and money was tight?"

"Yeah," Young Rafe said, dryly. "You were investing in treasure hunts. Salvage operations. We figured that out."

Big Rafe shook his head. "You figured wrong. I've been investing in the land around the island while property values were low."

Mason gasped just slightly, and I frowned over my shoulder at him, not understanding. His grip on my waist tightened.

"You've been buying *land*?" Gage clarified. "That was your plan all along?"

"Hell, no. At first, I was trying to help folks who needed the money to start over somewhere else. But a good plan means adapting along the way, right?" He looked over my shoulder at Mason and gave him a half-smile. "These days, I figure... this is my legacy. Jacob and Resolute wanted the island to be for the Goodmans and the Godfreys." He shrugged. "So I bought up what I could and put it in trust for my boys." His brown eyes came to rest on me. "All *four* of my boys, since being a Goodman's about more than a name."

I blinked. Mason buried his face against my shoulder blade and said, "Baby," so softly I don't think anyone but me heard it. Young Rafe shook his head at my expression and coughed, "Dumbass," before smiling broadly. But I just stared at Big Rafe, utterly dumbstruck. I'd realized Friday that I'd maybe been reading the man wrong for a while. I hadn't realized just *how* wrong until that moment, and once I did, it shed an entirely different light on every conversation we'd had... *ever*.

Every time he'd mentioned his boys. Every time he'd mentioned making things right for the Goodmans.

Well, shit.

"Aw! Look at Fenn having emotions," Beale said in a smug, satisfied sort of way. "How cute."

I pointed a finger at him. "Enjoy it now because we'll be adding this to the list of things we don't discuss."

Beale nodded. "I kinda figured."

Young Rafe ran a hand through his hair. "I'm still not entirely understanding, Dad. You own the island? The whole island?"

"Lord, no," Big Rafe said, frowning. "Just most of it from here north to, say, Margot Lane? Except Marius Wynott's place, of course, and the land around it. Not the inn. Not the Sundry. Couple other spots, too."

"So what's the problem?" Beale demanded, asking the question I was pretty sure the rest of us had been thinking. Big Rafe's eyes cut to him, and Beale shrugged. "Doesn't take *the sight* to see you're nowhere near as excited as you should be about this. You devoted your entire life to finding this treasure and finding the *Esmerelda*. Now half your life's work is done and you're all, '*Yeah. Whatever.*'"

"Because finding the treasure was *not* my life's work, Gage!" Big Rafe exploded. He jumped out of his chair and began to pace the yard. "Do you boys know what Gloria said to me on Friday when she was out in that bunker, unable to *breathe*?" He thrust a hand toward the back fence and the bunker beyond. "She told Mason she didn't want to go to the hospital because she knew I needed her help to plan the Extravaganza and she didn't want to let me down. As if she *could*! As if that were *possible*!" He shook his head wildly. "Fenn's said a hundred times, and Rafe has, too, that I'm a liar, a manipulator. That I care too much about my own plans and make everyone else fall in line. But I... but I... I figured you always knew that the *point* of the treasure was never the *treasure*. It was you boys. It was my Mary. It was our *family*."

He pushed his palms to his eyes and took a deep breath. "Gloria and I have been dating for a little while now. I wasn't gonna say anything until Gage came home for summer break and we could make an announcement, but I'm gonna ask her to marry me. I love her, and somehow, despite everything, she loves me, too. But even then, the woman thought I'd be upset about the stupid Extravaganza when she needed me. And it's made me start to wonder... all those times when you boys got mad at me, had you really not understood how much I loved you? How much more important you are to me than *anything*? This island could sink into the Gulf, and as long as you four were all right—" He broke off and turned around, staring at the tree line, one hand rubbing the back of his neck.

All of us were silent for half a minute, and even Rafe, who'd called *me* a dumbass for not recognizing that Big Rafe cared about me, looked completely poleaxed by his father's heated confession.

"Well, damn, Dad," Gage said. He lifted himself out of his chair and went to clap his father on the shoulder. "If you wanted me to cancel my plans, you should have just said so. No need to be all dramatic."

Big Rafe snorted.

"And just to say, Uncle Rafe," I called. "I *never* doubted for a second that you cared about your family." I just hadn't known I was a part of it.

"Well, *I* just want to say, I called this thing with you and Gloria *weeks* ago, and no one believed me!" Mason, my personal troublemaker, piped up.

Young Rafe punched Beale in the arm. "Are you hearing this? Dad and Gloria are in love. Mason shacked up with Fenn, God knows why. And even Gage has a date. It's just you and me, Beale."

Beale shook his head, and his face turned pink. "Or maybe it's just you."

"Oh, the burn!" Rafe gasped and clapped a hand to his chest. "And now he keeps secrets from his family, too? Beale, it's like I hardly know you."

"Beale should be allowed to date whoever he wants without teasing," Mason said stoutly. "And however *many* people he wants. Whatever makes him happy."

Beale snorted and ran a hand over his face. "I'm not in a poly relationship, Mason," he said. "Sorry to disappoint."

"You're not?" Mason *did* sound oddly disappointed.

"Wait, were you *ever*?" I demanded.

"For your sake, I'm really glad you two have improved your communication skills recently," Beale said, grinning at Mason and me. "Getting you two together has been a full-time job."

My jaw dropped. "*Pfft*. I have no idea what you're talking about."

"Same," Mason agreed. "We may have had some tiny, minor issues—"

Beale hooted. Young Rafe laughed out loud. Even Big Rafe shook his head and smiled.

"—but we've figured them out. I can't wait to see how *your* relationship progresses." Mason sat back in the chair and folded his arms over his chest smugly.

"Yeah, me neither," Beale said, rolling his eyes.

"So, wait, speaking of secrets... Dad, how'd you get the money to fix up the island?" Gage asked. "The small-business loans, the road repair... Did you mortgage some of the land?"

This was an excellent question.

Rafe opened his mouth to answer when a voice called from the side yard, "Yoo-hoo! Afternoon, Goodmans! And Doc Bloom!"

Rafe closed his mouth with a smile. "Guess a man should get to keep *some* secrets, shouldn't he?"

I wanted to protest, but before I could, nearly the entire population of Whispering Key invaded the backyard, and Mason jumped to his feet in surprise.

Max scurried in first, chasing after his soccer ball, which Marjorie leaped off the porch to run after. Taffy came next, smiling and shaking her head in apology for her son, carrying a tray of cupcakes she dropped on the table before giving Mason a hug. Lety arrived like a queen with her court, carrying a bouquet of flowers in her arms while Bubba and Juju hurried behind her carrying enormous platters of food in mismatched plastic containers. Lorenna and George McKetcham came next, followed by their granddaughter, Maddie, who held a rolled-up paper. Then more folks came, and more, and *more*, each one walking up to Mason to shake his hand, or give him a hug, or say a word of thanks about some ache or pain or worry he'd soothed in just the few weeks he'd been there.

"What's happening right now?" he whispered to me, wide-eyed, during a break in the greetings.

I smiled just a little at the stunned, *happy* expression on his face and shrugged. "The other night, when I thought you might be leaving the key, I figured it might be easier to convince you to stay if I had a little help, so I asked Maddie McKetcham to call a few friends." But honestly? Even *I* was stunned by just how many people she'd organized, just how many people Mason had touched.

And when Maddie unrolled a banner that said *Welcome Home, Mason Bloom* and Mason got legit tears in his eyes and turned to wrap his arms around me, I knew my incredibly hokey, cheesy plan had *worked*.

"I'm the *best* at plans," I whispered in his ear.

Mason laughed, just as I'd known he would, and lifted his green gaze to mine. "Unnecessary plans, maybe. I was already convinced." But when he pulled my head down to his and slid his tongue against mine, all breathy and wanting and *Mason*, I knew I was going to spend a little time every single day reconvincing him.

"Mason, *chico*!" Lety bustled up to us, wearing a bright orange dress and a happy smile. She grabbed Mason's hand and patted it lovingly. "I'm so happy you're staying! Just remember, my sweetheart, que *el amor es ciego, pero los vecinos no*, okay?"

"Okay." Mason nodded solemnly. "That sounded... really beautiful."

Lety smiled warmly and patted his cheek. "Don't change, my Mason. Don't change."

Mason looked at me blankly, and I shrugged. Sometimes I felt like I'd understand Lety better if I spoke Spanish, and sometimes I was convinced it was better that I didn't.

"Dr. Bloom!" Marius Wynott came over, wearing a three-piece blue suit and holding two arms full of fluff. "I'm so very relieved that you're planning to make your sojourn on Whispering Key more of a permanent affair! And Topaz is very excited that you'll be here to dog-sit."

Mason patted the squirming furball.

"I also must congratulate you two, finding the treasure the way you did." He sighed. "Like most mysteries, the answer seems so *obvious* now that all has been revealed."

I frowned. "You think? That was *never* where the treasure was meant to be. I figure there must have been an underground river that carried the treasure down from—"

Mr. Wynott's jaw dropped. "Oh, *no*, my boy. Oh, no no no. Don't you see? The answer was right there in Resolute Goodman's papers all along. He buried the treasure in *the garden of dreams*."

"Yes," I said patiently. "The dream garden he built his wife. But there was never anything in Sarah's—" But looking at him in that moment, I realized the answer. "Not Sarah."

Mr. Wynott shook his head.

"*Jacob*."

Mr. Wynott nodded. "I do believe so, yes. The garden at the Original Homestead."

"Wait," Mason said. "Wait, wait. Does this mean Resolute and Jacob were..." He widened his eyes meaningfully, and I poked him gently.

"Mason. *Words*."

"*Gay*," he said finally.

I grinned. I kinda hoped they were, if only because Jessica the "shipper" would be so thrilled.

"Oh, hard to say," Mr. Wynott said, waving a hand airily as he struggled to contain his dog, who desperately wanted to get down. "Men in those days spoke much more effusively than we do today, and that place may simply have called to Resolute as the place where he and Jacob had *dreamed* up their plans for the island. But I do admit there's a certain romanticism in the idea of them together." He nodded once, firmly. "Two imperfect men who found a unique way to spend the bulk of their lives together during a time when the world was less kind than it is now. If Jacob's spirit ever did haunt this island, I like to think he'll be at peace knowing another pair of star-crossed lovers have finally gotten together in their stead. Maybe that's why he finally allowed you two to discover the— *Oh, good heavens! Topaz!* You leave that cat *alone!*" he cried, running after the dog who was running after Marjorie.

"I don't believe in any of this," I told Mason, turning him to face me.

"Nope. Me neither."

"Not ghosts. Not portents. Not mystical woo-woo..."

"Not fate, not destiny, not the Universe?"

I hesitated. "Well..."

Mason laughed. Then his phone chimed in his pocket, and his laughter turned to a groan.

"What?" I demanded. "Reporter?"

"No, *worse*. Apparently some reporter got my name and printed it."

"Oh." I stroked a hand down his back. "That was always gonna happen, babe. Is it a problem? Are you worried people will know about us?"

Mason gave me a look so full of love, I literally couldn't have imagined it, in those fucked-up years after Texas Thad.

"Are you joking? I want *everyone* to know about us. In fact, if Gerry keeps looking over at you, I'm gonna get *Property of Loafers* tattooed on your forehead. But my brother made me promise I'd call him if I joined the mafia or ended up on the news." He brandished the phone in my direction. "Guess who made the news and didn't call?"

"Ohhhh." I glanced down at the screen where there was a link to an article followed by his brother's words.

> MICAH
>
> An IMPOVERISHED island? A buried treasure? A BOYFRIEND? What the actual fuck, Mason? You haven't been gone TWO MONTHS. I'm expecting A CALL.

"Oops?" I offered.

"No shit," he said, sliding the phone away so he could loop both arms around my neck. "Constantine and Micah will be expecting a visit soon, if I know them. God, and so will *Toby*." He leaned up on his tiptoes to bite the tendon in the side of my neck, and I hissed. "Which is why we really, *really* shouldn't waste any alone time now. As in, we should walk away *right this minute*. Because it's going to be a really busy summer around here, Fenn Reardon. Everyone's gonna want to come to Whispering Key. We've got sunshine year-round."

I laughed out loud and pulled him tighter. "It's basically paradise," I agreed.

And with Mason in my arms, that was the absolute truth.

Want to see what happens when Beale finally meets his soulmate? Grab On the Run, *book two in the Whispering Key series, here: https://readerlinks.com/l/3037614*

Want to know what happens when Fenn and Mason travel to O'Leary to meet Micah and Constantine from The Secret? Check out Unicorns Forever *here: https://readerlinks.com/l/3143036*

ABOUT MAY ARCHER

May is an M/M author who lives in Boston. She spends her days planning vacations, mainlining diet soda, avoiding the gym, reading M/M romance, and when all other forms of procrastination fail, writing it.

Visit her website at <u>mayarcher.com</u> to sign up for her <u>newsletter</u> to hear about sales and upcoming releases, freebies and behind the scenes info and more! Or join her Facebook group, <u>Club May</u>!

facebook.com/may.archer.author

instagram.com/mayarcherauthor

amazon.com/May-Archer/e/B075JQVGLX

patreon.com/MayArcherRomance

bookbub.com/authors/may-archer

ALSO BY MAY ARCHER

Get my <u>New Release Alerts</u>

Join me on Patreon

Follow me Everywhere Else

<u>Love in O'Leary Series</u>

<u>Whispering Key Series</u>

<u>The Sunday Brothers Series</u>

<u>Copper County Series</u>

<u>The Way Home Series</u>

<u>Licking Thicket Series</u>

(cowritten with Lucy Lennox)

<u>Champion Security Series</u>

(cowritten with Lucy Lennox)

<u>Honeybridge Series</u>

(cowritten with Lucy Lennox)

For a comprehensive list of titles, audio samples, freebies, suggested reading order, and more, visit my website at www. MayArcher.com!

www.ingramcontent.com/pod-product-compliance
Lightning Source LLC
Chambersburg PA
CBHW020323010826
48973CB00005B/1100